Praise fo[...]

"If you're entertained by sex, innuendo, and a few fantasies you'd like to see played out—and who isn't?—you ought to have Lucky and her extended Vegas family (*So Damn Lucky*, etc.) on speed dial."
—*Kirkus Reviews* (starred review)

"Coonts packs a fair amount of meat on the bones of this comic, fast-paced, and sexy romp.... With punny one-liners and irreverent banter, Lucky lovingly guides her entourage through Las Vegas's warped world."
—*Library Journal*

Praise for *So Damn Lucky*

"Whether tactfully dissuading a senior citizen from marrying her dog or discreetly extricating an amorous couple from their complex sex toys, Lucky proves first-rate at her job. Fans of lighter mysteries will have fun."
—*Publishers Weekly*

"Lucky is an irresistible heroine.... *So Damn Lucky* is wacky and witty, chaotic and compelling, and the title aptly describes how you'll feel after you've read the book."
—*USA Today*

Praise for *Lucky Stiff*

"Las Vegas is the perfect setting for this witty tale of misdirection and larger-than-life characters. Fans of J. A. Konrath's Jack Daniels series will love this."
—*Library Journal* (starred review)

"Fast-paced, witty, and full of colorful characters, *Lucky Stiff* is a sure bet to be a reader's favorite."
—*Booklist* (starred

W9-BNX-759

Praise for *Wanna Get Lucky?*

"Deliciously raunchy, with humorous takes on sexual proclivities, Vegas glitz, and love, though Agatha Christie is probably spinning in her grave."
—*Kirkus Reviews*

"This is chick-lit gone wild and sexy, lightly wrapped in mystery and tied up with a brilliantly flashing neon bow. . . . *Wanna Get Lucky?* hits the proverbial jackpot."
—*Booklist*

"Funny, fast-paced, exuberant, and brilliantly realized."
—Susan Wiggs,
New York Times bestselling author

Lucky Bastard

Forge Books by Deborah Coonts

Wanna Get Lucky?
Lucky Stiff
So Damn Lucky
Lucky Bastard

NOVELLAS

Lucky in Love
Lucky Bang

Lucky Bastard

DEBORAH COONTS

FORGE®

A Tom Doherty Associates Book
New York

NOTE: If you purchased this book without a cover, you should be aware that this book is stolen property. It was reported as "unsold and destroyed" to the publisher, and neither the author nor the publisher has received any payment for this "stripped book."

This is a work of fiction. All of the characters, organizations, and events portrayed in this novel are either products of the author's imagination or are used fictitiously.

LUCKY BASTARD

Copyright © 2013 by Deborah Coonts

All rights reserved.

A Forge Book
Published by Tom Doherty Associates, LLC
175 Fifth Avenue
New York, NY 10010

www.tor-forge.com

Forge® is a registered trademark of Tom Doherty Associates, LLC.

ISBN 978-0-7653-7044-0

Forge books may be purchased for educational, business, or promotional use. For information on bulk purchases, please contact Macmillan Corporate and Premium Sales Department at 1-800-221-7945, extension 5442, or write specialmarkets@macmillan.com.

First Edition: May 2013
First Mass Market Edition: March 2014

Printed in the United States of America

0 9 8 7 6 5 4 3 2 1

For Brad Gibson
and the hearing-impaired community

ACKNOWLEDGMENTS

As most writers discover, writing is an adventure. At the beginning of a story, the writer often thinks she is in control, that she knows exactly where the story is going. Nothing could be further from the truth. Stories are fluid journeys; each character takes on a life and will of its own. And, they lead their creator on amazing educational experiences, often introducing new worlds and incredible new people. Ultimately, stories, at their essence, are about people . . . and relationships, as is our journey through life.

People often hold on to misconceptions about Las Vegas. Sin City. Lost paycheck. A city where all your desires can be realized. While each of these may be true to some extent, the most interesting question is why do people come here? What do they hope to find? This question is what drives my Lucky series. The whole world, vast hordes of folks, wander through Vegas. And they all bring their hopes, their dreams, their failures, their successes, their joy, their despair. What they take away is up to them.

Here's my takeaway from the journey of bringing *Lucky Bastard* to life: as usual, many thanks are required. So, a heartfelt thanks must go out to:

Brad Gibson, a wonderful young man who educated me in profound ways. Brad is deaf. And he tackles life with vigor, enthusiasm, and confidence most of us would do well to harness even a fraction of. One of Brad's passions is poker. Watching him play, communicating with him about his life, opened my eyes to the world of the hearing impaired. Amazing. If I got anything wrong in attempting to present a bit of your world, please forgive me and know the mistakes are entirely mine.

Morgan and Everett Gibson, the two who brought Brad into this world and nurtured him on his journey, molding him into the wonderful, resilient spirit he is today. Thank you all for sharing your experiences, and most of all, thank you for your wonderful, continuing friendship. I am blessed.

Linda Bertuzzi, my dear friend who, despite all of my shortcomings, continues to give this writer a port in the storm of life. There is a special place in heaven and in my heart for you.

Tyler and Lisa Coonts, my kids. You two inspire me every day with your love, compassion, hard work, laughter, and support. The world is so much better with you two in it, as am I. I love you both more than you know.

Barb Nickless and Maria Faulconer, terrific writers and the best friends and critiquers ever! Your help in all things is immeasurable.

My publishing family at Tor/Forge: Bob Gleason, Tom Doherty, Linda Quinton, Patty Garcia, Whitney Ross, Aisha Cloud, and my agent extraordinaire, Susan Gleason. Dream makers one and all.

To independent booksellers, especially Murder by the Book (Houston, Texas), The Tattered Cover (Denver, Colorado), The Poisoned Pen (Scottsdale, Arizona), and Mysterious Galaxy (San Diego and Redondo Beach, California), who have supported this writer in her quest to make the dream of being an author a reality from the very beginning, sticking with me through thick and thin.

To readers. Without you there would be no stories, I'd have to spend every day in the real world, and my passion for storytelling would be unrealized.

To Tiger, Todd, Pierre O'Rourke, David Edgerley Gates, Carol Kahn, Jerry Lamber, Scott Largent, and Diane Mott Davidson. Your voices, your support, your friendship, and your sage advice save me every day. Thanks for putting up with me—you deserve hazardous-duty pay, for sure.

In short, thanks to all.

Now I'm off on the next Lucky adventure, this one set in the gourmet foodie world of Las Vegas, one of the gastronomic capitals of the world. I'm going to need more gym time when I'm finished with my research.

Lucky Bastard

Chapter

ONE

♡

"Wow, talk about killer heels." The words were out of my mouth before I could stop them. I dropped my head for a moment, then recovered. "I can't believe I said that."

Openmouthed, I stared at the body of a young woman sprawled across the hood of a candy-apple red Ferrari on display in our dealership, the heel of one of this holiday season's signature Jimmy Choos embedded in her neck.

"I can," growled Paxton Dane, the man who had summoned me to the scene and the only other living, breathing human within shouting distance at this ungodly hour of the morning. His tone held a not-so-gentle chiding.

Truth be told, he was right—very bad form. Normally I had a better filter but tonight it was on the fritz. At least I had an excuse.

Murder always made me twitchy.

"Death by Jimmy Choo," I babbled, riding a

building wave of panic. "Well, at least she went out with style." The words and thoughts gathered like dark clouds heralding an impending storm. "This is clearly a new twist on the stiletto-as-a-murder-weapon theme, don't you think? And can't you just hear Sherlock Holmes now? 'Come, Watson, murder's afoot.'" I choked back a nervous giggle but was singularly unable to rein in my runaway foot-in-mouth disease. What had the poor woman done to deserve such a hasty exit? Better yet, who could've done such a thing?

"It's 'Come, Watson, the *game's* afoot,'" growled Dane, "and you need to put a sock in it."

Again, he was right, but I wasn't about to tell him so. I wondered who the dead woman was. And how had the Vegas magic so deserted her? At Dane's scowl, I swallowed the comment on the tip of my tongue.

"The sock reference was unintentional." He raised a finger, silencing me. He knew me far too well for my comfort level. When he was sure he had my attention, he continued. "And if you can't stifle yourself . . ."

I struggled to get a grip. Focusing on breathing, I gulped steady, even, deep lungfuls of air. Finally, the morbid comedian in me beat feet.

Okay, maybe not. Clamping my lips together, I tried to think.

Anyway I looked at this . . . situation . . . it was *so* not good. Three A.M. A closed and presumably locked Ferrari dealership—in my hotel no less. A dead woman. A ruined shoe. And somehow all of it had landed in my lap.

Not entirely unusual, but certainly unappreciated.

My name is Lucky O'Toole and I am the vice president of Customer Relations for the Babylon, Las Vegas's most over-the-top Strip casino-resort. Drowning in the aftermath of a still deep and turbulent romantic tsunami, I had recently taken temporary residence in smaller quarters in the hotel—a decision I was currently rethinking.

Accessibility clearly had its downside.

Dane was a former co-worker, sometime suitor, and now awkward friend. Despite past skirmishes and unrequited affections (his, not mine, for once), we'd reached a grudging respect for each other, a détente, if you will. He had said little since calling me. Instead, standing quietly off to the side, he lurked like a gargoyle, waiting, observing, while I absorbed the scene. Shadows angled across his features, hiding his expression behind a mask of darkness and reflected light. Arms folded tightly across his chest, he hugged himself. Was he seeking comfort, or stilling himself from action?

Fight or flight? I was so there myself. Unfortunately for me, flight was not an option. Like it or not, I was the Babylon's professional problem solver in residence.

And the dead girl was clearly a problem.

Sometimes, being a grown-up sucked.

"Murder sort of refocuses you, doesn't it?" The normal comfort I found in the familiarity of my voice proved elusive. Dane had enough insight to know I didn't expect an answer.

Frozen for the moment, I watched as the car rotated on a raised platform in the center of the showroom, each detail captured in the accusatory beam of a single spotlight mounted above. The young woman wore a silver spandex dress, very short, strapless, hugging her every curve. Her feet were bare. A red welt marred the otherwise perfect skin of her neck. As she rotated past, I had an unobstructed view up her dress—no underwear. Of course, this being Vegas, most of the young women went commando—no muss, no fuss, no panty lines, no worry as to how to get them off or where you might have left them when the evening was over. Vegas survival skills they should print in the visitors' guide, if you ask me. Chasing runaway skivvies was part of my job description—the wrong pair in the wrong place could be a catastrophe of epic proportions. Trust me on that one.

Her eyes were open, sightless. They were blue—one a brilliant sky blue, the other a muddier, ocean-after-a-storm blue. I found the difference unsettling.

One arm flung over her head, her legs splayed, her shoulder-length hair a spun-sugar pillow under her head, she'd been beautiful. Stunning even. The champagne-colored crystals of the single shoe fractured the light like a disco ball in a cheesy nightclub. A beaded mini hobo—multicolored sequins stitched on silver satin—dangled from a chain wrapped around her lifeless hand. I'd bet my lifetime membership in the Conspicuous Consumers Club it was also Jimmy Choo.

Somebody had a fat wallet and impeccable taste.

Blood trickled from her wound, tracing a graceful path across the woman's bluish skin, then dropping silently to the hood of the car. The reds blended until it was difficult to follow the blood's meander down the smooth metal to the white faux-marble tile underneath where it pooled, a dark ominous stain. Following imperfections in the stone, tiny rivulets of darkening color flowed outward until they painted a freeform web.

But something important was missing: the other shoe. I bent down to peer under the car. Clean as a whistle. Boy, being Cinderella in Vegas clearly wasn't all it was cracked up to be.

"Who is she?" I asked Dane, hoping he had some easy answers.

With his hands jammed in his pockets, he shrugged but didn't look at me.

"You *are* going to tell me how you managed to stumble upon this young woman, in this position, after hours, in a dealership locked up for the night, in a hotel where you no longer work, right?" I pressed, casting a quick glance at him as he stepped into the light and parked himself at my shoulder.

He didn't look good. Well, that wasn't entirely true. Several inches taller than my six feet, with ax-handle wide shoulders, a narrow waist that hinted at washboard abs, wavy brown hair, and emerald eyes, he always looked good—especially in his creased

501s and starched button-down. Normally, one glance at the man could throw an unwary female into hormonal overdrive. Tonight, however, with dark circles under worried eyes, his brows furrowed, his face pinched with an emotion I couldn't quite read, Dane didn't look his best.

I didn't blame him. Even after years of dealing with the occasional dead person in my hotel, I still hadn't gotten used to it.

Of course, most of them hadn't been murdered.

Before Dane answered, he ran a shaky hand through his hair and avoided looking at me.

From past experience, I'd learned a thing or two about Paxton Dane, most of it the hard way. If he was good at anything, the long, tall drink of Texas charm was good at prevarication. Right now, I'd wager my future firstborn that Dane was framing his answer. Like a woman looking for the perfect pair of jeans, he'd try a few on for size until he got the fit just right. Only then would he trot out his choice for my perusal. With Dane, most of the time *what* he told you wasn't nearly as interesting as the stuff he left out.

"I was in the Poker Room. Watching." His eyes furtively sought mine, then skittered away. He nodded toward the dead woman. "She caught my eye."

"Understandable." I took a deep breath, marshaling my notoriously thin patience. "She was playing?" I prompted.

Dane grunted.

I took that to mean yes.

"She'd made it to the final table of the thousand-dollar buy-in, but she busted out about an hour ago and left."

"Alone?"

"As far as I could tell."

This time I gave Dane my full attention, leveling my eyes to his. He still wouldn't look at me for more than a few seconds. "What do you mean, as far as you could tell? You're a private investigator. Don't you guys notice that type of stuff?"

"I wasn't investigating, I was watching."

"Ahhh. So your powers of observation only function when you're on the meter?" I knew he was smart enough to recognize a rhetorical question, even when it was obscured in dripping sarcasm, so I forged ahead. "If you weren't . . . investigating . . . how did you mange to find her here?"

This time his eyes met mine. "I was on my way to the garage—my truck is parked on level three, row C. You can check it out if you don't believe me." The tilt of his chin held a challenge, but his eyes looked haunted. "I saw the door to the showroom was cracked open. I knew the place was closed, so—"

"You investigated." I finished his sentence, enjoying the minor victory. "Why didn't you call Security? After all, you used to work for them; you know the protocol. Or, better yet, why didn't you call the police?"

"I called you."

"Am I lucky or what?" I blew at a strand of hair

that tickled my eyes. Even at 3 A.M. and far from my best, I had enough functioning gray matter to realize he hadn't answered my question. Of course, I knew my in-your-face style always shut him down. It must be a Texas thing, those Southern men and their delicate egos. Unfortunately, coddling was rarely in my repertoire. "You weren't stupid enough to touch anything?"

A tic worked in his cheek as he ran a hand over his eyes. "I checked for a pulse. That's all."

"Uh-huh. I suppose that's your bloody footprint then?" I pointed to a half print under the driver's-side door—triangular with a pointed toe.

His head swiveled in surprise, his eyes following my finger. We both glanced at his feet—very expensive kickers made from some exotic skin. "Looks like it," he acknowledged with a deepening frown.

"Not messing with a crime scene—isn't that the first thing they teach you in investigator school? Right after they give you your very own decoder ring?" I asked, but Dane didn't take the bait.

None of this was adding up, and Dane didn't seem inclined to offer any clarity. And to think, thumbscrews weren't included in my vice president's superhero utility belt. An oversight I'd have to remedy. But until then, I'd have to wait for answers. Not one of my best things. Especially since I had no doubt that, while *what* Dane had done would make interesting reading, *why* he had done it would keep me riveted.

But I'd leave Dane's questioning to the police—

surely *they* had a set of thumbscrews somewhere. Or, better yet, a water board.

"Well," I said, my word choice matching my brain function, "it seems a bit late to muster the in-house cavalry, but don't you think it would be wise to call young Romeo?"

Detective Romeo was the ace up my sleeve at the Las Vegas Metropolitan Police Department—Metro to the locals. Romeo was definitely a high person in a low place.

The still-wet-behind-the-ears detective and I had met chasing a weasel. We'd bonded over an odds-maker who had become a tidbit for a tiger shark, and cemented our working relationship while investigating a disappearing magician. He'd do his job, but he'd watch my back as well.

Loyalty, a precious commodity in a fickle world.

Having one of Metro's finest on speed dial spoke volumes about my life, but I refused to think about it. Instead, I flipped open my phone and pressed his number.

The kid was going to have a field day with our Ferrari girl.

DANE and I had boosted our butts onto the dealership's Parts and Service counter and now sat, hands tucked under our thighs, feet swinging. My thoughts whirled as I concentrated on my alternating white ankles and studiously avoided looking at anything else. My feet, which protruded from the ends of my purple flannel pajama pants, were tucked warmly into fuzzy slippers. A departure from my normal vice president costume, but at this god-forsaken time of morning it was all I could muster. I was particularly proud of the faded UNLV tee shirt that rounded out my ensemble—a Vegas fashionista to the end.

The whir of the motor turning the Ferrari's dais and the imagined drip of blood mingled with the distant echoes of fun and frivolity leaking in from the casino beyond the closed doors, thankfully keeping silence at bay.

Quiet would have been way too creepy.

Unable to resist the draw of the macabre, I cast a furtive glance at the girl's body as if half expecting her to push herself to a seated position, remove the shoe from her neck, and laugh at a really great practical joke.

But she didn't.

"Do you normally sleep in flannel pajamas?" Dane's voice sliced like a knife through my carefully constructed calm.

I flinched, then shot him a sideways glare. "Why would you care?" I snapped. "We resolved that issue, as I recall."

"Not entirely to my satisfaction." He gave me one of his famous grins although it lacked its normal wattage. Still it seemed out of character, not to mention out of place and inappropriate.

Too antsy to sit any longer, I hopped down from my perch and turned to face him. "I'll have you know there are numerous factors that influence what

I sleep in." Hands on my hips, I paused and looked at him. A smirk lifted one corner of his mouth. Smirking was not on my list of acceptable responses. "Why are we talking about this? It seems . . . irreverent or something. Not to mention that it's none of your business what I sleep in or who I sleep with." Now where had that come from?

"You don't have to rub it in." Dane eased himself to his feet. "But somehow talking about something normal . . ."

I knew what he meant, comfort in the mundane. Not that my sex life was mundane—it was nonexistent—but that was another story. And not that Dane and I normally talked about it, but there had been a time, fairly recently, in fact, when he'd been in the running.

Standing in front of me, with a finger under my chin, he lifted my gaze to his. His eyes were dark, troubled. His expression serious. And he was *way* too close for comfort.

While I was wise to his charms, I wasn't immune. I wanted to step back, but his hand on my arm held me.

"Lucky," he said, his voice shaking. "I'm going to need your help."

For a moment time stopped. The empty room crowded around us. I stared at my friend and for the first time truly saw.

Red scratches on the side of his face—one deep enough to draw blood that had dried to a dark crust. A tortured look in his eyes. The stern slash of his mouth. The slight tremor to his hand as he quickly stuffed it into the front pocket of his jeans.

The touch of his skin on mine was unexpectedly cool.

Oh God, what *had* he done?

We both jumped as my former lover Teddie's voice shattered the silence singing "Lucky for Me." My phone! Dang! And why had I chosen that song as my ringtone? It skewered my heart every time I heard it.

The jump-start surge of adrenaline pegged my heart rate. My hand closed over the offending device, jerking it from my pocket. I shot Dane what I thought might resemble a rueful look. "Self-flagellation." I flipped the thing open. "What?"

"Lucky?" The delicious French intonation, the voice as smooth and rich as a homemade hollandaise, could belong to only one person: Jean-Charles, our new chef and, if he had his way, the new man in my life. But once burned, twice shy, I was riding the brakes. "I am thinking you are not sleeping," he continued. "I did not awaken you, then? Yes?"

"No." For some reason, or perhaps for a multitude of reasons, I seemed to be struck monosyllabic at the moment. His voice suffused me to the core with warmth. Taking a deep breath, I struggled to apply pressure to those brakes. But they'd gone all mushy . . . along with my brain and other body parts that I won't mention. Apparently my self-control had thrown in the towel as well. Toss a handsome man with empty promises in my path, and I'd take the bait, hook, line, and sinker. Swallowing it whole, I'd lose my heart only to have it handed back to me on a platter. I knew the drill. Why couldn't I just grab some local hunk and have wild, meaningless sex like everybody else?

Unfortunately I apparently lacked the moral fortitude to be immoral.

"*Non?* You were sleeping then?"

"No. I mean yes, you did not awaken me." Exactly when did I lose the ability to speak proper English? "I'm sorry, I'm a bit muddled at the moment." I scrunched my eyes shut and tried to block out the scene around me—Dane's stricken face, the dead woman on the car. Turning my back to them, I conjured a mental picture of the Frenchman in a vain attempt to recapture a sense of normalcy. "Are you just now heading home?" I attempted to infuse a casual, warm tone to my voice, but I wasn't sure I pulled it off.

"Yes, I am driving on the Fifteen." A car horn sounded, then faded, as I heard Jean-Charles's sharp intake of breath. The American form of offensive driving was a skill the Parisian had yet to master. He'd spent most of his adult life in the great cities of the world where owning a car was not only superfluous, it bordered on the insane—New York parking fees regularly equaled the rent for a studio. I shuddered at the thought of him at the wheel while on the phone.

"A late night then?" I chatted as if I hadn't a care in the world. They say compartmentalizing is one of the first signs of mental illness.

"*Oui*, the restaurant, it was very busy. These Americans, they like food," Jean-Charles said with classic European understatement. Another car horn sounded, this time answered with a muttered Gallic epithet, which made me smile.

"The American way: Treat each meal as your last," I said, finding my equilibrium.

Jean-Charles had opened a gourmet burger joint in the shopping area of the Babylon called the Bazaar while he perfected the menu and finished out the space that would be his signature restaurant.

"Precisely! So many, many burgers, *pomme frites*, shakes. And I am working on the new dishes for the Vegas *Last Chef Standing*. My kitchen here, she is, how do you say it? A poor stepchild?"

"Found wanting in every way?"

"Yes, this is it. I need my kitchen at Cielo."

"We are at the mercy of the contractor, you know that. He is working."

"Perhaps you can do something?"

"Wave my magic wand?"

Silence stretched between us. "I have made you angry." His voice held a note of defeat.

"No. I'm just . . ." I looked at Dane, his face pulled tight, the woman on the Ferrari, still dead. "It's just not a great time."

"For this I am sorry. Perhaps tomorrow would be better?"

"Right now, it's not looking so good, but we'll talk about your kitchen soon, I promise."

"You must help me, you see, I am also nervous."

Jean-Charles said the words haltingly, as if confessing a major sin—one he couldn't believe he'd committed. "This is a very public stage. My reputation and that of your hotel hang in the balance. This is not only a competition with my fellow chefs, the media is turning it into a circus."

"Vegas and reality television—a perfect storm of bad taste."

"Yes, well, with your help, I will adjust and we can make it better. However, right now I am, how do you say it? Wrecked?"

"That will do." For some reason I enjoyed his struggle with American slang—sometimes his choices made the mundane charming.

"I am looking forward to sleep." His voice sounded tired as he deftly changed the subject. "But I could not end the day without hearing your voice."

I felt like a ping-pong ball being smashed from one side to the other. On one side I was the potential romance, on the other, the hotel exec standing in his way. How this game would play out—and which me would win—was anybody's guess. "I'm glad you called."

"Yes, but why are you awake?" He sounded as if the thought that normal people were asleep at this hour had just occurred to him, which was probably accurate.

"I had to answer my phone." I know, I know, playing fast and loose with the truth. Not good. But to be honest, I was having a real hard time with reality right at the moment.

. . .

AFTER finishing the conversation, I reluctantly hung up and repocketed my phone, taking my time to savor the sweet taste of a very real fantasy. Turning, I glanced at Dane. He still looked like hell, maybe worse. Underneath it all, he looked . . . guilty. Which doused my French glow pretty nicely.

"Are you going to tell me what's going on?" I hissed, my temper flaring again. Add playing games to the long list of things that piss me off. Dane was a master.

"I wish I knew." His face remained a blank slate, a study in self-control.

"Cowboy, you know . . ." I was reaching for something to say, measuring my words, trying to resist closing my fingers around his neck, when the doors opened. Instinctively I turned, squinting through the darkness. Like a Hollywood version of a near-death experience, figures moved toward me silhouetted by the bright light behind them.

There was someone here near death, but it wasn't me. So I wasn't too alarmed.

"Lucky?" Romeo called, his voice hushed as if he had wandered into a church and was afraid to awaken the dead. He needn't have worried.

At the sound of the detective's voice, Dane stiffened. Stepping back, he straightened, throwing his shoulders back. With practiced ease, he arranged his features into a bland, impenetrable mask.

The man could be as stupid as a bull thrown in with the cows.

Lying to me would land him in the doghouse. But lying to the police would move him up the food chain to the Big House . . . if I didn't kill him first.

And he wanted my help?

He acted as if he'd find my name under the word *doormat* in the dictionary. Just another bit of proof to my all-men-are-pigs theory. Yes, it's a sad commentary that the survival of the human species rests solely on the low expectations of females.

Been there, done that, bought the tee shirt. But thankfully, I'd never done the nasty with Dane. One minor triumph, all things considered.

"Over here," I called to Romeo. My voice sounded strangled, as if Dane had put both his hands around my neck and squeezed. Of course, if he did, it might save us both a ton of trouble.

Out of the darkness, Las Vegas's finest young detective materialized in front of us, followed by a half dozen officers in uniform and three people in civilian clothes. With his rumpled beige raincoat, wilted shirt, a dark suit that hung on his thin frame, his tie knotted but hanging loosely around his neck like a noose ready to be tightened, Romeo looked as if he hadn't seen a decent night's sleep or a good meal in a month of Sundays—something I suspected was closer to the truth than I'd care to think.

His sandy brown hair, mashed down on one side, held the evidence of a recent wetting and combing. A cowlick stood at the crown of his head like a defiant thistle. The hint of sleep lingered in the corners of his cloudy blue eyes. One cheek held the imprint of something, his hand perhaps, or the corner of a stack of papers—remnants of a quick catnap.

When we'd first met, Romeo couldn't hide his emotions. Each one would march bold and unbidden across his face, much to his chagrin. Now he eyed our dead girl with the blank, businesslike stare of someone who had seen more than his share of the bad things in life.

A fact that broke my heart just a little.

I watched and listened as Romeo instructed his men to secure the scene. He supervised them until, apparently satisfied, he turned to me. Pulling a spiral-bound pad from his inside coat pocket, he flipped it open, then wetted the end of a stub of pencil on his tongue. Glancing between Dane and me, he said, "I should separate you two, go by the book. But with our history, why bother?" He turned, focusing his words on me. "You're probably eight steps ahead of me already anyway. You gave me the overview on the phone, so just give the rest to me straight, okay?"

"When have I ever not . . ." I trailed off. Better not to open that can of worms. So I did as he asked—straight as I could. As I talked, trying to remember every detail, even the seemingly unimportant ones, the young detective scribbled, his brows furrowed. "The call from Dane came in at . . . ?"

Dane started to answer.

Romeo silenced him with a frown. "You'll get your chance, cowboy."

I raised my eyebrows at my detective friend. Like a spark, a hint of humor flared in his eyes, then quickly faded. The kid was growing into his badge. Somehow, I didn't feel like celebrating. One more cockeyed optimist thrown under the reality bus.

Scrolling through my phone directory to the most recent calls, I said, "Two forty-two."

Romeo made a note. "This dealership is a concessionaire, right?" He glanced up from his notes. At my nod he continued: "I need to know who owns it, and who has access."

"Frank DeLuca owns the place. Give me an hour to get you the rest."

"DeLuca?" Romeo's brows snapped together, making him look older than twelve and somehow a bit more serious. Perhaps he ought to think about that as a permanent look. Could they do that with Botox?

Stress and panic had clearly fractured the few functioning brain cells I had, leaving loose random thoughts to ping around my empty skull. Terrific.

"DeLuca? As in the pro poker player?" Romeo continued. "I went to Bishop Gorman with a couple of his kids." A local Catholic high school, Bishop Gorman had educated the best and brightest of most of the old Vegas families.

"One and the same."

"I'd like to talk to him," the kid muttered as he made a note. "Although after that dustup with his daughter . . ." Romeo's cheeks reddened as he glanced at me and shrugged.

"Nothing like having history in this burg, huh?" I said with a hint of resignation and a sharp nip of reality. "A lot of people live here, but it's still a small town."

"Tell me about it." Weariness hung heavily in his voice. The kid looked barely old enough to drive. How much history could he have? "Would you happen to know where I might find Mr. DeLuca?" he asked, his pencil poised.

"You're in luck. He qualified for the Sin City Smack Down."

Romeo's face creased with puzzlement. "Smack Down? Isn't Mr. DeLuca a bit old for cage fighting?"

"Poker. It's a poker tournament almost as important as the World Series of Poker. What rock have you been living under?" I felt like a creep the minute I said it—I don't normally feast on unseasoned detectives. The hurt look flashing across his face didn't help. "Sorry, I forget not everyone lives in my happy little corner of the universe. The Smack Down is the Super Bowl of Texas hold 'em and this weekend is the final table. The hordes descend today—the nine players who qualified, the media, celebrities wanting some face time, the hookers hoping to land a whale, and folks just needing an excuse to misbehave. Tournament play starts day after tomorrow. Each interminable moment will be televised to the world from Teddie's old theatre."

There, I'd said his name. Teddie. I held my breath, waiting for a reaction. Nothing happened. My pulse remained steady. My heart didn't constrict to the size of a raisin. Wow. Maybe I was over him. As I let my breath ease between my lips, the ache in my chest returned. Okay, maybe not *completely* over him.

"Oh." Romeo chewed on his lip as his eyes turned toward the ceiling and his brain shifted gears. "No cameras in here?"

"It's the only place in the hotel without internal monitoring, if that's what you're getting at. Look around," I swept my arm toward the showroom. "There's nothing in here but some expensive Italian iron. Nothing much to pocket and take home. So only the external door alarms, the front door into the Bazaar, as well as the exterior doors, are wired into hotel security." As the detective opened his mouth to speak, I silenced him with a raised finger. Flipping open my phone, I pushed to talk. "Jerry?"

"Lucky? You ever go to bed, girl?" The voice that came back belonged to Jerry, our head of security. Me and Jer went way, way back . . . all the way back to the beginning. I kept the guests happy; he kept them safe—flip sides of the same coin.

Feeling the burn of their penetrating stares, I turned my back to Romeo and Dane. "Sleep isn't part of my job description. Nor yours, apparently." I pressed the phone to my ear and lowered my voice. "Did you guys get an alarm on the front door to the Ferrari dealership?"

"Funny you should ask. I was just heading down there."

"Why?"

"According to my staff, the alarm lit up at . . ." He paused, then said, "Two oh three."

"You guys didn't respond?"

"No, the alarm was silenced with a code shortly after. As procedure dictates, we called down there. The woman who answered the phone had the magic word. But this is coming to me secondhand. I was dealing with what's looking to be more and more like an inside ring of thieves working the guest rooms when I was called away to handle one of the poker players in town for the big wingding. Not only is he a whiz at poker, he's a pretty good card counter too."

"So you enlightened him as to the dim view we take of that skill?"

"Hell, he'd already been enlightened—we had him under contract to not play blackjack. Guess the lure of a new shoe, a young dealer, and the time of night got to him."

"What did you do?"

"I'll probably regret it, but I gave him a slap on the wrist and let him go. I didn't finish up with him until just a couple of minutes ago—wanted to scare him a little."

"You're going soft on me. If that gets around it'll be regarded as an invitation," I half joked.

"Yeah, well, maybe they'll give me my gold watch. They'd be doin' me a favor. But before you put me in for early retirement, the kid was deaf. I cut him a break. Some of the other players had been hassling him and it ticked me off."

"Gotcha. Had he qualified for the Smack Down or was he a hanger-on?"

"Neither. He's a player but he missed the final table by a few spots—finished pretty high in the qualifying as I understand it, though. He was flashing a wad around."

"Inviting attention. Thankfully, not my problem, but this alarm at the dealership? That one has landed in my lap. Anything more you can tell me?"

"Not much, that's why I was coming to check it out myself."

"If she had the proper word, what piqued your interest?"

Alarms were double-checked with a phone call. Each authorized person was assigned a unique code word. If they could repeat that word when Security called, then all was clear and Security had no other duty to perform.

"The time of night raised a red flag, although test-driving a Ferrari at two in the morning isn't that odd of a request. Seen it before." Jerry sounded like he was reciting statistics as he gave me the rundown. "But to be honest, a woman with the owner's code word? I know DeLuca's a player—runs through the ladies like a slot addict through quarters. But the kid who took the call didn't ask to speak to Mr. DeLuca—a breach in protocol—he shoulda known better. At least he had the sense to find me and tell me about it. I reamed him a new one, then called the dealership back, but the gal didn't pick up. When I finished with the deaf kid, I thought I better check it out myself. Your call caught me in the lobby heading toward the dealership."

"I got this one covered." I stared at the girl on the car—thankfully someone had stopped the rotating. "But our system apparently has a fatal flaw. What was the code word?"

"You and I both know that if someone's intent on jumping into a buzz saw there's not much we can do to stop them. Hang on." I waited, then Jerry's voice came back on the line. "The word was, well, it was actually a phrase: *dead man's hand.*"

"DeLuca drew to that one year to win a World Series of Poker bracelet—the stuff of legend, but it's sorta creeping me out right now. So no one asked the woman where DeLuca was?"

"Apparently not. I didn't bother trying again, I figured she'd left by now."

"She's gone all right." I glanced at the girl.

Two technicians were bagging her hands. One of them pawed through her jeweled feedbag of a purse. The tech pulled out a lipstick and a couple of condoms in pink wrappers. He shook his head at Romeo.

"Do you happen to know when you called down here?" I asked Jerry.

"Yeah." Jerry paused. "Two twenty-one. These iPhones are amazing—all the information at your fingertips."

"Got it." Eighteen minutes after the alarm sounded. Then another twenty give or take until Dane called me.

"You going to tell me what happened?" Concern crept around the edges of Jerry's weary voice.

"Your woman didn't leave. Somebody buried the heel of a shoe in her neck—the pointy end punctured something important. She bled out all over a new California. I'll need a list of everyone who had access, keep all the tapes from the cameras in the hallway, and those outside showing the external doors to the dealership, you know the drill." I rattled this off as if murder were as common as a drunk locking himself out of his room.

"They killed her with a shoe?"

"Has a certain style," I said. "Romeo's here. Are you going to be around for a while?"

"Now I am." Jerry sounded as if the world had just been dropped on his shoulders. "Besides, I got some paperwork to do on this rash of room robberies, but I was going to ignore that until tomorrow."

"Sitting behind the desk where the buck stops is overrated, isn't it? Can I meet you in Security in an hour?" I glanced at my watch. Wow, apparently time also flew when you *weren't* having any fun. I thought this was a good thing, but I couldn't marshal the brainpower to think it through. "Make that an hour and a half."

"You got it."

As I closed my phone and stuffed it into the pocket of my pajama bottoms, I turned back to the young detective who stared at me with old eyes. I gave him a quick and dirty recap of my conversation—he'd already heard my side of it. Glossing over the code word thing, I bartered a bit of self-respect for some sniffing-around time.

"If you're done with me," I said, trying not to feel guilty about my contribution to his downward spiral into the morass of cynicism, "I've got to dress for the day, then I have some other fires to put out."

He nodded. "But—"

"I know," I said, interrupting him. "Don't leave town."

Finally, that got a grin out of the kid, which made me feel hopeful. "Your leash isn't that long," he fired back.

I was about to bite off a stinging reply when the kid's grin faded. "I started to ask if you have any idea who this woman is. No ID in her purse." The look on his face telegraphed his desire for easy answers.

"Since she had a code to silence the alarm and call off the dogs, one could assume she either worked here or knew someone who does. And, if that is the case, whoever that is has some answering to do." I'd pointed him in the right direction, which made me feel a little better about not giving him the whole story. As an insider myself, I owed Frank DeLuca a chance to explain how the woman ended up with his code word before I turned the cops onto him—that's the way the game was played. But holding out on Romeo didn't sit too well either—that's not how our game was played. I'd make it up to the kid somehow. "Mr. DeLuca isn't going to like this one bit."

Romeo paled. From the looks of him, his fracas with Mr. DeLuca's daughter had included a run-in with the man himself, which was good. Knowing the kid, he'd put DeLuca at the bottom of his interview list, buying me some time.

I put a hand on his arm. "Before we go any further, could you do me a favor? Check her bra. A lot of the girls carry their licenses and mad money there to outfox the purse snatchers and pickpockets."

"Mad money?"

"If your date gets mad, you can still pay a cab to take you home. It's a girl thing."

"I see." Romeo didn't make a note of that little tidbit. "We'll look, but even still, I'd appreciate it if you could do a bit of digging, maybe come up with a name."

Great. The young detective who had barely graduated from training wheels was throwing me in with the wolves. Of course, that was the role I played. After all, being Albert Rothstein's daughter did open a few doors . . . and would give me a few minutes' head start before anyone started shooting.

Dane cleared his throat, making me jump. He'd been so quiet and still that I'd forgotten he was even there, which, given his considerable charms, I had heretofore considered an impossibility.

"I can tell you who she is," Dane said, his voice flat, hard, yet with a tremor of emotion.

Romeo and I turned toward him.

"You know her?" I asked, not even trying to keep the incredulity out of my voice.

"Unfortunately." Dane's eyes captured mine. "She's my wife."

Chapter

TWO

♡

$\mathcal{F}$ ighting to keep calm, I stared at the man I had known for almost six months. The man who had tried numerous times to worm his way into my life, not to mention into my pants. The man I had kissed in the Garden Bar, for chrissake!

He had a wife!

In my book, there are different levels of lying by omission—gradations starting with the little white lie that did no one any harm and could be overlooked. Progressing to holding your cards close until you knew who could be trusted, which was potentially forgivable. And culminating with the omission so glaring, so deceitful, that drawing a terminal amount of blood was a given.

Dane had just shot that arrow, an arrow tipped with the poison of betrayal.

Just as I was working myself up to homicide I remembered reading somewhere that losing a spouse is one of life's most devastating events, which inched me back from the verge. Ah, the delicate tightrope one walks when a friend turns out to be far less than expected.

Disappointment, one of life's greatest conundrums.

And I could be big . . . in theory. So I'd try to be appreciative of his pain, but I needed some answers. Even if I had to hog-tie the man and threaten him with a branding iron, I was going to get them.

Dane took a deep breath and ran his fingers through his hair. "Her name is . . . was Sylvie." Staring over my shoulder at his wife's body, his carefully constructed mask slipped away, leaving raw emotion, but not the pain I expected. I fought the urge to reach out, squeeze his arm. "Actually, it was Svetlana. She was from Latvia. We met during my first tour in Afghanistan. She wanted to come to the U.S. I was lonely, naïve . . . a stupid cowboy from Lubbock."

Riveted, Romeo and I didn't move a muscle. I wasn't sure either of us was breathing.

"The base commander married us, and that was the beginning of the nightmare." Dane gave a half laugh, rueful and self-deprecating, as he glanced at me. "As my mother never misses a chance to remind me, bringing Sylvie into our family was like letting a coyote in with the sheep."

Several emotions traveled across his face—anger, fear, something else. . . . "After my first tour ended, we came back to the States. She was as sweet as the scent of sage under the warm sun . . . until all her paperwork came through. Then she turned on me like a cornered rattler. She hated West Texas. Hated me. Hated my family. After a couple of brushes with the law, she disappeared. And good riddance."

"You didn't divorce her?" Why this was the question I chose to ask, I couldn't fathom. Maybe it was because his rating on my creep-meter hinged on his answer.

"I was sent back overseas, this time to Iraq. Not having anything to come home to, I volunteered to stay. The army wasn't about to turn me down. They were in desperate need of war-tested officers who spoke the local lingo. I'd only been out six months when I showed up on your doorstep."

"I see."

"I hired a lawyer when I got to Nevada, but since I had no idea where Sylvie might be, I couldn't exactly send a process server to hit her with papers. So I had to publish notices in the paper, a long rigmarole, which took time. But the paperwork has been done and the first notice is due out in the *Review-Journal* this Sunday."

"Whoever killed your wife significantly streamlined the legal process for you, didn't they?" said Romeo.

If Romeo's question knocked Dane off center, I couldn't tell.

"I didn't kill her, if that's what you're driving at. This is a no-fault state, divorces are easy to get and certainly not worth a felony conviction."

The detective paused for a moment, staring at Dane, measuring. "Your wife wasn't trying to shake you down or anything, was she?"

"I'd hear from her periodically. Always a hurried phone call from some truck stop or cheap motel. She moved around a lot." A hard look flashed across Dane's face. "Of course, she was always running low on funds and in some trouble. Although, she never sounded too panicked. Believe me, the woman could take care of herself."

"Did you give her money?" Romeo didn't even glance up from his pad as he scribbled notes.

"Sometimes. I'd wire her just enough to get out of the scrape she was in, but not enough to run too far. I thought if I could get a bead on her I could . . . well, I could solve a few of my own problems. But she was always one step ahead."

"What kind of problems?" This time Romeo looked up, his eyes steady, unreadable; his expression open, encouraging.

"Once in a blue moon, she'd call my folks, hassle them. My father has a bad ticker. Her last call put him in the hospital for a week. I told him she was blowing smoke—she wouldn't hurt them and couldn't hurt me. But he's a stubborn cuss, tough as an old boot and as ornery as a longhorn."

"Apparently not as tough as he thinks," I said. "Why would she care about them?"

"She was looking for me." He trailed off. "They wouldn't tell her where I was. The whole thing upset them tremendously." He paused, collecting himself. "Once she got the bit in her teeth, she took it and ran with it. She wouldn't let go."

"A beautiful face with a mile-wide mean streak," I summarized. "Pretty isn't always as pretty does, is it?" I asked, because apparently I needed to rub a little salt in his wound as salve for my own. Not a proud moment. The minute the words escaped I felt the flush of shame. I needed to get a grip.

"If you found your wife, what was your plan?" Romeo prompted.

"Divorce her ass and hand her over to the Immigration and Naturalization Service." He glanced at me. "They're the ones who kick the illegals out, right?"

"In theory," I said, not wanting to open that can of worms. Vegas had more than its share of illegals and I'd never seen even one of them shipped back to wherever they came from. But that was above my pay-grade. We rounded them up. What the government did with them after that was anybody's guess. Whatever it was, most of them were back within a day or two, with new identities, applying for the same job.

"They can send her to Hell for all I care."

"That'd be one heck of a bus ride," I remarked, because sarcasm hid the hurt.

"This time when Sylvie called, it was different, wasn't it?" Romeo probed. Once the kid latched on he was like a tick on a dog.

"Yeah. Not only was she right in my backyard, but this time she was scared, really spooked, you know?"

Dane looked at me. I nodded, but again resisted any show of sympathy—even if I believed him, I wasn't letting him off the hook that easily.

"Someone was following her—at least she thought they were. And they wanted to kill her." He glanced at the lifeless form of his former wife. "Guess that much she got right."

"What'd she get wrong?" I asked.

"Huh?" Dane went still as his eyes met mine

"You said, 'that much she got right.' That implies she got something wrong. What?"

"I didn't mean it literally." Dane's eyes shifted to look over my shoulder. "It's just a saying."

"I see," I said as I captured his eyes and stared him down. Why did I have the feeling the guy was being as honest as a cardsharp in a rigged game?

"Did she say who was after her or why?" Romeo asked. He paused in his note taking as his gaze drifted between Dane and me.

Shifting his attention to Romeo, Dane pressed his lips into a thin line and shook his head. "No. She called me during the poker game, around one. She said she'd play for a while, maybe an hour more, pretend everything was business as usual—her words, not mine."

"So somebody was watching her?"

"That was the impression I got, not only from her comment, but from the way she talked. She was holding her cards close, acting like maybe somebody was eavesdropping."

"Was she still playing when she called?"

"No, taking a break."

"So it could've been anybody in the room who was listening," Romeo said under his breath, as if talking to himself as he jotted a note. When he'd finished, he looked up, meeting Dane's eyes. "She wanted you to meet her here?"

"No." Dane's eyes held steady, his voice didn't waver. "She wanted to meet me in Delilah's."

"Then how—"

"She didn't show, okay?" Dane bit off the reply. Taking a deep breath, he paused and ran a hand through his hair. "I fell for it, even after all this time. Christ, I'm a fool."

"Fell for what?"

"If that woman was a pro at anything it was giving me the slip." He chewed on his lip and turned inward. From the look on his face the conversation he was having with himself was heated. "I had given up finding her and was on my way to the garage when I noticed the door to this place. It hanging open at this hour didn't seem right."

Personally, none of this seemed right, but I didn't say that part. I was willing to acknowledge that the time he spent looking for her could explain some of the time gap in his story, between the alarm and his call to me.

"Did she work here?" I asked.

Dane shook his head. "Sylvie didn't work. She found a sucker, then bled him dry."

"Did it ever occur to you that you might be walking in on something going down?" I asked Dane.

The guy should have had *stupid* tattooed on his forehead.

"It occurred to me." Dane shot me a glare. "But I'm pretty good at taking care of myself."

"So you went and pulled a Lone Ranger."

"I thought I could handle it."

"Well, cowboy, it didn't quite work out so good now, did it?" Didn't the guy know even the Lone Ranger had Tonto?

Then it hit me: Was that the role he expected *me* to play?

WITHOUT a glance at Dane, I turned on my heel and forced myself to walk calmly toward the land of the living. Wringing the man's neck was starting to look like a viable solution to several problems, which had me worried. Usually I didn't resort to contemplating homicide this early in the game. A killer had recently been in this room, breathing the same air. Was murderous intent communicable? Who knew? Regardless, with bloodlust coursing through my veins, I knew I needed to put some distance between me and Prime Suspect Number One before I creased his skull with a tire iron.

Once I was out of the showroom, rational thought trickled in, filling some of the emotional gaps in my logic. Calmness—okay, a diminished level of murderous intent—returned as I ducked under a paper sign that had come loose from its mooring and now dangled, one end still firmly affixed to the ceiling, the other dragging on the ground. The sign, hand-painted in red on butcher paper, welcomed all the poker players. I wondered what nimrod had approved it. Had the request come through my office, I would have required the banner to be professionally printed.

Quality control, a never-ending quest in an increasingly tacky world.

Crossing the hallway, I pushed through the service doors, turned to the right, and headed down a back hallway leading toward the main building of the hotel. Somehow I didn't have it in me to traipse through the public areas in my purple flannels and ripped and worn Rebels tee shirt, even though the hotel would be sparsely populated at this hour. And, to be honest, no one would pay any attention anyway.

My thoughts returned to Dane and homicide. It's funny how often those went hand in hand, like peanut butter and jelly . . . or guns and bullets.

Perhaps I was overplaying my hand, making the punishment worse than the crime. I wasn't that mad . . . well, maybe about the Lone Ranger thing . . . and the lying thing . . . and the being married but not wearing the hardware thing . . .

Okay, I was seriously steamed. And scared. Yup, the emotions were redlining. Not good. And so not helpful when trying to problem-solve.

A set of spring-loaded double doors on my left flew inward. I dodged two housekeepers staggering under armfuls of neatly folded, bright white towels. Pressing my back to the wall, I waited until they passed. From behind their towers of terry cloth, they never saw me, jabbering as if they hadn't a care in the world. What was that like? I couldn't remember. And why did it feel as if I had an anvil sitting on my chest? My knees threatened to buckle under the weight.

Leaning my head back, I closed my eyes and focused on the cool hard surface of the wall under my shoulders. I took a moment simply to breathe, pulling as much air into my tight chest as possible. With each breath, the panic subsided ... and I started seeing stars. Too little air will kill you, too much will make you hyperventilate. There was a lesson in there somewhere, but balance had never been my forté.

Pushing myself from the wall, I continued toward the main hotel, willing myself to walk slowly, to think—there was very little worse than an emoting female who threw logic out the window. And that was so not me—at least not the me I used to be. The before-Teddie me.

But I didn't want to think about that now. I *couldn't* think about that now.

I needed to figure out where I stood on Mr. Paxton Dane. Assuming I swallowed his story, there were gaps in time and evidence at the scene, not to mention a circumstantial case that was starting to look pretty incriminating. And the whole song and dance about Sylvie needing money didn't jibe with her Jimmy Choos—not only the shoes but the fancy handbag as well. Of course, they could've been gifts, but . . . any way I looked at it, the man had *murderer* written all over him. And I didn't have to be Judge Judy to figure out that's exactly where the police would take it. They had to.

But Dane couldn't be a killer. Could he?

I'd seen enough of life to know that we all could resort to homicide if properly provoked. After all, my mother, Mona, had pushed me perilously close so many times that now my neurons automatically flipped to the pissed-off position when excited by the electrical snap of her aura.

Had Dane crossed the line?

After ducking up the service stairs to the mezzanine, I paused at my office door. Stilling myself, I turned my focus inward.

When all else failed, I'd learned to trust my gut instinct, my intuition. It hadn't let me down yet—at least not when I'd been smart enough to listen.

This time, obviously under the influence of a serious case of wishful thinking, my gut told me Dane couldn't be a killer. A creep maybe, something he shared with most of the Y-chromosome set, but he wasn't a shoe-wielding madman.

My gut also told me the stakes were, well, life and death. Death for his wife and life without parole for Dane.

I needed answers and I needed them fast. Once Romeo started poking around, I'd be SOL. Nothing made casino people clam up faster than a bunch of nosy cops.

. . .

AFTER a quick dance between the droplets in my office shower, I dressed for battle, trading flannel and fuzzy slippers for silk and Ferragamos. Although it was only 4 A.M., give or take, my day had started, like it or not.

With one last glance in the mirror on the back of the closet door, I fluffed my hair, not entirely sure the woman who looked back was, in fact, me. My hair had been bottle-blond for so long, I still wasn't used to the natural light brown, the result of a fairly recent makeover. Despite the improvements, recent history had taken its toll. Wrinkles had sprouted, creasing previously unmarred skin. My eyes were tired. My expression, cautious. My smile, a memory.

No doubt some of this was due to Teddie—I had handed him my heart and he . . . well, he left. And when he'd left, he had taken a part of me. I leaned closer to my reflection and narrowed my eyes. Apparently he'd taken the good part.

We had unfinished business, that man and me. And when I saw him again, I hoped I'd be smart enough not to shoot him, but all bets were off—taking the high road wasn't my best thing.

After making a halfhearted attempt with some eye shadow, blush, and other still-foreign potions, I gave up. Nothing was going to save this face. Not today, anyway. Guess I'd have to count on my blue eyes and high cheekbones to keep from scaring small children. Not much to hang the shreds of feminine vanity on, but it was all I had, so I went with it.

In a vain effort to look polished and professional, I stuck the big, square-cut diamonds in each earlobe—gifts from my mother in a weak moment. Then I latched around my neck a large matching diamond on a platinum chain, a gift from myself in a weak moment.

Out of ideas for further self-improvement, I kicked the closet door shut on my reflection, grabbed my sweater from the back of a chair, then shrugged into it as I made my way to the front of the office. The message light on my assistant, Brandy's, desk phone blinked—a scolding red eye in the semidarkness.

I ignored it. It was probably bad news and I'd had enough of that already.

Bounding down the stairs two at a time, I pushed through the fire door at the bottom into the main lobby of the Babylon. At this time of night, it was a veritable mausoleum—okay, not quite the right metaphor. Briefly I squeezed my eyes shut, but being very visual, I couldn't chase away the sight of the girl, Dane's *wife,* Sylvie, on the car.

Covering ground with long strides, I charted a course through the casino. With a practiced eye, I took stock of my surroundings—tonight with a bit more attention to detail than usual. Of course, I didn't *really* expect to find a murderer lurking behind a potted palm, but with me, hope always sprang eternal.

The Babylonian theme redolent in the rest of the hotel was on full display in the casino. The carpets, brightly colored woven mosaics grand enough for a royal's tent, provided a comfortable cushion, muting the noise in addition to setting the stage. The walls were painted a dark, rich purple and trimmed with gold. Torches, real flame encased in blown glass at the ends of bundles of faux reeds, hung from the walls and the columns dotting the casino. They cast a subtle, flickering light, as inviting as logs on a fire.

Multicolored cloth tented above Delilah's Bar, which sat on a raised platform in the center of the casino. A wall of water cascaded down a sandstone wall behind the burnished mahogany counter. Flowering bougainvillea climbed trellises, giving the space a hidden, secretive feel.

Action in the casino was winding down. Guests filled no more than half of the stools in front of the slots. Play at the various tables had been consolidated. Piped-in music, a low, thumping beat, struggled in vain to keep the energy level high. Only a few brave souls, too drunk or too tired to go to bed, still pressed buttons on the video poker machines set into the bar top in Delilah's. The baby grand in the corner sat silent, abandoned.

Teddie used to play that piano.

I shut my heart to the pain as I sailed past.

A lone bartender wiping a glass with a rag returned my nod. Cocktail waitresses shivered in skimpy uniforms as they balanced on high heels. I caught myself looking at their feet—not one of their most ogled body parts, I felt certain. I didn't think I'd find a pair of Jimmy Choos. They weren't exactly work shoes designed for a day spent on your feet. Nor were they within financial reach of the normal working girl— well, maybe the working girls, but not the cocktail hostesses. Although in Vegas sometimes those lines blurred.

Stilettos graced the feet of the few girls who remained—they were part of the uniform, the illusion. One pretty young thing sported a pair of kick-ass, bright red, there's-no-place-like-home slingbacks with peep toes. She looked world-weary and anxious— it was long past a decent hour. Probably a new hire stuck on the graveyard shift, but those shoes were grade A. When she turned and walked away, I glimpsed a red sole. Loubous! I was momentarily overcome with shoe lust. However, heeding the call of duty, I resisted stopping to ask her where she had bought them and kept looking. No sparkly Jimmy Choos. Not a one.

And one was the critical number. Since I actually knew where one of the shoes was, I was only looking for its mate. How would that work? I had no idea. Where was Prince Charming when I needed him? He had plenty of experience with one glass slipper.

Guess I'd leave that to the police as well—the shoe part, I mean. Despite my miserable track record, I still felt I could handle the Prince Charming part.

Self-delusional to the end. A fitting epitaph.

But I wasn't going to think about that either.

IN contrast to the subdued vibe of the casino, the Poker Room was firing on all cylinders. The mood was hushed, but energy shimmered off the crowd clustered at the railing dividing the Poker Room from the main casino. Worried about cheating, most casinos prohibited nonplayers from huddling too close to the action. Ours was no exception. Tonight the throng was at least three deep.

The thousand-dollar buy-in Sylvie had played in had finished up—the table was empty. Presumably a winner had been declared and the players had wandered off to find more action, celebrate their winnings, lick their wounds . . . or die on the hood of a Ferrari.

Vegas, the town of endless possibilities.

The high-stakes marquee action played out at the tables nearest to the railing. At the front table eight players matched wits and nerves at a high-stakes game. Among the players I recognized two pros, both trying to look bored as they listened to music through earbuds, and a top-ranked amateur who had won a World Series of Poker bracelet several years ago and made serious money through an off-shore Internet poker site he'd formed. Two of our regular high-roller whales were seated across from each other. One of them looked less than confident—a fact I felt sure had the pros circling like wolves around a wounded fawn.

The other players hadn't hit my radar, but among them was an older woman. I liked it. High-stakes poker was notoriously unwelcoming to women, as if somehow a dose of estrogen would completely counteract all that testosterone and render the men ineffectual. Oh, if wishing would make it so!

Each player carefully guarded the stacks of chips in front of him, the number and color of which provided an easily readable measure of the player's success. It looked like the amateur was just joining the game. One of the pros had drawn the most blood, but the older woman was holding her own. All in all, the stacks weren't too disparate in size or color, so the game was just ramping up. Far from an expert, I did a quick calculation. Each stack ran to the hundreds of thousands.

Hence the crowd. Hence the energy.

As I eased through the small, gated entrance, raised voices captured my attention. One of the voices seemed a bit garbled, yet while the words weren't sharp, the anger came through loud and clear.

The other voice, low and demeaning, I recognized instantly. It belonged to our longtime Poker Room manger, Marvin J. Johnstone—a pain in the ass who kept his job simply because the casino manager was too scared to fire him. I would have been delighted to can his ass, but from my perch on the corporate ladder, such a task was beneath my pay-grade.

Marvin, who preferred to be addressed as "Marvin J.," but who was mostly not so fondly referred to as "the Stoneman," had attached himself to the Big Boss, our fearless leader, back before the earth was cool. As the Big Boss moved from property to property, clawing his way up the food chain, so too did Marvin. But Marvin, a parasite living off the host, reached his high-water mark at middle management, where he had been abusing the staff ever since.

He was a small man, nattily attired in black tie. With sallow skin, a long, pinched face, and closely set, dark eyes, he reminded me of a ferret—well, a ferret with a really bad comb-over.

The Stoneman and a young man in blue jeans sporting a head of shaggy dark hair, a soul patch under his lower lip, and an angry stare, faced off behind the lone open chair at the high-stakes table.

"Forgive me, sir," the Stoneman said, not looking the least bit sorry, "you may not play at this table."

Arms moving animatedly, the young man opened his mouth and spoke, but the words sounded as if they'd been spoken under water.

Red faced with a sheen of perspiration, the Stoneman raised an eyebrow as he ran a finger under his collar, tugging as if it were too tight. He crossed his arms, a look of exaggerated patience tinged with a hint of disdain settling over his features. Clearly, Marvin considered dealing with the young man an act of kindness worthy of canonization.

With his patience obviously held by a thin tether, the young man whirled to a man standing behind him and began signing rapidly. I never knew anger could infuse silent, signed words. When the young man was done, he whirled back to the Stoneman as his friend interpreted for him.

"Mr. Johnstone, my friend here has all the prerequisites with this hotel to participate in this game. I can only assume that you are denying him the open chair because he is deaf."

"He doesn't have the star power to play at the

premier table. I mean, who wants to watch some . . . handicapped kid play?"

My anger instantly redlined. My eyes closed to slits as I advanced on our Poker Room manager. "Is there a problem?"

The Stoneman started to bite off a reply, but when he saw me, his eyes widened and he clamped his mouth shut. Wise man. I had him by about six inches, thirty pounds, seventy IQ points, and multiple rungs on the corporate ladder.

The young man's interpreter needlessly explained the situation. The Stoneman, flying in the face of every corporate policy I was aware of, and I knew them all—I'd written the book—was using his own biases to deny a legitimate player, fully vetted and fully funded, a place in the primo game.

Because the kid was deaf.

And in doing so, he not only exposed the hotel to legal ramifications, he offended me on every level.

I turned to the Stoneman, pulled myself to my full height, conjured Donald Trump, and said simply, "You're fired."

Normally, firing people gave me hives. This was not one of those times.

The room fell silent. The games stopped.

Marvin J.'s already red face flushed crimson as he breathed heavily, putting a song in my heart. Hey, shallow is my middle name. I take my jollies where I find them—a character flaw I've learned to embrace.

Defensively, the young poker player took a step back, giving us space.

"You can't fire me," the Stoneman hissed. Nervously, he wet his lips with his tongue. I half expected it to be forked.

"I just did. You've been begging for it for years and tonight you happened to hit me when I am hardwired to the pissed-off position." And the planets had aligned to make me the right person, in the right place, at the right time. How I love synchronicity. But I didn't say that part. Holding his gaze with mine, I flipped open my phone and pushed talk. "Security, please send a team to the Poker Room. Mr. Johnstone has been fired and I wish you to escort him off the premises."

"You are a god among mortals," Jerry said with an awe-filled chuckle. "Once the staff gets wind of this, you could be elected emperor."

"A thankless job. More work, less pay, and generally terminated with a beheading."

"Giving credence to the adage that no good deed goes unpunished."

"Perfect, I just *love* being the proof to a cliché." Actually, cliché whore that I am, that did have a sort of perverted appeal, but I'd never admit to it.

"Your security team is twenty seconds away."

"Thanks." Enjoying this far more than I should have, I snapped my phone shut with a flourish and repocketed it.

"The Big Boss will have your head," Marvin spluttered, his face mottled, his breath coming in short gasps. When he leaned in, his breath smelled like Amaretto or something nutty and his eyes were a bit wild.

I wondered if he'd been drinking. "Just because you're his daughter . . ."

My eyes narrowed even more as I lowered my voice and whispered into our now former Poker Room manager's ear. "Before you play that card, I'd think it through."

Marvin snapped his mouth shut and for the first time, realization dawned in his eyes. His demeanor changed, his face softened. He wrung his hands as he looked up at me with those tiny, feral eyes. He squinted like a rat seeing the sun after a night in the sewers—or like a man with a serious hangover. He was sweating pretty good now—beads of water trickled off his forehead. "There's been a misunderstanding, Miss O'Toole. You're reading this all wrong. I was planning to call someone from the list, so the young man couldn't have the seat."

"Policy states you resort to the list to keep the table full only if you don't have any qualified players waiting to play." I raised a questioning eyebrow at the young man. "Mister?"

"Weston," the interpreter said.

"Mr. Weston is to take the chair." I waved to the two security guards pushing through the throng at the railing. "And the only misunderstanding is yours, Marvin. A grant of power does not include the license to abuse it. You're finished here. And if you don't leave now, I'll see that you're finished in Vegas." I'd always wanted to say that. And much to my delight, I sounded like a petty hood from one of those horrible old mobster movies. That wasn't my

Vegas, but I was having fun, so I went with it. However, I did resist rolling out my Robert De Niro impersonation. "But I wouldn't go too far, the police are going to want to talk to you."

One of the guards grabbed Marvin by the arm and urged him toward the exit.

The guy was a reptile, but he was smart enough to know my threat was far from hollow. "I'm not done with you," the Stoneman spat as he allowed the guard to lead him away.

All eyes followed the threesome until the crowd swallowed them. No one said a word as I sighed and blew a lock of hair out of my eyes. Boy, getting to be the one who finally fired the Stoneman! I was living at the foot of the cross.

The sound of clapping broke the silence. Starting in the back of the room, at first only a few hands came together. Then, like a wave hitting the shoals, the sound grew until the whole room joined in the crescendo. Startled, I slowly rotated. Everywhere I looked I gazed into smiling eyes. The staff, the players, all stood as they applauded . . . me!

Rachael, the assistant Poker Room manager, rushed to my side. Not yet out of her twenties, she looked at me through red-rimmed eyes as big as saucers. Puffy and bloodshot, her eyes reminded me of long nights spent dealing with people betting more than they could afford to lose. "You have no idea what you have done," she said, her voice breathless as if after a long sprint.

I rolled my eyes and swiped at that stubborn

strand of hair once again. "I have an idea," I sighed. What I had done was create one more major pain in the ass to be dealt with. Preferring dignity, Marvin might have left the room quietly, but he wouldn't go without a fuss. Poker Room manager was a cherry job. Most would sacrifice body parts to keep it. I had no doubt Marvin J. Johnstone was no exception . . . and the body parts sacrificed would be mine. The rodent would take a few bites out of my ass before I was rid of him.

Oh well, that's why they paid me the big bucks. Not to mention, my ass could use a little whittling.

"Rachael, you are now the acting Poker Room manager. Can you handle that?"

"Yes, ma'am," she said with conviction.

Youthful enthusiasm. Mine had left so long ago and so quickly I don't even remember it packing for the trip. "You understand I don't have the authority to make your position permanent. The casino manager will make that decision."

She nodded curtly then turned to the room. With a few nonverbal signals, she launched her staff and they busied themselves ensuring the games currently in play resumed with the minimum of fuss. Timers needed to be reset. Cards and chips checked. And every player needed to be reminded where their game was in the betting, what the blinds were, and when they would increase. Rules needed to be rigidly followed. The Gaming Control Board was sticky about that.

I turned to young Mr. Weston.

A handsome kid, he eyed me with a mixture of disdain and amusement—a hard, steely stare tempered with challenge. His arms hung at his sides. His fingers twitched as if he were muttering under his breath, aching to tell me off. One shoulder seemed to dip under the weight of the chip it carried.

Couldn't fault him there. This called for serious sucking up.

I looked him in the eye and touched him lightly on the arm. The deaf people I knew spoke as much with touch as they did with their hands. Since he played poker, I assumed he could read lips. "I am so sorry. I apologize for the rudeness of my former colleague. Please, the seat is yours." I pulled out the chair for him.

With a slight nod and enough hesitation to make me think he might refuse, he accepted my invitation. A steward brought a tray of chips and set it in front of him. Now all business, the kid fell to counting his chips and arranging them to suit himself. He didn't make eye contact with any of the other players. They seemed to be ignoring him as well.

Part of the game.

However, I'd played enough to know, through their feigned disinterest, every player was meticulously noting habits and expressions of his fellow warriors. During at least the first hour of play, they would play tight, going to school on each other. Each one would be looking for tells, subconscious signs a player might give that would indicate what kind of hand he was holding, whether he was bluffing or not, whether his card had come on the river, or whether he was betting the bundle on less than stellar odds.

To me, watching a poker game was as scintillating as trimming the lawn with nail clippers. But for reasons best not explored, the game seemed to hold men spellbound.

"You may converse with Mr. Weston prior to the game starting and during the breaks," I said to the interpreter. "In fact, it would be beneficial if you could interpret the rules as they are being given to the table. But I would appreciate it if you would not communicate while the game is in progress. One hand, one player, I trust you know the drill."

"Understood."

I raised an eyebrow at the game steward, who was standing within earshot. He nodded in understanding.

Leaving the operation of the game to the pros, I wandered to the back of the room to observe the play occurring there. Sidling in next to the game steward, I stopped and watched for a moment. The gamesmanship was subtle, but it was there. It took guile and cojones to play poker.

Something it seemed the former Mrs. Dane had in spades.

"How long have you been monitoring play?" I asked the steward at my side.

"My shift started at midnight. I rotated to this table an hour ago."

Stepping away from the table, I motioned for him to follow me. With a nod he summoned another steward to take his place.

"Do you remember a young woman, platinum hair, silver dress?" I asked when we were comfortably out of earshot. "She busted out of the thousand-dollar buy-in a few hours ago."

The young man gave me a grin. "Ms. O'Toole, I'm young, male, and have a pulse."

I fought back a grin. "I'll take that as a yes. Did you notice anything unusual about her?"

"She wasn't at my table, but I could tell she played pretty aggressively, for a girl." Pausing, he blushed when he realized what he had said. "No offense, ma'am."

"After that remark, it's 'sir' to you." At his stricken look, I said, "I'm kidding. Anything else you notice about her?"

"Well, not that jumped out, but she did cause a bit of a dustup between Rachael and the Stone— Mr. Johnstone." He colored at his near faux pas.

This time when I fought with my smile, my smile won, surprising me—I thought it had gone on tour with Teddie. "Really? What about?"

"I don't know." The kid cast a furtive glance at Rachael. "I'm speaking out of turn here, but since it's you. . . . Whatever it was, it was pretty serious. Mr. Johnstone was really angry. Rachael was crying when the silver dress lady left."

"Did you notice the silver dress lady leave with

anyone? Did anyone pay more attention to her than they should?"

"Half the room couldn't keep their eyes off her. And she left while I was dealing with a break and a reset of the blinds at my table."

"Anything else you notice?"

"The game broke up pretty soon after she left. The amateur cleaned everyone out. Nobody was too happy about it—excepting him, of course." He paused, pursing his lips and narrowing his eyes in concentration. I let him think. Finally, he said, "There was one other thing. I don't know if it's important, but Mr. Johnstone left the Poker Room right after."

"Left?" I crossed my arms and leveled a stern gaze on the young man. "Really? Managers don't just abandon the room when high-stakes games are getting under way."

"I thought it was weird, too." The kid's eyes widened; sincerity infused his features. "He wasn't gone long. And when he came back, he ducked into the back for a minute. If you ask me, he looked sorta spook-eyed, like he'd seen a ghost or something."

I struggled to keep my face a mask—news of Sylvie Dane's fatal foot fetish was still under wraps. "Anything else leap out at you?"

The kid chewed on his lip, then shook his head slowly.

"So you didn't happen to notice she was cheating?"

Chapter

THREE

♡

"*C*heating?" The young man's Adam's apple bobbed up and down as he paled. "How?"

"What color were her eyes?"

Now, in addition to looking half sick, the steward looked confused . . . and a bit dreamy. "Blue. She wore sunglasses, but I'm sure they were blue," he announced like a lovesick schoolboy.

God, responsibility was so wasted on the young.

"Yes," I said, feeling ancient. "But not the same color of blue. One was light blue, the other a muddier blue."

Still the light didn't dawn.

"A red contact lens," I said, dispensing with the clues.

"But that's illegal in Nevada," the young man said, a bit louder than I'd have liked. Heads turned in our direction. With a finger to my lips, I shushed him as I pulled him farther from the action.

"Cheating is certainly illegal. While fitting anyone with a red contact lens isn't technically against the law, it's certainly strongly frowned upon." The thought made my blood simmer. A magical place, Vegas painted a pretty picture when folks colored between the lines. "She was marking cards. The red contact lens allowed her to see the mark. I know it may come as a shock, but people do nefarious things all the time here."

He looked at me as if he didn't know what *nefarious* meant. "But if she was cheating, why did she lose?"

Before I could wrap my brain around that, my father's voice sounded at my elbow and the young steward eased back toward his table. "Isn't it a bit early for you to be causing your usual ruckus?"

A Las Vegas legend, Albert Rothstein, otherwise known as the Big Boss, had been in the casino business so long he could wax poetic about the days when the Strip was a two-lane road, the Rat Pack was the hottest ticket in town, and Sinatra used to hang out at the Garden Room at the Sands, chowing down on the ninety-nine-cent special and abusing the staff. My father's start in the business was a bit murky, adding to his mystique. But with a nose for money, an uncanny knack for managing his balance sheet, and an unerring ability to avoid even the hint of impropriety, he had risen to the top of the heap in a dog-eat-dog world. A glamorous position . . . if you didn't mind mongrels nipping at your heels.

Of course, when he'd hired me as a cabana girl when I was fifteen and had lied about my age, I didn't know he was my father. A little secret he and my mother had only recently let me in on. They'd had their reasons for keeping it to themselves and, while I sort of understood, I still hadn't quite forgiven either one of them. But no one is guaranteed a perfect life and, all things considered, mine was darn close. Well, if you ignore my unerring penchant for picking the wrong guy. However I couldn't blame anyone else for that—although I'd really like to.

A short man, as fit as a boxer in his prime, with a head of salt-and-pepper hair, my father exuded a quiet confidence and a steely resolve that endeared him to his employees and struck fear in the hearts of his competitors. Tonight he wore creased black slacks, Italian loafers, no socks, a starched white shirt, and a smile for me. How anyone could be un-crumpled at this ungodly hour was an enduring mystery. It wasn't hereditary, that was for sure.

"If you've come down here about the girl in the Ferrari showroom . . ." I glanced around, making sure no one was paying particular attention to our conversation, but everyone seemed to be focused on his or her own tasks.

He pursed his lips, then shook his head. "I figure you've got it under control. Turn it over to the police and then manage their interference. You've done it a thousand times."

Well, not quite that many, thankfully, but I wasn't going to argue. Through the years the Big Boss had seen stuff I didn't even want to think about. "Death has become mundane, has it?" I said, trying to make light, but with my heavy heart I don't think I pulled it off.

"As long as it's not imminent," my father shot back.

He had a point, I guess. Not one I could identify

with, but I'd learned long ago the Big Boss was who he was. For a long time I'd wondered whether he knew where any bodies were buried. Vegas being what it is, he'd done business with the mob back in the day and the whispers still followed him. He'd never cultivated that reputation, but he didn't work to dispel the rumors either. So he remained surrounded by mystery—something I think he got a big bang out of. Personally, I couldn't see my father throwing his lot in with Tony Spilotro, Lefty Rosenthal, and the boys, but as recent history had proven once again, I was not the best judge of character—especially when it came to men. However, family was family—blood thicker than water and all that. I looped an arm around his shoulders, gave him a quick squeeze, then stepped back. In heels, I had him by at least six inches—a fact that always surprised me. He just seemed . . . bigger.

"Poker, a game that totally eludes me." He nodded toward the two pros now engrossed in the game the young Mr. Weston had just joined. "Give me some dice to throw and I'm all in."

"Nothing like the rush of a pure, unadulterated gamble?"

He gave me a knowing look, the sort a father shares with a child. No words were necessary. For some reason, the exchange gave me a warm fuzzy. We'd had those moments before, when I hadn't known of our blood relation, but somehow, the father-daughter thing changed things in a subtle, insidious, heartwarming way. Working my head from side to side in an attempt to move muscles that felt like tight steel bands, I rolled my eyes at myself. What was it with me lately? *Soft* and *mushy* were not adjectives anyone would use to describe me, of that I felt certain.

I must be hormonal. Meaningful sex would be a good cure for that. But given my lack of a meaningful relationship, that was a pipe dream. However, even a dog with a bad nose eventually found a bone, right? Easily amused, I smiled at the puns.

"What?" my father asked.

"What?" My face fell into a mask of guilty innocence.

"What were you smiling at?"

Once again ignoring the impropriety of touching my boss—it sent all the wrong messages to those who cared enough to notice—I hooked my arm through my father's. "That you will never know. There are simply some things a father should never know about his daughter."

"Probably so. I shock easily," he teased.

"So, how was the party?" I asked in a deft change of topic. Each year before the Smack Down begins the Big Boss hosted a party for all the big guns in the poker world. Most of them had been longtime friends so the party usually wound up late and involved a king's ransom in single-malt and Habanos.

"Exhausting. Back in the day I could hold my own, but not anymore. Now they leave me in the dust—even the old farts. I can't tell you how good that makes me feel." He shot me a grin, which took the whine out of his statement.

"Was Frank DeLuca there?"

"Sure, but he left early."

"How early?"

My father gave me a shrewd look. "A little before midnight. Why?"

"You know why. We've got a dead girl in his dealership. Inquiring minds are going to want to know his whereabouts between two and two thirty this morning."

"Frank's been around."

I didn't know exactly what he meant by that. I wanted to pursue it, but there was a time and a place, and his clipped tone told me this was neither. "Anyone else interesting there?"

"The usual suspects." The knife-edge slid from my father's voice. "Funny thing though. This year Shady Slim was a no-show."

"That's not like him."

"No, it's not. And he hasn't checked in yet . . . I looked into it myself." A shadow of worry passed across my father's face. "His health hasn't been good, but still, normally he would let me know if he couldn't make it."

"I'll follow up tomorrow." I gave his arm a squeeze just because I felt like it. "Tonight you may be feeling your years, but I bet you were the only expectant father in the room."

Like a kid caught out after curfew, he blanched and shot me a worried look. "Shoot, I forgot."

"Forgot what?"

"Your mother," he said, weariness creeping into his voice.

"How could anyone forget Mona? She'd never allow it." Another thought wiped the grin off my face. "She's okay, isn't she?"

My mother, the former owner of Mona's Place, the self-styled "Best Whorehouse in Nevada," had recently had a life-changing experience. My parents, afraid of offending those holding the keys to the kingdom—marrying an underage hooker would have catapulted my father right off the fast track, and probably have landed him in jail—had carried a torch for each other for half a lifetime. After a recent health scare and with the realization that they no longer had anything to lose other than perhaps their last chance at happiness, my parents had married. And now, after years in the sex trade, Mona found herself inexplicably with child—at an age where normal mothers are looking forward to bouncing grandchildren on their knees. Of course, *normal* was never an adjective used to describe Mother.

Call me shallow, but I took a perverted delight in the cosmic justice, the laughable irony of it all.

Except when I had to deal with her.

A one-woman weapon of mass destruction, a pregnant Mona should have come with a biohazard warning label.

I took a good hard look at my father. He seemed to be holding up well. Of course, he was made of sterner stuff than his daughter.

"How exactly would you define *okay*?" my father asked with a tired grin. "She's alive and well, propped up in bed, miserable, unable to sleep—so that means neither of us gets any shut-eye. Now she wants ice cream and something covered with mustard. I've been wandering around for half an hour trying to figure out what that might be."

Every Achilles had his heel and Mona was my father's.

"Is it really going to matter? She won't be hungry when you get back, so get her a bowl of raspberry gelato, her favorite, and a big Coney dog with mustard." My stomach roiled at the thought. "And perhaps a double hit of single-malt for you."

"You wouldn't like to—" My father shot me his hangdog look.

I fought the urge to cave and give him what he wanted. If only there were a vaccine against handsome men. "Do I look suicidal?"

"Well, there's a rumor floating around that you took down the mighty Stoneman, so I had high hopes that, fortified with the thrill of victory, you might be willing to wade back into the fray."

"Please, Marvin is a piker compared to Mother. She would be less than pleased at the comparison. I'd love to walk with you, but I still have some tidying up to do." I caught Rachael's eye and motioned for her to come over. My father gave my hand a quick squeeze then left to continue his mission. I didn't envy him—a thankless, dangerous job trying to mollify a pregnant woman. "Rachael," I said, turning my attention to the young woman as she rushed to my side. "Do you remember a blonde in a silver dress playing in the thousand-dollar buy-in?"

"The one who was cheating?" Rachael said it so matter-of-factly I almost blew right by.

"You knew?"

"Of course. The game had been in progress an hour when my shift started. I was to take over from Mr. Johnstone." The girl stared over my shoulder, her eyes unfocused as if she were reviewing an internal tape. "I wanted to remove her from the table. That's standard procedure," she said unnecessarily. "But I was overruled."

"Is that what you and Mr. Johnstone argued about?"

"He wanted to fire me. He said I was being insubordinate." Rachael's eyes welled up. "Ms. O'Toole, I was just trying to do my job."

"I know you were." I gave her a pat.

"And now she's turned up dead and all." A tear leaked out despite her best efforts to fight it back. "I feel terrible."

"Dead?" I asked, feigning innocence.

"That's what I heard."

"From whom?"

"Mr. Johnstone."

"When?"

"I don't know. The lady in the silver dress had just left and her game was winding up. It was after that

that Mr. Johnstone asked for twenty minutes of personal time—I had to get the high-stakes games under way myself."

"I see," I said, which was a bald-faced lie. "Was it normal for Mr. Johnstone to leave like that?"

"No, but we all have emergencies." Rachael wiped her hands down her pants as she regained her composure a bit. "We all cover for each other."

"You're sure Mr. Johnstone didn't notice the lady . . . in question . . . was cheating?"

"Apparently not, and he refused to question the woman about it." Rachael worried with the end of a strand of hair, twisting it around her finger. "I would've been fired if you hadn't fired Mr. Johnstone first."

Her weak smile torpedoed mine, and my mood sank with it. I had a real bad feeling about this. "Did you call Security?"

"Mr. Johnstone was livid, but yes, I called them." Rachael nodded. "He was here in a jiffy."

"He?" It had been my experience that Security usually came in twos.

"Yeah, it was sorta weird, but since I'd seen the guy around, I didn't think too much of it at the time."

"Much of what?"

"Well," the girl again tugged at a strand of blond hair. I resisted the urge to take her hand and make her stop. "Like I said, after I called, this guy shows up real fast."

"Can you describe him?" If she couldn't, I'd bet all my worldly possessions that I could.

"Yes, a tall, handsome man, green eyes, brown hair,

jeans—the guy with the whole cowboy thing going on. Give me a minute, I'll remember his name." A slightly goofy, dreamy look flashed across her features. I'd seen that look on a woman's face before. And I knew who'd put it there.

"Dane?" I offered, knowing the answer.

"That's it! How'd you know?"

"Lucky guess." Sometimes it sucked to be right. My voice took on a murderous tone. "You said all this was weird. What exactly did you mean?"

"I don't need to tell you, Ms. O'Toole, that Security usually comes in pairs, so it was odd he showed up alone. Then, when a security team showed up a bit later, I knew something wasn't cricket."

"You turned them away?"

"I told them what happened, but they didn't seem alarmed so I let it go." The girl worried with the medallion she wore around her neck, sliding it first one way then the other on the long gold chain. "Looking back, maybe I should have done something else."

"I don't know what." I resisted reaching out and grabbing her hand to stop the worried motion. The girl was as twitchy as a dog with fleas. "So, Dane shows up. What happened then?" I asked even though I knew the answer.

"Mr. Dane and the woman left together. He said he could handle it from there."

DANE had handled it all right. And now he was trying to handle me. Not a good idea if longevity was part of his future plans. Running on high-octane adrenaline, I covered ground through the casino in long, angry strides. I hated to be played. I hated to be lied to. Guess that made me pretty normal. *Normal*—what a mediocre word—and not something I especially aspired to, which somehow made me even angrier.

But Dane could wait.

Right now, I needed to track down Frank DeLuca before the cops rode up on my tail.

Grabbing my phone from its hip cradle, I pushed talk. "Jerry, you got a bead on Frank DeLuca?"

"Gimme a sec. I caught a glimpse of him on one of the feeds not too long ago." Jerry sounded tired, not that I was surprised—we both were rowing the same boat.

"You think he's still around?"

"Poker dudes are nocturnal creatures. Besides, as one of the last nine players in this weekend's shindig—he's basking in the attention."

"With everything else, I'd forgotten about that."

Jerry whistled under his breath as I waited. I could picture him scrolling through the feeds. "Yup, there he is. Garden Bar, top tier. From the looks of him, he's been there a while."

"Thanks." I reholstered my phone and ran.

At this time of morning, the crowd in the casino consisted of either those too drunk to find their rooms, or those winning or losing big. Music thumped in the background. Glasses clinked in the bar, not from frivolity but from the bartender washing, drying, and putting away. Vegas might be the city that never sleeps, but the energy level did have its own circadian rhythm. Right now it faded to a low ebb allowing for regenerating, recharging, and for me to actually make it across the hotel and out the back in near record time.

The Garden Bar hung in the branches of a huge tree overlooking the pool area. Reminiscent of the Swiss Family Robinson tree house but on steroids, the bar consisted of several levels, each with a counter in the middle surrounded by barstools. A rope and mesh fence that was stronger than it looked ringed the perimeter and protected patrons from a plunge to sure disability. At appropriate intervals, two-tops cozied up to the rope enclosure.

The real trick here was not finding the place, but getting to it. A wobbly plank and rope footbridge connected the structure to the mezzanine level of the hotel. Late at night when I was feeling particularly sadistic, I loved to park myself next to the bridge and watch the patrons who had sampled too much of the local firewater negotiate a bridge that moved. Tonight my mood ran more to homicidal, so I didn't stop.

DeLuca hadn't moved. Slumped down in his chair, he reminded me of a rag doll, slack and forlorn. One hand fisted around a glass firmly anchored him to a two-top next to the railing. By all accounts he was a handsome man, thick and broad, oozing virility and a hint of impishness when he smiled. Women flocked to him, eager to run their fingers through his thick, black hair or to discover the joke that lit his eyes. And, through some divine lack of spine, he'd never been able to resist a pretty face, tight body, large rack, curvaceous booty, or any combination thereof—at least, not that I'd ever been able to tell. Married several times, Frank was an eternal optimist and self-delusional to the end. He seemed genuinely surprised each time a wife would take umbrage with his dalliances.

Guileless, a child in a man's body, Frank was the kind of guy a woman hated to love . . . but one they couldn't resist. Thankfully, since I'd called him Uncle Frank for as long as I could remember, I'd been inoculated. Besides, he was my father's age, but as I recall, Wife Number Four had been two years behind me in school. She'd worked flat on her back under Frank for a few years, until she was certain the courts would give her a solid stake. I'd heard she'd bought a high-end jewelry store at one of our competitors, but I wasn't sure. As far as I knew, Frank hadn't married again.

Frank looked up when I eased into the chair across from him. He flashed me a pale imitation of his famous smile.

"You okay?" I asked, reaching across the table and squeezing his arm.

"Sorta shook, you know?" Red-rimmed, his eyes were wet. His hand shook as he wiped away any trace of a tear. "I didn't have anything to do with that girl." His expression reminded me of a kid trying to convince the authorities he hadn't blown up the chemistry lab despite the M-80 in his back pocket.

"My father tells me you left his party early. That's not the last-to-leave-Frank I know and love."

"I gotta call from Slim's plane. He wanted me to meet him at the airport."

"Why?"

"He was all riled over the political wrangling around legalizing Internet poker and bringing it back onshore." Frank turned his glass in his hand, then took a long pull. "You know they got that legislation before Congress. Everybody's pickin' sides. A huge pile of money is at stake."

"We've all been trying to figure that one out. But why'd Slim want to talk at midnight when both of you were supposed to be at the Big Boss's party?"

"He'd gotten wind someone was fighting dirty, trying to kill the legislation."

"Why'd he care?"

"You know how he is, guarding the sacred game of poker."

"The cheaters ought to be shot at dawn?" I said, smiling at the memories. How many times had I heard Slim say that as he pounded the table? "Do you know where he is now?"

"I left him on the plane. He said he was 'hittin'

the hay,' as he put it." Frank motioned to the cocktail waitress hovering nearby. "I'll take another. Lucky, you want anything?"

Needing breakfast, I nodded. "Wild Turkey 101, make it a double." I waited until we both had our libations in hand before continuing. "So you met him at, what? About midnight?"

"A bit later, maybe half after. We talked for about an hour, I guess."

"Where'd you leave it?" I took a sip of whiskey, looking for courage. "And where'd you go after?"

"Lucky, girl, you're getting awful personal."

I didn't say anything. Instead, my eyes sought his. Holding them, I didn't blink.

Finally he broke our gaze. "I hadn't talked any sense into him. I had the feeling he was going to be proactive, if you get my drift, with or without my help."

"Did he name any names?"

Frank shook his head. "After that, I went home . . . alone."

"You didn't come back to the hotel?"

"I didn't have anything to do with that girl, if that's what you're driving at. She came on to me, you know. We met playing poker—she beat the pants off me." He tossed me a weak grin. "Never had a girl do that to me before."

"I bet."

"At poker." He gave me a semisuggestive look. With Frank, flirting was his default language. "Boy, she was a pretty thing." He shook his head as he stared into his drink. Whatever he was looking for, I doubted he'd find it there.

"And?" I took a sip of my liquid sustenance. For some reason I wasn't ashamed—if beer could be a breakfast food . . . well, this was just the natural progression.

"Nothing," Frank said with forced casualness.

"Any idea how she came to know your code word to the security system at the dealership?"

Shock registered in his eyes, turning them from a light blue to a distant gray. "The cops didn't tell me that part."

"You talked to the cops already?" This time the surprise was mine.

"They called me about the . . . murder." He shivered. "I raced right down to the dealership. But nobody mentioned the code thing."

My heart rate slowed. Dodged that bullet. Romeo's was the last shit list I wanted to find my name on. "They didn't know."

Frank pushed himself up in his chair. "I appreciate you not telling them, Lucky. That'd make it real bad for me."

"You understand I'm going to have to tell them eventually?"

He shrugged, his reluctance poorly hidden.

"Come clean, Frank. The sooner we catch the killer, the better for all of us." Even the whiff of murder threw the media into a feeding frenzy. My entire staff and all their considerable talents might not be enough to keep us from being sucked into the maw of public opinion and digested whole.

"Nothing to tell, really. Me and Sylvie, we got drunk together a few times. Had some laughs."

"Where?"

"The dealership once or twice, but home mostly."

"And do you have your code word written down anywhere, or is it on a computer or something?" Frank was old-school—I doubted he knew how to turn on a computer much less use one, but I had to ask.

"I keep all my personal stuff in a notebook in my desk drawer at home." His brows furrowed, but he didn't look too worried. "The drawer's locked."

"Personal stuff?"

"Bank accounts, brokerage accounts, the odd investment or two, the security code word, passwords, stuff like that." Frank shrugged as if he couldn't imagine anyone stupid enough to tamper with his stuff. Personally, I couldn't imagine someone that brazen either. Frank might play the clown, but when it came to business, he was anything but. And he had important friends.

"And your money?"

"All accounted for. I checked a little while ago. I got this app on my iPhone." He pulled the device out of his pocket and pushed it across the table toward me. Along with it came a Baggie containing a few recognizable blue pills, which he hurriedly grabbed and stuffed back in his pocket.

I raised an eyebrow and gave him what I hoped to be a disapproving look.

"Don't want to go falling down on the job. I'd sure hate to disappoint the ladies with a lackluster performance." He had the decency to blush as he grabbed his phone and pushed it into his pocket also.

"Up to you," I said as I revised my opinion about Frank and computers—and because not only was I fluent in sarcasm, but I dabbled in innuendo as well. "You said you entertained her in the dealership. Could she have overheard you using the code word then?"

The corners of his mouth turned down. "I suppose. I'm not that careful, especially after throwing back a couple. Besides, being in the company of a beautiful woman, code words and silly shit like that weren't exactly uppermost in my mind."

I resisted crawling up on my soapbox. Casual sex gives me hives. And disdain for security punches my buttons. "Any idea why she would take the code?"

"She didn't take it. She wanted me to change it—thought it would be cool. Dead man's hand . . . sorta creepy now, like she knew or something. All we got in there is cars, and the keys are locked tight in a safe every night. We don't carry much cash."

"Anything missing?"

"No." He sighed. "And now I'm gonna have one hell of a time unloading that car. I thought I had it sold to that amateur, but now . . ."

"Amateur?"

"Yeah, that Slurry kid. He test-drove it yesterday and was all hot to go. He had the jack, too."

"If he doesn't want it, feng shui it and sell it overseas," I said, half joking.

"You can do that?"

"Who knows?" I waved his next question away, interjecting one of my own. "You don't know what Sylvie was doing in your dealership? What she wanted?"

"Haven't a clue."

"Well, whatever it is, someone was willing to kill for it."

Chapter

FOUR

♡

*A*s promised, Jerry was still reigning over Security when I pushed through the door and entered his fiefdom. Pausing for a moment to allow my eyes to adjust to the relative darkness, I casually scanned the banks of monitors that dotted the long wall opposite the door. They formed an electronic mosaic, an ever-changing glimpse of life in all parts of the casino and hotel—other than the guest rooms and the bathrooms. Don't ever let them say there are no boundaries in Vegas.

At this time of the morning, with action across the property winding down, only a few of Jerry's staff sat in front of the wall of monitors searching the feeds for anything unusual. This being Vegas, *unusual* was a relative term. Perhaps it would be more accurate to say they were looking for anything criminal, as were the others seated in front of a smaller bank of monitors on an adjacent wall. These were the gaming experts. More often than not, they were former cheats, experts at scamming the casinos. After paying their debt to society, they helped us ferret out those in their former profession.

Jerry stood behind his staff, his hands clasped behind his back, his feet spread like a captain manning the bridge as his ship rode the swells. A tall, thin black man with a closely shaven head, an open face, wide, warm eyes, and a ready smile, Jerry had been my port in a storm through the years. Often, he'd been a surrogate father when I thought I didn't have a real one, doling out wisdom and keeping confidences.

Somewhere along the journey from yesterday into today, he had abandoned his suit coat and loosened his tie. His trousers and the back of his shirt were creased from too much sitting and too much stress. Even though I doubted it was possible, I swore his skin held a sallow tint from too much fluorescent light and not enough of the full-spectrum kind. Although all parts of the hotel except the casino had been declared a smoke-free environment, a cigarette dangled from his lips. He seemed oblivious to the ashes as they grew into a feathery cone, then fell to the carpet.

"Finally, I found someone who looks like I feel," I said as I moved to stand beside him.

His eyes were red and tired as he gave me the once-over. "Sorry to break it to you, sweetheart, but you also look like you feel. If you feel like shit, that is."

Pleasantries exchanged, we grinned at each other.

Jerry led me to his office, a small, glass-walled cubicle in the far corner of the room. We each took a chair in front of a single computer monitor. After I had filled him in on the high points of my evening, he cued the tape.

"You're not going to like this," he said as he fast-forwarded, scrolling through the time line for the appropriate spot. He stopped the tape and the screen went white.

"What is that?"

"Someone hung a paper banner in front of the camera, blocking it from recording the traffic into and out of the Ferrari dealership."

The cheap butcher paper sign that was hanging by one corner when I left! "When?"

"Early evening. Somebody stuck it down in Maintenance. Hotel staff put it up."

"On whose authority?" My voice had a sharper tone than I intended.

"Yours."

The head of steam that was building vanished in a whoosh as my breath left me. "Mine?" I leaned back in the chair and cocked an eyebrow at him. "I didn't authorize that . . . monstrosity."

"They're looking for the maintenance order now. So far, they haven't been able to find it."

"They won't. It doesn't exist."

"So how come they think the request came from your office?"

I eyed my friend. "You really expect me to have an answer to that?"

"Well, whoever hung it added a bit of premeditation to the evening's frivolity, didn't he?" Jerry ran a hand over his bald pate as if smoothing the hair no longer there—an old habit not easily broken and one he resorted to when stress levels spiked. "And I checked the feeds after the poker game, just for grins. Dane and his wife split at Delilah's. The chick headed toward the showroom. Dane ducked out of sight and he never cropped up again."

"Where'd he go?"

"That's what I'm tellin' you, girl. I haven't a clue."

"So he avoided the cameras?"

"Incriminating, isn't it?"

"The way this thing is going down, Dane couldn't be any worse off than if he'd appeared on national TV and told Katie Couric he did it." I blew at a strand of hair while I stalled for thinking time. But thought proved elusive. "If Dane has a death wish, I can't save him. So, let's focus on the feed from the Poker Room. I'd like to know who was playing with our dead girl—both figuratively and literally. And, maybe we can pick up who might have been watching her."

Lost in thought, I watched Jerry work through

some pull-down menus. He shouted across the room and one of his staff rushed to push various buttons on the main console. So far we had one dead girl married to a friend who was acting stranger than normal. The girl was cheating at a card game but didn't win. She claimed she was in some sort of trouble—that much seemed to be true. The Stoneman was either so incompetent he shouldn't have been allowed within a hundred yards of a poker room, or he was up to his ass in alligators. But what was the connection?

Beat the heck out of me.

"I'll start the tape around one A.M.," Jerry said. "That's right after the break where your girl takes a phone call. I presume that's the one from Dane. You said she didn't bust out until close to two?"

"Two, right, but I said she *made* a phone call."

"No." Jerry shook his head and cued the feed. The monitor flashed to life. "Here, watch it for yourself."

I'd been right, Sylvie Dane had been a real looker—style and class with just enough trashy thrown in to call attention to herself in Vegas. Pale, her face drawn, and the look of the hunted in her eyes, she played aggressively for sure, but more than that—she played with reckless abandon. And from the reaction of some of her compatriots, they were starting to smell a rat. Bad beats were part of the game, but when one player hit a string of luck that defied the odds, the others began to get twitchy. And there were so many ways to cheat. . . . Of course, I knew how Sylvie did it. But during the game, she kept her eyes averted behind glasses

with lenses just gray enough to obscure the color difference.

Jerry was right. Clearly annoyed, Sylvie fished her
phone out of her handbag—the same one she'd died
holding—and answered the call, cupping her hand
around her mouth as she spoke. The conversation
had been brief.

I wondered who had called her. "Are there any
more calls?"

Jerry shook his head. "I checked twenty minutes
either side. Nothing. You can always check her phone."

"Funny enough, that was missing from the crime
scene."

His eyes widened a bit as he looked at me and
took a long pull on his cigarette. He didn't have to say
anything, I could tell we were both on the same
page—Dane had time to lift the phone from her purse.

One thing I didn't know: Was lying a protective
habit or a calculation with Dane?

Either way, it *so* did not work for me.

But now was not the time to think about Dane—it
just pissed me off. And when I was pissed, I couldn't
think. I turned my attention back to the poker game
unfolding in front of me. While Sylvie was a curiosity,
I knew her story—at least I thought I did. On the other
hand, a couple of the others at the table were more
interesting. I tapped the screen. "That guy there."

"Kevin Slurry." Jerry answered as he took a pull
on his cigarette, then blew a ring of smoke.

I watched the ring dissipate. "They call him 'the
Hawk,' right?"

"Yep. A big-stakes amateur who loves to slow play, then swoop in for the kill."

"He had just bought in to the big game when I had arrived in the Poker Room and had my altercation with the Stoneman. I find it curious that he was playing the thousand-dollar buy-in before that. Doesn't his motor run on higher-octane adrenaline?"

"He doesn't normally go for the satellite games. But from the looks of it, he's cleaning everyone's clock." Multicolored chips stacked high in rows in front of him formed a wall of money gaudy enough to get all the attention.

"The cat who ate the canary," I commented as one of the pros motioned the Stoneman over to the table and had a whispered conversation with him. I couldn't tell what was said—the cameras in the Poker Room were not equipped with audio—but the conversation was heated and left the pro red faced with anger.

"What's that guy's name again?" I tapped the pro's image on the screen. "I've seen him around."

"Morton." Jerry pulled on his cigarette, then gazed with narrowed eyes through the smoke at the image on the screen. "First name Felix, but no one calls him that to his face if they value their skins. Most refer to him as 'the Professor.' He's from somewhere back East, I think. Chases the big money."

"Stop the tape," I said a bit louder than I had intended, making Jerry jump. "Who is that?"

"Where?" He leaned forward.

"There." I pointed to a fuzzy image. A pair of jean-clad legs.

Jerry pushed buttons and searched other feeds until he found the right one to back out. Blurry but recognizable.

"Well I'll be damned," Jerry and I said in unison.

We looked at each other. "You first," I said.

"The kid who was counting cards . . ."

I'd forgotten about that. "What time were you tangled up with him?"

"A little after two. He told me that he'd left the Poker Room because some of the players were hassling him, not letting him play."

"Not only the players." I crossed my arms and leaned back. "He's the kid I fired the Stoneman over." I would've said the plot thickens, but that was too much of a cliché, even for me. "He must've been on break from one of the other tables or he wouldn't have been allowed to stand there." As I said it, the steward hustled him away from the table.

But he'd been there long enough.

"He was with me when Sylvie Dane was killed, so he's off that hook. But you think he was in on whatever scam was going down?"

"It would be interesting to find out, wouldn't it?"

"You done with this one?" Jerry asked. At my nod, he rekeyed the original feed.

I pointed to the man sitting opposite Sylvie Dane. "River Watalsky. I didn't know he was back in the game."

A muscular guy with sandy brown hair cut military short, small angry eyes, and thin lips, Mr. Watalsky had a killer instinct, and an uncanny knack to get his card on the river, hence the nickname. Unfortunately, River's luck ran hot and cold, and he was the last one to realize when it had turned icy. He'd won and lost so many fortunes even the oddsmakers in Vegas had quit laying odds on him. When he'd been down on his luck, I'd gotten him a job or two. Last I'd heard he'd been driving a cab.

"Yeah, surprised me, too," Jerry mumbled as he took the last drag on his cigarette—his fifth since I'd arrived but who was counting? "He's a good guy. Nice to see luck smiling on him again."

Tonight, from the size of the stack in front of River and the fact he had a grand to buy in, I guessed Lady Luck had visited him once more. I didn't know who won the tournament, but from the stack of chips in front of him, I'd bet he'd at least made it into the money.

Jerry reached for his pack and shook another cigarette out. He lit it with the butt.

"I thought you'd quit." On the theory that second-hand smoke was worse than the filtered stuff, I scooched my chair away.

"I've tried everything. Even some laser hocus-pocus, if you can believe that."

"No way."

"I knew it wouldn't work when I saw the pile of butts in the bushes by the front door to the place, but I'm desperate. I'd try hypnosis if I wasn't scared

of what other suggestions might be implanted—
I've seen those hypnotists on the Strip. My insurance premiums are through the roof. My wife is
hounding my ass. Gotta love her, but she's driving
me crazy."

"My kind of gal." I tapped River Watalsky's image on the screen. "That guy can ferret out a cheat
better than anybody I know. I wonder how come he
was hoodwinked by the looker."

"He wasn't." Jerry let smoke out through his
mouth, then sucked it back in through his nose. I
didn't even know that was possible. "He got pretty
steamed at Sylvie Dane."

"Really? What'd he do?"

"Not much. The Stoneman stonewalled him, what
could he do?"

"Take matters into his own hands?"

"Watalsky?" Jerry's voice rose an octave as his
eyebrows shot north. "No way."

"People kill so often for money that it's become
hackneyed. You know that."

"Yeah, but she was losing, remember?"

"True, but something was going down, that much
seems obvious. So, the two were in it together and
she'd get the split later. I don't know. There's lotsa
ways this could've worked."

"But Watalsky? If that guy has a mean bone, I've
not seen it." Jerry had dug in his heels.

I shrugged. "Farfetched, I know, but feasible." I
made a sweeping motion. "For God's sake, the whole
table knew Sylvie was cheating."

"Seems like everyone knew except the Stoneman, the little shit." Jerry squashed out the butt of one cigarette after lighting another from the glowing embers.

I tried to ignore his chain-smoking, but wasn't very successful. "When did the game end?"

"They broke it up right after Sylvie left. The Hawk took the pot."

"Thanks to Sylvie and her little game, whatever it was," I scoffed. "I'm going to want to talk to Watalsky."

"Sure. You pick the time and place."

"This morning, my office." Neither of us took our eyes off the video feed.

"It's already morning. Better make it afternoon," Jerry said, the cigarette held between his lips bouncing with the words. "He's on a roll. You know him, with money in his pocket he'll play until he's tapped out or thrown out."

As we watched, Sylvie hooked a finger under the chain around her neck and pulled what looked to be a pocket watch out of her cleavage. I'd heard that was a great place to stash stuff, but having no cleavage of my own, I wouldn't know. "Can you zoom in on that?"

Jerry gave me a sly grin as he toggled a few switches. "My pleasure."

In no mood to play, I ignored the exaggerated leer that followed.

Besides, nobody in Vegas really cared about cleavage anymore. These days, everyone had a set of first-class, custom jugs. Five grand and serious pain just to be like everyone else. There was an interesting irony there.

Made of white gold, with what appeared to be a rather ornate pattern in precious stones on the cover, the watch looked expensive.

"Interesting bauble for a girl always low on funds. I wonder what happened to it. It wasn't around her neck when I saw her on the Ferrari."

"Dane took it, maybe?" Jerry commented, his eyes never leaving the feed. After a few moments, he froze the picture. Tapping it, he looked thoughtful. "There's something . . ."

"What?"

"Hang on." His chair shot back as he stood. Without a word, he strode from the room, leaving me alone with the silence and the ticking of the clock hanging on the wall.

Not much time passed, not even enough for me to get nervous, before he burst back into the room, waving a piece of paper over his head. "That watch rang a bell." He thrust the paper at me. "It's stolen."

"Really?" I snatched the paper from him, smoothed it on the table, and began reading. Two weeks ago. From one of our nicest suites. "Do you know these people?"

"Big fish from Toledo. The suite was comped." He turned the paper back around and read from the second page—I hadn't made it that far. "The watch they reported stolen had been in the family several generations, they were pretty upset. Apparently some famous ancestor had inscribed his initials on the inside cover."

"I wonder how it ended up in Sylvie Dane's possession?" I also wondered what happened to it, but I didn't voice that. If Jerry knew, he'd have told me. But I knew who might be able to shed some light. Dane had some answering to do—he hadn't mentioned the necklace, nor, come to think of it, the missing shoe. "Could you get me a photo?"

"It'll be grainy, but your wish is my command." Jerry moved the cursor over an icon and pressed. Somewhere in the darkness behind us a printer whirred to life.

After flipping open the cover on the watch, Sylvie made a show of checking the time, then snapped it shut and tucked it back into its nest. Most of the men at the table were riveted. Even the Hawk. Even Marvin Johnstone, who stood off to the side.

For the next forty-five minutes, Sylvie played fast and loose until her stack was gone. Rachael escorted her from the table, as she said she had. Sylvie didn't look afraid, just . . . angry. When Dane joined her, she narrowed her eyes as she grabbed his elbow, whirling him around. Her mouth set into a grim line, with an in-your-face tilt to her chin, she ushered him toward the exit.

Dane and his wife made a striking couple as he untangled his arm and grabbed one of hers just above the elbow, turning her skin white from the grip of his fingers. Neither of them looked pleased to see the other. No, they both looked mad as hell.

Not what I expected, but somehow that didn't surprise me—disappointed me, perhaps, but surprise? Not so much. I could be really stupid, but I was a fast learner—with Dane everything was smoke and mirrors, a clever game of misdirection.

Forcing my focus back to the screen, I watched for a moment. Something else wasn't right, but I couldn't pinpoint it. "Rewind that section, would you?"

I kept my eyes on Dane and his wife as Jerry did as I asked, "Again."

By the third time I had it.

Her shoes. Slingbacks with a peep-toe. There's-no-place-like-home red. With a red sole. I'd seen those shoes before.

"Damn." I leaned back in the chair and let my breath out in a whoosh.

"What?" Jerry asked as he crushed the butt in the ashtray. He seemed oblivious to the fact it was over-flowing.

"I saw those shoes on a girl in the casino." I closed my eyes, playing back my mental tape. What had she looked like? Leaping out of the chair, I squeezed my eyes shut as I paced across the small cubicle—not much room to think. Trying to picture her face, I could only conjure vague details. Brunette, I thought. His-panic, maybe. Medium height. Medium weight. Average everything. Well, *that* really narrowed it down. She'd seemed nervous, anxious . . . and tired. I'd passed all that off to a new job and a late night. Why hadn't I paid more attention? Because I was fixated on the friggin' shoes, that's why. Boy, I sure had a case of the stupids. And it was getting worse. Not a good sign.

"Dane's wife was wearing them, then they show up on some chick in the casino?" Jerry asked as he rose and stepped out of his cubicle. Returning a few moments later, he handed me the print of Sylvie Dane's watch, which I folded and pocketed. He parked one butt cheek on the edge of the console and pulled a handkerchief out of his back pocket, wiping his brow before he stuffed the bit of cloth back where it had come from. "You think Dane's wife has somebody else's shoe planted in her neck? And, do I need to point out that those red shoes on her feet in the video and the ones you saw could be different pairs?"

"Even with my diminished IQ I considered that, but it'd be one heck of a coincidence, don't you think?" I tapped the screen that still showed Sylvie Dane frozen in time. "Those shoes are a special, limited-edition kind of thing. I've seen them in the holiday fashion mags. Christian Louboutin. And expensive beyond the reach of us commoners. Can I have a print of that still shot also?"

It took him only a moment to get me what I wanted.

"Get some of your guys on those shoes right now," I barked at Jerry in my best follow-those-shoes voice. "Last I saw her, the girl was near Delilah's. That would be around four or four thirty. Sorry I can't be more precise—time is getting away, lately. With a picture, HR can give us a name." Before he could grab his box of cancer sticks, I snatched it. With a flourish, I squashed the thin cardboard in my fist as I held it under his nose. Then I let the remnants sift through my open fingers into the wastebasket.

"I've had enough folks dying on my watch, thank you very much."

Chapter

FIVE

♡

On autopilot, I tapped my foot as I waited for the elevator. Unable to handle even the tiniest glimpse of reality, I studiously avoided looking at myself in the mirrored surface of the bronze doors. One floor down to the lobby—even though Security was on the same level as my office, there was no direct route between the two. I should've taken the stairs, but my recent enthusiasm for self-betterment seemed to be flagging. Somehow, while I had been busy actually enjoying myself, life had done a one-eighty and galloped into the gloom.

Teddie was gone. Bodies were piling up.

Along with "the bad die young" I should add "the good times never last" to the Lucky O'Toole Book of Wisdom—a very thin volume, but each sage, clichéd, tidbit learned the hard way.

Silently the elevator doors slid open and I stepped inside. With my shoulders pressed against the back wall, I crossed my arms over my chest and closed my eyes, letting my head lean back. I took a couple of deep breaths. The truth of it was, I was running on fumes. I couldn't sleep, hadn't been eating, and had been drinking more than even *I* thought was healthy. The only exercise I got was running from one crisis to another. I had a sneaking suspicion that my friends were thinking of staging an intervention.

After a moment of unfamiliar introspection, it dawned on me that, given the option, Sylvie Dane would probably want to change places with me. A very real example of my mother's frequent admonition that things could always be worse. Clichés apparently ran in my family. Too bad it couldn't have been something useful like long legs or a sunny disposition.

I needed to get over myself. This whole down-in-the-mouth thing was so not me—well, not the old me, anyway. But the new me was definitely a whiner—so much so, even *I* didn't like hanging out with me.

So no more pouting. No more pity party of one. Time to get my life back.

Pushing myself from my leaning position, I threw my shoulders back. Chin up. Chest out. For a moment I felt better, stronger. More . . . me.

Then the crushing weight of bitter disappointment fell on my heart once again. Hope abandoned me as quickly as it had come as I sagged against the wall.

One foot in front of the other, my father always used to say. Clichés on both sides of the family . . . lucky me. And some days, survival was the best I could do. This apparently was one of those days.

A bell dinged my arrival at the requested floor and the elevator doors slid open. I launched myself through the opening and strode into the lobby.

Even with the bad visual of Sylvie and the shoe, and even though I'd walked through the lobby a gazillion times, it still took my breath away. Gleaming white marble floors and walls inlaid with brightly colored, intricately patterned mosaic, and peaked cloth in rich, multicolored hues conjured a sultan's vision of ancient Babylon—the sultan in question being my father. All of this was his creation.

Reception ran along one wall, the brightly tented cloth above it reminiscent of the tents of a Persian oasis. At the far end of Reception, the one closest to the front entrance, a vaulted, brick entranceway invited all passersby to come enjoy the bazaar that lurked beyond. Our humble marketplace, the Bazaar, offered all the baubles to satisfy any self-respecting royal's most outrageous desires—from glittering jewels, to Italian sports cars, to French couture, to gourmet hamburgers.

Gourmet French hamburgers.

An insult to every self-respecting French gourmand.

I don't know why, but there was something so satisfying, so heartwarming, about poking a hole in Gallic culinary snobbery that, even as grumpy as I was, I mustered a thin smile. Perhaps I found it appealing because I had dealt with so many arrogant French chefs. . . .

However, there was one French chef who was not at all distasteful. My French chef. For a moment, my thoughts drifted. Jean-Charles was truly *très magnifique*. But was he the man for me? In addition to the complication of mixing business and pleasure, which kept me perpetually off balance, there was another . . . unknown . . . in the mix: His five-year-old son, Christophe, would be arriving soon. I hadn't met him yet. Would he like me?

Full of questions and short on answers, I wasn't going to think about that either. The list of things I wasn't going to think about was longer than a kid's list at Christmas.

Opposite the reception desk, a wall of glass carved off one side of the lobby. Behind the glass, which was really very thick Lucite, a mountain of man-made snow beckoned all willing to pay a sultan's ransom to ski in the desert. Not exactly consistent with the whole Babylonian theme, but no one appeared too troubled by that. Right now, the hill was barren, closed for grooming in anticipation of the hordes that would descend once the sun actually rose today.

The false light of night on the Vegas Strip held back the darkness outside the front entrance. The valets darted to retrieve cars for the few clusters of guests waiting after what I hoped was a night well spent.

High above the grand lobby, blown-glass creatures arced in flight. A flock of multicolored humming-birds and butterflies—a huge rainbow of color that always brought smiles. Even I wasn't immune. I paused, my neck craned. Somehow those friggin' birds and insects always made life seem better.

The Big Boss was a genius.

I turned left, away from the front doors, and headed toward the entrance to the casino. A placid stream flowed at the far end of the lobby, providing the demarcation between the lobby and the casino beyond. Our own rendition of the Euphrates, it meandered tranquilly. At least a dozen different types of waterfowl floated with their beaks tucked under one wing, a leg curled under them, and the other leg acting as a keel while they slumbered, drifting with the slight current. Flowering plants and shrubs lined the banks with papyrus reeds lending an air of authenticity—which was all you needed to create an illusion in Vegas—although the architects of some of the newer indiscretions seemed to have missed that point. Bridges arced over the stream at discrete intervals, providing perfect photo opportunities and a bit of ambience.

The combined effect was warm, soothing, inviting all to pause, spend some time . . . and some money.

Like I said, the Big Boss was a genius. I only hoped it was hereditary.

Along with this hotel, my responsibilities extended to our new property, Cielo. A renovation of an aging Vegas property formerly known as the Athena, Cielo was to be my concept of an environmentally friendly hotel with a European emphasis on quality and customer service—something usually reserved for the high rollers in Vegas.

A daunting project that could suck every second out of every day.

Yes, I am my own worst enemy. If I'm good at anything it's burying myself.

Bury myself in my job; ignore life. It used to work.

One thing that was impossible to ignore no matter how deep I dug myself in—my office was a hardhat area. After receiving my own promotion to vice president, I bestowed my former job as Head of Customer Relations for the Babylon on Miss Patterson, formerly my most able and loyal assistant. Her assistant, Brandy, moved into Miss P's former position. Cleverly, I had seen to it that we all moved one step up the food chain. Unfortunately, I had clevered myself right out of an office.

Miss P had taken my old one—it went with the job. So we carved out some space in a storage area adjacent to our old offices and two guys with one hammer spent their days trying to give me a headache. At the rate they were going I'd have to have wheelchair ramps installed by the time they were done. My first lesson in the vagaries of construction: Take the architect's time estimate, double it, then pray. My second lesson? The more you complain, the slower the work goes.

My life clearly was running me.

After a punishing dash up one flight of stairs that left me at the point of apoplexy, I found the office door was open, as I knew it would be. With a gaping hole cut in the wall where my future office door was to be, what was the point of locking up? A single bare bulb dangled on a wire from the fixture in the ceiling, providing a weak circle of light. Every time I flipped the switch I thought fifty thousand volts would sizzle through my body, which, come to think of it, was sounding sort of appealing at the moment.

Stepping around buckets of drywall paste, trying not to trip on the puckers in the tarp, I headed toward a lump in the corner. Carefully I lifted the plastic the painters had tossed over my beautiful burled black walnut desk and peered under it. As I feared, the piles of paper had propagated. Whoever thought being a hotel executive was glamorous had better think twice. Signing my name was so ingrained by now I should be a rock star or at least a minor celebrity. But alas, I was just a corporate grunt . . . who apparently wallowed in pity parties of one.

Add a phone complete with texting, e-mail, and a push-to-talk walkie-talkie thing, and I was tethered to my job no matter how far I ran. Teddie had been convinced the thing was also a blood pressure monitor—it had a habit of ringing at the most unfortunate moments. The memory of his hands working through the buttons on my shirt, the pounding of my pulse, the heat in his skin where it brushed mine, the look in his eyes when the ring of the phone interrupted us assaulted me, crushing my heart and stealing my breath.

Instant access had its downside.

I don't know why I even bothered going home. Come to think of it, now that I had moved into the hotel, I didn't—go home that is. Life and work had merged until one was indistinguishable from the other.

And I had disappeared.

THE pile of papers on my desk was diminished by over half when I heard noises in the outer office. Scuffling sounds, then, "You fuckin' bitch!" Newton, our multicolored macaw, had a serious potty mouth. Miss P usually uncovered his cage in the morning and was rewarded for her efforts with a string of epithets. Newton had apparently had a rough-and-tumble upbringing before he adopted me. When I moved out of my apartment, the bird had to take up temporary quarters in the office. A fact that probably entitled my staff to hazardous duty pay—if they didn't mutiny.

"Friggin' bird," Miss Patterson muttered. "I swear I'm going to have you stuffed."

"Asshole!" Newton sang out. It was his best word and he said it with feeling.

I couldn't help smiling. Leaning back in my chair, I closed my eyes and listened to the noises in the outer office. A drawer opening—Miss P stashing her purse. The squeak of wheels on the floor, then the creak as she settled into her desk chair. A beep—she was checking the messages.

"This is for Lucky . . ." Teddie's voice. A dagger to my heart.

"Turn that damned speaker off," I shouted, perhaps louder than I needed to.

He'd left. How could his voice still make me feel so . . . happy, sad, angry, thrilled, and all at the same time? My pulse quickened as I flushed with anger. I hated him for leaving, for breaking my heart. Yet I had loved him so . . .

Love and loathing. Two powerful emotions separated by such a thin line.

"Christ! Lucky, is that you?" Miss P sounded less than pleased at being startled yet glad I was there, both at the same time—like a rebuke with a hug. It was one of her best things. I had no idea how she did it.

I didn't think she expected me to answer, so I didn't.

Her chair banged into the wall, then she filled my doorway. Trim yet curvy in all the right places, Miss P sported a brown sweater with gold flecks that was just tight enough to get the right kind of attention. Her slacks of white winter wool looked pricey. Bronze Loubous with a semi-sensible heel and closed toe graced her feet. Cascades of David Yurman silver and gold filled her décolletage, and matching earrings sparkled in the light of the single bulb. Her spiky blond hair and subtle makeup completed the picture. The angry eyes and frown were new additions and I wondered what had gotten her knickers in such a twist.

Hands on her hips, she glared at me. "Don't sneak up on me like that."

"Sneak up? On *you*?" I raised my head and

opened my eyes wide. "For your information, I've been here for the better part of two hours. Here, take care of these." I stuffed the pile of signed papers into her hand. "And get the Beautiful Jeremy on the phone. I need his help."

Mention of the Beautiful Jeremy Whitlock, Vegas's premier investigator and Miss P's live-in boy toy brought a brief smile to her face as she tucked the papers under her arm, pen poised to take notes.

"And Brandy? She knows American Sign Language, doesn't she? Her parents were hearing impaired, right?"

"I believe they still are," Miss P said with a slight air of superiority.

Teddie's voice droned on in the background. The machine beeped through several messages, all from him. All saying the same thing: He missed me, he'd made a mistake, please call him any time, day or night.

Too much water under that bridge. And his recent recognition of something that had been so obvious, so vital to me for a long time, did little to improve my mood.

"Fine. Brandy's job today is to find a pro poker player we've got wandering around here. Cole Weston. He's young, handsome, and deaf."

"And what should Brandy do with him when she finds him?" Miss P looked at me over her cheaters, her face a blank slate.

"Bring him to me. Whatever she does, once she finds him, I want her to stick to him like glue."

Miss P scribbled. Teddie's voice finally stopped.

"I've been busy," I said, apropos of nothing.

"And you deserve a gold star," Miss P noted with a sardonic lift to one eyebrow.

It was way too early for attitude. I opened my mouth to give her a . . . readjustment, but she cut me off. "I was just going to stash my stuff, then come looking for you. The pilots caught me on my cell on the way in. We have a problem."

"And this is news?"

She gave me a look of exaggerated patience. "Don't you ever take anything seriously?"

"If I did, I would explode." That statement had a ring of truth to it that I hoped Miss P didn't hear. Avoiding her penetrating stare, I pretended to be interested in a Lucite paperweight, one that contained a golden cockroach—a gift from the employees after dealing with a guest and his pests. Finally I hazarded a glance at my assistant. "So, where's the fire?"

"The airport. They got a dead guy stuck in the lavatory on one of our G550s."

THE Executive Terminal at McCarran International Airport was no more than ten minutes from my office door—on a good day. With Paolo driving our limo, we made it in less than five—and we didn't even take out any tourists or bend any metal. After narrowly missing a post holding a section of chain-link fence topped by several rows of barbed wire, Paolo skinned the big car through a tight opening onto the tarmac and then screeched to a halt.

With no momentum to fight, I loosened my white-knuckled grip on the armrests and settled back into the comforting embrace of the deep leather seats. Behind tinted windows, shadowed by the darkness of morning that brightened the eastern sky but had yet to reach the ground, I savored a few moments of peace.

My mother always said death came in threes.

So far I'd racked up two. What if, for once, Mona was right? Who would be next? A cool breath of a breeze tickled my cheek. I didn't know where it came from, which creeped me out. Feeling the specter of death at my elbow, I bolted upright and threw open the door, surprising Paolo, who had stepped around the car to help me out. He jumped aside in the nick of time.

"Ms. O'Toole! Let Paolo help you." With one arm tucked regally behind his back, his chauffer's hat clutched between his elbow and his side, he bent at the waist and extended a hand to me. Not wanting to offend, I accepted, even though it was like letting a pony pull a freight train.

A small, dapper man, with jet-black hair brushed straight back, dancing black eyes, and a thousand-candlepower smile, Paolo took his job seriously. His uniform was spotless. Even at the end of a long shift, his pants still held a sharp crease. A twenty-five-year service pin, his only jewelry, sparkled in his lapel. Grasping my hand, he helped lever me from the bowels of the limo—and he did so without a grimace. I'd have to remember that at Christmas.

Taking a deep breath, I stretched to my full height and filled my lungs with fresh air. Even though it was tinged with jet exhaust, it was a far cry better than the recirculated stuff wafting through the hotel. We did our best, but there were limits to just how much sin could be filtered from the Vegas atmosphere.

The airport was just awakening. Like lumbering giants moving quietly in the half light, planes taxied to the runways. The inbound red-eyes hung in the sky, a glittering string of landing lights above the ever-brightening eastern horizon. Personal jets of varying sizes already dotted the parking area behind the private terminal. Our G550 was the largest of the bunch.

If God had money, she would have a G550.

The Babylon had two.

Bathed in phosphorescent glow from the arc lights, its directional lights still illuminated, the plane waited like a living, breathing beast. Sleek and elegant, reeking of adventure, it looked ready to leap into the wild blue yonder at a moment's notice—which was not too much of an exaggeration.

This one was the oldest and had already been sold to one of our investors in the Macau operation, pending the delivery of a G650. Stairs had been lowered from the doorway just aft of the cockpit on the left side of the plane. It looked like we'd beaten the police, which was an unusual stroke of luck. But I didn't have much time, of that I was sure. Soon, the place would be crawling with cops. I hoped, for once, they could be discreet, but I wasn't holding my breath.

Men in jumpsuits clustered at the bottom of the stairs, wringing their hands, looking lost and worried. Please! It was just a dead guy in the bathroom. I could handle that with my eyes shut. Come to think of it, that was probably not a bad idea. Although sometimes welcomed, death is rarely pretty.

The men parted as I approached and said nothing as I started up, taking two steps at a time. At the top I paused, collecting myself, then ducked through the doorway into the plush interior. Even though I'd been one of the privileged passengers a few times—a particularly vivid memory of a trip to Macau to check on our property when it was under construction sprang to mind—I'd never quite adjusted to the whole *Architectural Digest* thing going on inside. Gulfstream made beautiful machines—efficient, luxury condos that could deposit you anywhere in the world you desired. The ultimate extravagance.

The aft portion of the plane housed a stateroom with a double bed and private lav, which included a massaging shower and other high-end appointments. Club seating for ten or twelve of your closest friends, depending on the exact configuration, filled the forward section of the main compartment. A galley and small lavatory for the three-person flight crew separated the passenger compartment from the flight deck.

Stepping farther into the plush interior, I found

myself between the passenger seating on my right and the galley on my left. The door to the lav was open, but I couldn't see inside. I let my eyes adjust to the soft lighting as I took stock of my surroundings. All the comforts of home—assuming you lived in a Four Seasons. With soft Italian leather upholstery, 1,400-thread-count Egyptian cotton sheets, thick Turkish terry cloth towels, burled black walnut accents, the plane was beyond the reach of most of us mere mortals.

With flat-screen televisions streaming live satellite feeds, communication capabilities to anywhere in the world, food service in the finest five-star tradition, wines from the best houses, top-drawer spirits, all served by a beautiful young man or woman depending on the passenger's preferences, the G550 was reserved for only the best customers of the hotel, certain executives, or, on occasion, personal family friends.

I figured the odds that I would know the dead guy in the lav at better than even.

One of the flight crew slumped in a seat across from the forward lav. The bars on his shoulders indicated he was the low man on the totem pole. Regardless, I doubted his job description included handling dead bodies. That sounded more like something in my contract. Assuming every job was a stepping-stone to another, I briefly wondered what position mine was preparing me for? Who knew? And it was too terrifying to speculate.

Our young flight engineer was fast asleep, his legs sticking out in front of him, his hat pulled low over his eyes, his chin resting on his chest, his breath coming in long, even pulls. I envied him—only saints and sinners were awake at this hour. And fools like me, who unfortunately qualified as neither.

With a toe, I nudged his leg. "Excuse me?"

He raised his head and tipped his hat back, exposing the most incredible dark eyes. His face was angles and planes with a square jaw that, in the proper venue, either begged to be hit or kissed. With a sexy two-day stubble and full lips curving into a slight smile, he most likely found his current profession a nice respite from adoring females. Young females. His twentieth birthday couldn't have been too far in his rearview. Too bad cradle robbing wasn't within my skill set. Sometimes it was hell to have standards.

"I'm here to see about your passenger stuck in the lav," I said, trying to muster a pleasant tone.

A blank stare. Those puppy-dog eyes.

Damn. I swallowed hard. "The dead guy?" I prompted, willing my mind to focus. An overactive libido could be such a bother. Wrong time. Wrong place. Wrong guy. Welcome to my world.

Realization dawned and the young man jumped to his feet. "Sorry." He wiped his palm on his pant leg before extending his hand. "I'm Benton Miles."

A grown-up name for a not-so grown-up, I thought, and prayed the words hadn't come out of my mouth.

He still smiled, so I assumed they hadn't. "Lucky O'Toole. From the hotel." I took his hand. He had a strong, firm grip.

His eyes widened a smidge. I swallowed hard.

"I've heard about you," he said, holding my hand a bit longer than propriety dictated.

I didn't know whether that was a good thing or a bad thing and I didn't really want to know. Pulling my hand from his, I inclined my head toward the lav. "Show me what you got."

"It ain't pretty."

"Didn't expect it would be," I replied with a bravado that quickly evaporated when I peered into the small space.

"Christ." Normally, being right was a good thing—tonight was not one of those times. I knew the guy all right. I knew him well. "Shady Slim Grady. Damn."

My heart sank—the Big Boss. The two of them went way back. So far in fact that, had Shady Slim Grady had a normal name, I'm sure I would have been instructed to refer to him as my Uncle Whatever—although, in Vegas that could have led to interesting misinterpretations.

A poker legend, Shady Slim was bald as a billiard ball, with a ready grin, ubiquitous cowboy hat, and alligator kickers. As a young man, he had presided over the birth of Texas hold 'em. Now semiretired from competitive play, he dabbled in the periphery and contented himself with being wined and dined as one of the gods of the game.

A native Texan hailing from Corpus Christie, he had played that shtick for all it was worth, calling me "little lady" each time he saw me. I'd liked it—especially since I'd never been . . . little, that is. Probably not much of a lady either, come to think of it. But in Vegas, nobody noticed—I was lucky that way. And I'd liked him. With an effusive personality, height to match my own, in heels, and a substantial girth that had expanded with the passing of the years, Shady Slim had been larger than life, both figuratively and literally.

Now it seemed the figurative aspect alone remained. Abandoned by its life force, his body had collapsed in on itself. His bones appeared to bend as if unable to withstand the assault of gravity. He sagged like a puppet with no strings, his height expanding into width. Oozing over the sides of the toilet seat onto the bench underneath, his ample flesh filled the tight space between the walls. His shoulders braced the small space. With legs splayed, his knees pressed against the cabinet under the tiny sink on one side and the outside wall on the other, effectively wedging him into the tiny space.

Aircraft designers! Why they felt compelled to make each lav small enough so everyone could throw up into the sink while still seated on the throne beat the heck out of me. Rather Machiavellian for us larger than normal types. And I don't think they anticipated someone would actually die in the bathroom, although I thought that a bit shortsighted. In my experience, people did it all the time. I guessed there were worse ways to go, but right at the moment, I couldn't imagine one. Since he was stuck tighter than a cork in a bottle of twenty-year-old wine, Shady Slim's extrication was going to be very public. Of course, I doubted Shady Slim cared, but Miss Becky-Sue would have a cow.

I turned to Benton, who was fidgeting behind me. "Did Miss Becky-Sue come with him?" I asked, knowing the answer but hoping I was wrong. Wherever Shady Slim went, Miss Becky-Sue trotted four paces behind.

The kid nodded, a flash of panic lit his eyes. I knew the feeling—I'd tussled with that little bit of Texas trash before. Between you and me, I was still a trifle snakebit—although I would never admit it.

"They got her in the back there." The kid stammered, looking a bit wild eyed. "She's . . ."

"I can imagine," I said, patting him on the shoulder. "No worries. My shots are up to date, I'll handle her."

After a moment, he rewarded me with a grin. Dimples. Damn.

Forgetting I was in a plane, I straightened quickly—at six feet plus four-inch heels, I needed a pretty good clearance. Thank God it was a G550 or else I would've broken my neck . . . or perhaps knocked some sense into my empty head. "Call the maintenance department. Get them to tow this beast into a hangar away from prying eyes. Then, ask them to send some folks proficient in dismantling a G550."

"Ma'am?"

I stepped aside and gave the kid a good view of Mr. Grady. "The only way we're going to get him out of here is to take this lav apart. The door is going to have to come off." I peered around the side and knocked on the partition. Even I was smart enough to know none of the walls in a plane were load bearing. "And probably this wall as well. We'll need a crane."

"Where are we going to get that?" the young pilot asked.

"Leave that to me." I reached for my phone. Very rarely does luck swing my way, but this was one of those times.

The funeral directors were holding their annual convention in our main ballroom.

"First, find me some privacy. The cops will have their go, then we'll deal with getting him out of there."

LIKE a rabid pit bull, Miss Becky-Sue whirled on me the minute I slid back the stateroom doors, but I was prepared. At least I thought I was. Silly me.

"You!" she snarled. "This is your fault." She pointed a long, painted blue talon at me. It reminded me of the knuckled finger of death.

"Of course it is." I tried to look appropriately sympathetic. "I'm sorry for your loss, Miss Becky-Sue."

I guess she'd been expecting an argument because that stalled her for a moment. Precious seconds I used to gird myself for battle. I had the woman by at least a foot, and a disturbing number of pounds, but she still scared the life out of me. Logical, I can deal with. Hysterical, I can manage—as long as someone hovers nearby with a ready hypodermic or a stun gun. But Miss Becky-Sue was neither consistently logical nor consistently hysterical . . . ever. Instead she gyrated wildly between varying emotional extremes. Dealing with her was like riding a roller coaster: just when you thought you'd stabilized, the bottom fell out and you were plunged into oblivion, your stomach in your throat.

Stretched and tanned, peroxided and waxed, sheathed in fringed leather and cowboy boots, and painted in primary colors, Miss Becky-Sue looked like Dale Evans on crack. Texas trashy on the outside, tempered steel on the inside, she was a barracuda with a bimbo fetish. If she had a heart, I hadn't seen a hint of it.

From her eyelashes, to her blond beehive—she always said, "The bigger the hair, the closer to God"—to her generous tits and her smile, she was as fake and as overprocessed as Velveeta.

The name on her law degree from some lesser law school in Texas read "Gloria Axelrod." But the Axelrods had disowned her after an ugly skirmish with the State Bar Grievance Committee—the last in a long list of embarrassments. The feeling was mutual. So Gloria had reinvented herself as Shady Slim's bimbo, which was probably a better fit, all things considered.

When I was younger, I couldn't understand the

pairing. My father told me that if you put tits on a warthog and taught it to bat its eyes, Shady Slim would've jumped it. Being visual, I never got rid of that image, but I did get it . . . sort of. Like so many of his clan, Shady Slim did most of his thinking with the wrong head. And I'd wager Miss Becky-Sue knew some tricks that the rest of us weren't privy to. If only . . .

Pride, Lucky. Pride.

"Now," I said, pulling my mind out of the gutter and wading into battle. "What can I do to make you comfortable? The police are on their way."

"I ain't talkin' to no pigs," Miss Becky-Sue spat, her veneer slipping.

"I'm afraid that's nonnegotiable." I motioned to the two pilots cowering in the corner, making themselves small. "I'll take it from here. Thank you. But stick around. I'm sure Metro will want to talk to you both as well."

The two men came within an eyelash of knocking me down in their haste to leave. They jammed in the doorway when they both tried to go through it at the same time. The older of the two finally forced his way through first, followed by the other. And I was alone in the lion's cage.

The look in Miss Becky-Sue's eyes made me wish I had searched the cabin for firearms. I'd sell my mother for a Taser. Or even a chair and a whip. Or a chunk of raw meat laced with sedatives. "Why don't you take a seat and let me pour you a drink?" I said in what I hoped was a conversational, nonincendiary, yet forceful tone. "Single-barrel, one cube of ice, if I recall?"

Turning to the bar, I felt her eyes bore into my back. Glancing at her briefly, I watched her lower herself into a dainty chair. In addition to the lavs being a tight fit, the furniture on the plane was Lilliputian. I felt like I was playing inside a dollhouse. Thankfully, the bottle of Jack was full sized. I splashed a generous amount into a Steuben crystal tumbler and extended it to her.

Her hands shook as she took the glass then drank deeply, wiping her mouth with the back of her hand. Her red lipstick an angry smear, she lifted her eyes to mine. They were dark, dead eyes—lethal and heartless.

"Why don't you tell me what happened?" I said before she could jump in.

"Why should I tell you anything? You can't bring Slim back." She plucked a tissue from the box by the bed and dabbed at an imaginary tear, presumably for my benefit.

"No, while I'm pretty good at pulling rabbits out of hats and drawing to an inside straight, resurrection is definitely not part of my repertoire." I glanced around for a place to park my carcass, but I didn't think anything would fit, or hold my bulk. Probably not true, but I wasn't in the mood to be proven right. "I'm going to have to tell my father something, so whatever you can give me—for the Big Boss—will help."

Eyeing me over the rim of her glass for a moment,

she then threw back the rest of the sour mash and extended the glass for a refill. I complied as she started in. Her voice seemed to have warmed a bit, but I might have imagined that part.

"Slim, he was fidgety. Like a young bull sensing the knife, you know?"

I winced and nodded. Talk about letting her steer the conversation. Okay, puns pop up when I'm under pressure. I'm not proud of it, but I've learned to deal with it. With no desire to explain and no way to protect myself, I bit down on the inside of my mouth, stifling the grin that threatened to explode.

"No matter what I did, he wasn't spilling." Miss Becky-Sue crossed her arms across her ample chest. She glanced through the small window next to her while she gathered herself.

"Why did you arrive so late?" I asked. "I haven't checked the log, but I'm sure the plane was sent to pick you up and deliver you in plenty of time for the Big Boss's party."

"I bought this outfit special." She brushed down her white leather skirt, and then raised her eyes to mine. "We ran into some storms or somethin' around Wichita Falls and had to detour halfway to Canada to get around them. We were way late. I got tired and fell asleep."

"And Slim, was he feeling okay?"

"Seemed to be. He spent the whole time yacking on the phone. Got pretty steamed a time or two, but that's nothing new." Miss Becky-Sue chewed on her lip as she continued to stare out the small window.

She had to bend down a bit; it couldn't have been comfortable.

"Do you know who he was talking to?"

She shrugged, then turned and tried to stare me down—it didn't work. Finally she broke. "What, you think I can keep track of all the pies that man has a finger in?"

From what I knew of Miss Becky-Sue, I'd have to say she could run a small country single-handedly, but I let it slide. Sometimes giving folks a long rope was a great way to get them to hang themselves. Maybe I'd get lucky.

I expected to see something in her eyes. Sadness. Pain. Anger. I should've known better, but hope springs eternal. At the very least, Shady Slim deserved someone to cry at his funeral. But Miss Becky-Sue wasn't exactly conjuring the grieving widow.

"I remember landing. Slim was still on the phone. He told me to go back to sleep—it was too late for the party and, besides, he was expecting someone." With a long, blue fingernail, Miss Becky-Sue scratched at a pimple on her arm as she pursed her lips. Thinking perhaps, but it was hard to tell.

"Frank DeLuca." At her startled expression, I felt a need to explain. "He told me."

"Well, if you know so much, what're you talkin' to me for?" She stopped picking and used the tissue to dab at a small spot of blood. "Besides, I don't know if he was the one Slim was expecting, but he was the one who come . . . came."

"What time was that?"

Miss Becky-Sue shrugged and avoided my eyes. "Around midnight, I guess, a bit after. I wasn't payin' much attention, bein' pretty steamed about the party and all."

"What did they talk about?"

She waved her hand. "Business stuff, you know. I don't bother myself with none of that."

I started to ask another question, but red lights strobed through the small windows. My time was up. The police had arrived.

Chapter

SIX

♡

*H*eld tightly, my body pressed to his as we swayed to the music. Intoxicating, romantic music that held the promise of love . . . of life. Scent infused the air. Gardenias, I thought. Or maybe magnolias. And the hint of Old Spice. My head on his shoulder, I nuzzled his neck and was rewarded with a tighter squeeze. Held tightly, I felt free. Love filled my heart and completed me. I lifted my head and leaned back slightly. Teddie's face swam into view, then faded. Then I was looking into the warm, solid face of my chef, Jean-Charles, his eyes alight with an emotion I felt.

"Lucky?"

The voice was wrong. The accent wasn't French.

"Lucky?"

No, the voice was decidedly middle-American. I felt a hand on my shoulder shaking me.

My eyes fluttered open and the lovely vision shattered in the bright light of reality. I squeezed my eyes shut again, but the dream was gone . . . he was gone. Damn. Wrapping my arms around myself, I tried to remember, to hold on to the feeling, the emotion, the peace, but it slipped away, like smoke on the wind, leaving a hollow place where my heart should be.

"Sleeping on the job," Romeo teased. "Not like you."

"Since all I do is work and sleep, it seemed only natural to combine the two." I pushed myself up in the seat, trying to get my bearings. From the view through the cockpit window, it seemed I'd fallen asleep in the captain's chair on the G550. Squinting against the full wattage of a day now under way— the nose of the plane stuck out of the hangar that concealed the rest—I had no idea how long I'd been out, not that it mattered. If life as we know it was on the verge of extinction, my office knew where to find me.

"Reasonable," Romeo said as he sagged into the copilot's chair. "You think we could steal this thing and go somewhere far away?"

For a moment the idea seemed irresistible. "I took flying lessons once."

"No shit?" Romeo lost the hardened cop voice and sounded like the kid he was, which restored my confidence in the balance of the universe.

"Yeah, the Big Boss thought it would be a good idea. Something about having a Plan B if the hotel management thing didn't work out."

"He thought you'd be a good corporate pilot?" Romeo clearly thought this was funny.

"That was his tack. I had no idea he was my father then, but he always took an interest in my career. Between you and me, I think he was really thinking military pilot. He had visions of a drill sergeant molding me into shape." I ran my fingers over the switches and marveled at the glass displays. Most of the instrumentation was unrecognizable. Gone were the vacuum and electrically driven dials of that ancient Cessna 172. So far in my past, flight school seemed like it had happened to someone else. "I was a bit of a handful." I shot a cockeyed grin at the young detective.

"Were?"

"I am who I am. And I'm too stupid to pretend to be anybody else." Leaning back, settling into the sturdy chair, I tried to recall what it felt like to fly. One hand on the throttle, the other easing the yoke back, my feet dancing on the rudders as the plane gathered speed. Each time the machine left the earth, I remembered being so happy, so free, I couldn't resist laughing.

"So you have a pilot's license?"

I shook my head. "Not finishing the training is one of my few regrets." Opening my eyes, I turned and looked at my friend. "I soloed and was working on the required hours, the cross-country, night flying, all that stuff."

"It sounds like you liked it. What happened?"

"Loved it. Funny enough, it was one of the few things I've ever encountered that I was perfectly suited for. But I let life get in the way." Reaching across the center console, I put my hand on his arm and squeezed. "No regrets, Romeo. Live each day . . ."

Understanding flared in his eyes. Then he turned and with both hands, grabbed the yoke as a kid would the steering wheel of his parents' station wagon. "What's it like? To fly?"

I joined him in his fantasy, grabbing the yoke on my side—two escapees taking the corporate iron for a joyride. If only wishing could make it so. . . . "Like having your own magic carpet."

"To take you as far as your credit card limit will allow."

"There is that." Leave it to the youngster to add a dose of reality.

Giving up the game, I leaned my head back and closed my eyes. "So, where do we stand?"

Pages rustled as Romeo flipped through his notebook. "According to the tower log, the plane touched down a bit before eleven last night. Mr. Grady sent the pilots to the hotel. He told them he and the . . . lady . . . would spend the night on the plane. It took the pilots some time to get the plane squared away, give instructions to the line, call in a breakfast order— you know all the stuff."

I didn't but I could imagine.

"The pilots reported that, after they'd done all their paperwork and stuff, which took about a half hour or so, a guy showed up to talk to Mr. Grady."

"Frank DeLuca." I opened one eye to gauge Romeo's response. If he was surprised, he hid it well. He was either tired or getting used to my uncanny skills.

"Yeah. He showed up—"

"About midnight," I said, stealing his glory. "But when the pilots were called back after Shady Slim was found dead, Mr. DeLuca was nowhere to be found."

"Lucky, I swear, are you going to let me finish?" While he tried on a stern expression, his voice held a hint of humor. "You are just like your mother."

"Low blow, Detective Junior-Grade." I grinned back at him even though I tried not to. "You know, if I thought you were serious about me sharing any trait with my mother, I'd be curling my toes over a very high ledge while contemplating the concept of terminal velocity."

"Retracted. But it got your attention."

The kid seemed proud of himself, so I handed him victory. "I'll shut up now."

"Thank you." I heard Romeo flip a page. "According to Miss Becky-Sue, he stayed about twenty minutes . . ."

"Plenty of time to get back to the dealership."

The detective sighed heavily.

"Sorry. Change at my advanced age is very difficult—I'm working on it." Opening my eyes, I pushed myself upright. "Please, go on."

"Miss Becky-Sue said she went into the room in the back when DeLuca arrived—apparently Shady Slim wanted privacy. She said she fell asleep. When she woke up, she found Shady Slim in the lav and you know the rest."

"What time was that?"

Romeo consulted his notes.

"Two hours, give or take."

I raised my eyebrows. "Pretty sound sleeper. She stayed asleep while the pilots freaked and called my office? And if she was asleep the whole time, as she says, how did she know DeLuca only stayed for twenty minutes? DeLuca himself told me he stayed for an hour."

Romeo deflated. "Good question."

I looked for a mirror to check my appearance, then realized a plane would have no need of a rearview picture—if it wasn't going forward, it would be going down, so behind was irrelevant. "And another thing: She said Shady Slim talked on the phone the whole ride, and something in the conversation made him angry. He must've used the satellite phone—his cell wouldn't work from over forty thousand feet."

"You sound like you think his death was from something other than natural causes. The guy was as big as a barn. I'm betting his ticker quit. What would make you think something else?"

"Curiosity, that's all—and a strange little bit of synchronicity. We have one dead woman in a dealership owned by Frank DeLuca. Then the man himself shows up here and we end up with another dead body." I eased myself out of the captain's chair—a tight squeeze between the armrest and the yoke. Romeo had to strain to look up at me as I continued. "It may be nothing other than bad coincidence, but it's worth a look, don't you think?"

"I'll get the call log," Romeo offered. God bless him. "And I'll see if the coroner can run a quick and dirty tox. Money's getting tighter and tighter, autopsies aren't done regularly anymore. I can't promise anything, especially with no signs of anything other than a heart attack or something normal. Pretty soon, the only way we'll make murder one stick is if we catch them red-handed." The kid followed me out of the cockpit—I noticed he didn't have as much trouble getting out of his chair. The expansion that came with age, stress, too little sleep, and too many carbs was a total downer.

"Let me know what you get." I stood tall and stretched. The snooze had been marginally restorative.

"Miss Becky-Sue isn't being completely honest with us," Romeo said, ever the master of understatement. "How do we get her to come clean?"

"The same way you milk a rattlesnake—very carefully. Leave that part to me, kid, snakes are my specialty."

· · ·

THE process of removing Shady Slim Grady went more smoothly than I'd thought, not to mention faster. We even managed to do it all inside the hangar, far from prying eyes. The funeral directors had come through. I'd never really thought about moving dead bodies around, at least not until today. The picture of Shady Slim's lifeless body dangling in midair wouldn't leave me any time soon, of that I was sure.

When Romeo was finished with her, I sent Miss Becky-Sue to the Babylon, giving instructions that she be parked in the Sodom and Gomorrah Suite— somehow it seemed appropriate. Security was keeping guard and Romeo had restricted her to a short leash. But as they would a rabid dog, most people gave Miss Becky-Sue a wide berth and as much latitude as she wanted, and she was used to that.

While the young detective was tying up loose ends, I wandered into the Fixed Base Operator, the FBO to those who flew general aviation aircraft. These were the folks who took care of the planes and the pilots, providing fuel, weather information, access to Flight Service for flight-plan filing, and a place to crash while waiting on clients or waiting out weather. I was looking for the line guys who had been on duty when the plane came in—I hoped shifts hadn't changed yet. For once, luck worked in my favor—they were still there, catching a bite to eat in the break room.

The bagels looked good, so I split a blueberry one

and plopped the halves in the toaster. Grabbing a mug, I prayed the coffee was still as strong as I remembered it to be. After adding a touch of cream and resisting the sugar, I took a hit and groaned in delight.

One of the line guys appeared at my elbow. "Man, coffee, it's like essential, you know?"

"A drug of necessity."

His coffee now cold, he tossed the remnants into the sink, then replenished his mug. He blew on it for a moment, then took a tentative sip. Satisfied, he gulped a bit more. "You know that dead guy?"

"Yeah, he was an old family friend." The toaster dinged and I set about covering my bagel with butter—if I was going to sin, I was going to sin big.

"Sorry to hear that," the kid said, sounding sincere.

"Let me ask you something." I took a bite out of my bagel as I contemplated my approach. "Did anything happen before I showed up?"

"How do you mean?"

"People coming and going. Anything unusual?" Soft yet chewy, the bagel was worth every calorie, so I paced myself, relishing every bite.

The kid boosted himself up onto the counter, then topped off his coffee again. "A guy came to visit."

"Frank DeLuca."

Recognition dawned on the kid's face. "I thought he looked familiar."

"Anything else?" I reached for a napkin and dabbed at some butter that had dribbled down my chin.

"Well, nothing unusual, really. After Mr. DeLuca left, we'd just gotten everything buttoned up for the night and that lady came in demanding the courtesy car."

I dropped my hand, my bagel forgotten . . . almost. "Miss Becky-Sue? She took the car?"

The kid nodded. "I gave her the keys myself."

"Where'd she go?"

"I don't know, but she wasn't gone long, maybe a half hour."

A half hour. Plenty of time to get to the Babylon and back . . . with time to kill.

CHRISTIAN Louboutin had a signature boutique in the Forum Shops at Caesar's Palace. A long shot, but I had to chase that pair of shoes. Even though I'd told him to go home a long time ago, Paolo still lurked out front of the FBO, staying way past his shift to see I got home. With a nod I acknowledged his kindness—he knew grateful when he saw it.

I settled in the soft embrace of the leather back-seats, afraid I might not have the energy to get out again. When Paolo was settled in front, I pressed the intercom button. "Would you mind stopping at the Forum Shops on the way back to the Babylon?"

His eyes swiveled to the rearview mirror. "Which entrance?"

"The middle one, on the through street near the spa. I've got my eye on a pair of shoes."

Riding the escalator from the dark parking area into the high-ceilinged, beautifully lit, high-energy

Forum Shops was a bit like being pulled from the dungeons and thrown to the lions. Blinking at the lights, I tried to time my jump into the flow of humanity without much success. Dodging patrons, I worked my way upstream to the Christian Louboutin boutique.

This was dangerous territory for me—I'd never met a stiletto I didn't like. Keeping my eyes focused straight ahead, I moved quickly past the displays to the counter in the back. Thankfully, a young lady jumped to help me, leaving me no time to linger into trouble. "May I help you?"

I introduced myself. "I'm looking for a pair of red shoes. Strappy slingbacks?"

She tried to frown but her forehead didn't move—Botox, a Vegas affliction. "Red. Too bad. This season's signature shoe sounds like it would've been a perfect fit." She reached for a large ringed binder and started flipping pages. "As all the signature shoes are, it was a limited edition. We only received two pair." She stopped at a page, then turned the book around so it faced me as she pointed. "That's it there. If you're interested, perhaps I could get them from another store?"

I unfolded the photocopy Jerry had given me and smoothed it on the counter. The shoes were identical. "Would anyone else in town have sold these shoes?"

"Our other styles, yes. But the signature shoes are limited to the official boutique."

"You wouldn't happen to know who bought the pairs you had, would you?"

The sales lady glanced around, then lowered her voice. "I really shouldn't give out that information."

"It's part of a murder investigation. I can get a warrant, if I need to, but that would be so . . . public, don't you think?" I patted her hand. "We can keep it between you and me."

"Murder," she whispered, her attention clearly piqued. Funny how a good killing did that. "If they paid cash, I probably can't help you."

"If they paid cash you'd probably have the shoes back." Regularly johns wanted to buy gifts for their high-end hookers. The ladies preferred cash purchases. When the john went back to the wife and kids, the escort would return the gift and take the cash refund.

"Good point." The salesgirl's mouth puckered in distaste at the thought. "We're in luck, my manager has gone to lunch."

She disappeared through a hidden door.

I tapped my toes, my arms crossed tightly across my chest, as I exerted heroic willpower, keeping my eyes averted from the enticements in the display cases.

She didn't take long. Glancing around furtively, she looked guilty. Thankfully, there wasn't anyone around to see, if you ignored the cameras, which I did. "You know, I've always wanted to work at the Babylon." She pushed a scrap of paper across the counter. "One pair of shoes came back, we sent them to Corporate."

"When did they come back?"

Her eyes hit mine, her confusion apparent. "Last week. Why?"

"And the other pair?"

"We sold them right after they came out—a special order. These were a really hot, limited-edition kind of thing. I remember delivering them myself. And, curiously enough, he paid cash." Her face paled as she looked over my shoulder. The manager must've returned.

I palmed the paper. "Thank you so much for checking on the availability. I'll send my guest at the Babylon over later."

Turning, I grinned at her look of relief, then sashayed out of the store as if I hadn't a care in the world—an Oscar-worthy performance, if I do say so myself. I didn't look at the name until I was once again settled in the limo, this time en route to the Babylon. Carefully I unfolded the scrap. There, in a flourishing cursive, was one name, a name I recognized:

Frank DeLuca.

FRANK DeLuca—his dealership. But what dummy would kill someone on his own turf. I know . . . murder is often a crime of passion and opportunity. And now his shoes. I sure needed another tête-à-tête with the good Mr. DeLuca.

But first, I needed to find my father. The news of Slim's departure to the Poker Room in the Sky should come from me—I owed him that. Heck, I owed them both that. But I wasn't about to tackle that job solo; I needed reinforcements. Mother could help soften the blow, but she hadn't answered the phone at her apartment.

Miss P answered on the first ring. "Customer Relations. How may I help you?"

"I need to find my mother."

"If you're going to kill her, I refuse to be an accessory."

I filled her in on Shady Slim. "Mona hasn't been looking for me or anything, has she? It's still pretty early. I thought I'd find her at home, but no such luck."

"She's in Mrs. Olefson's suite. They called to invite you to tea."

"Tea? How civilized. I smell a rat."

"Nothing ventured, nothing gained."

"That's what my day was missing—a platitude. Have you ever thought about doing one of those calendars? You know the ones with one page for each day and they have like a joke or a word or something? Yours could include a platitude."

"Why don't we do it together? One day a platitude, the next day a cliché?"

"Now that's really gilding the lily." Somehow the banter righted the ship of my day, filling my sails. "Personally I'd rather do a Handsome Men of Vegas Uncovered kind of thing, but that's just me. I'll be with my mother and Mrs. Olefson. Pray for me."

"I'll light a candle."

"Even better. Oh, before I go, has Brandy had any luck finding Cole Weston?"

"Not yet. She did get a bead on him, though, from one of the players last night. He said he last saw Cole leaving the property early this morning."

"Interesting. Any idea where he went?"

"None."

"And he hasn't been seen since?"

"No."

"Why am I not surprised? Let me know if he appears, okay?"

When I ended the call, my step was lighter. I don't know why, but I felt the glimmer of a song in my heart. Even a meeting with Mona couldn't dim my newfound joie de vivre. This being my life, I knew it couldn't last. Someone would rain on my parade, I was sure of it. The director of my life never could resist shouting, "Cue the catastrophe" every time I hit a happy stride.

Dane caught me at the elevators.

Am I clairvoyant, or what?

"Lucky, can I have a minute?" His reflection appeared next to mine in the polished bronze doors.

"Shouldn't you be in jail?" Looking at him would probably turn me to stone or something, so I didn't take the chance.

"Apparently, they didn't think I'd be a flight risk." He cleared his throat. His voice sounded hollow.

"Since you have so many ties to the community," I fired back. Sarcasm is my best thing. Followed closely by my ability to spend the bulk of my time in the company of less than stellar men.

"Lucky . . ." His voice broke. Tentatively he touched my arm.

I pulled away as if I'd been poked with a cattle prod. "Don't."

He dropped his hand; his arms hung at his sides; his shoulders drooped—like a scarecrow with no backbone . . . and no brain, but that last part was my personal opinion. Either way, it wasn't a look I would associate with the former army über officer. I felt my resolve slipping. I am such a pansy-ass. Like a drunk with a bottle, I found it next to impossible to resist a problem that needed solving.

And Dane was most definitely a huge problem.

But he wasn't mine.

"Look, cowboy," I said, summoning fortitude I didn't know I had. The elevator doors opened and he followed me on. "I got a hotel full of problems to solve and yours isn't one of them." I waved my pent-house access card. "I've got to find my mother, then deliver some real bad news to my father, and you're not invited."

Dane refused to budge. From the looks of him, he'd dug in his heels like a roped calf. "I want to explain. I *need* to explain. You owe me that much."

"Owe you!" With hands on my hips, I whirled to face him. The man had cojones; I'd give him that.

I must've looked like a banshee from Hell—he retreated into a corner, his color and his courage receding. "Even a condemned man gets a last wish." He trailed the words out like a flower girl dribbles rose petals—a reluctant peace offering.

"Hollywood hogwash," I growled. "You need to leave."

The elevator doors closed and we remained immobile. I figured we had twenty seconds at the outside before someone called the car. I'd been taken for enough rides lately, so I stuck my card in the slot and punched the appropriate button. "Okay then. You got fifty-one floors."

Dane slapped my hand away, then mashed the emergency stop. Grabbing my shoulder, he pulled me around to face him. "I need your help. I didn't kill her and I need to find the SOB who did before your buddy Romeo digs a pit and throws me in it."

He looked scared. And mad as hell.

The fight trickled out of me like water through a rusty pipe. "Give me one reason why I should help you."

He deflated. "I can't."

Not the answer I expected. I found it a bit redeeming. Somehow, I'd known from the beginning I'd help him. And I'd also known it could be my undoing. If I was wrong; if my gut was leading me astray; if he really killed his wife . . . well, there was nothing like the prospect of being hoodwinked into helping a murderer cover his tracks and frame somebody else to dampen life's little joys.

"I'll listen, but not now." I released the emergency

stop and pressed the button for an intermediate floor. "Meet me in Delilah's in an hour."

When the elevator stopped and the doors opened, Dane stepped off. His hands stuffed into the pockets of his jeans, his shoulders hunched up around his ears, he didn't look at me.

As the doors closed, I stuck my hand out, holding them open for a moment. "And, cowboy . . ."

Dane turned to look at me, his face impassive, his eyes haunted.

"No guarantees."

MRS. Olefson, the hotel's resident grandmother, lived in a corner room on the forty-first floor with a nice view of the Strip and the Spring Mountains beyond. We'd met when she'd asked to marry her dog in the Temple of Love at the hotel. I intervened, and made a wonderful friend in the process.

Widowed, well into her tenth decade, and with no real family, Mrs. Olefson and Milo, her Maltese, had asked to stay permanently. God knew we all could use a den mother. Sometimes life gives you a gift. We set her up in a sunny room where she held court every day, serving tea, biscuits, and sage advice to all visitors. She was happy. We were happy. And Milo was getting fat.

Giggling greeted me as I raised my fist to knock on the door.

I knocked firmly and the giggling stopped. Heels clacked across the tile floor, then the door flew open.

"Oh, Lucky! I knew you'd come!" Mona, resplendent in a dark purple peasant skirt and a flowing peach top that swooped precariously off one shoulder, grabbed my arm and pulled me inside. Holding my arm to her side, she kicked the door shut. "Come, come. We have that tea you like—the peach one from Teavana. And you're in time—we're just getting started." A smile danced across her face, then sparkled in her eyes. Pregnancy had filled the hollows of her face, rounding the sharp edges. Her dark brown hair fell in soft waves curling lightly at her shoulders, bangs barely tickling her doe eyes. Like a Rembrandt Madonna, she glowed. And she looked like my sister—my younger sister.

Just getting started, she'd said. I didn't even take the bait—I'd find out what she was up to soon enough. Giggling usually meant mischief.

With Mona, naughtiness was a gift—a natural aptitude bestowed on her at birth.

At some point in the normal course of life, the roles of parent and child are expected to reverse, with the child assuming a parental caregiver role. I had been born into the role. Lucky me.

Mrs. Olefson beamed when she saw my delight as I took in all the touches she'd added to her space. "You like it, I can tell. I'm so pleased." A tiny woman, she all but disappeared in the overstuffed chair. As usual, with her white hair perfectly coiffed, her face painted to accent not alarm, and dressed primly in a St. John suit and sensible pumps, she looked prepared for an audience with the queen. Milo, a ball of white fur with a black nose and a red bow, curled at her feet. He'd pricked one ear at me, then had lost interest.

The tea service, made of exquisite bone china glazed with a pretty floral pattern and arrayed on a silver platter covered with a linen doily, was placed on a table within Mrs. Olefson's easy reach.

Trotting out her best Emily Post, she delicately pinched the curved handle of a tiny cup with one hand and the larger handle of the pot, covered with a crisp white napkin, with the other. Holding them both up, she raised a questioning eyebrow at me.

"Yes, please. One lump, a touch of milk."

"Traditional. I thought as much." She smiled as if I'd earned a gold star.

While she performed her duties, I glanced around, taking in my surroundings more completely. Yup, Miss Marple's drawing room. That's what this whole thing reminded me of. Something very British, very proper.

"Here you go." She extended the cup to me.

Reaching, I cradled the delicate porcelain with both hands, as I would a baby bird, afraid to crush it. Steam and the subtle scent of ripe peaches filled my nostrils as I breathed deep. Blowing briefly, I then took a tentative sip. Still a bit hot.

Mona ruffled her skirt around her as she kicked off her shoes, then pulled her feet up, tucking them under her as she settled into a corner of the couch.

She worried a stray thread and refused to meet my gaze directly. Squirming like a child under adult scrutiny, she chewed on her lip.

I waited, biting down on my smile. If Mona was good for anything, she was good for a laugh. But she would also interpret a grin as a sign of weakness. And history had taught me that I never, ever wanted to give my mother the upper hand if I could help it.

So I remained calm, detached. "Mrs. Olefson, I love all the personal touches you've added."

"Thank you, dear." Her hand shook a bit as she grabbed a cube of sugar with the silver tongs, then dropped it into her own cup. She added a dollop of milk, then settled back with a smile of self-satisfaction as she gazed around the room.

"Is that your husband?" I nodded toward an oil painting on the wall of a smiling man with a round face and happy eyes.

"Oh, yes. It wouldn't be home without Ollie."

"Ollie Olefson. That's . . . memorable."

"Ollie is his nickname. His given name is Randolf and he just hates it." She spoke of him as if he'd just gone off to work for the day and would be home soon. Her loss made me sad, but her memories filled my heart. At the end of the day, that's all there really was.

"Lucky, we have something we want to talk to you about." Mona had apparently filled her quota of quiet time.

"Then this isn't a purely social visit? I'm shocked." I grinned as I lifted my cup to my lips.

Mother straightened. Sitting tall, she made herself big then leveled her gaze, but her eyes didn't meet mine. Instead she looked to my left out the window, leaving me with the distinct impression she was following the instructions on what to do when confronted by a grizzly. "You know how I gave up Mona's Place because you told me to?"

"That's not exactly how I remember it, but go on." I took another sip of tea—it had cooled nicely.

"Well, I've been at loose ends since then." She worried a bright pink toenail. Finally she looked at me. Her eyes held the expression one would expect from a dying man pleading for his life. Mona and her drama. "I've been so bored, honey. I just don't know what to do with myself."

"Apparently you've engaged in some forms of . . . recreation."

She paused, a quizzical look on her face.

"Oh for heaven's sake, Mona, the horizontal cha-cha?" Miss Olefson gave a surprisingly throaty laugh.

Mona's face reddened a little. "Well, one can't do that *all* the time."

I'm not sure that had been her opinion when she ran the brothel, but I didn't point that out. I had no intention of being perforated with a pair of sugar tongs today. "Mother, in a few short months, you are going to be busier than a bookie during March Madness. I think you'll have plenty to do when the baby comes."

"I'm not talking about busywork. I'm referring to something more intellectual. Mrs. Olefson and I have decided to go into business together."

"Doing what?" I eyed her warily as I relished another large gulp of tea. Somehow I just couldn't get past the words *Mona* and *intellectual* in the same sentence.

"Phone sex."

My tea spewed out my nose. "*What?*" I reached for a linen napkin. Blotting at the tea dripping down my face, I worked at composing myself. "How?"

"A nine-hundred number through the main switchboard should do it." Mona had done her homework.

"You want the Babylon to be a conduit for nine-hundred-number phone sex?" My blood pressure didn't even spike—I must have been dead. Either that or I had been inoculated against clear idiocy. Regardless, I found it next to impossible to work up a good case of red ass. Which was a good thing. I had a feeling it would be like yelling at a couple of two-year-olds—I'd wear myself out and end up with a mess I didn't want to clean up.

Mona mistook my silence for complicity and drove right into the impending storm. "Here, let us show you."

Like children practicing for the school play, each woman pretended to hold a phone to her ear. Then Mona whispered, "I'll be the john."

Mrs. Olefson, her eyes as big as saucers, nodded, her perfectly coiffed white curls bouncing. She worried a finger through her pearl choker, twisting it.

"Ring, ring," Mona said.

"Hulloooo." Mrs. Olefson lowered her voice at least an octave, infusing it with warm, sultry undertones. "Honey, who do you want me to be tonight?"

Like a passenger in a car watching the accident in slow motion, I was powerless to stop the scene unfolding in front of me. I bit down hard on the inside of my mouth and turned toward Mona, waiting expectantly. The price of admission to this show had been cheap, so I might as well enjoy it—before I shut it down.

"I'm a fireman," Mona growled. "I need a hose handler."

My cup rattled in its saucer.

Mrs. Olefson held her imaginary phone away from her ear and whispered, "Is this where I tell you what I'm wearing?"

Mona rolled her eyes and hissed, "Just like we practiced. You remember."

"I'm not sure if I'm dressed properly . . . to be a hose handler, I mean." Again that sexy voice.

If I closed my eyes. If I didn't know she'd grown up long before Las Vegas had . . .

"Tell me what you're wearing." Mona's fireman needed work.

"Well, I'm not wearing any underwear." Mrs. Olefson couldn't quite get the note of incredulity out of her voice. I'm certain the woman had never gone commando—the premise clearly confused her.

"Tell me more," Mona encouraged. Then she

turned to me and whispered. "The delivery needs a bit of work, but the voice is great, don't you think?"

"Words fail me, Mother."

"Well," Mrs. Olefson dropped her voice, "I'm wearing a black lace nightie my husband gave me—"

"No," Mona corrected. "No husbands. Remember?"

"No husbands?" Mrs. Olefson crinkled her brow and snatched a glance at Ollie hanging over the fireplace.

The laugh, so long held in my belly, burst forth. Struggling to catch my breath, I swiped at the tears. Then I dabbed at my nose, which had started to run. Mona glared at me, which made me laugh harder.

Mrs. Olefson hung up her imaginary phone. "I really suck at this."

That pronouncement cracked Mona's stern veneer. Laughter started slowly, then built, doubling her over. Mrs. Olefson remained above the fray, serving us all fresh cups of tea and gracing us with a beatific smile.

Finally I thought I could hazard a conversation without convulsing. "Mother, what ever gave you the idea?"

"Sex is all I know."

Well, that little bit of honesty was a showstopper.

"Mother." I put my cup and saucer on the silver tray, then rose. "You know that's not true. But we need to go, I'm sorry. I need your help."

When I asked for help, which was usually the last act of a desperate woman, Mona was front and center, no questions asked. We made our exit with appropriate thank-yous and promises to come back soon.

Once safely in the elevator, I punched the button for the penthouse, then turned to face my mother's questioning stare.

I proceeded to fill her in on my morning.

She listened without interruption, nodded once as the elevator doors opened, then hooked her arm through mine and gave me a comforting squeeze. "We'll get through this. Your father and Shady Slim . . ."

"I know. Two horses cut from the same herd."

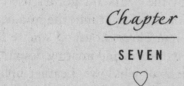

Chapter

SEVEN

Delivering bad news always tied me in knots. Delivering bad news to my father made me feel sick, like the condemned—blindfolded, back against the wall, the acrid taste of my last cigarette lining my mouth like cotton. Of course, smoking was probably the world's only vice I had managed to escape, but I was pleased with the analogy, so I went with it.

Even with Mona providing for-once-silent support, dread coalesced into a cold ball in the pit of my stomach. Sweat trickled down my sides. A case of serious brain freeze paralyzed my thoughts as words left me. After all this time, I should be used to it—as the chief problem-solver at the Babylon, bad news was a big part of my vocabulary. And the Big Boss handled it better than most—at least, up to this point he'd resisted shooting the messenger. Even still, I'm pretty much of a happy-ending kind of gal.

As the elevator slowed, I straightened, then smoothed my slacks and retucked my shirt. I buttoned one more button at the top, I don't really know why.

As the doors opened, I took a deep breath, which wasn't as steadying as I'd hoped. Motioning for Mona to precede me, I let her step out to take the first bullet. Through the years I'd gotten used to stepping out of the elevator right into the middle of my father's great room. Three thousand square feet of luxury, the space felt warm and inviting despite its high ceilings and walls of windows. Leather upholstered walls and rich mahogany floors lent a richness further enhanced by brass sconces casting diffused light. Richly hued Persian rugs, hand knotted in the finest tradition, each with a cluster of furniture fashioned from exotic woods and covered with hides from successful safaris, provided cozy entertainment areas—assuming one could get over the fact that some poor beast paid the ultimate sacrifice so your butt could be coddled, something I could never do. I preferred the overstuffed couch by the window.

Paintings, lesser works by the great masters from the Big Boss's handpicked collection, dotted the walls, each perfectly lit.

"Albert," Mona called. When no one answered, she headed toward the hallway leading to their private wing. "Let me check our room. Make yourself at home, honey. Of course, I don't need to tell you that."

Bright sunlight streamed through the floor-to-ceiling windows that defined the room on two sides. Lured by the view, and comforted by the fact the room appeared empty, I wandered to the windows. The Las Vegas Strip stretched at my feet and angled toward the horizon. To the west, the Spring Mountains hunkered down, a ragged scratch defining the horizon. Carol Lombard had lost her life in a plane crash in those mountains. Clark Gable had never recovered from the loss. Ever the romantic, I thought about the tragedy more than I would admit to.

My stomach told me it was long past feeding time but I wasn't certain. My stomach often led me astray. The bagel had done nothing but stoke the fire in the hunger machine. Clearly, I needed food, but I also needed to find my father.

Preoccupied and in desperate need of a moment of peace, I stared at my city, its lights now dimmed in deference to the sun. Daytime wasn't Vegas's best time. Sunlight doused the neon magic and made everything appear . . . normal, mundane even, as if the city turned in on itself, regenerating, restoring, awaiting the rebirth of nightfall.

Shutting my eyes, I took a deep, quieting breath.

My mother returned, shaking her head. "I don't know where he is." She settled on the couch. Patting the cushion next to her, she said, "Come sit. You look exhausted. Rest for a minute. Your father usually comes to check on me about this time of day, after his lunch meetings."

Her suggestion was a good one. I settled into the couch's soft embrace. Leaning my head back, I closed my eyes. We fell into a thoughtful silence.

Somewhere I had heard about a relaxation technique where you concentrated on relaxing one muscle at a time. They might have kicked me out of yoga class, but I wasn't above trying some of the stuff on my own. First my neck. I rolled my shoulders and turned my head slowly from side to side. The tension eased. Only a bit, but I'd take it. Now my breathing. I slowed the rhythm, willing my body to relax. In. Out. The world retreated.

The sound of the elevator whirring to life penetrated my consciousness, hitting me like a Taser. My father. Shady Slim Grady.

When the doors to the elevator opened, I was standing in front of them. My father looked up, surprise on his face. Before he could say anything I stuck out my hand. "Your wallet?"

"What?" He gave me a half laugh as if he thought I was joking.

"Can I have your wallet, please?"

With a sardonic grin and no questions, he reached into his hip pocket with two fingers. After extracting the worn leather billfold, he handed it to me.

I opened it, plucked out a hundred dollar bill, and handed both back to him. "Make me something."

He kept the bill in his hand as he stuffed the wallet back into his pocket. The amusement in his eyes disappeared as he looked at me. "That bad, huh?"

I nodded as I took his arm, leading him over to the couch. Mona patted the spot where her feet had been. "Sit by me, Albert."

He did as she asked. "What'll it be? An elephant for luck?" he asked.

"Luck is always in short supply." And Shady Slim's had run out, but I didn't add that part.

With Mona absentmindedly kneading his shoulders, my father began to crease and fold the money, his fingers working the paper with the quiet sureness of years of practice. Instead of worry beads, the Big Boss turned to origami to ease the tension, to take his mind off unpleasantness. As he folded, refolded, and creased, a small form took shape. This miniature elephant would have its trunk raised . . . for luck.

With one hand he grabbed mine, opened it, and dropped the tiny shape into my palm. With both hands he closed my fingers over it and held them there. "The two most important people to me are in this room, alive and well, so don't look so stricken. Whatever it is, I can handle it."

"It's Shady Slim. He's dead. I'm so sorry."

A tic worked in my father's jaw as his face clouded. Mona reached for his hand and squeezed, her eyes reflecting his pain. He worked his hand from hers, then patted it as he rose. I stepped out of his way. As he moved to stare out the window, I stepped in beside him.

"Heart attack?" he asked after a few moments. Shady Slim had been asking for one for years. Everyone, including Slim, had known it was a matter of when, not if.

"Don't know. There weren't any obvious signs of foul play." I left out the part about him dying on the throne. Somehow I didn't think my father needed to be burdened with that bit of indignity. "Romeo questioned everyone. There will be an autopsy, but with budget cuts and the fact that no foul play is indicated, it could be a while before we have any results. I'll let you know when I hear."

"Arrangements will need to be made."

"I mentioned that to Miss Becky-Sue."

My father flinched. "Slim always said he wanted to be buried here. I think he has a plot at Palm Mortuary. He said no funeral."

"No funeral?"

My father shook his head, then gave me a faint grin. "No, Slim wanted a party. He didn't want anybody going all soft and weepy. I believe that's how he put it."

"A wake?"

"From the sounds of it, he envisioned something bigger, something definitively Vegas."

A themed party in lieu of a funeral?

My father sounded hopeful but not certain. "I think it's called a Celebration of Life."

But of course.

THE increasing energy level in the lobby assaulted me as the elevators deposited me in the middle of the fray. With long strides, I covered the vast marble expanse, taking in every detail while pretending not to. The lines in front of each registration station were several customers deep but moving quickly. With ready smiles, bellmen jumped in to help with baggage. Cocktail waitresses in their tiny togas with gold braided cord balanced on stilettos while darting in and out, supplying the oil that kept the squeal out of the Babylon's finely tuned engine. Clusters of admirers gathered under the flocks of blown-glass hummingbirds adorning the ceiling. Others wandered, window-shopping, holding hands, relaxing. A gallery of spectators ringed the large windows in front of the ski slope and rewarded a successful run with raised glasses and a cheer. A spectacular wipeout earned a collective groan and cringe.

Midafternoon was well under way. No wonder my stomach was staging a revolt. Liquid refreshment before dawn and one bagel slathered in a cholesterol-raising amount of butter was hardly sufficient sustenance—at least for this body.

Something told me there was a yummy, juicy, gourmet . . . French . . . hamburger in my very near future. The lone bright spot in a deadly day. I'd been sidestepping Jean-Charles's issue of an appropriate kitchen—it was time we came to some sort of resolution, although I had no idea what. But first I probably ought to put in an appearance at the office and at least pretend I was in charge. And there was Dane. . . .

Feeling the need to move, I took the stairs, two at a time, to the mezzanine. Miss P didn't give me a glance when I burst through the office door. Her eyes were riveted to the six-foot-four, two-hundred-and-twenty-five-pound hunk holding down a corner of her desk—the Beautiful Jeremy Whitlock. For a nanosecond, envy perched on my shoulder. To have a guy like that. I could almost resort to mooning, too . . . almost. He bent down and whispered in her ear, making her blush, then giggle. Mooning, blushing, and giggling—the woman had no shame! I should be so lucky. . . .

As a challenge to females everywhere, Jeremy had been graced with light brown hair, brown eyes flecked with gold, a ready smile hanging like a hammock between a pair of the deepest dimples, and a body begging to be . . . Well, I slammed my mind closed on that visual. Suffice it to say he was the kind of male populating women's fantasies since the beginning of time. I wasn't immune. I could easily picture Jeremy in a kilt wielding a broadsword, or astride a white steed. But he was Miss P's knight, and there are certain boundaries no friend would ever cross. Especially not this friend.

"Jeremy, great. I need to talk to you," I said as I breezed by on my way to my office. Two steps through the door, I realized it wasn't my office anymore—it was Miss P's. But she was sitting at her former position out front, which was where Brandy should be. Old habits are hard to break. And I had a hard enough time keeping up without my staff playing musical desks. I backtracked and this time, under the amused expressions of Miss P and Jeremy, stepped through the makeshift doorway to my new office—or what would someday be my new office, perhaps not in my lifetime the way things were going, but someday.

Miss P followed me with notepad in hand and Jeremy on her heels.

"Take a seat." I motioned to a tarp-covered form against the wall as I settled into my desk chair. Early this morning, which now seemed a lifetime ago, I had uncovered my desk. Like powdery snow, a fine layer of white now dusted the rich burled walnut.

A cloud of fine grit floated and danced in the shafts of light that filtered through the doorway and shone weakly from the lone overhead lightbulb as Jeremy folded back the cloth over the couch. Miss P sank into the soft cushions as Jeremy straddled the arm, folding one leg over the other so his ankle balanced on his other knee. Holding his leg in both hands, his foot bounced as he glanced around the construction zone.

"I love what you've done to the place," he said, his dimples deepening. What is it about an Australian accent that runs through a woman like molten chocolate?

"Nothing like that personal touch," I said as I tried to marshal my thoughts—the morning had left me reeling. Two dead bodies are two more than I'm used to dealing with.

Leaning forward, I placed my hands on my desk, idly swiping at the dust. Then, focusing on a point on the wall—not making eye contact somehow made the telling easier—I summarized the events of the morning. Miss P scribbled notes. Out of the corner of my eye I saw Jeremy staring at me intently, a small frown marring his otherwise perfect visage, but neither interrupted me as I filled them in on the dead woman on the car—Dane's wife—the poker game, and my Poker Room showdown with the Stoneman.

After I finished, the two of them stared at me with owl eyes. Jeremy was the first to break the silence. "Hooley-dooley, Dane has a wife." He reached across the space between us and grabbed my hand. "Lucky, you have to believe me, I had no idea."

"You work together."

"He was a right-up guy."

I looked at him and wanted to believe him. "That's like telling me he slaps his wife around a bit, but he's really a great guy."

Jeremy's eyes widened and he started to say something, but I silenced him with a raised hand. "Don't mind me. I'm not exactly feeling kindly toward the Y-chromosome set these days. Nothing personal."

He gave me a wink. "Of course not."

Dane was a championship liar and men historically weren't great at ferretting out the bad apples in their barrel, so I let Jeremy off the hook. "I need you to find a needle in a haystack: an optician somewhere in this town willing to fit red contact lenses. I know Sylvie could've gotten those things anywhere, but if we're lucky . . ." I let the thought hang.

"That all?" he asked with just a hint of sarcasm, which made me grin.

"Child's play for a man of your skills." Nervous energy overflowing, I picked up a pencil and began tapping a rhythm on the desk. Irritating I know, but it was a far sight better than wringing necks or shooting someone, and I figured Jeremy and Miss P would get that. "I have no idea what to make of any of this. I need you to get me a toehold, at least."

"What can I do?" Miss P asked.

"Someone hung a banner outside the Ferrari dealership—a hand-lettered, butcher-paper sign designed to block the camera recording the traffic in and out of the showroom. Security says the work order came from this office."

Miss P's eyebrows snapped into a disapproving line.

"Could you follow up on that?"

Miss P, familiar with my order-framed-as-a-question style, didn't bother to answer. "Then get Flash on the phone," I went on. "Somehow we've managed to keep Shady Slim under wraps, so give it to her. Tell her to handle it appropriately—she'll know what you mean. It's sorta interesting Miss Becky-Sue hasn't tried to sell the story to *People* or something."

"Maybe she's honoring Slim's memory?" Miss P offered.

I paused, pondering that imponderable. "Possible, but the high road isn't her usual route." I turned to Jeremy. "Can you find out where the Stoneman lives, the places he hangs out in when he has free time, and anything else you deem pertinent? We need to find him ASAP. It also wouldn't hurt to get a snapshot of his finances." I pushed up out of my chair. The others rose out of habit. "When you are ready to go round him up, call me; I'd like to ride along."

He nodded, but his eyes had lost focus as if he were already three steps ahead of me in the thinking game. Apparently not hard to do these days. Being blindsided by life was getting really tiresome.

"Oh, and Brandy? Has she caught up with Cole Weston yet?"

"He staggered in not too long ago, muddy and dead on his feet. He's asleep in his room. If he sleeps as soundly as most young men I know, she won't be able to get his attention with the light over the door. And he certainly won't hear the phone or a knock, so she's waiting until he appears. Do you want her to get Security to let her in his room?" Miss P looked like she knew the answer.

"No. Barging in there half-cocked would open the hotel to serious liability."

"They're supposed to meet up at five."

I glanced at my watch. "It's almost five now. When they appear, give me a heads-up and I'll meet them in the Burger Palais. The food's on me."

"You got it. And I'll get on that sign as you asked. Where will you be in the interim?"

"Whomping rats."

BY the time I hiked up the steps to Delilah's, a thumper of a headache pounded behind my right eye. Great. A migraine, a putrid pit in my stomach, two dead bodies, one of them a good friend of my father's, another a former friend's wife, a Poker Room manger playing games, and that former friend hell-bent on proving my all-men-are-pigs theory was actually true and not the result of rampant cynicism. Could today get any better?

Pulling my phone from my hip, I flipped it open and hit Jerry's direct dial. He answered on the first ring. "Jer, where's Watalsky? Did you tell him I want to see him?"

"I put the bug in his ear, but he said he had plans. I didn't think it was critical."

"He's peggin' my interest meter."

"I'll try to roust him—he was here until after dawn. Left with a pile."

"Any idea who he took it off of?"

"DeLuca. And he wasn't happy about it."

"DeLuca. He's next on my list. Do you have a bead on him?"

"Girl, he won't be here at this hour."

"Keep an eye out for him. Let me know the minute he hits the property, okay?"

THE sight of Dane sitting at the bar, his back hunched, two empty Buds in front of him and draining a third as I approached, did nothing to brighten my less than sunny disposition.

Thankfully, business was light at this hour. The only other patron sat at the far end of the bar mechanically punching buttons on a video poker machine embedded in the bar top. I thought I remembered seeing the guy here yesterday, and the day before that. I wondered if he ever went home . . . or if he had one to go to. But in my line of work, it was best not to dwell on those kinds of questions, so I didn't. I was only one problem-solver swimming in a sea of problems—drowning wasn't a possibility; it was an inevitability. So it was best to pace myself, delay the inevitable.

"Drinking's really going to help," I snarled as I slid onto a stool next to Dane.

He set the third empty next to the others, carefully aligning them before he spoke. "You'd be surprised."

The water cascading down the sandstone wall behind the bar, the flowering bougainvillea trailing from trellises, the soft music, warm colors, and muted lights were supposed to be welcoming and soothing. I wasn't buying any of it. Apparently I must've looked ready to chew through a tanned hide or something because Sean, our head bartender, kept his distance as he lifted a bottle and an eyebrow at me. I shook my head—just the thought of a Wild Turkey fireball in my empty stomach convulsed me with anticipatory pain. "Club soda with lime, please." If he tried to hide his smirk, he didn't try very hard.

Sean put a tall glass filled with clear liquid and bubbles in front of me. Bubbles really weren't my thing—unless they were rising through a golden liquid from a very specific region of France. However, I'd been trying to cultivate a taste for water—part of my anemic effort to improve my health—so champagne had been downgraded from an everyday thing to a special occasion thing. And bubbles were an attempt to make a tasteless beverage palatable. Why did everything that was good for you have to be so unappealing?

"If anyone wants to know what a lying creep looks like," I said, glancing at Dane as I took a tentative sip of the soda water, grimaced, then placed the glass back on the bar and pushed it away. Bubbles didn't help. "I'll just send them your picture."

If my verbal arrow hit his soft underbelly, I couldn't tell. I hoped it had, but felt bad if it did. What can I say? Conflicted is my natural state. Apparently I am incapable of feeling a pure, unadulterated emotion without wallowing in ambivalence.

"I take it you looked at the security tapes." Dane motioned for another beer.

"Convicting. And that's ignoring the serious

issues you have with the truth for a moment. Those tapes alone are more than adequate for a grand jury. The two of you leaving the Poker Room, heading toward the dealership, where she was found dead—you were the last person to see your wife alive."

"Only if I killed her." He glanced at me, then focused on lining up the fourth beer with the others. He didn't take a sip.

"How much money were you guys wrangling over in the divorce?"

He glanced at me. "Enough."

"And those scratches on your face."

With a haunted look in his eye, he raised a hand to gently probe the angry red gashes on his right cheek. One of them was deep enough to have drawn blood.

"Did Sylvie give you those?"

"She was pissed when I showed up in the Poker Room."

"Why?"

He gave a snort. "With Sylvie, the rising of the sun each day could piss her off. I know it looks bad."

"Bad!" At a loss, I stared at him. Clearly his reality wasn't mine and words weren't bridging the gap. I grabbed his arm, swiveling him around so he at least half faced me and had to meet my eyes. "Cowboy, let me give it to you straight: You are so far up shit creek even a Mercury outboard wouldn't help."

"But you can." This time, when his eyes met mine, they held.

"Dane, I'm a customer relations person. If you've got a pesky rash, an ill-advised marriage to be annulled, your bathroom is too small, your bed too hard, your dinner unacceptable, your show tickets for the wrong show, your wife needing to be rubbed the right way, I can fix that. But you're looking at twenty to life with no parole. What you need is a pit bull with a Bar card and a healthy dose of divine intervention."

"Or someone who can uncover the truth."

"A concept you seem curiously divorced from." Throwing caution to the wind, I grabbed the full bottle in front of him and drained half of it before coming up for air. Beer, not my beverage of choice—a bit low on octane—but it was a darn sight more bracing than water with bubbles. "I can't help you," I said as I slammed the bottle on the counter. I resisted wiping my mouth with the back of my hand as being a wee bit tacky.

"Can't or won't?"

Unwilling to answer, I shrugged and refused to meet his gaze. Conflicting emotions waged a battle in my churning belly. Of course, the beer hadn't helped. And it also wasn't helping me fight my Pavlovian response to other people's problems.

Dane reached for the bottle still clutched in my hand. I relinquished my hold and he drained the remaining beer in one swallow. "I've lost your trust," he said as he again carefully aligned the bottle with the others as if keeping score.

"One of the many downsides to lying."

"If I promise to be square with you, will you at least listen before deciding whether you will help or not?" He gave an almost imperceptible nod to Sean, who popped the top on a fresh longneck, then slid it down the bar where it stopped, still upright, in front of Dane—a skill I marveled at.

"Cowboy, I would like nothing more than to hear the truth. But how do I know when you're giving me the straight skinny and when you're shining me on?" I asked, even though I knew he had no answer. Trust, once lost, can be regained but never fully restored. And picking the right horse in this race would be critical. If I picked poorly, I'd be in desperate need of a get-out-of-jail-free card.

With a weak grin, he crossed his heart. The smile didn't reach his eyes. "From here on out, no matter what, no more lying."

"You know what this is like?" I focused on the television hanging in the corner while I fought a losing battle with myself. Even with the sound muted, I could tell the talking heads were discussing our murder. In Vegas, while good news traveled fast, bad news traveled at the speed of light. The one bright spot appeared to be that Shady Slim Grady's demise was still under wraps. "This is like one of those word problems in freshman algebra: If a liar tells you he's not lying, is he?" My resolve weakening, I gave Dane a tepid smile. "I never got that answer right."

Sensing my weakness, he went for the kill. "Help me? Only you can fix this."

Manipulation at its best and most obvious. Why

didn't it put the fear of God in me? I must have a death wish.

"Against my better judgment, I'll listen, but we take it one step at a time." Relief washed over him, easing the tension from his features, relaxing his posture, and breaking my heart a little bit. "However, if you try to hook a ring through my nose and lead me down some path, I'll bust your ass. Are we clear?"

"Crystal." He grabbed my arm and squeezed. "Thank you."

"As a token of your good faith, give me Sylvie's phone."

"I don't have it." He shook his head. "Before I called you, I looked for it. That's why my boot prints were around the . . ." He swallowed hard, then cleared his throat. "The car."

"Give me her number." I boosted myself up and leaned across the bar. Sean had a bunch of pens stashed in a glass next to the register. I grabbed one, then handed it to Dane. He wrote the number on the back of a cocktail napkin, which I folded and pocketed.

Fire burned in the pit of my stomach. My body was trying to tell me something, something more than it was hungry, but I ignored it. "Sean, do you have some peanuts or something back there?"

"Peanuts, please! This is the Babylon. We have plump whole cashews and dates from the finest Persian markets. Extra-virgin olives . . ." The kid's smile lit his face as he pushed a bowl of the delicacies in front of me. With blue eyes, a receding hairline, and short-cropped brown hair, which he spiked up, Sean had an easy rapport with customers and, apparently, us corporate types. He loved to tell young ladies that his last name was Finnegan and he was Black Irish. I knew the truth: His last name was really Pollack and he was from New Jersey, but far be it from me to bust his myth.

Even though I knew there was no such thing as an extra-virgin olive, I played along, appreciative of Sean's attempt to lighten my mood. "Then those olives are the only thing extra-virgin in this town." I pretended to grouse as I picked at the nuts Sean set in front of me. I popped a few in my mouth and said to Dane, "Okay, let's try to figure out who's playing whom. Why don't we start with the poker game? Tell me everything you know."

"I got pieces, but I don't see how they fit together." Resting his elbows on the bar, Dane sipped his beer as he settled in. "Sylvie called me a week ago. To be honest, I was surprised to hear from her. Our relationship, if you could call it that, was acrimonious at best and over a long time ago. After being granted an early discharge, I started the formalities, as I told you."

"Early discharge?"

"Cost-saving program."

I tested a few of the dates as I listened. "What made Sylvie call you now?"

"She was scared, I think. Although, with her it was hard to separate the truth from the bullshit."

"At least you two had something in common: lying, the bedrock of a solid marriage." I avoided the olives as being far too healthy while I contemplated another beverage choice.

"Do you ever give it a rest?" Now it was Dane's turn to snarl.

"Not when I'm angry," I said matter-of-factly, then turned my attention back to the bottles behind the bar. "Sean, how about a split of Veuve Clicquot?"

After rooting in the refrigerator under the bar, he popped the cork, filled a crystal flute, and set it in front of me. "Celebrating something?" he asked me with a quick glance at Dane, who continued to scowl into his beer.

"The demise of good judgment."

"Always in short supply," he said as he wiped his hands on a bar towel. "But you're lucky, in this town, it's not valued." With a nod and a raised eyebrow at Dane, he wandered to the end of the bar to check on his other guest, leaving us alone.

"What is it with bartenders?" Dane snarled when Sean was out of earshot. "They're always spouting some profound philosophical bull they've overheard."

"Wisdom gained from vicarious experience—the safest kind." One sip of champagne and every nerve ending jumped with joy. On some level I knew that should bother me. However, caring was an insecurity I hadn't the time or the energy for—coping took everything I had. "What was Sylvie doing in that poker game?"

Dane didn't answer immediately. Instead, he stared into his beer. I could almost see the wheels turning—the truth shouldn't be that hard. "I don't know," he finally said, "but she was as twitchy as a dog before a storm. She bought in for cash—she wouldn't tell me who staked her—she never had that kind of green."

"Anything you *do* know?" What I meant was did Dane know anything important that I couldn't find from another source, but I was betting he knew that. The guy hid plenty of IQ points behind the aw-gee-shucks cowboy routine. I'd learned that the hard way—which was pretty much my MO, especially when it came to men.

"Someone was watching her, I know that." Dane glanced at me as if trying to see if I was buying it or not; then he refocused on his beer.

"Who?"

"She didn't say."

I grabbed his knee and spun him around. Face-to-face with him, I leaned in. "Don't play me, cowboy. I didn't ask you what she said; I asked you what you know. I'm five seconds from walking."

"Okay, okay." He rested a hand on my knee as if anchoring me to my stool. "I don't know who exactly was watching her. Several of the players in the game showed more than even the normal amount of interest my wife generally drew, but nothing that seemed odd. Everyone seemed pretty focused."

"With those guys, it's about the chase," I said, thinking out loud. "Winning is everything. There is no such thing as enough. The games they play when the stakes are high are subtle, but very serious. And the Poker Room manager, did she mention him?"

Dane thought for a moment. "Not that I recall. Why?"

"I just find it odd, that, with all his years of experience, he didn't figure out she was cheating. After that much time, you just develop a sort of sixth sense, you know?"

Dane shrugged. So he knew she had been cheating. "She was slick."

"Maybe the manager wasn't that smart, but if anyone else knew . . ." I let the thought dangle. Vegas was a boat riding on a river of money. Anyone messing with the flow was a marked man . . . or woman. One possible motive, and a tableful of "persons of interest." "You told Romeo that she called you during the game, but we both know that isn't true. Why'd you call her?"

"I wanted her out of there. I could tell the noose was tightening—someone was onto her." His voice cracked. Swallowing hard, he cleared his throat.

"Saving damsels in distress is your thing, isn't it?" Dane had run to my defense a time or two so I knew the drill. "But she didn't want to be rescued."

"No, she was pissed." His brows snapped down. "Damned independent women."

"Excuse me?"

He shrugged, but didn't meet my angry gaze. Nor did he look sorry.

"You two left the Poker Room together. It's not too big an assumption to believe you stayed together, but that would make you the killer. You say no. So, what's your story? Lead me through it."

Dane worked his shoulders, stretching. "I'm a fool." I detected a hint of defeat in his voice, but I wasn't about to argue—I happened to agree with his assessment. "Once we were out of sight of the Poker Room, she . . ." Again he rubbed his cheek and winced. "Like I said, she was pissed. Said we should split up. She didn't want anyone to see us together and it would give me a chance to see if anyone followed her."

That sounded reasonable . . . I guess, since I'm such an expert in this arena and all. I nodded for him to continue.

"We were to double back and meet in Delilah's. She promised she would lay the whole thing out for me." His eyes narrowed and his face shut down. "Guess she had no intention, really. She didn't show."

"So how'd you end up in the dealership?" I took another sip of my champagne—much better bubbles.

"I really was on my way to the garage—my truck is still there if you want to check. I saw the dealership door ajar and the rest is history."

"Not quite—there are some giant holes in the story. You didn't smell a rat?"

He shook his head.

"Bad time to be wrong." I resisted diving in for more nuts—champagne with anything other than beluga was like a crime against the god of good taste or something. No need to add my name to the shit list of another minor deity—I was on enough of those lists already. "Did she clue you in to her need to detour through the dealership?"

"She was pretty good at keeping me in the dark."

"A skill you seemed to have picked up," I said as I sipped my bubbly and eyed him over the top of the glass. "Do you have any idea why she would go there?"

"None."

I let the silence stretch between us. "The cameras in the hallway leading to the front door of the dealership weren't any help—they were blocked."

"Yeah. I saw the sign." He moved to get Sean's attention, then apparently thought better of it—I guess five was his lucky number. I did *not* smile at the pun.

"Do you have any idea how she got in? Did someone let her in?"

"Your guess is as good as mine."

"Doubtful."

"I've told you all I know." He reached over and squeezed my hand. "Trust me."

"Said the spider to the fly. Where men are concerned, trust isn't good for my health." I finished the flute of champagne and poured the rest of the contents of the bottle into my glass before I spoke again. "Did you see anything odd? Anyone hanging around looking nervous?"

"Odd? In this loony bin?"

My patience at an end, I leveled what I thought was my best stern gaze on him. "Anything that looked . . . I don't know . . . wrong?"

He pursed his lips and shook his head.

"And you didn't show up on any of the security feeds after you and Sylvie split up. Where'd you go?"

"I doubled back. I wanted to see if anyone followed her."

"So why did you avoid the security cameras? That looks a bit suspicious, don't you think?"

"I wasn't avoiding them, it just looks that way." Dane took a deep breath and looked at me, conjuring his most sincere look. "Lucky, it all looks bad, but I'm telling you the truth. You have to believe me." His eyes skittered from mine as he hailed the bartender. "Sean, what do I owe you?" he asked as he reached into his back pocket for his wallet.

Sean glanced at me and I shook my head. "It's on the house," he answered.

Dane backed off the stool, then pulled a hundred out of his wallet and tossed it on the bar. "This ought to cover it." Then he turned to me. "If you find out anything, you let me know."

"You didn't seem surprised she was cheating. You wouldn't happen to know why she was also losing, would you?"

That got his attention. His eyes snapped to mine and widened in surprise. The most amazing color of green, those eyes were his best feature—emerald whirlpools that captured the weak and unsuspecting. Conscious effort was the only thing keeping me from surrendering my sanity and succumbing to the pull.

Leaning back, putting a few more inches of distance between us, I nodded in answer to the question I saw lurking in his expression.

"She busted out," he said. A statement, not a question.

"Curious, isn't it?" I knew I'd never keep the sarcasm out of that simple statement, so I didn't waste the effort.

"It doesn't make sense."

"Amazingly, that much I'd figured out all by myself. Do you have any idea why she would cheat, then not win?"

"Something scared her? It was part of a bigger plan?" He rubbed his eyes and for a moment he let his mask slip and I saw the toll all of this was taking. Not that I felt pity, but I'd be lying if I said his pain didn't squeeze my heart a tiny bit. "How the hell do I know?" He made it sound like an epithet as his shoulders drooped in defeat.

"Go home, cowboy." I picked up his Ben Franklin from the bar and stuffed it in his shirt pocket, then patted his chest. "This mess will be waiting for us tomorrow. Maybe a new day will bring a fresh perspective." In my experience, that was rarely the case, but a little ray of hope is a powerful thing.

Taking my hand from his chest, he raised it to his lips—his skin was cold. With a sardonic grin, he let my hand go.

I watched Dane saunter away—he really did have a Grade A ass. Too bad he *was* one as well. Even though he hadn't answered my questions, he'd shown a few of the cards he was holding. He hadn't told me about the necklace . . . or the shoes. He hadn't explained dodging the security cameras—a skill we all had—at least not to my satisfaction. Although he acted surprised, he hadn't asked how I knew Sylvie had been cheating or how she had done it. Yup, there was a lot he hadn't shared. But he had told me one thing loud and clear—we weren't partners. Like a TV cop working his snitch, Dane wanted to keep me close, letting me do his work for him.

He might think me a fool, but he had met his match. Coming up through the casino ranks, I'd cut my teeth on inveterate liars, cheats, cardsharps, and other vermin. Compared to them, Dane was a piker.

"Did he kill her?" Sean's voice at my elbow startled me out of my reverie, which was a good thing as my thoughts had done a one-eighty toward committing a murder rather than trying to solve one.

"If he did, he's dead meat."

Chapter

EIGHT

*T*he intoxicating aromas of beef cooking over charcoal, of onions glazing in a buttery skillet, hit me halfway through the Bazaar. Salivating in earnest now, I walked faster, unsure as to which I wanted first—a juicy hamburger or a juicy chef. It was a toss-up. I doubted the order would matter significantly, so I surrendered myself to anticipation.

But before I fully relinquished myself, I put in a quick call to Jeremy. Reading from the napkin on which Dane had scrawled Sylvie's number, I recited it to him, then double-checked it as he read it back. "Can you find out who she called and who called her?"

"No worries."

"Wow, really? That easy?"

"I know people you don't want to know."

"You won't get any argument. Thanks." I terminated the call and reholstered the phone. If only all my problems were that easy to solve. But they weren't. And if I was going to be of use to anybody, the hunger beast needed to be fed.

Working in the hermetically sealed environment of a top casino where nary a window or clock could be found, I'd developed other ways to keep track of time. One of them was watching the crowd. Judging by the thickening flow of humanity, older couples dressed for the evening strolling hand in hand, pausing occasionally to drool over the extravagant offerings in the shopwindows, and the younger crowd, sunburned and still in pool attire, I guessed afternoon had segued into the refreshment hour.

Even though each day in Vegas seemed to be a random walk through alcohol-fueled chaos, it actually had a subtle regularity to it. The older crowd generally dined early, then hit a show, and were tucked in before the younger crowd had even decided what to wear. Nightclubs didn't open until ten thirty or eleven—the cool folks wouldn't show until well after midnight. The morning lull gave all of us time to recover, restore, and rejuvenate—in theory.

For me, it was just enough time to catch my breath, and perhaps a couple of winks, if luck was running my way, which wasn't the normal flow. Even though I kept hiring assistants, the load kept growing, over-taking any free time into which I could fit a life.

Of course, recent history had me rethinking the whole having a life thing—it wasn't all it was cracked up to be.

The short line in front of the Burger Palais told me my guess as to the time wasn't too far off. Guests occupied more than half the tables—the place would be packed in an hour with a line out the door. Apparently hamburger joints and reservations didn't go together—at least according to the gospel of Jean-Charles Bouclet. He felt a line of anxious diners and a reasonable wait fueled demand. By all appearances, he knew what he was talking about, so who was I to quibble? I hated lines. What was it Yogi Berra said? The place was so crowded nobody went there anymore. I so got that. Apparently I was in the minority.

A beckoning combination of rough-hewn wooden floors, mortared brick walls, brass sconces, tables draped with checkered cloth, the restaurant reflected the refinement of its proprietor, tempered with his sense of fun. A bar, hand-carved of the finest wood in Scotland and imported piece by piece, curved from the right-hand wall. Bottles lined the shelves—Jean-Charles preferred quality rather than quantity at each price point. Something for everyone, he said, but not so many to choose from that the choice became daunting. A glass wall ran the length of the dining space opposite the bar. Behind the glass, Jean-Charles and his staff toiled in a carefully choreographed dance. Tonight, the proprietor worked the stove while barking orders. I sifted through the early dinner crowd already gathering at the entrance. With a nod and a knowing smile, the hostess stepped out of my way as I breezed by her. Halfway down the far wall, I made a left turn into the kitchen and entered another world.

Steamy and laden with temptation, the air was at least ten degrees warmer. Like a kid timing her entry into a turning jump rope, I watched for a moment then eased into the dance of waiters, prep cooks, and chefs. His back to me, Jean-Charles didn't notice as I stepped in behind him. His soft brown hair, which he wore a trifle too long, curled from under his toque and feathered over his collar. My hand on his shoulder, I leaned in and pressed a kiss to the tiny square of exposed skin under his right ear. He tasted like hamburgers, go figure.

Jean-Charles didn't turn. Instead, he reached up, took my hand in his, held it to his lips, then murmured, "Ah, Lucky, my love. My day is now complete."

His touch jump-started my pulse, which now raced to a staccato beat. "And I thought I was so sneaky. How'd you know?"

"Your Chanel No. 5. And you are the only woman in my life who has that subtle, special *je ne sais quoi*."

I wanted to ask him if I was the only woman in his life, but he would have found the question odd.

As a Frenchman, he failed to understand the peculiar insecurities of American females—our preoccupation with the future to the detriment of the now. Besides, I still wasn't a 100 percent sure whether I wanted to be the only woman in his life—that would come with expectations. The kind of expectations I sucked at.

He let go of my hand as he continued working the grill. How he kept all the orders straight, cooked all of them to the temperature requested, and melted my heart, I hadn't a clue.

Rinaldo, the only other human on the planet Jean-Charles would trust at the grill unsupervised, stepped in to flank his boss on the side opposite me. A large man with a round face, sparkling dark eyes, and an easy smile, he gave me a wink as he said, "Boss, why don't you take a break?"

With a nod, Jean-Charles handed him a spatula and began rattling off the details of the orders he was working on. Of course, all of it was displayed on a computer screen embedded in the backsplash.

"No worries. I got it, boss." Rinaldo eased into position, effectively moving my Frenchman out, and the dance continued with nary a step lost.

"Come." Jean-Charles placed a hand in the small of my back and guided me toward the door to the restaurant. "I have a wonderful Viognier on ice. Crisp and refreshing, it is from the Willamette Valley. You will tell me what you think, yes? But you will like it."

Once he had me installed at the bar, Jean-Charles

moved behind the counter. Tall and trim, with robin's-egg blue eyes and high cheekbones bracketing a square jaw that lent an air of ruggedness to his face, Jean-Charles was not what he seemed. A pompous prima donna in public, he played the role of the chef from Central Casting ready for his eponymous show on the Food Network. But when the klieg light of public performance dimmed, the camera eye of public opinion blinked out, he let a few of us see behind the façade to the private man underneath. A kind, driven man who loved his son, he would forever carry the scars of losing his wife to a dissected artery shredded during childbirth.

A sum total of our previous experiences, we all had our baggage, I guess. And life is simply the process of repacking, then unpacking, and repacking again until our baggage could fit easily into the overhead. Jean-Charles seemed to have folded everything neatly into a small carry-on. Time would tell. And, of course, I needed time to discard a particularly hurtful bit of excess baggage—a crooner who preferred the adulation of strangers to the love of a good woman. Yeah, right now my baggage would need a stateroom of its own.

Not a great time to start a new relationship. I knew that, but . . . throwing caution to the wind is another one of my best things. Foolhardy, my mother used to say, but she was just being nice. Stupid beyond belief would be more accurate, if you ask me. But thankfully, nobody ever did. They just picked me up, brushed me off, and sent me into the fray one more time. Perhaps just once I'd get it right. Of course, once was all it took.

With the slight frown of concentration, Jean-Charles reached for a glass and set it in front of me. Next he pulled a bottle out of the ice bucket, wiped it down, then, with practiced ease, popped the cork. His fingers cradled the bottle, his thumb stuck in the indentation in the bottom. With appropriate reverence, as if making an offering to the gods, he poured me a healthy dose of amber liquid. His eyes held mine for a moment—the warmth there took my breath. "You will like this."

I swirled the wine, then took a sip. Crisp, fruity, but with a body that would complement even a heavy meal. "A nice addition."

He nodded then poured himself a glass. As he lifted it to his lips, his eyes met mine over the rim. "Your day, it is nice, yes?"

My day? Reality crashed over me in a towering wave of emotion, fatigue and ravenous hunger.

Clearly I hadn't hidden my feelings as Jean-Charles's face clouded with concern. "You will tell me."

"First, I really need food."

"Your wish . . ." With a flourish and an exaggerated dip from the waist, he disappeared toward the kitchen.

Past caring, I drained my glass and poured another as I contemplated my reflection in the mirror behind the bar. Curiously my exterior remained unruffled—a perfect contrast to the tumult inside.

My nerves were as raw as the meat Jean-Charles threw on the grill. Like a beast tearing his way out, hunger gnawed inside my stomach. A wary, weary look folded the skin around my eyes. Still, with my hair in place, makeup subtly applied, laugh lines ready to bend for a smile, I bore an uncanny resemblance to me—even though I didn't feel like me at all.

I nursed the second glass of wine as I worked to quiet my thoughts, smooth my ragged nerves. The events of last night and today had left me punchy. I felt disconnected—strangely removed, as if I were merely a spectator and not a participant. Disassociation, the ultimate survival skill. My motto: If you can't figure it out, pretend it doesn't exist and maybe it will go away. Never happened that way before, but as Mona warned, there was always a first time. Someday I'd probably lose my tether to reality and sanity would slip away like a balloon drifting toward Heaven.

In the mirror, I watched Jean-Charles weave his way from the kitchen back to me. Balanced on his open palm, he held aloft a platter piled with sliders, making me salivate—of course Jean-Charles alone was enough to do that. Several patrons called to him, and he stopped momentarily at each table. With an easy manner and quick smile, he greeted everyone, making new fans and, hopefully, repeat customers. He loved to remind me that, even though he sold a product, his was a service business. I wasn't a hundred percent convinced, but it was hard to argue with success—and with a string of exclusive eateries in all the major cities of the Western world, he was certainly that.

Stepping behind me, he paused to nibble my ear, then slid the platter in front of me and stepped around the bar to replenish my glass. If he noticed I'd refilled it once in his absence, he was kind enough to keep his observation to himself. "Your day. It was bad, *oui*?"

"Can grown-ups run away from home?"

Concern darkened his eyes from their normal lighter blue to a deeper, more sensuous shade. "You are joking, yes?"

I shrugged but didn't answer. He would be appalled at how alluring I found the idea of packing the credit cards and heading for a part of the world that hadn't heard of 4G or Wi-Fi. Summoning courage and resolve that I didn't know I had, I gave him a lopsided smile and reached for a slider oozing cheddar and sautéed onions—manna from Heaven and food for the soul.

"My day? Perhaps a bit worse than usual, but nothing life-threatening." At least not to me . . . yet, but I didn't say that part. Chicken that I am, I decided not to mention that I was on the trail of a Jimmy Choo–wielding madman.

"Hmmm, you don't want to tell me?" With a critical eye, my chef perused the offerings on the platter, finally settling on what looked to be a tiny turkey burger. He popped the whole thing in his mouth, chewed for a moment, then washed it down with a slug of wine—American expediency apparently could override a lifetime of European refinement. How many times had I heard him tell me Americans eat, but the French dine?

Before I said anything, he held up his hand and gave me a warm look. "Burgers are to be eaten. If we are to dine, it will be on something more refined. With enough time to savor . . . everything."

Was the guy reading my mind? I paled at the possibility. Or was I simply as transparent as usual? Either way, it wasn't good.

My breath caught and I swallowed hard, shutting my mind to all the possibilities the word *savor* conjured. "I'm good with that." I reached for another slider—tenderloin, onions, cheese, and French-made thousand-island dressing—the real thing. "Let's talk about the kitchen facilities you will need for the *Last Chef Standing*." Vegas, amazingly enough, was actually a foodie paradise. Not only did we boast locations of most, if not all, of the major restaurants in the world, we also had ongoing competitions featuring the city's best chefs, culminating in Vegas Uncork'd. A huge blowout to raise not only awareness of the city's fine food offerings, but also raise money for various local charities the event was hugely popular, a coveted showcase.

"You wish to talk about this now?" Jean-Charles looked dubious.

"My day couldn't get any worse." I held up my hand as he started to argue. "I know, there's a time and a place. But I assure you I can be reasonable despite having an . . . interesting . . . day. And this is clearly bothering you, so I'd like to address it."

Jean-Charles seemed to weigh that for a moment, then gave an almost imperceptible shrug and dove in. "My kitchen at Cielo . . . it is in pieces. It must be completed in a week, ten days, but no more. Then I will have what I need."

Of course he asked the impossible. I decided not to get into the nuances of code inspections and green tags—he wouldn't understand. "Two problems." I held up my hand as he started to argue. "Hear me out, please. I know we plan to open Cielo in phases with your restaurant part of the first phase. But the demolition on the rooms has just begun and opening the first phase is well, at least two months away—*if* the gods smile on us." I took another sip of wine as I watched Jean-Charles's face turn an interesting shade of pink. *No* wasn't a word he was used to hearing.

"I must have my kitchen. The other chefs, Boulud, Ducasse, Keller, Mina, they all have their kitchens and their staffs. I will be made the fool."

"If you do not wish to be made a fool, then don't allow it," Brandy announced as she eased onto a stool next to me. Under the full force of our scowls, she withered a bit. "At least that's what my grandmother used to say, if it's helpful."

"Not in the least," I brushed her off after I made sure she in fact had Cole Weston in tow. He straddled the stool next to my young assistant, who needed to stay out of conversations she wasn't invited into.

Jean-Charles lowered his voice. "You promised."

"I promised the kitchen would be ready to go when we open phase one—even that will probably take a special dispensation by the pope, presidential fiat, and an act of Congress." Pausing, I took a deep breath. His worry was easy to read . . . and easy to understand. His reputation was really all he had. Of course, our reputations were all any of us had, but right now his livelihood rested on his. I put a hand on his arm and softened my look and my tone into hopefully one of understanding rather than confrontation. "I understand. Let me work something out, but it's the county that's keeping us out of the building, not me. Governments are all alike and they all work at a glacial pace."

"Money, it often can move mountains." He gave a Gallic shrug, which, incomprehensibly, I found charming.

"Perhaps in Provence. However, in the States we pretend bribery is a bad thing, which requires a more circumspect approach. I said I'll do my best—I have nothing more to offer."

Perhaps realizing there was nothing else to say or do but to trust me, Jean-Charles nodded . . . once. But he didn't look too pleased.

Just another happy victim.

"Okay," I said as I turned my attention to Brandy and her charge. "Please tell Mr. Weston that I saw him showing a particular interest in the poker game the dead woman was playing last night. I want to know why."

Younger than I remembered ever being, Brandy was tall and lithe with a stripper's body and the look of innocence in her big, brown eyes—a contrast men found irresistible. A black belt in some mystical form of deadly martial art took care of the unwanted attention. Today she wore a prim and proper business suit of steel gray with subtle turquoise pin stripes—vintage Versace. Her ubiquitous pair of smoky Loubous on her feet, a single diamond at her neck and matching ones on each earlobe, she looked every inch the up-and-coming hotel exec she was. Loose and free, her shiny brown hair cascaded past her shoulders. Her face, open and disarming, held not a trace of the passage of time.

Could today be any more depressing?

Brandy turned to Cole, who was eyeing a platter of hamburgers a waiter carried by. She put a hand on his arm to get his attention. While she signed my request, I turned to Jean-Charles.

Before I spoke, he held up a hand. "A platter of hamburgers for your friends. I will prepare them myself, if you will excuse me." He gave a stiff little bow and a rueful half grin dialed back from its previous warmth. I watched him work his way through the tables, his practiced façade of charm falling into place, and wondered how to have a relationship with a man who bristled at the first barrier in his path.

Brandy and Cole were deep into a silent conversation, so I sipped my wine and pouted. Just being able to express a simple, albeit juvenile, emotion was so much better than my normal routine of bottling them inside. My job required eating too much crow as it was. I'd be damned if I'd conduct my personal life the same way.

Brandy snapped her fingers in front of my eyes. "Do you want it word for word, or will a summary do?"

"A summary."

"Well," Brandy settled herself on the stool, "Cole plays a lot of Internet poker."

"Isn't that illegal?"

"Isn't that irrelevant?"

Oh, she was turning into me, just as Miss P feared. "I seem to have a particular gift of bringing out the pissy in everyone I talk to today." Reaching across the bar, I grabbed the bottle of wine and freshened my glass. "Now, continue, but without the attitude."

Clearly immune, Brandy gave me a look that said "Whatever," then continued. "For a long time now, he's been playing on Aces Over Eights."

"The site Kevin Slurry's recently sold."

She nodded. "Right. And Cole noticed some anomalies."

"What kind?"

"Someone was cheating."

"How the heck do you cheat in an online game?" The criminal mind always eluded me. If the bad guys spent as much time trying to fix the world as they did thinking up ways to defeat it, we'd all live above the poverty line and be settling Mars.

"Cole figured that Kevin Slurry must've kept a back door when he sold the site."

"Back door?"

"An opening into the software algorithm. With that he could see other players' cards, he could monitor and track betting, the source of the funds, how winnings were distributed."

"He had access to all the information in the whole site?" Wow, talk about a cheater's paradise.

Brandy nodded.

"Cole can prove this?"

Brandy turned, her fingers racing through words. Then his did the same in reply. She turned back to me. "He has all the data, but it would take the police to legally access the Web site records to see if he is correct."

"The police." There was something there, a connection. What was it? I took another sip of wine while I tried to let my mind free-wheel. The tickle of an idea started to form. "Ask Cole if he knew Sylvie Dane personally."

He read my lips and nodded, then Brandy translated as he signed his story. "He knew her through poker, and he knew she had some background in law enforcement."

"Wait." I threw up a hand, stopping her. "Law enforcement? Which side of the fence?"

Cole rolled his eyes and signed rapidly—I'd forgotten he could read lips.

Brandy translated. "He's not sure, Sylvie wouldn't say."

"I bet."

"Anyway," Brandy continued, "after watching her for a while and satisfying himself she wasn't in bed with Kevin Slurry . . ."

Brandy paused, her eyes grew a trifle wider as she watched Cole's fingers fly.

"What?" I asked.

The girl ducked her head shyly, her face pinkening. "Nothing. That part was personal."

"What's personal?" Detective Romeo asked a bit roughly as he pushed through the gathering crowd. Stopping behind Brandy, he put a hand possessively on her shoulder. If he felt half as bad as he looked, I could understand his mood. His clothes were rumpled probably beyond repair, an old coffee stain trickled like a dried tear down the front of his shirt, and remnants of a meal dotted his tie. The kid had gone seriously downhill in the last twenty-four hours. If he'd been home, he hadn't bothered to change clothes. Fine stubble dotted his cheeks, which were hollower than I remembered. Deep grooves bracketed his mouth, tension pulling his lips into a thin line. His hair had been hastily combed into place—even his cowlick had succumbed somewhat, bending weakly. His voice hard, his expression less than pleased, he hooked a thumb at Cole but focused his attention on Brandy. "Is this guy hitting on you?"

Cole smiled as if he thought the whole thing a wonderful joke.

Brandy gave Romeo a quick kiss. "Forget about

it. He was just playing. Besides, it's not like he's the only guy who's going to hit on me today."

Oops.

Romeo turned his glare on me. "You allow your staff to be bait for every . . ."

"Enough." I could be stern when I wanted. "You know better than that."

Clearly miffed, Romeo struggled with his emotions. "Sorry. I don't want her left alone with this guy—or anybody else, for that matter."

"Sit, Romeo." I patted the stool next to mine. "Trust is the foundation for a good relationship, remember that. Besides, you're going to be interested in Mr. Weston's story."

"This isn't making me happy," he groused, but he did as I asked.

"As I was saying," Brandy drawled. "Cole knew Sylvie from playing poker. Once he was sure she was on the up-and-up, he took his data to her."

"What data?" Romeo whispered. I filled him in. "Wow, the plot thickens," he mocked—his version of pouting. Or maybe he'd tracked down DeLuca and wanted to take a chunk out of my hide. I wasn't going to ask.

"Cole wanted Sylvie to take it to the next step, get a warrant, whatever, but Sylvie refused."

"Why?" Romeo and I said in unison.

Cole's fingers flew as Brandy watched. "He says she was working her own angle and wanted some time."

"And he doesn't know what she was after?" I asked.

Brandy pursed her lips and shook her head. "No." Cole tapped her on the shoulder to get her attention. She watched him for a moment, her eyes growing wide.

"What is it?" I asked, unable to contain myself.

"After the poker game, Cole went to an underground game over in the warehouse district just across the Fifteen."

"I won't mention those are both illegal and unsafe," I scolded.

Cole shrugged and gave me a cockeyed smile. He was cute, no doubt about it, with a charm he knew how to use.

Brandy looked at me, her eyes as big as plates. "There was a girl there, at the underground game. She had the necklace that Sylvie Dane was wearing."

"Sylvie's necklace?" I spluttered. "How?"

Cole shrugged and shook his head.

"Do you know her?" I asked. Again a negative response. "Was she young, Hispanic, long dark hair?"

This time a vigorous nod of his head as he pulled Brandy around.

"He tried to follow her after the game, but he lost her. He wants to know if you know her."

"No. So far, she's just one more dead end," I said, hoping only figuratively.

"Was anyone else there that we should know about?" I asked routinely, never expecting to know anyone at one of those games. I was wrong.

After watching Cole for a moment, Brandy, her voice hushed as if conjuring an evil spirit, announced, "River Watalsky."

Romeo snapped out of his romantic funk, his cop sensors on alert. "Watalsky? What was he doing there?"

Cole rolled his eyes as he signed.

"Playing poker," Brandy interpreted, fighting a smile.

"Thank you," Romeo countered. "Anything else? Anything unusual?"

"He seemed awfully interested in the girl," Cole said this himself, the words a bit muffled, but understandable. "And the necklace."

"I bet," I offered—so helpful, I know.

Jean-Charles reappeared with the promised platter of hamburgers. His mood seemed to have improved as he cast a smile in my direction—a smile that looked like he meant it. With youthful metabolisms to feed, Brandy and Cole dove in with gusto. Initially hesitant, Romeo finally dismounted his high horse and pushed his way to the trough as well. The three of them moaned in gustatory delight, making the chef who stood next to me smile, although I suspected he was accustomed to that reaction.

"Those three are my perfect demographic—young enough to eat so many calories, old enough to appreciate the nuances of the flavors."

"And to pay for premium burgers."

"That as well." Jean-Charles gave me a smile. "I am sorry to be difficult."

I leaned into him, savoring the spark where our bodies touched. "Trust me."

Once a lead dog, the habit was hard to break, and I watched my chef struggle with the concept of letting someone else pull the sled for a bit. "The kitchen, it must be . . ."

"Professional, I know."

"But most chefs with that sort of kitchen will not . . ."

"Share, I know."

Those robin's-egg eyes went all milky and soft, turning my heart inside out. "Yes, I can see that you do."

"Your son, Christophe? He comes soon?" I said, changing the subject as I watched him pour us both another glass of wine. Three or four, I'd lost enthusiasm for counting, and apparently for moderation. Whatever the number, it was past my limit—when I used to have a limit, that is.

At the mention of his son's name, all the hard lines softened. A smile lifted the corner of Jean-Charles's mouth. Reaching into his breast pocket, he pulled out the creased and worn picture of his five-year-old I had seen countless times before. Although I had yet to meet him, I could easily pick the boy out of any kindergarten lineup.

Sandy curls, blue eyes like his father's, a smile to melt even the hardest heart—he terrified me. If he didn't like me, I was screwed. Well, if experience had taught me anything, it was that life would lead me down the path I was meant to follow. And whether I went willingly or screaming bloody murder with my heels dug in never seemed to make a difference.

Jean-Charles lingered over the photo before stuffing it back in his pocket. "He comes soon, yes. My sister's daughter, Chantal, is bringing him from France. My mother is already calling me, threatening to keep him. She is making fun with me, of course, but like all mothers, she enjoys, how do you say it? Pulling my rope?"

"Jerking your chain. Mona is a master."

"I have not seen this side of your mother." Jean-Charles snagged another slider, this one made of ahi tuna.

I let it go, but between you and me, creating a hamburger from raw fish . . . okay, rare fish . . . was a culinary crime. *Hamburger* and *healthy* should never even flirt with being synonymous. "Of course not. She would never let a handsome Frenchman see her practice the subtle art of manipulation."

"Then, there are benefits to being in my company?" His smile lit his whole face, reaching his eyes.

"Many." Something in his eyes made my heart beat faster, my skin flush. When he reached for my hand, a connection jolted through me. Why did life always serve up more than I could handle? Just lucky, I guess. Maybe I could change my name—then all these stupid puns wouldn't apply. Maybe that would help. Who knew? "Your mother is enjoying her grandson, then?" I asked, veering the conversation away from my mother—not the best topic for a bad day.

Jean-Charles turned his eyes toward Heaven and blew in the way that the French do when they think you are the master of understatement. "They are like . . ." He paused for moment, searching. "They are like two people with one soul." He crumpled his eyebrows together, questioning.

At my nod, he continued. "My mother, she likes the earth, the animals. My son, too, likes the animals, especially the babies. My parents have many on their farm." Jean-Charles chuckled as a faraway look flashed in his eyes. "In the beginning, the animals were to be raised organically. Then, when the time was right, they were to be slaughtered and served in my father's restaurant. You know, of course, how this would end?"

Taking a sip of wine, I relaxed and smiled, enjoying the story.

"My mother, she gave them all names. This, my father said, was the death kiss. And he was right." Jean-Charles laughed at the memory and shook his head. "All their animals die of old age."

"And your father's restaurant?"

"He buys his meat from a local farmer with a more hard-hearted wife."

"I would like them, I think." My phone sang out at my hip—actually it was Teddie doing the singing.

I didn't meet Jean-Charles's eyes as I reached for my phone.

I didn't have any answers, but one thing I knew: My fun was over.

Chapter

NINE

♡

*A*s I raced out of the restaurant, I clung to the tenuous threads of a cheery mood that threatened to evaporate in the face of worry. Jerry's call had been brief—he refused to share over the phone. He said only that I needed to meet him at the front desk, I'd better hurry, he hoped I hadn't eaten anything, and I would not like whatever it was he hadn't told me.

My pulse still racing from the kiss delivered with meaning by my chef, I dodged and darted through the ever-thickening crowd, arriving at the appointed spot in near record time. But Jerry wasn't there. My back to the counter, I leaned on one elbow and scanned the crowd, cooling my heels, waiting for a man who was never late.

Taking measured breaths and pretending this was just another day, much like all the rest, I reminded myself that all problems, no matter how large, had solutions, but I just wasn't buying it. That's the problem with arguing with yourself—nobody ever wins.

This was so not going to be good—I could feel it. Like smoke under a door, an ominous sense of foreboding filtered through the edges of my consciousness. My heart skipped a beat, then raced to catch up.

Surprises, especially bad ones, were among my least favorite things—Jerry knew that. I'd shot people for less—okay, I made that part up—but I'd felt like shooting them. For him to risk running afoul of my notoriously short temper and twitchy trigger finger meant it had to be bad. Real bad.

I should've known—today could get worse. Silly me. At least Brandy and Cole were safe under the watchful eye of Detective Romeo as Cole went off to play poker in the High-Stakes Room. At least, that's where they had said they would be, but I had left in a hurry.

Brandy, Romeo, and Cole. The three of them. Together. Perhaps I should rethink that "safe" part.

"Ms. O'Toole?"

I whirled, even though I knew Jerry would never call me that, and found myself face-to-face with Sergio Fabiano, our front desk manager.

Dark and delectable, with bedroom eyes, a mop of jet-black hair that he constantly flipped out of his eyes, full, pouty lips, and a body Rodin would have immortalized in marble, Sergio was the perfect frontline face for the Babylon, or so said the Big Boss. Admittedly, he was a tasty bit of eye candy, but he was a tad fussy for my tastes.

If you ask me, it wasn't his animal magnetism but rather his mystical ability to tame the customers with a firm but gentle hand, like Siegfried and Roy with their white tigers, that endeared him to the brass, me included. As long as he continued beating back the hordes from my office door, I was good. And, as his direct superior, I guess my opinion counted for something, although, at times, I wasn't so sure.

"Ms. O'Toole, are you busy?" Sergio asked as he grabbed my arm and pulled me toward a couple standing off to the side. "I have some people I'd like you to meet. They are such good customers."

Something about his manner kept me from shrugging him off. I was as far from being in a social mood as was humanly possible, but he looked like he was having fun. Right now I could use even just a hint of joy, so I let him maneuver me to the far end of the reception desk.

The couple—I guessed them to be somewhere around forty, give or take a few years—stood apart, several feet separating them. To the casual observer, they didn't look like they were together or that they even knew each other. They didn't make eye contact, or any contact for that matter. They didn't chat or exchange flirty looks. In fact, they appeared to be studiously avoiding each other.

The man looked ill at ease, antsy, as he shifted from one foot to the other. I guessed him to be a trifle over six feet since, with me in my sensible Ferragamos with their one-and-a-half-inch heels, we were eye to eye. Casual in his pressed jeans and open-collared shirt, he looked up as I approached. He had kind eyes and a corn-fed, middle-American wholesomeness.

As we stopped in front of the two of them, Sergio

motioned toward the woman and said, "This is Mrs. Jacobs."

Shorter than the man, but not by much, and dressed in a chic Diane von Furstenberg wrap dress and flats, the woman was long and lean, with black hair, penetrating onyx eyes, and porcelain skin.

A quiet mirth sparkled in her eyes and the hint of a grin tugged at the corner of her mouth as she made a shushing sound, then said, "Myrna, please."

When I took her extended hand, the warmth of her skin surprised me.

Sergio dropped his voice, adopting a conspiratorial whisper. "Right. My apologies." He gestured toward the gentleman. "And this is Mr. Jacobs."

"Toby, please," he said as he grasped my hand and pumped it up and down. "And we don't know each other. I mean, I know I don't know you . . ." He paused, flustered, as his cheeks reddened and he started over. "I was referring to this lady here." He tilted his head toward the woman who I thought had just been introduced as his wife.

We hadn't even successfully navigated the how-do-you-dos and I was already at sea. Lately I'd been spending so much time behind the eight ball, I might as well have hung out a shingle and called it home.

Pausing, I blew at a lock of hair that tickled my eyes, hoping for an epiphany . . . or an explanation. When neither was forthcoming, I looked between the two of them, then raised a questioning eyebrow at Sergio.

He shrugged and grinned—so helpful.

"I'm Lucky O'Toole," I said to the couple, "part of the customer relations team here at the Babylon." My face flushed when I realized I still clutched Mr. Jacobs's hand. Trying not to call attention to that fact, I let him have it back. If I had breached protocol, he didn't seem to care. "Welcome to our hotel. I take it this isn't your first stay with us?"

"Oh, no," Myrna said in a theatrical whisper. "We come here every year."

"But you don't know each other?"

"Not yet. We meet tonight for the first time." Myrna glanced at her watch. "Oh, I have to hurry. They're holding some things for me at the mall. You'll have to excuse me." She pecked her husband-who-she-had-yet-to-meet on the cheek. "Bye, honey." Then she waggled her fingers at us as she stepped away and melted into the crowd.

Toby seemed energized as well. "Gotta scoot. I need to make some . . . preparations." He too melted into the crowd although I could see the top of his head as he moved toward the elevators.

When I turned my attention back to Sergio, he pressed his lips together as if trying to stifle a laugh.

"Am I the butt of a joke?" I asked.

Sergio seemed aghast. "But Ms. O'Toole, I would never make you the butt."

"Trust me, I don't need your help. I am able to do that all by myself with alarming regularity." I thought I felt the glimmer of a smile tickle my lips, but I wasn't sure.

Sergio must've seen it as he relaxed a bit, the

tension easing from his shoulders as his body settled into its normal insouciance. "I wanted you to meet them—to me they are . . . wonderful."

"Certifiable, if you ask me."

"Perhaps." Sergio nodded, his dark eyes dancing. "But they have fun. Twice a year they come here together, then pretend to not know each other."

"A mutual time-out vacation?" I'd met plenty of folks who came to Vegas to take a respite from their marriages—a few even with their spouse's blessing. But I'd never met a couple traveling together to cheat on each other. Sounded like a prelude to justifiable homicide. "A cheating trip," I said, not sharing Sergio's glee.

"Exactly." Sergio adopted a sage attitude. "But they don't cheat *on* each other, they cheat *with* each other."

"Really?" This time I know I managed a smile as the pieces fell into place and it all made sense. Marriage therapy, Vegas-style. Once again love triumphs. Just the thought proved a strong antidote to an abysmal day, so I wallowed a bit. "They role-play—I like it. Do you know if their tastes include a French maid's outfit? I've heard that can be fun—although, between you and me, I'd laugh myself silly. Somehow that would probably break the mood, don't you think?" Captured by the visual, I glanced at Sergio.

Momentarily struck dumb, he stared at me with owl eyes.

"What?" I kept my face impassive. "You know what they say about all work and no play."

Sergio still couldn't rally, which made me proud. Never one to gloat . . . much . . . I decided to let him down easy, especially since this wasn't exactly the sort of professional repartee a corporate type should have with the staff. Even in Sin City we had sexual harassment sensitivity training. However, I never understood whether it was something we were being taught to avoid or to do—lines blur somewhat in Vegas.

"Sorry," I lied. "Recently, I've developed this proclivity for oversharing." Unfortunately, that last part wasn't a lie. For some reason, I wasn't as embarrassed as I should have been. Apparently my give-a-damn had gone AWOL. I wondered if that was a good thing or a bad thing, but I didn't seem to care.

My front desk manager swallowed hard, then continued, "Myrna buys trashy clothes and dresses as a . . . how should I say it?"

"A hooker?"

He shot me a look. "If you wish to be crass, yes. She waits for him at Delilah's. He picks her up. What happens from there . . ."

"I can only imagine," I groused, my fleeting frivolity crushed under the returning weight of reality. That was the problem: I could only imagine.

Leave it to me to live in the Sex Capital of the Western Hemisphere and not be getting any.

APPARENTLY underwhelmed by my mood, Sergio left me there contemplating my nonexistent sex life. For a moment I was perplexed by the conundrum of ruminating on something that didn't exist, then decided I was making a simplicity into a complexity—one of my better skills.

That's when Jerry appeared at my shoulder and whispered in my ear, "Come with me. You are so not going to like this." Gripping my elbow, he held me close to his side as he steered me toward the garage elevators.

"Oh goody, a surprise," I managed to choke out, but I swallowed the rest of my sarcasm when I turned and got a good look at his face.

Dark circles half-mooned his bloodshot eyes. Like denim on a twenty-year-old, his skin stretched taut and tight over the frame of his face, bone and sinew barely concealed. Life was sucking him dry. To be honest, our days were filled with herding rattlesnakes. You never knew when the bite would come, but eventually it did—that final venomous sting of reality that would have us chucking it all for a flower stand on a beach in Tahiti. My bags were half packed, Jerry's too, from the looks of him.

"This is what happens when they don't let you out to play in the sunshine," I whispered, but his tight lips didn't bend.

We took the stairs instead of the elevator, Jerry pulling me after him. Two flights left me light-headed. And that, as it turned out, was the best I would feel for the rest of the night.

We burst through the door onto the third floor of the garage and into another world. Like toys abandoned by a two-year-old, police cars rested at odd angles, defining a loose perimeter. Uniformed cops patrolled the periphery while plain-clothes detectives huddled near a dark pickup and stared at the ground between the truck and the yellow Ferrari parked next to it. Crime scene tape draped around the two vehicles. Like vultures eyeing a kill, large lights on stands perched over the area, capturing the scene in stark, unforgiving light.

As we moved to step over the tape, one of Metro's finest stopped us with a meaty hand to Jerry's chest. Tall, with broad shoulders and a gut straining the buttons on his wrinkled uniform, he rested his other hand on his service revolver hanging on his hip. With his beady eyes half hidden under a ledge of bushy brows, he perused us with the casual interest of a natural predator already sated but always willing to eat. The gun on his hip seemed ill-advised, but what did I know?

"You two, I don't know who you think you are but you got no place here," the man-mountain growled as if talking to the village idiots. My tax dollars at work—I was so proud.

"I'm the head of security at this hotel," Jerry growled back. "I got more years dealing with crime scenes than you've been walking and talking—I know the routine. Don't tell me where I can and can't go." I couldn't remember the last time Jerry had let someone raise his hackles.

To be honest, I was looking for a fight as well. If the cop had even the hint of a glass jaw, I would've been tempted. At least then I'd have a problem I understood.

Before I could do anything rash, Romeo's head appeared above the bed of the pickup—he must've been crouched down between the two vehicles. When he looked at me, our eyes caught and I got a brief glimpse into an old soul. Where had the kid gone?

"Officer, let them through." Romeo covered the distance between us, stepped on the tape, and motioned us over. "Donovan," he read from the officer's badge. "I'm going to recommend you for a stint in the Protocol Office."

Donovan's face fell as the kid gave me a hidden wink. It was the only hint of mirth in his demeanor.

"Are you getting a complex?" he asked me as I stepped over the tape and brushed by him as he held it down for Jerry.

"No." I eyed him, searching for an explanation. "Why?"

We stepped around the end of the pickup. There, on the ground, in a contorted position of pain, lay a man—from the looks of him, a very dead man—his face turned away. Balding, a ring of dark hair, thin, wearing a black suit jacket . . . no, a tuxedo jacket and pants with satin down the side.

Romeo motioned for the gloved tech to roll the body. "Do you know him?"

I stepped closer and bent down to get a good look at the man's face. My heart stopped. "Shit." I fought the urge to leap back. "Marvin J. Johnstone. He used to work for us as the manger of our high-stakes poker."

"Used to?" Romeo raised one eyebrow as he pursed his lips.

"He was fired last night . . . early this morning."

"Really? By whom?"

I swallowed hard. "Me."

"You?" A spark of something lit his eyes then died as the chatter quieted and all heads swiveled in our direction.

I nodded, blinking fast, unaccustomed to the accusatory glare of the limelight. Nothing like being the center of attention in a murder investigation.

"You do realize," Romeo said as he leveled his gaze to mine, "I got three dead bodies and you are a pretty good link?"

"Me?" My blood ran cold. Surely he didn't think . . .

You could've heard the blood pounding through my veins as time stopped.

"I wasn't anywhere near any of the bodies," I stammered, feeling helpless. "I'm sure that would be easy to prove."

"I am going to need to establish your whereabouts at the times of all the relevant deaths."

"As opposed to the irrelevant deaths?" I asked, cocking an eyebrow at him. As quickly as it came, my bravado fled. My heart leaped into my throat as the blood rushed from my head. Bending at the waist, I put my hands on my knees and took deep breaths.

Romeo made a motion with his hands trying to calm me down. "Protocol, nothing more. That way we can definitively remove you from the suspect list."

Okay, that did it. Anger spiked. Blood pressure elevated. Sanity returned. I stood and, placing my hands on my hips, leveled my anger at the young detective. "Do what you have to do, but spare me the insinuations."

Like a plant absorbing the full force of the summer sun in the Mojave, he drew in, withering . . . a bit, but not as much as he used to. "You and your hotel are a link between the three."

"Romeo, we provide a link between three thousand guests, several thousand employees, and plenty of others who just wander through the doors. And that's on a slow day. You'll have to do better than that. Speaking of connections, where did you leave Cole Weston?"

"Playing poker under the watchful eye of *my* girlfriend, thanks to you."

"*My* assistant."

We faced off for a moment, then he returned to the relevant business. "You have to admit, you do seem to have a connection with all three of the stiffs."

"For chrissake! I have a connection with three-quarters of the residents of this valley." I ran a shaky hand through my hair as I tried to process all of it. Marvin. God. I felt the bile rise in my throat as I looked at him. Under the harsh light, his jacket had the shiny look of well-worn fabric. His tie loosened, his collar torn open—the button was missing, a small tear in the cotton the only hint of its former presence. Mud had dried into a light brown ring on his white bucks. He'd thrown up and soiled himself. Pain had traveled through his every feature, etching a lasting contortion. An abnormal shade of pink, his skin still held the sheen of dampness. Perspiration perhaps? Do you sweat when you die? Who knew?

His open eyes stared but saw nothing. What I would give to pull the last images from his retinas and the last sounds he heard from some inner tape. It would make this murder thing a whole lot easier to solve, but science hadn't yet bridged that impossible gap.

My experience with death was limited, but I'd say Marvin's hadn't been quick or merciful.

"Why the odd color?" I asked. The guy looked like he'd been dunked in the Easter egg–coloring tank—pink, brown, green . . . I shut my eyes and swallowed hard.

"Cyanide," Jerry answered.

I stared at him for a moment as the dam of self-control finally broke, emotions tumbled, panic reared its ugly head. "You have got to be kidding. Cyanide? Are you sure it wasn't a curare-tipped umbrella? Or an arsenic-laced beverage from the bar? And let's not forget strychnine . . . Where's Miss Marple when you need her?" In danger of losing control completely, I clamped my mouth shut and squeezed my eyes tight for a moment, blocking the world out and my racing thoughts in.

Jerry put a hand on my arm and softened his voice. "You okay?"

"Sure." I glanced at him, studiously avoiding the Stoneman, and the fact that his nickname was now curiously apropos. "Just another ho-hum day in paradise." I ran a shaky hand through my hair and gave him a rueful smile. "But you must admit, the body count is a bit elevated—alarming, even."

"Sarcasm," Jerry remarked to Romeo with a satisfied nod. "She's fine." Then he turned back to me. "His skin color. Pink or red is a pretty good indication of cyanide. The stuff interferes with oxygen absorption. So, the lungs remain hyperoxygenated while you suffocate. Not a good way to go."

I felt my blood becoming severely unoxygenated as stars whirled before my eyes.

With one arm, Jerry circled my shoulders and held me tightly. "Probably more than you wanted to know."

He was batting a thousand.

After a few deep breaths, I regained my composure. "Cyanide. How the hell does someone get his hands on that? I thought you'd need a top-secret clearance or a double-zero classification and 'God Save the Queen' tattooed on your butt or something."

"You can buy it on the Internet," Romeo interjected.

"What? At murder.com?" I asked, struggling to

somehow put the last twenty hours and three dead bodies into perspective. I was singularly unsuccessful.

"No," Romeo scolded as if talking to a small child—which wasn't far from the truth, if we were going strictly by intellectual capacity. "Cyanide has some industrial uses, primarily in the jewelry business."

"Well, this being Bling Town and all, that really narrows the field." Needing some time to think, I wandered over to the nearest staircase and sat, not the least bit concerned over what I might be sitting in. At this point, what did it matter? Pulling my knees to my chest, I crossed my arms, resting them on my legs. It dawned on me that this was as close as I could get to the fetal position without looking like I'd gone completely loony. A subconscious coping mechanism. Well, if that's what it took to keep from pulling a Humpty-Dumpty, I could live with it.

Coping in his own way, Jerry stood off to the side smoking one cigarette after another while he fielded phone calls and watched the forensics team do their thing.

Time lost all relevance as Romeo talked to an endless stream of people, taking notes.

I tried to marshal my thoughts, but all I seemed to come up with were questions that pinged around my empty head like lotto balls—all with the number zero on them.

I have no idea how much time had passed when

Jerry dropped his final butt, ground it out with the toe of his Italian loafers, and wandered in my direction. His legs seemed ready to buckle when he stopped in front of me, weaving slightly. Too much nicotine and not enough food or sleep—a life out of balance. Familiar with the affliction, I empathized—although alcohol and caffeine were my drugs of choice.

"The security tapes don't help us at all. Apparently after we escorted your buddy Marvin to the exit last night, he didn't leave. When he reached his car, he went down. No one caught it—it would have been a real lucky break if the camera had cycled to this view right as he fell, but it didn't."

"And he's been here all that time?"

"Cameras couldn't see him between the cars like that. And, if no one walked right by . . ."

"Hell of a way to go." I hadn't liked Marvin, but I wouldn't wish that kind of exit on anyone. "Do you have any idea how he got poisoned?"

"Well, guests aren't dropping like flies, so we can feel good about that."

Under normal circumstances I might have found that slightly humorous.

"Sorry." Jerry could always read my mood, no matter the subtlety.

"So we can assume he was singled out on purpose?" I said, trotting out my flair for the obvious.

"I'll resist pointing out that that is redundant." Jerry patted his pockets, looking for something, but he'd already inhaled all the cigarettes he had. I didn't know whether to be thankful or horrified. "Cyanide is fairly purposeful," he added as an afterthought.

"There is that." I watched Jerry sort of stagger in place, trying to find his equilibrium—the walking dead. "Why would someone want to kill Marvin . . . I mean, besides the fact that everyone on this planet, and probably a couple of others, hated his guts?"

"I'm tapped out," Jerry said. "Care to speculate?"

"Well, we've got a poker game where Sylvie Dane was cheating and losing and Marvin did nothing to stop it. Either he was stupid or in on it."

Jerry looked back and I followed his gaze. They'd body-bagged Marvin and were now stuffing him in the coroner's car. "I'm thinking we can probably rule out stupid—I don't think people kill for stupid."

Personally, I thought people killed for stupid all the time, but I didn't say it. "If you got a spare set of eyes, you might want to check some of the video feeds. Apparently right after Sylvie Dane left with her husband, Marvin asked for some personal time. Sure would be nice to know where he went."

"With the Smack Down, things are pretty tight, but I'll get somebody on it." Jerry watched the proceedings until the car pulled away and disappeared around the corner. "Oh—" He rooted through his pockets, searching. Finally he found the right one. "I've got something else for you." He extracted a folded bit of paper from his inside jacket pocket and extended it to me.

"What's this?"

"Take a look. I pulled it from some of the footage from the casino."

I unfolded it and for the first time in a long time, hope surged through me.

"Is that your girl?" Jerry asked, looking just the teensiest bit smug.

I stared at the grainy photo. Dark hair, haunted eyes, young, with those red shoes. "That's her!" With energy I didn't know I had, I jumped up and wrapped him in a bear hug.

"Whoa, now." Jerry eased my arms from around his neck. "You're jumping the gun here."

"This is great." I couldn't resist grinning like a fool as my glance kept shifting between the photo and Jerry. "Who is she?"

"Ah, there's the rub." Jerry pulled his handkerchief out of his back pocket and wiped his brow. "You don't have any cigarettes, do you?" He asked, his expression a mixture of hope and guilt.

I gave him a dirty look. "The girl. Who is she?"

"I haven't a clue. HR had no idea." Jerry stuffed his handkerchief back into his pocket. "But I can tell you one thing: That girl is not employed by the Babylon. She may have something to do with Sylvie's murder, I don't know, but I'd bet my pension she could tell me a few things about the theft ring operating in the hotel."

"Damn." Hope so easily dashed. I folded the photo and pocketed it. "I'll give Romeo a copy to run through the databases. Who knows, maybe we'll get a hit."

"Do that, but she looks young. My bet is that, if she's been through the system, she was a juvie and her records are sealed."

"Aren't you a ray of hope." I refused to let him drag me down. We were making progress, baby steps, but in the right direction. Positive thinking is a powerful tool, my mother used to say. Probably a crock, but it made me feel better. "Go home." Too tired to move, I stayed rooted where I was. "All this'll still be here in the morning."

"Which is flying at us with the speed of light. You and I have both put in two days' worth of work in the last twenty-four hours."

"If we'd left when we started, we'd be half a world away by now." Ever since sitting in the G550, I'd been tormented by thoughts of escape.

"Home's about as far as I've got energy to get to. And I for one plan to spend some serious rack time with a pillow stuck in my ear. What about you? You heading home?"

"This *is* home, remember? When Teddie took a powder . . ."

Jerry's brows crumpled into a frown. "Oh, yeah." I could tell he still wanted to bruise Teddie a bit, which warmed my heart.

Even though a month or so had passed—almost two now, I guess—I still hadn't completely unpacked and settled into the apartment next to the Big Boss and Mona. I don't know why. Everything in my life seemed to be in suspended animation.

Jerry reached up and touched my cheek. Then, with

a faded smile, he turned and did as he was told. With a curious detachment, I watched him walk away.

Needing sleep, but not wanting to face the loneliness of an unfamiliar, empty place, I once again sat on my step and leaned back on my elbows. My chin on my chest, I guess I was half dozing because I wasn't aware of Romeo until he spoke.

"If you show me yours, I'll show you mine."

I opened one eye.

His hands clasped behind his back, he loomed in front of me.

"Like combining strip poker with Clue? Sure, I'll play." I sat up and patted the step next to me as I struggled to open both eyes and get my bearings. "Sit down before you fall down."

My attention switched back to the crime scene as Romeo settled in next to me, his shoulder touching mine. For a moment we both watched the activity, which was winding down. One cop motioned a rollback into place to begin pulling the two cars onto the flatbed.

"We're impounding both of them," Romeo said, although that fact seemed obvious. "The Italian iron belongs to your Poker Room manager. I had no idea those guys made that kind of green."

"It's a cherry job that pays well. But a late-model Ferrari like that one will set you back a quarter of a million brand-new. I don't care who you are, that's a serious chunk of change."

Romeo whistled. "We did find something interesting."

"You mean besides a dead body that looks like it's been parboiled?" I leaned back again and swiveled to look at him, my eyes too tired to focus up close.

Wise to my act, he ignored me.

With a blank look, he reached into the pocket of his coat, pulled out a large Baggie, and dropped it in my lap. Smoothing the bag revealed its contents.

I gasped.

The missing Jimmy Choo—all champagne-colored rhinestones and nary a drop of blood.

Adrenaline surged through me. "Where?" Oh, how I hoped it was in the Ferrari.

"The F-150," Romeo said as he squinted at the truck. "Want to guess who owns that particular ride?"

My heart fell and my anger spiked as the pieces fell into place. "You think Dane is still here? At the hotel?"

"Hell no," Romeo snorted.

"I saw Dane about thirty minutes before Jerry called me to come down here. At that point, I thought he was heading home."

"The first call about the body had come in by then." Romeo looked like he was mentally working backward in time. "He could've come for his ride, seen all the attention this area was attracting, and decided to boogie. Kind of incriminating, like he knew of the body here, don't you think?"

That was the problem, I didn't want to think. And I sure didn't want to think Dane was . . . well, a killer. So since I didn't have anything sarcastic to add, I said nothing.

"Your cowboy is in a heap of hurt," Romeo added unnecessarily. "When I find him, I'm going to have to take him in."

"Do me a favor—when you do, keep him locked up. It'll keep me out of trouble."

Romeo grinned. The kid so got me. Stretching his legs in front of him, he massaged his thigh with one hand. "My whole body hurts."

"Get a few more years under your belt, then talk to me about it."

He gave me a shrug. "You want to compare notes and see where we are?"

"You first, I'll fill in with what I know."

He appeared to think about it for a moment, then pursed his lips. Nodding, he started in. "Let's begin with the dead girl on the car, Dane's wife." I think he threw in that last part to keep me from going all mushy at some point. He needn't have worried.

Romeo pulled out his notes and scanned them before continuing. "The coroner puts her time of death at about two A.M., which we'd pretty much figured based on the security tapes and Dane's call to you."

"Anything out of the ordinary? Besides the shoe in her neck? I assume that's what killed her?"

Romeo nodded. "Yeah, whoever swung that thing had good aim—they buried the pointy end in her carotid."

"Pointy end—by that you mean the protective thingie was off the heel?"

Romeo looked at me with that vacuous look most men donned when confronted with the nuances of high heels and high fashion.

I pulled off one of my heels to show him. Even though the heel was low, it still had the little protective cover on the tip. "See this thing?" I wedged my fingernails under it and worked it a bit until it came loose, leaving a tiny metal spike, sharp as a nail. "Is this how the shoe in her neck looked?"

"Yeah," Romeo said as his brows creased in thought. "What does it mean?"

"I don't know. You didn't find one of these, did you?" I opened my hand and showed him the tiny piece I'd pulled from the tip of my shoe's heel.

"No, and my team went over that showroom pretty thoroughly—it took us the rest of the night and half the morning. Mr. DeLuca was practically apoplectic. I caught him at a bad time, or so he said. Something about the cleaning crew not doing their job or something." Romeo pulled a quarter out of his pocket and began working it through the fingers of one hand then back again. A minor magician, he liked to practice while he was thinking.

"So you found Frank?"

"He found me, more like." Romeo looked a bit stricken.

"Kid, I'll let you in on a secret, these guys who have been around a while are used to barking, but they rarely bite. And they certainly don't dine on detectives. If you act like you're in charge, they'll give you some room to run before they shoot."

"I'm not sure I'm comfortable with that analogy." Romeo glanced at his notes again while I waited. "I want to get the times right," he said, as if he needed to explain. "DeLuca said he was at your father's party until about midnight, then he went to see Shady Slim at the airport."

"Which jibes with Miss Becky-Sue's story," I chimed in—apparently my mute button was still on the fritz.

"He acted like none of this was that important, but you don't go visit someone the minute they get into town, at the airport at almost midnight just to gas."

"Poker players are nocturnal creatures, so midnight isn't that late for them." To be honest, I thought it a bit coincidental, but I kept that to myself. "When do you think you might have the preliminary tox screen on Slim?"

"DeLuca being less than honest with me pushed it to the top of my list and I pushed it to the top of the lab's." He reached into his inside jacket pocket and pulled out a crumpled piece of paper that he thrust at me. "Some of the boys in the lab in Reno owe me."

With the hint of a grin I didn't know I had, I took the paper. "I won't ask why."

"Probably better you don't." Romeo didn't look like he was kidding. As I let my eyes traverse the page, he continued, "Nothing abnormal leaps out. Normal meds for a guy with a bad ticker. Alcohol was a bit over legal limits, but he wasn't driving.

Heart stuff. Sildenafil. Nothing else of any substance."

"Sildenafil?" I asked.

"Pecker-power stuff. Every guy I know above a certain age pops those things like candy. They must have perpetual hard-ons."

"Scary thought." I refolded the paper and handed it back to him. "So, natural causes?"

"Yeah. You mix nitrates and sildenafil, you're asking for a heart attack eventually. The combo can cause a serious drop in blood pressure that can trigger a heart attack—we see it all the time in this town. Old guys hit the city limits hoping to score big."

"I've heard men think about sex every seven and a half seconds." I took a deep breath. "Who knew even monogamous sex was such a high-risk activity?" I glanced at Romeo. "Don't answer that."

Romeo reddened just a bit—the kid still lurked under that hardened exterior. "At least he's one piece of the puzzle we don't have to find a fit for."

"Nice," I said, only half listening as the wheels spun. "Did DeLuca say where he was when he got the call about Mrs. Dane?"

Romeo didn't even break stride. "He swears he was home asleep when he got the call about the . . . problem . . . in the dealership."

"Alone?" Since there were several former Mrs. DeLucas but no current one, I had to ask.

"So he says."

"And what time was that?"

"About three thirty," Romeo said after checking his notes. "That much I can confirm—I called him myself."

"Do you think he's telling the truth?"

Romeo leveled his gaze at me. "Lucky, you know better than most, it's not what we think . . ."

"It's what we can prove," I finished his sentence— the teacher parroting the student. "Did Frank offer a story to cover his whereabouts from the time he left the airport after talking to Shady Slim and three thirty, when you got him on the phone?"

"He said he was home and he didn't turn the house alarm on until he went to bed, which was at two twenty." Romeo glanced up from his notes. "Yes, I checked. Someone activated Mr. DeLuca's home alarm at two twenty, so that much of the story jibes."

"He could easily have doubled back and met Sylvie at the dealership. If he used the outside door, avoiding the perimeter cameras would have been easy." I also decided to share the whole code-word thing with the young detective—now seemed as good a time as any.

When I'd finished, Romeo ran a hand over his eyes, but thankfully didn't feel the need to comment on the obvious. Not to mention that, had I been him, I would've been really steamed at me.

"Someone I count among my best friends recently told me that trust is the foundation of a good relationship." Romeo tucked his notebook in his jacket pocket.

"I know. But if you want me to use my sources to get information, you're going to have to let me do it my way."

"I know. But don't keep me in the dark too long." He glanced at me. I could tell he wasn't really mad. "Remember we'd like to think all this is about truth, justice, and the American Way. You know as well as me, when the lawyers get hold of it, it'll be about playing a game."

"Believe me, I know how the game is played." I threw my arm around his shoulders and squeezed. "With the old guard, there are unwritten rules." I let go of him. "You could use more than the occasional burger, Detective. Thin always looked good on you, but now you're down to skin and bones. You need to take Brandy out to dinner. I hear we have some nice dining establishments in this town."

"With her schedule and mine we're lucky to squeeze in coffee and a roll somewhere."

"That's net negative calories—if your roll is vigorous."

"What? Oh." He ducked his head as his cheeks turned a rosy pink.

Satisfied, I got back to business. "Now, about Sylvie." I ran my fingers through my hair and worked my shoulders, trying to loosen the muscles.

"Dane's wife."

I shot him a look. "Yes, Dane's wife. I got it. But is there anything else? Like trace under her fingernails? Unusual marks on her body?"

"The mark around her neck, you already know about."

I nodded. "From the missing necklace." I rooted in my pocket and pulled out the photo Jerry had given me of the necklace. "This is what it looks like. And it was stolen from a guest room here at the Babylon two weeks ago." Romeo started to say something, but I cut him off. "Then it ends up with our shoe girl at an illegal poker game in a warehouse across the Fifteen."

"I'd sure like to find that girl," Romeo muttered as he glanced at the photograph, then refolded the paper and stuck it in his notebook.

"Stand in line." Then I remembered the photo Jerry had given me. "Oh, this might help." I handed him a second bit of crumpled paper.

Hope flared in his eyes.

"We already ran it through our database. The girl doesn't work here—not legitimately anyway." I told him Jerry's suspicions regarding the theft ring. "But . . ." I paused to make sure I had his attention. "I'll tell you one thing. Those shoes were on Sylvie Dane's feet when she left the poker game."

Romeo's eyebrows shot up. As tired as he was, interest still fired in his eyes. "Seriously?"

"The security feed proves it." I held up a finger, silencing him. "And . . . if my source is right, those shoes were purchased by Frank DeLuca."

"Wow. Remind me not to try to shorten your chain again." He looked at the photo for a moment, then held it as if divining answers through osmosis really was an option. "I'll run it. Maybe we'll get lucky." Romeo gave me a resigned look then glanced at his notes. "To answer your previous question, there was no trace under Sylvie's fingernails."

I straightened. "Really? You sure? No skin or anything?"

"Nope. It'll be a couple of days for the full tox reports, but I don't expect anything weird, although with this cyanide thing, that doesn't seem quite so straightforward anymore."

"You've told me it's pretty easy to get your hands on the stuff, but getting it into Marvin, wonder how they did that?" I pushed myself to my feet and struggled for a tentative balance. Then I reached a hand out to help the young detective.

"Could have been a thousand different ways." Romeo took my hand. "Nothing seemed to jump out when we searched his car. He had a bag with stuff from his locker—a stained shirt, still wet—we're testing the substance now—some toiletries, what you'd expect."

"I didn't give him long to clear out. The guy had it coming, trust me."

"I'm guessing there's a long list of people with a motive then?"

"A bunch of people hated him, but murder? That takes a special kind of hate, don't you think?"

"Not as special as you might think." Still holding my hand, Romeo looked up at me expectantly.

I pulled him to his feet. "If you're trying to make me feel better, it isn't working."

"Do you think the girl killed Sylvie Dane?" Romeo ran his fingers through his hair in a halfhearted, self-conscious attempt to unruffle his exterior.

"I have no idea." I resisted straightening my own hair—even to attempt it would be a wasted, futile effort. "If she didn't, she might have seen who did."

"*If* she was there and *if* the killer saw her . . . two big *if*s . . . but—" I didn't need to finish the sentence.

"We better find her first." Romeo was exhausted but he wasn't stupid. After studying the picture of the young woman again, he carefully folded it and put it in the same pocket as his notebook. Then he seemed to deflate. "This job is beating me up." Romeo brushed his jacket down and made a feeble attempt to straighten his tie, then gave up. "I'm heading home, if only to shower and change."

I felt like giving him another hug, but resisted. A hug no longer seemed appropriate—I was no longer the teacher. Romeo was my equal now. Of course, I'm not sure he would be overly pleased with my assessment, so I didn't mention it. "You know, kid, there is an air about you."

"If it would keep people off my back, I'd make it a habit."

"Man, you're like a verbal backboard—everything I hit your way comes blazing back. Better be careful, I'm rubbing off on you."

"And, as we know, that can be deadly."

. . .

"I'M assuming the police have the murders under control?" Miss P asked when I staggered through the office door.

I thought that a bit optimistic, especially considering it was Metro we were talking about, but I didn't say so. Instead, I shrugged noncommittally. "I see the grapevine is operating at its normal blinding pace."

"No matter how bad things get, we can always count on the rumor mill."

"Gossip, the glue that holds us together." I shifted from one foot to the other in front of her desk—tired yet amped on adrenaline.

Miss P consulted her notebook. "Mr. Watalsky came by this afternoon looking for you. He said to find him if it's early. I told him you were tied up at the airport." She glanced up at me with the hint of a smile, then continued. "Jeremy will meet you for breakfast. He said he had some leads to check out. Eight o' clock at Jamm's. Does that work?"

"Eight o' clock? In the morning? He can't be serious? Does the man ever sleep?" Morning is not my best time, but Jeremy knew that. "Luring me with fresh-baked cinnamon bread, is he? Swine."

Miss P knew a "yes" when she heard one. "Fine, I'll let him know that your price is one pot-o-bread. Mr. Watalsky said if he doesn't see you tonight, you could catch him tomorrow in the Poker Room any time after noon."

"What's he doing tonight? Did he say?"

"He said he had plans."

I had a good idea where he was headed—the illegal poker game. Cole had told Romeo where it was last night, but being smart and prizing their skins, the promoters moved the game every night. The young detective had prevailed upon Cole to try to get a line on tonight's game. Maybe he'd come through, maybe not. Regardless, it wasn't my game to play.

"Now." Miss P pushed herself to her feet so we were essentially eye to eye and her tone turned a tad frosty. A closed-down expression replaced her open one as she put her hands on her hips in an exaggerated show of displeasure. "About Teddie."

I threw up one hand. "Not to worry, I won't add to the body count . . . yet. He might become a future homicide—if he's foolhardy enough to show his tight little ass around here. But since he's half a world away, I shouldn't think his demise is imminent."

Miss P scowled at me. "Lucky . . ."

"Don't." I looked for a chair to fall into, then thought better of it—I always think better on my feet, or at least I can turn and run faster from a standing position. Either way, I'm money ahead. "You know better than anyone, after all the years of sucking up I've put in, I've developed an immunity to attitude."

She weakened. "But he says he's sorry. Doesn't that mean anything?" Like the crust on cooling lava, her frosty demeanor cracked, revealing the warmth of a caring friend. "He loves you."

"He left. Interesting way of showing it."

"He made a mistake."

"He made several." I sighed. This was the last thing I wanted to talk about. "The funny thing about words, you can take them back, but they can never be unheard."

"He hurt you. He's human—it's not a capital crime."

"We've established that."

Miss P threw up her hands. "Will you ever forgive him?"

Now that was the sixty-four-thousand-dollar question, wasn't it? And lately I hadn't had much luck with answers. I stepped to the window overlooking the lobby below. Couples wandered hand in hand—the shows had let out only a short while ago. Clusters of stylish young males and females eyed each other and jockeyed for attention. At this time of night, the clubs were just revving their engines, advancing to full throttle.

And I was completely out of gas.

Teddie. The memories assaulted me, tearing at me, ripping my heart open like a bloodhound with a rabbit. Wasn't time the great healer? The sands of time were sifting through the hourglass, yet my emotions were still as raw as the day he walked out. How did you ever put a patch over that? Scar tissue was thick and tough—not the stuff to wrap a heart in, not if I hoped to love again. "Forgiveness," I sighed, the concept totally foreign. Grudges weren't my thing, but once someone pushed me too far, I'd never found a way back.

"Is next to godliness," Miss P added. A platitude for every occasion.

I gave her my best dirty look. "I can't tell you how much better that makes me feel. And it's cleanliness, not forgiveness."

"What?"

"Cleanliness is next to godliness."

"Whatever. You know what I mean."

A few moments of silence, pity written all over her face, and I caved. I opened my arms, pleading. "It would never be the same."

Miss P stepped into the hug. "Honey, nothing ever is."

Chapter

TEN

Even though the night had long since barreled into a new day, I still had work to do. The funeral directors would be setting up for their conference expo and I owed them a thank-you.

Moonbird Ridgeway, Moony to most of us, stood, back to the door, hands on hips, staring at a job only half done when I eased myself inside the cavernous exhibit hall. After a couple of decades working together, you'd think I would be used to Moony by now, but she always made me grin. Competent and to the point, she was as unexpected as a cool breeze in July. Raised on a cattle farm outside Carson City, she was as tough as boot leather and as callused as a cowboy after a summer spent pulling fences. Like a sheepdog working the herd, she ran her department with a bark and a nip, but she had the lowest turnover of any department head, so I stayed out of her way and let her do her thing. She liked that about me—she'd told me so on numerous occasions.

Overalls and a white tee shirt hid her tiny frame, lending her a no-nonsense air, which she cultivated with an ever-present frown. Her steel-toed work boots had probably been broken in before I was born. Part Paiute, her large eyes and dark skin evoked American Indian, but silver now streaked her jet-black hair. Still, she wore it in a thick plaited tail down her back. Her face, a wide-open expanse, had never seen even a touch of makeup that I was aware of. Perhaps that's why her skin still held the luminous glow of a youth. But no matter how distant a memory her youth was, wrinkles had yet to defy the force of her vigor. With careful scrutiny, I couldn't find even the hint of a laugh line.

Forklifts maneuvered, the operators reacting to barked orders. Crew members, festooned with tool belts and hardhats, hammered together the displays, pulling the puzzles together from the pieces scattered around them. The light crew adjusted spots and colors in a dizzying display. The whole thing was taking shape but remained far from done.

I stepped in next to Moony and adopted a similar stance, although I crossed my arms over my chest. "When does this thing open?"

"Noon." She didn't look at me. Instead, with brows scrunched into a frown, she focused her attention on a forklift. Putting her two pinkies between her lips, she let out a shrieking whistle that stopped everyone in their tracks.

Eyes swiveled in our direction.

"Otis, that flat goes with the Source of Comfort display—it's marked right on the box you're carrying big as day. Booth two-forty-two." She motioned toward the far right of the hall. "Over there."

The driver grinned then gunned the engine, narrowly missing a display of thematic caskets on velvet. The NASCAR and the NFL caskets I understood—heck, the last Celebration of Life we'd held had been for a guy who insisted on being buried in his white Steinway, so I was not a themed-burial virgin. But the *Twilight* casket messed me up. When one died was it prudent to surround oneself with the undead?

"And cool it on the Mario Andretti impersonation, Otis," Moony yelled, cupping her hands around her mouth like a megaphone. "Your ass is a grape if you run over anything. Got it?"

"Or anyone," I added as I watched a group of exhibitors scatter as the forklift bore down on them.

"Hell, people we got." Moony tossed off the line like she meant it. "It's those displays that can't be replaced—they're like friggin' works a' art, each piece molded to fit into another. We so much as bend a piece, we're screwed." The forklift problem addressed, Moony's focus shifted to another. This one apparently needed her personal touch. "You wanna talk, girl, you gotta walk." She threw the words over her shoulder as she turned and bolted.

As she charged across the hall, I had trouble keeping up. "I want to thank you for the use of the body-mover thing. How you talked the funeral guys into letting me use it, I'll never know."

She waved me off. "You'd a done it for me. Probably have a time or two."

"You're not still paying me back for sweeping that episode with Fred Rainwater under the rug, are you?"

She stopped and whirled around so fast I almost rolled right over her. She trained her eyes on me as if she were leveling a shotgun. "You promised never to breathe a word."

"Yes, but I'm not above a good goading every now and then." At least I got her to stop loping so I could pause and catch my breath. "How is Fred, by the way?"

"Sorta like an old rodeo bronc—good for a buck every now and again—if you catch him before he's finished a six-pack."

"Too much information."

"You asked." She whirled and charged off again, this time stopping at a booth under construction.

"So, you think you'll get this circus up and running by noon?" The colorful display at an already finished booth caught my attention.

"By breakfast." She turned and gave an animated instruction to one of the workers, then focused on me again. "Stop touching things."

At her scolding, I dropped the framed flyer I had been reading, then righted it and stuck my hands in my pockets. "I was curious. Those folks develop interactive home pages for the deceased. You know, that begs a lot of questions."

Moony sighed and shook her head, then started talking and walking. "Actually, it's sorta fortuitous you showed up—even if you are as much trouble as a hungry calf. I have a pesky little fly I could use your help with."

"What?" As I worked to catch up with her, I wasn't sure I'd caught what she'd said. "A guest?"

Like a quarter horse separating a cow from the herd, Moony darted to the right, then to the left, dodging a workman swinging a ladder into place, then she hurried on. "She's staying in one of them big-bucks rooms, so I didn't want to go messing with no big shot."

"Who?" As I dogged her heels, I cast around, but couldn't see anyone who looked out of place.

"Hell, I didn't take her name. But she came breezing through here acting like this was some sort of one-stop shop." Moony stopped as she pointed and barked at another one of her crew.

I picked up a small item from a display that had been completed. It looked like some sort of a plug. "What is this for?"

Moony grabbed it from my hand and put it back. "You do not want to know. Anyway, about this guest—she needs your magic touch."

Then I heard it. A shriek, then a shrill voice raised in anger. My heart stopped. "This guest, does she have the whole fake cowgirl thing going on?"

Moony nodded. "Real cowboys would rather swing on the end of a rope than be seen in public in that getup. What's that woman thinking?"

"Thinking's not her long suit." I grabbed Moony's arm as she started to launch off again, holding her in place. "What'd she want?"

"Far as I could tell, someone close to her just passed and she wants to throw a party."

Before I tackled Miss Becky-Sue, I looked for some fortification. I know, a warning sign if there ever was one, but Miss Becky-Sue was above and beyond—at least that's what I told myself as I stopped in front of a display of tiny little caskets designed to hold bottles of wine. I didn't know whether the wine thing was meant to show folks that indeed they could take it with them, or whether it was for the morbid among us who might think this would be fun to have on the buffet in the dining room at home. Either way, the wine looked promising. But there was nobody there and I didn't feel like adding larceny to my list of transgressions for the day, so I moved on.

I found the little piece of Texas trash, head tilted to one side, absentmindedly picking at chipped polish on one fingernail as she contemplated a banner that said IMPLANT RECYCLING. She glanced at me with a frown as I stopped beside her. "What're you doing here?"

"I could ask you the same thing. This is a showroom for a convention that opens tomorrow." Actually, it was later today, but I didn't feel the need to clarify, so I didn't.

"Right convenient, don't you think?"

"It's not open to the public."

"Money opens most doors." She shot me a shrewd look that cracked the bimbo mask, giving me a glimpse behind it. She tilted her head toward the banner. "What'd'ya think they'd give me for a well-used penile implant? Slim don't need it no more."

A lot of responses sprung to mind, none of which were appropriate. "I hear you want to throw a Celebration of Life?"

"Day after tomorrow—the night before the final table." Her eyes held a challenge when they met mine. "Kinda fittin' by my way of thinkin'."

"And the theme?"

"Clearly brains wasn't a requirement for your job."

I agreed with her assessment, so I didn't even pretend to object.

"Poker, of course."

"Of course." With one arm under her elbow, I eased her toward the doors. "Why don't you come down to my office in the morning? We can help with that."

As we walked by, she reached out and palmed a silver locket off a display. The locket was designed to hold some of the dearly departed's remains so the loved ones left behind could "hold a source of comfort next to their hearts." Words failed me.

"I want it big, with a band and dancin'—all of it."

"Beer, barbecue, and boot-scootin'—an appropriate send-off." I pulled her to a stop outside the Exhibit Hall. Extending my hand palm up, I stared her down.

Rolling her eyes, but not offering any explanation, she pulled the locket out of her pocket and dropped it into my open hand.

As I watched her sashay away, my phone sang at my hip. Reflexively I reached for it and flipped it open. "O'Toole."

"Lucky? It's Brandy." Her voiced was hushed, male laughter sounded in the background.

"Brandy. How's the poker going?"

"Uh, well . . ."

I heard a male voice raised in anger, but I couldn't make out the words. No music. Anger. My blood froze.

"Where are you?"

Her voice dropped to a whisper and it sounded like she had cupped her hand over the phone. "Lucky, we're in trouble."

Chapter

ELEVEN

♡

The warehouse looked abandoned—a dark hulk shadowed by the dim light from a lone streetlight halfway down the block. The closer ones had been shot out. Jagged edges of broken glass jutted from holes that had once been windows at the top of the building. A tattered chain-link fence circled the property—a porous defense riddled by neglect. Whole sections sagged, holes gaped, two strands of barbed wire curled back where they had been cut. A cool breeze skittered an unseen can in the darkness.

"All we're missing is a black cat to run across our path," I whispered to myself as I staggered when my ankle turned on a buckle in the asphalt. "Shit." I gritted my teeth and tried to make myself small. The last thing I wanted to do was alert the folks inside to our presence. "Not until everyone is in place," Romeo had said before he'd disappeared in the darkness.

Taking shallow breaths, I tried to ignore the stench of garbage left too long in the sun. Downwind of the putrid smell, my eyes teared, my stomach turned. Of course, the fact that I was like a racehorse in the starting gate anticipating the gun could have had something to do with my anxiety.

Lacing my fingers through the fence, I knelt, one

knee on the ground, the other bent and ready to spring. My nerves were caught between hoping for the best and fearing the worst. Goose bumps competed with a sheen of cold sweat. My heartbeat kept a steady rhythm in my ears as I fought the urge to do something. Surprise was on our side. We needed to wait—get everyone in place. I knew it, but I wanted to ignore it just the same.

Like a wraith, Romeo materialized at my shoulder. "Backup got here pretty quick. I've got a couple of teams at each door ready to move in on my mark."

"Okay, let's go." I started to rise, but Romeo grabbed my arm, pulling me back down.

"You're staying right here." Romeo lowered his voice to a growl. "No way in Hell am I letting you traipse into harm's way."

"Traipse?" My voice matched his—I knew he couldn't see my slitty eyes.

He blew out a breath. "Lucky, you stay right here. I mean it. You'll be nothing but in the way. And if you got hurt? I could kiss my ass good-bye."

I wanted to point out that it wouldn't do my ass much good either, but that wouldn't help—it really was Brandy's and Cole's asses on the line here. And if I argued, the more likely he would be to assign me a keeper. "Fine. Just get them out of there in one piece, okay?"

I must've sounded sincere because he bought it. "That's my job."

"You better get going, then."

"Patience. We get one shot at this, Lucky. We need to make it count."

"Your guys know we have a couple of innocents in there?"

"If there is an illegal game going on and Cole and Brandy are playing guppy, swimming with the big fish, they're gonna get caught in the same net as the sharks." Romeo sounded like the cop he was. Impressive, considering one of the little fish was his girlfriend.

I reached through the darkness and fisted a hand in the front of his shirt, pulling his face close to mine. "If anybody's going to kill them, it's going to be me. Got it?"

"You'll get your chance." In the half-light I could see he was as scared as I was. As a detective, I guessed, it was his job not to show it. "Stay here. For once, do as you're told."

I waited until he disappeared into the darkness, then, crouching down, I followed him. Pulling aside a section of fence, I stepped, trying to be quiet. On the other side, I stayed close enough behind that I could hear him whisper instructions into the radio mike affixed to his shoulder, although I couldn't make out the words. Clicks were the only response. Hiding in the darkness, I watched as he eased up three steps to the door on the east side of the building. Taking a deep breath, Romeo closed his hand around the doorknob. His back to the door, his gun held chest high at the ready, he thumbed off the safety. He gave the knob a turn. The door clicked open and he pushed it in a few inches. For a moment he waited, listening.

Voices rode the air—diffuse, distant, but not too far. Light filtered into the darkness from our left.

Pressing his lips to the mike, Romeo whispered something I couldn't hear, then motioned with his head to someone out of my line of sight toward the glow and the voices.

I slithered through the doorway behind him, then ducked into a shadow. First, I eased one foot out of a shoe, then the other, and kicked the pair to the side. Nothing to make noise. The bare concrete was cold and damp, a discomfort I welcomed as we moved farther into the building. The walls creaked as the wind moved outside. I thought I heard scurrying sounds in the darkness, but I might have been imagining that part.

"Let the deaf kid play. Hell, he knows his way around and he's got green we can take." That voice I knew—River Watalsky. I'd been right about his plans, a small comfort. Which side was he playing?

Time would provide the answer, but for now, at least Cole was alive and kicking.

Some grumbling met his announcement, then the sound of a chair scraping back. The kid was in the game.

Crouched, I followed Romeo, keeping a safe distance between us, as he worked his way closer, one careful step at a time.

"What about the girl?" Another voice, unfamiliar and with a hard edge. "She's got a body on her."

Brandy! So both of them were okay . . . for the moment.

"Throw her into the pot." Watalsky again. "We'll play for her."

"But the kid's on the button. He has an advantage."

"Who the fuck cares? He's just a kid and he can't understand a word we say." Watalsky knew that wasn't true.

The voices fell quiet. Silence for a moment as cards were dealt. Chips clattered as players made their bets. I moved in next to Romeo. To his credit, he didn't act too alarmed—in fact, he looked like he'd been expecting me. He shook his head and rolled his eyes. Taking our position just outside the perimeter of light cast by a lone bulb hanging from the rafters, Romeo and I turned away from the game as we sat, our backs against a large pile of wooden pallets.

Romeo again clicked his mike and waited for the sets of two answering clicks. Four sets for four pairs of officers in place, they came quickly. Everyone was ready.

His mouth set in a grim line, he slid the bolt back on his gun, chambering a round. Then he raised a questioning eyebrow at me. He mouthed the words "Stay here. I mean it."

I nodded. It's not like I was armed or anything.

And if we didn't get the show on the road, the pounding of my heart would give us away any minute.

Romeo pushed himself to his feet. Holding his gun in both hands, he brought it to level in front of him, the pile of pallets providing a shield of sorts. Aiming at the group of players, he shouted, "Metro Police Department. Don't move. Hands in the air."

Still hiding behind the pallets, I don't know exactly what happened next. All I do know is that chairs scraped back. Shouts. Then bullets started flying.

On my hands and knees, I peeked around. Pandemonium. Romeo, his gun in front of him, launched himself into the fray. Other officers darted, hiding themselves, then risking a shot.

The players overturned the poker table, using it as a shield. Backs to it, they popped magazines from their pistols, rammed new ones in, then turned to fire at the officers again.

Crawling forward, I moved toward the center of the room, keeping Romeo in front of me. Desperate for a glimpse of Cole and Brandy, I stuck my head out farther and scanned the room, my heart in my throat.

A bullet whizzed by, embedding itself in the wooden pillar next to my left ear. "Shit." Why is it that every time I feel like shooting someone, my gun is not in my hand? Probably a stroke of luck, but it didn't feel like it right at the moment.

One of the players took a step toward me, then whirled and squeezed off a round. Another pop. The shooter let out a yelp and clutched his leg. His gun clattered, then skidded in my direction. Just as I reached for it, a foot kicked it out of the way.

"Don't you dare," Romeo growled. "Get the hell away from here. You don't need that kind of trouble."

Not the thing to say to me as another bullet hit too close and I saw red. I dove for the pistol. A Beretta 9mm, it felt good in my hand.

I inched around and got a good look. Most of the players had surrendered their weapons and now knelt, hands clasped behind their heads. Only one fool had any fight left. The cops had him pinned down behind the poker table. As I stepped into sight, the player behind the table turned on Romeo and me, catching the young detective with nowhere to hide. He ducked. I aimed. A pop. The gun jerked in my hand.

A grunt. The shooter fell back, blood on his shoulder. His shooting arm dropped.

His buddy, the guy who had been hit in the leg, raised his hands but stayed where he sat. "Don't shoot, man. I got no gun."

Romeo stepped to him and pushed him face-first to the ground. "Hands behind your back. I got a feeling you know the drill."

As he cuffed him, Romeo gave me a half grin and a shake of the head. He didn't have to say anything.

As the dust settled, I caught sight of Watalsky on his chest, lying flat on the ground. My heart leaped. I rushed to his side. Kneeling down, I scanned the room as I asked, "Are you hit?"

"Hell, no." As he pushed himself up, another set of arms and feet stuck out from under him. He'd been lying on someone. "Darn near took one in the ass trying to get this guy to the ground." Watalsky rolled off the body underneath.

Cole!

Fury reddened the young man's face as he pushed at Watalsky, who was twice his size and probably three times his weight. I reached down and grabbed Cole, bringing him to his feet with one jerk. "Brandy? Where is she?"

Panic on his face, Cole scanned the room. My eyes followed his.

Behind me Watalsky asked Romeo, "How many do you have?"

Romeo paused as he got a good picture of his officers and their captives. "Six."

"There's one more."

"I didn't kill her." The voice was low, angry, but it held a plea.

All heads turned toward the sound as a figure stepped out into the light. I stepped back into the shadows.

Kevin Slurry. The Hawk. The former owner of the Web site that seemed to be at the center of things, Aces Over Eights, a dead man's hand. Sylvie's code word. That went from being merely creepy to totally terrifying. Had she been trying to tell us? Warn us?

He held Brandy, her back to his chest, like a human shield, the muzzle of his gun pressed to her temple.

Romeo made a move toward him. Slurry re-aimed his gun at the detective's chest. "Don't be a hero."

Romeo froze. He raised his hands, his gun pointing at the ceiling.

"I want all of you to put your guns on the ground, then kick them over to me."

Unsure, the officers glanced at Romeo. He slowly knelt and did as Slurry asked. The other officers followed. In the shadows, I stepped farther back, hiding myself in the darkness and hoping that the bright light over Slurry made it hard for him to see.

"I didn't kill Sylvie Dane." Slurry's voice shook. Under the harsh light of the exposed bulbs, it was easy to see he was nervous. Perspiration trickled down the side of his face. Raising his shoulder, he wiped it away, but the panic in his eyes remained as they darted around the room.

"This is no way to get us to believe you," Romeo said. "Put your gun down. Let the girl go. Then we'll talk."

"They're going to kill me," Slurry said as he once again pressed his gun to Brandy's temple. "She's my ticket outta here."

"Who's going to kill you?" Romeo asked.

"The same ones who killed Sylvie." Slurry was starting to lose it now. I could see the wildness in his eyes as he gripped Brandy to him with an arm across her throat.

"Who are they?" the young detective pushed.

"Hell, if I knew that do you think I'd be here? I'm looking for answers the same as you." Slurry motioned with his gun for the officers in front of him to move to the side. With a nod from Romeo, they did as he requested. "I was helping her."

"With what?" Romeo asked.

I kept my eyes glued to Brandy. She didn't struggle. Finally, her eyes locked with mine. Big and bright, they mirrored her fear and something else . . . resolve. I gave her a questioning look and pointed to the ground. She gave me a half smile.

We'd get one shot at this. I didn't smile—lately puns had been losing their luster. Half hidden from view behind Romeo, I pulled back the slide on my gun, then curled both hands around the grip, one finger resting lightly on the trigger.

As Romeo kept Slurry's attention, I gave a quick nod to Brandy.

I raised my gun. She sagged in his arms, fighting against his hold. Caught by surprise, Slurry's grip loosened. Brandy shrugged him off and dropped to the ground.

To me, everything happened in slow motion. I stroked the trigger and the gun jerked in my hand. Kevin staggered back. A red stain ballooned on his chest.

Romeo pivoted, looking at me, his eyes as big as saucers.

For a moment time stopped.

"I'VE never shot a man before," I said, apropos of nothing, really. Huddled in a blanket, sitting on the fender of an ambulance, I tried to control my shaking. Cops and paramedics rushed in and out of the light cast by the headlights of the vehicles clustered around the ambulances. They'd circled Brandy and Cole before I'd had a chance to shoot them myself. The Flight for Life helicopter carrying Slurry lifted off. Quickly, its landing light dimmed as the night swallowed it. A couple of the other players, including the one I had winged, were being treated, then transported to UMC at a more sedate pace, their injuries deemed non–life threatening.

Holding a cup of coffee by the rim, Romeo handed it to me. Cupping my hands around the Styrofoam cup, I sought comfort from the warmth steaming from the liquid. I tried to raise the cup to my lips, but my hands shook so badly I was worried about scalding myself. Of course, then I might be able to sue for a huge sum, like that lady who sued McDonald's, and retire to some obscure island in the South Pacific. But with my luck, I'd probably just get a burn, a scar, and bad publicity, so I contented myself with absorbing the warmth rather than ingesting it.

If Romeo noticed my struggle, he kept it to himself. "The first time is the hardest, but it never gets easier. That guy had it coming for sure, but he's someone's child or brother, or something."

"If you're trying to make me feel better, please stop. You suck at it."

"So I've been told." He scooted me over, then squeezed one cheek onto my fender, propping himself there. "I'm just saying we all feel the same way.

But look at it this way, if you hadn't shot that guy in the leg, I might not be sitting here."

"Working so hard to improve my mood."

Romeo nudged me with his shoulder and grinned. "You did the right thing. Even though you shot him before he could tell us what he was helping Sylvie Dane with."

"As you said, I had one shot at saving Brandy, so I took it."

"And a good thing you did, too."

"Do you think he's going to make it?" My voice came out all hushed.

"Slurry? I don't know." Romeo snaked an arm around my shoulders, pulling me tight. Somehow he must've sensed that offering platitudes would just ring hollow, so he stayed quiet.

I'd finally managed to negotiate a sip or two of coffee without scalding myself or decorating my front when Watalsky appeared, trailed by two officers. "Detective, you gotta tell your goons I'm one of the good guys."

"Really?" Romeo let go of my shoulders, but he didn't move from his perch. "Convince me."

"Me and Jerry over at the Babylon have been trying to get a bead on the cheating that was going on the other night. Those two, Slurry and Sylvie Dane, had to be in cahoots, I just can't figure out why."

I pulled the blanket tighter around me—for some reason I couldn't get warm. "Did Jerry know you were here?" I asked.

Watalsky looked at the ground as he scuffed his toes in the gravel. "Not really."

"Didn't think so."

"We're going to take the lot of you to the station. You'll be there until we get the truth out of you." Romeo motioned to the officers, who had each taken one of Watalsky's arms, bracketing him. They didn't need him to spell it out. Without a word, they led Watalsky away.

"You're in for a long night."

Romeo looked resigned. "Yeah, well, you know how it is." With the excitement over, the adrenaline waning, the kid looked like he could use a month of good shut-eye. His hair slicked to his head, his face haggard, a stubble scratching his cheeks, a decade had been added to his appearance since the last time I'd seen him—and he hadn't looked so hot then. The clothes were different. A new suit, but the same wilted white shirt noosed by a tie loosely knotted and covered by his same tan overcoat—he looked like Clark Kent in need of a phone booth. With a casual glance, he assessed the area. "Things are under control here."

"Saying those kinds of things does nothing but tempt fate," I groused, thinking my emotions were far from under control—they still spiked and dove, twisted and flipped, a dizzying roller-coaster ride.

As Romeo started to say something, Brandy appeared out of the darkness and threw her arms around him, burying her face in his neck. Romeo grabbed her with both arms and held tight. Cole, hanging back in the shadows, didn't look too pleased. Finally, out of patience, he strode into the light and tapped Brandy on the back. When she turned, he signed something to her.

"Right." Her brows crinkled in worry as she glanced between Romeo and me. "Is the other girl okay?"

"What other girl?" we said in unison.

"The girl with the necklace."

I dropped my coffee as I leaped to my feet. "She was here? Where?"

"She was in the game. She used the necklace to buy in."

"Really?" Romeo was openly skeptical. "Why would anyone bring a red-hot piece of ice like that here?"

Cole rolled his eyes, his fingers flying.

"Where better?" Brandy interpreted. "Here nobody cares who you are, or where you got it. No records and it disappears into a melting pot at some local chop shop."

"Can't argue with the logic," I said to Romeo.

Romeo turned to Cole. "You wouldn't have any idea where she went, would you?"

"When the shooting started, she rabbited." Brandy appeared to be picking up some interesting lingo hanging with the poker crowd. "God knows where."

"And the necklace?" I asked out of curiosity.

Cole reached into his pocket. Then he grabbed

Romeo's hand, turned it palm up, and dropped Sylvie Dane's pocket watch into his open hand.

"**WELL**, we have the watch," I said to the audience clustered in my office as I held it by the chain and watched as it twirled, fracturing the light like a disco ball. Romeo had dusted it in vain—any meaningful prints had long been obscured. "A pretty bauble. But no girl."

Miss P and the Beautiful Jeremy Whitlock sat molded together, Jeremy underneath, like a human stacking game. Entwined, they looked tired, but happy.

"Fuckin' A!" Newton, never one to be ignored, trotted out the epithet with abandon. "Asshole! Asshole! Asshole!" He ducked and shimmied from one side of his cage to the other.

"What's with the bird?" Miss P asked.

"A shiny bauble and an audience—bird heaven."

"Gimme, gimme, gimme." Newton's vocabulary was clearly growing. The worst part of it was that his word choices seemed to be appropriate—well, if four-letter words were ever appropriate.

Dropping the watch on the corner of Miss P's desk, I reached for the cover to the birdcage. "Time for you to go to sleep, kiddo."

"Bitch," Newton murmured, making everyone laugh as I wrapped him in darkness.

"Where are the kids?" Jeremy asked as he snaked out a hand to grab Sylvie's watch. He turned it over in his hand, then popped the cover. "Sweet."

"Brandy and Cole went to the station with Romeo," I explained as I plopped into my desk chair, kicked off my shoes, then put my feet on my desk. "He's got Watalsky on the hot seat and wanted to use the kids' stories to keep him honest."

"Gotcha." Jeremy grinned as Miss P nuzzled his ear. "Honey, that's really distracting."

"Go get a room, you two. I hear we have a few that are pretty nice." I watched, wishing for an ear of my own to nibble . . . perhaps one with a French flair. "As I was saying, Romeo is going to get everyone's story straight, then he's going to bust Dane's ass with it."

"Assuming that happens, what's going to happen to Dane?" Jeremy asked. I wasn't sure whether anger pinched his face or another emotion.

"Once Metro finds him . . . *if* they find him . . . he'll be escorted through the criminal justice system, to much media fanfare, unless we can conjure up a killer." Wiggling my toes, I pretended to be interested in them for a moment while the room fell silent, each of us lost in our own memories, our fears. "I hear a grand jury will be convened on Monday. It's my guess they have enough evidence, albeit circumstantial, to indict."

"I'm chasing some interesting money trails for your dead Poker Room manager, Johnstone." Jeremy shook his head as he ducked away from Miss P. "It's pretty convoluted, highly sophisticated. But it's looking like he had his hand in a pretty large cookie jar."

"Any offshore connections?" I asked. Sometimes a shot in the dark actually hits something.

"Why would you think that?" Jeremy's eyes narrowed, his interest piqued.

"Kevin Slurry seems to be at the vortex of this hurricane. And he owned an offshore poker site. Money flows through there like shit though a goose, but comes out clean as a whistle on the other side."

"Really?" He boosted Miss P off his lap. He set the watch back on my desk. "You might want to check the inside of the cover there." He pointed to a section of the metal that was less shiny than the rest. "It looks like something's been removed. Some initials or something—I can't tell without a magnifying glass." As I bent to look where he pointed, he grabbed his cell and started dialing, then disappeared through the office door.

Miss P brushed down her skirt, then pulled her shoulders back, stretching. Taking a deep breath, she leveled her gaze at me. "Is there anything I can do for you? Anything you need?"

"Any info on that sign in front of the dealership?"

"Maintenance is looking for the work order, but you know how they are."

"Organization is not their strength."

Jeremy had finished his call and poked his head back in the office. "I've got some preliminary news on Sylvie Dane's phone. It was a burn phone, a prepaid cellular, untraceable to any source, not that I expected to find any. And she didn't make any outgoing calls, except to one number."

"What was the number? Could you trace it?"

Jeremy nodded. "Don't get all excited. The number is registered to a local charity that hands out phones to homeless kids."

"Homeless?" That was a turn in the road I didn't see coming.

"Don't ask," Jeremy shut my questions down. "I haven't tied any of this together—still working on it."

"Gotcha. Maybe you'll know more when I meet you for breakfast tomorrow. Jamm's, right?"

"Eight o'clock."

I turned my attention to Miss P. "Take your Aussie boy home. We've done enough for today."

She didn't argue. Miss P hooked her arm through her honey's and they fell into easy conversation. She grabbed her purse off Brandy's desk as she went by, then both of them stepped through the hole in the wall, my future office door. Quiet descended as their voices retreated down the hallway.

Alone with myself, I picked up the watch and held it to the light. The stones shattered the weak light into colorful sparkles. Flipping open the cover, I held it so it caught what light there was. On my second pass, I saw the scuffed patch of metal on the inside where it appeared something had been removed. The initials Jerry had mentioned. Why remove them? Whatever the reason, the deed had been done fairly recently from the looks of it.

I had no idea what it meant or if it was relevant at all. Like a blanket thrown over a smoldering fire, the quiet semidarkness pressed around me as I contemplated all the pieces to the puzzle. Despite my best efforts, my brain flipped to shutdown mode. Too little sleep, too many murders, too many elusive connections . . . and too little life. Not to mention I'd shot someone today. Okay, two someones.

Caught in the daily current of chaos, it was easy to avoid myself. Perhaps that's why I sought the craziness—no time for introspection. But according to the experts, sanity is based on a balance between life at full tilt and reflective time. God knew I had a tentative hold on reality as it was, so I relinquished myself to the silence and let my world turn inward. And like horses galloping to the barn, when I let my thoughts run unbridled, they ran straight to my most personal problem—Teddie.

Someday I'd have to face him, I knew that. But with multiple time zones between us, I'd been avoiding the inevitable. The searing heat of his betrayal still burned at the touch of a memory. Yes, Miss P was right, Teddie used to love me; he probably still did. He just loved himself more. And if the best I could do was a distant second, I wasn't entering the race, thank you very much.

In need of moral courage, I wandered into the kitchenette—Miss P kept an emergency ration of medicinal Wild Turkey 101 in the top cabinet, way in the back. Dropping one cube of ice in the double old-fashioned glass, I filled it with the golden elixir— nothing like Kentucky mash to dull the pain.

Dousing the lights, leaving the light filtering in from the lobby below as the only illumination, I sagged into Miss P's chair. Pulling out the bottom drawer with the toe of my left foot, I rested both feet on it and tilted myself back. History had taught me, the first sip of whiskey is always the worst, leaving a trail of fire all the way down until it explodes in a ball of warmth. As I braced for the pain then relished the comfort, an inner voice sounded a warning that went unheeded.

I didn't want to think. I didn't want to feel.

So I did what any sane person would do: I hit the replay button on the message machine, then leaned back, bracing for the hit.

Like a sucker punch, Teddie's voice hit me hard, leaving me gasping for air.

"Lucky," he began. "I've been practicing this over and over, rewriting it in my head, trying to find the words. Finally, I realized, words are inadequate. Anything I say will fall so far short of what I feel. But words are all I have."

He paused. I could hear music in the background. I had no idea where he was, but he lived life to an accompanying soundtrack, subtle background music to set the mood. Perhaps that assessment was a bit unfair, but I wasn't in a magnanimous mood. Sue me.

"When I left, I thought I was doing us both a favor." He sounded like a lawyer for the accused pleading his case in summation.

My heart fell. Great. So this was my fault. Somehow I'd had a feeling he'd lay the blame—no, not the blame . . . the justification . . . at my feet.

"No," his voice interrupted my pity party. "Lucky, don't go there. You know it's not what I meant. This one is all on me."

Apparently I was as easy to read as a billboard—even from half a world away. That gave him quite an advantage. But he wasn't the only clairvoyant . . . I had seen the end from the beginning. I'd warned him about spiking the cauldron of friendship with two hundred-proof love—a potent punch that would leave us with nothing but a headache . . . and a heartache.

"But," Teddie continued, "I convinced myself that cutting you loose would be the best thing. Then I could let go of the guilt. It didn't work out the way I'd planned."

The games we play. The lengths we'll go to justify really bad behavior.

"I told you so!" I threw the verbal dart into the darkness, but this was a one-sided conversation—he didn't hear it. Of course, if I had the nerve to pick up the phone, which I didn't, I could tell him myself. I just didn't see the point—we'd worn a path through this ground before.

"You always told me, like the young woman who tried to leave Shangri-la, you'd die before you hit the city limits of Las Vegas. Point taken—your life is there. You were always honest about that. And you were honest about wanting a man to come home to every night."

Yes, I'd wanted all of that. And while we were dreaming, some of his mother's coconut oatmeal raisin cookies wouldn't be bad either.

For a moment I had had that—life with Teddie, even the cookies. Life had been perfect. In retrospect, a lie, but a perfect lie. Tired of fighting the memories, I relinquished myself to them: I could feel his arms around me, and I remembered lying awake in the dark listening to him breathe, comforted and content—a Norman Rockwell picture of the past.

"I thought I could be that man, writing my music. But I forgot what it was like to be in front of a crowd, feeding off their energy. Man, it's electric, intoxicating." He sighed. "And I chose."

Open and raw, I was no match to fight off those memories either. The pain flared as his words, his callousness, assaulted me once again. He'd come home unexpectedly—one last fuck before saying good-bye. Pig.

"They say you never really appreciate what you have until you've lost it."

Christ, the guy should be with Miss P—they could share a lifetime trading platitudes.

"I know that's one of those corny things you hate." He chuckled, presumably at a memory. "What is it you say? Platitudes are lies the world wants you to believe? I think that's it."

I took another long drink, then closed my eyes and rested my head on the back of the chair. The guy got me. I used to love that about him; now I resented it. This would be so much easier if I could work myself up to hating him, but I couldn't.

"Anyway, I have no idea whether you will ever hear these words, but I had to say them."

He sounded so sad, and sincere. Fuck.

"For a smart guy, I can be incredibly stupid." He took a deep breath.

I could picture him running his hand through his hair, making it stick out in all different directions, his blue eyes dark with emotion, wearing his Harvard sweatshirt with the collar cut out—the one I used to sleep in when he wasn't home. Home. Something twisted in my gut.

"And here's the kicker." His voice caught. "I thought performing was my calling, food for my soul—all that I would need. I was wrong."

A tear trickled down my cheek. I didn't wipe it away.

"I knew it the minute I left. I've spent the last couple of months trying to run from the truth, but I can't. Lucky, you are my tether. Without you I am adrift, at the mercy of the tides of life, lost. You are the words to my melody. You give me meaning."

I took a ragged breath and drained the last of my drink in one gulp, then slammed the glass on the desk.

"I love you," Teddie said. He'd always said it so easily, while I had stumbled over the words. "I need you more than you can imagine. And I am so very sorry I hurt you. I pray that someday you can find it in your heart to forgive me."

Forgiveness. There was that word again.

"You know my parents; stupidity runs in the

family. Let me back in, Lucky. Please. I won't hurt you. Not this time. That I promise."

He'd promised that the first time.

The line went dead. The machine beeped. The message was complete.

Men. Can't live with them, can't shoot them with a gun. Well, today had proven that sometimes you can, but that wasn't in the cards for Teddie. What had the Big Boss said? The man worth having would never make you cry?

As emotion overwhelmed me, I buried my face in my hands, fighting it. But I didn't have any fight left. Relinquishing myself to the tears, I cried. For me. For Teddie. For what we'd had, for what we had lost, and for what we would never have again.

Chapter

TWELVE

♡

*L*ike a diver struggling to reach the surface, I swam toward the light, pushing the darkness away. Slowly, awareness returned. For a moment I didn't know where I was—drop cloth, shrouded furniture, all illuminated by light filtering in from the room beyond. A hole in the wall. A single lightbulb on a cord.

My office.

What was I doing here? Apparently I had fallen asleep on the couch. Tentatively I moved, stretching first one arm, then the other. Man, I was too old for this. My joints creaked in protest. My neck would punish me with a headache later.

In the windowless, eternal half-light, I had no idea what time it was. I pushed myself to a seated position; I didn't dare stand until the feeling returned to my left foot. Groping for my phone, I found it firmly affixed to my hip and tugged at it. I didn't remember putting it back in its holster, but I must have. When it came free, I held it up and squinted at it.

Seven A.M. One hour to pull myself together, find my car, and meet Jeremy for breakfast halfway across town—piece of cake.

After far too long under the assault of a seriously hot shower, some of the kinks in my muscles loosened. A few more minutes and I'd be able to turn my head fully in each direction—a small thing, but right now I'd take all the positives I could find. Murders awaited and I needed to stoke my fortitude— however one did that. I was making it up as I went.

"Lucky? Are you in here?"

The familiar voice put a smile in my heart. "In here."

"Fuck." Flash let loose the epithet as she collided with something solid. "What the hell are you doing taking a shower in your office? You have a perfectly wonderful one upstairs. I've been looking for you all over. Are you hiding from someone?"

Reluctantly, I killed the water. After wrapping a towel around myself, then squeezing the water from my hair, I stepped out of the shower. Steam filled the small bathroom and I could just make out the filmy visage of my good friend peering through the doorway. "Yeah, I'm hiding from myself."

"How's that going?"

"Not so good. I seem to know all my best hiding places." With a hand towel I wiped the fog from the mirror. "Apparently so do you."

"If I admitted how long it has taken to find you, my rep as an investigative reporter would go down the crapper." Flash moved into the small room, lowered the cover on the toilet, and took her position on the throne.

Flash and I went way back—if she wasn't my best friend (and I suspected she was), then she was my longest-running friendship. We'd met while attending UNLV back before the earth was cool when each day had held the promise of untold adventures. Of course, being who we are, we'd found a few. I'd kept us out of jail and Flash, who was known then as Fredericka Gordon ("Flash" was pinned on her after an interesting night with a busload of NBA players), kept our names and photographs out of the paper and off the eleven o'clock news. We'd been watching each other's backs ever since.

From the looks of her, Flash was in total man-killer mode today. Like lava from Vesuvius, her bright red hair erupted from the top of her head in a cascade of unruly curls. And she was dolled up—

from her war paint to her six-inch heels, which still put her barely a few inches over five feet. Her double Denvers threatened to explode out of a threadbare tee shirt advertising the last tour of the Grateful Dead. I knew where she'd gotten that—hidden under Miss P's Iowa exterior lurked a die-hard Dead Head who still refused to tell me whether she had really slept with Jerry Garcia.

Flash could've bought the Lycra mini at any hooker emporium on Trop. Her pink nails, diamond loops, and Chanel J12 encrusted in diamonds added a touch of class—not nearly enough, but a touch, and that made me suspicious.

"Where are you headed looking like that? Or are you on your way home?" I leaned in to the mirror to examine my reflection. Bad idea.

"Today's a shopping day." Flash crossed her legs and leaned back, her elbows resting on the top of the toilet tank. The limitations of physics made it impossible for her to cross her arms over her chest. "Starbucks, nine A.M."

"I may not be fashion-forward, but shopping at Starbucks?"

"I made it to the go-see. My first time ever." Even though she seemed to be using a dead language or something, she looked pleased.

"Is the appropriate response, 'good for you'? I'm a bit unclear." I let the towel fall to the floor—I never could keep the damned things up anyway—and I began applying my mask for the day.

"Lucky, you can't be serious." Flash looked at me

with amusement and pity—her normal expression when dealing with me, so I didn't take it personally. "Online dating? Hello?"

"But of course. How silly of me."

"Don't tell me you've never tried it." Flash actually sounded serious. I opened my mouth to fire off a brilliant retort, but Flash stopped me with a raised hand. "I forgot, it's you I'm talking about, Miss All-Work-and-No-Play."

"Should I ask what a 'go-see' is, or would I be shocked?"

That got a howl out of Flash. She had a great, bawdy laugh—sexy with a hint of naughty—that men loved. "It's not what you think. I'm meeting a guy for coffee. Up to now we've just exchanged e-mails."

"And exaggerated profiles."

Flash looked at me with big eyes. "Why do men do that?"

"Same reason they buy sports cars they have to squeeze into."

"Compensating." Flash nodded sagely. "Well, I hope this guy is real."

"I'm sure he's real, the question is a real what?"

"He might even be The One." Flash said it with the reverence of a true believer contemplating the Second Coming.

"Please." I snorted. "To you, fishing for men is strictly catch and release."

She let loose another of those infectious laughs. This time I laughed with her. It felt good to laugh—

until I almost blinded my right eye with the mascara wand. "Damn. I feel as phony as a kid playing dress up."

"If you pretend long enough, it becomes real."

I didn't ask my friend to elaborate on what was a very profound observation. Although Flash was bimbo on the outside, she was a curious combination of Einstein and Freud on the inside. I wasn't sure I could handle her full explanation—not today.

"So, not that I'm not thrilled to share my bathroom with you, but to what do I owe the honor?" A little lipstick in a subtle gloss of pink, smoky gray on my eyelids, and I was done.

"I got my marching orders from Miss P on the Shady Slim Grady story. Another byline thanks to you—above the fold even. He was a bit of a Vegas creation, you know. I think you'll be pleased with how I handled it."

"With a deft touch, I'm sure." I opened the folding door to my closet and perused my emergency wardrobe. Not much to choose from—too many recent emergencies, too little recovery time. "The Big Boss will be pleased."

"I figure we're even." Flash moved to stand next to me. She reached in and extracted two hangers, which she thrust at me. "Here, you need some attitude today. I can see it in your eyes."

A hot pink boat-necked sweater that sagged seductively off one shoulder and a pair of silver satin pencil-leg pants. I raised an eyebrow at her. "The knock-me-down-and-fuck-me Jimmy Choos and pink lace bra and undies?"

"You rock that and the world is yours."

"That might be overstating, but I'm never one to turn my back on unbridled optimism." I set to work putting the outer me together. The inner me was what it was and I didn't think anything as simple as kick-ass lingerie would fix it.

When I'd finished, I turned to my friend, who nodded her approval. "Okay, we've gone through the niceties, why are you really here?" I raised my hand before Flash could jump in. "Wait, let me guess. You want the skinny on one dead girl on a Ferrari."

Flash's voice dropped to a conspiratorial whisper. "Is that not the best?"

I turned and walked out of the bathroom and went in search of the Jimmy Choos. "Perspectives probably differ on that."

Flash seemed not to have heard as she followed me into my office then deposited her ample backside in one of the chairs in front of my desk. "I mean, what a way to go. If it'd been me, the only thing that would've made it better was if I'd spent my last hours fucking Hugh Jackman."

Words failed me as I stared at my friend, so I leaned down and dug through the bottom desk drawer—the last place I'd seen those shoes. I saw a glint of silver. Hooking my finger around a strap, I pulled. One shoe came free. I held it up in victory as I fished for the other. "We all have our little fantasies. Frankly, yours scare the hell out of me."

"Poo." She waved her hand as if shooing away a fly. "But I'm getting off topic. What can you tell me?"

When I didn't respond immediately, she leaned forward and snapped her fingers in my face. "Come on. Dead girl. Ferrari. Hello?"

Shoes in hand, I resurfaced. With numerous straps and buckles, the shoes would take me a while. I might as well use the time to fill her in. What could it hurt? If she took the story and ran with it, maybe, just maybe, it might make somebody nervous. Nervous enough to show their hand. "I got twenty minutes and it's a heck of a story, so listen and listen good."

TEN minutes by Ferrari, Jamm's Restaurant lurked half hidden in a strip mall on Rainbow just south of the Ninety-five. Traffic was light and I let the horses run while my thoughts struggled to keep up. After all these years I should have known better than to tackle Flash before being fully caffeinated. After a nonstop grilling, I felt like a run-out racehorse, put away wet—tired, stiff, and in need of a good meal.

Flash, on the other hand, had bolted out of my office like the race favorite with the bit in her teeth, leaving me not only choking on dust but with the distinct impression that she liked Dane even more now that he had a wife. Dr. Donner, the chief coconut-cracker we kept on retainer to try to keep our entertainers on the functional side of crazy, would have a field day with her. Of course, I'm sure he'd love to crack my nut as well, but that would never happen. I wasn't convinced that crazy wasn't a good way to go.

Self-delusion: a sugar coating on the bitter pill of reality.

Flash was my sister from another mother, but her observations and choices usually left me praying someone would throw me a rope. Today was no exception.

Jeremy's black Hummer squatted in a space at the back of the parking lot—two spaces, actually. Wheeling in beside him, I angled the Ferrari across another two spaces and killed the engine. As I climbed out and shut the door, I paused, running my hand over the smooth metal. There was something about a fine sports car—a precision instrument designed to assault the highways, delivering the escape of an all-consuming task. A few minutes behind the wheel of the Ferrari lightened my load. Someday, I'd point that car toward points unknown and never look back.

Today wasn't that day, so I parked that dream and turned to the task at hand. Kathy waved to me as I pushed through the door. "He's in the booth by the window—Sandy's section. Shirley's off today."

Sandy apparently had seen me walk in. A tall, thin woman with a ready smile and long strawberry-blond hair pulled back into a tail arrived at the booth the same time I did with a cup of steaming coffee in her hand. "You want your usual scramble and pot of cinnamon bread?" she asked as she set the mug on the table.

"I am a creature of habit. Eggs, bacon, spinach, and mushrooms." I slid in across from Jeremy and began sweetening and whitening the dark witch's brew. "And keep the coffee coming, I'm running from the back of the pack this morning."

"You got it. Jeremy, what'll it be?"

"Bangers and mash?"

"Honey, the cook would have a coronary—you know what they say about English food. How about a nice American heart attack on a plate? Chicken fried steak, perhaps?"

Jeremy looked a little ruffled—so unlike him. He pushed the menu toward her without opening it. "A couple of eggs, over any way the cook wants to make them. And a ham steak."

"The boy's off his feed," Sandy said, turning to me, then she bounded away to greet another table full of new friends.

"She's right." I took a test sip of my coffee, then added more milk. "Any leads on the red contact lenses?"

Jeremy brightened just a little. "Actually, you're in luck. My crew combed the town and came up empty-handed. So I played one more card. I've got this friend at Nellis . . ."

"The Air Force? How do they factor in all of this?"

"Not Air Force specifically. My friend works at the medical center—they treat all the branches."

"I knew that," I groused.

"We got someone up there who will swear a woman fitting Sylvie Dane's description came in two days ago with a letter and she left with a set of red contact lenses."

"The implication, which is all we have, I might add, is that she was legit, working some government angle." I breathed in deeply as Sandy walked by with a tray of bread hot out of the oven. "I find that ludicrous."

"An emotional reaction." Jeremy gave me a stern look.

"Yes, an emotional reaction." I wilted. I had no idea why making Sylvie out to be a bad guy was so appealing—that sort of thing was beneath the me I wanted to be. "Curiously enough, Cole mentioned to me that he had the impression that Sylvie worked in law enforcement. Don't know if the two are related, but either she was a consistent liar—which is a distinct possibility—or she was one of the good guys. Either way, I don't need to tell you that we are long on suppositions and real short on proof."

Jeremy's shoulders drooped. "You don't have to tell me. And to top that, the cops have run me ragged looking for Dane. As if I would know where he is." Jeremy leaned back in the booth and swiveled his head like a fighter loosening his muscles before the championship fight. He put his hands flat on the table, took a deep breath, then raised his eyes to mine—they were as bloodshot as a drunk's after a bender. "Did you know he was under investigation by the Gaming Control Board?"

I didn't miss a beat—which had me worried. Apparently nothing about Dane surprised me anymore. "Of course he is. Murder is so ho-hum these days.

Guess he needed to embellish his résumé. What exactly are they investigating?"

"Monetary improprieties."

I pursed my lips downward. "So pedestrian. You'd think our boy would've aimed higher."

"He is a bit of an overachiever." Jeremy seemed to relax a little. Nothing like humor to diffuse the tension—except I didn't find any of this particularly amusing.

Dane had worked for us in Security, but he'd been hired by the Big Boss so we could keep an eye on him—I don't think anyone had paid a lot of attention to his particulars. "Is the case still open?"

"They wanted to see my cards, not show me theirs." Jeremy ran a hand through his hair.

I felt nothing. Letting the bad stuff numb me to life's little pleasures was not a good thing. I needed to work on that—but balance usually proved elusive in my world.

"One can assume the case is still open, though," Jeremy offered as an afterthought. "If it was closed, they either would've arrested him or moved on, so why bring it up?"

"I haven't a clue. If there was any part of anything that has happened over the last couple of days that I understood, believe me, I'd tell you." Too tired to reach across the table to give his hand a comforting squeeze, I didn't bother. "I don't have to tell you how much trouble he's in."

Jeremy nodded, those gold-flecked eyes dark and serious.

"I need you to tell me where he is." My coffee held a light brown color—I might have overdone it on the warm milk.

"What makes you think I know?"

"A friend in need. If I was him, I'd turn to you—you're the best friend he's got."

"Along with you. But that'd be obvious, though, don't you think?" Jeremy stared into his coffee mug, which he held cradled in both hands as if trying to draw strength from its warmth, or insight from its murky depths.

I could tell him neither worked well. "You don't know?"

"I haven't laid eyes on the bloke since before his wife was killed."

We both fell silent as Sandy arrived with our food. I guess we gave off a vibe or something—she slid our plates in front of us without a word, then beat a hasty retreat.

"You know him better than I do," Jeremy said as he grabbed a knife and attacked his ham. "Does he have any other place to go?"

Overcome with a sudden, intense hunger—I couldn't remember the last time I'd had any solid food—I peeled off a chunk of warm, gooey bread and stuffed it in my mouth. Vices were my thing and, in this carb-conscious world, bread was at the top of the list. Another chunk followed the first as I savored the sin. As the sugar hit my bloodstream, the brain cells fired and the light came on. It didn't take me long—another place? Of course! Granted, it was a long shot, but long shots were all I had, so I went with it.

"Eat up, Aussie boy. You wouldn't happen to know anything about automatic weapons, would you?"

"**ARE** you going to tell me where we're going?" Jeremy asked as he rode shotgun in the Ferrari. We needed to move fast and his Hummer wasn't exactly built for speed, so we'd left it. "I don't think I've bolted my food that fast since I battled with a bunch of Boy Scouts. And, for the record, I'm fluent in all calibers."

"Then you'll feel right at home in this toy store." When I hit the ramp onto the Ninety-five, I hit the gas. "Dane took me there once—to teach me how to shoot." I didn't know how many Gs one could pull in a Ferrari, but I intended to test the limits. Dane had a jump on us, but five hundred horses could close the gap.

Of course, I hadn't planned on rush hour. The spaghetti bowl was a nightmare with everyone jockeying for position to head south on the Fifteen. So I maneuvered to the left and took the 515 around the east side of town—a bit out of the way, but not by much. The wind whistled past, cocooning us between twin rushing streams as the car cleaved through the dry air like an arrow shot from Robin Hood's bow. Vibration from the engine mounted directly behind my shoulders reverberated through me, accelerating my heart rate, setting me free. An adrenaline junkie,

I longed for the rush, waited for it, needed it. Hands clutching the steering wheel, my fingers worked the paddle shifters, the transitions so smooth I almost didn't miss the clutch . . . almost. As the speed increased, the world fell away as if I could outrun the past and avoid the future, leaving only the now. Even if only for a while, it was enough.

Jeremy took his eyes off the road for a split second to shoot me a glance, although I noticed he didn't loosen his white-knuckled grip on the armrest. "Dane wanted to teach you how to shoot? That's rare. Everyone knows that's part of the Nevada citizenship test." He exaggerated, but not by much.

"That cowboy has a few things to learn." I raised my voice slightly to be heard over the wind and the machine. "But the fact that he knows I can perforate his hide and not think twice isn't an altogether bad thing." I downshifted, my left foot instinctively seeking the clutch but finding none, and blasted around a truck pulling three top loaders full of stone and barely making thirty miles an hour in a sixty-five zone. "Those things ought to be outlawed—talk about dangerous."

"You on the loose with ammo and an attitude ranks right up there," Jeremy continued.

I shot him a grin as the speedometer once again leaped past a hundred. I wanted to say "'Dangerous' is my middle name," but I didn't have any silly flirt left in me—another bad sign.

"Don't you worry about the cops?"

A reasonable question considering I was weaving

in and out of traffic as if it were an obstacle course. And, since he was a fixture in my office, I kept forgetting Jeremy was still pretty new to town. "Considering all the other things I have to worry about, the cops don't even make the top ten. If they want me, they'll have to catch me."

The cops and me, we went way back, but Jeremy didn't need to know that. Speeding tickets really didn't get them all lathered up anyway, unless it was the end of the month and they hadn't met their quota. Regardless, I regularly did favors for most of them, from the brass right down to the lowliest cop patrolling the Strip on a Schwinn—show tickets for special occasions or a nice meal out with the wife or girlfriend, but preferably not both at the same time—even I had my limits. So when I blew by a radar trap in the Ferrari, they usually just waved.

One lone pickup occupied a spot in the parking lot behind The Gun Store when I angled the Ferrari over the grade up from the road into the lot and killed the engine. A cinder-block building painted white against the unrelenting assault of the desert sun, the gun store looked like most of the other buildings along this section of Tropicana Boulevard. While not completely gone to seed, the neighborhood had certainly seen better days—some of the storefronts were shuttered, but several still clung valiantly to the hope of returning prosperity.

I didn't check the license plate of the pickup—I'd seen it before. A vanity plate, it read SHOOTR.

"Food, then firearms. You do know how to show a guy a good time." Jeremy unfolded himself from the low-slung car, eased the door shut as if he were handling Baccarat, which made me grin, then followed me around to the front of the building. "Teddie is a fool." At the look on my face, he quickly recovered. "Sorry, but he is."

"You won't get any disagreement from me, but thank you."

He eyed me for a minute, one eye shut against the glare of the sun, then he turned his attention to the building in front of us. "What is this place?"

"A mercenary's paradise. For a modest fee, you can throw lead with the weapon of your choice from a Glock to an Uzi and everything in between." Business hours were still an hour away. I raised my fist, but before I could knock, the door opened.

"The Captain figured you might show up here," Shooter Moran said with a smile that didn't chase the wary look from his eyes. Tall, sporting appropriate military muscles, with dirty blond hair worn military short, a shy smile, and a guarded manner, Shooter didn't ooze the warmth of a friend, but he didn't seem like a foe either—although I had no illusions as to where his allegiance would fall if forced to choose.

"He did, did he?" I pushed past Dane's former army buddy—they both had been Special Forces or Rangers or something. I didn't know which and I didn't know the difference. I only knew they'd seen and done stuff I couldn't even imagine, had I wanted to. Shooter always referred to Dane as the Captain, so I figured Dane must've had him by a few rungs on the food chain, not that it mattered a whit out here in the cold reality of civilian life, where money mattered far more than honor or bravery . . . or loyalty. But I bet those mattered to Shooter. In fact, I was counting on it.

"Shooter, this is Jeremy Whitlock, Dane's employer and friend. Jeremy, Shooter Moran."

The men shook hands, sizing each other up—one of the male friendship rituals I found particularly amusing. I could almost see their white knuckles as they tensed their arms and squeezed.

"Okay, you both pegged the testosterone meter and passed the manly-man test. Can we move on? I feel Father Time breathing down my neck." Both men gave me their attention, which surprised me, but I wasn't about to look a gift horse in the mouth. "Is Dane here?" I asked, peering around Shooter into the shooting bays, which were dark and silent—no Dane.

"Was," Shooter said, his eyes swiveling to Jeremy. "Dane said you were straight up."

"What else did Dane say?" I asked, putting myself between the two men and eye to eye with Shooter Moran. I actually had him by an inch or two, which gave me a false sense of security.

"He said to not look for him."

"Bullshit."

"He said you'd say that, too." Shooter shot me a fleeting grin. "The Captain's in a heap a hurt, isn't he?" The feral look of the hunter flashed in his eyes, replacing the wariness.

"Big-time. He needs our help. Although I don't know the details, I get the feeling he saved your ass in Iraq or Afghanistan, or some other god-forsaken shit hole. Now's the time for you to return the favor." I wanted to say semper fi and all of that, but that was the marines and I was pretty sure that would be crossing some invisible boundary—the branches of the service didn't cross-pollinate. The army had something similar, everyone needed a battle cry, I just didn't know what it was. I resisted the whole all-for-one-and-one-for-all thing as a bit dated.

"What can I do?" Shooter asked, his face a mask, his eyes dark and blank.

"You can start by telling us where he is," Jeremy said.

"I really don't know." Shooter glanced at him, then turned back to me. "Believe me."

I eyed him for a moment. I had no idea whether he was telling me the truth or feeding me a line—did they teach that in army school? "Say I believe you, for now. Why did Dane come here? He must've had a reason."

Shooter chewed on his bottom lip as his eyes skittered away. "He wanted a piece."

"You sold him a gun? The guy is wanted in connection with a murder and you sold him a gun?" My voice rose despite my best efforts to keep my tone low with a hint of menace. I stepped into Shooter. I don't know what I planned to do—wring his neck, pummel him into submission—irrational thoughts. The guy probably knew fifteen ways to kill me with only the things that were within easy reach.

Jeremy grabbed my arm, stopping me. "Lucky."

After taking several deep breaths and counting to twenty—twice—I said, "Okay, okay." I looked at Shooter. I felt my eyes go all squinty—not a good sign. The folks who knew me well usually turned and ran when my eyes got all squinty. Shooter stood his ground. "What did you sell him?"

"A beat-up Beretta nine millimeter."

"Registered?" I glanced at Jeremy—he understood. If not, the gun would be untraceable.

Shooter nodded.

"Serial number?" I asked, just to be sure.

Shooter nodded. "Of course."

I'm not sure whether that made me feel better or worse. The fact that Dane intended to shoot someone and he didn't care if they could trace the gun back to him didn't bode well. Of course, none of this gave me a warm fuzzy.

I really couldn't blame Shooter for selling Dane the gun—he'd done a friend a favor. The way Shooter saw it, it was the least he could do—a debt owed, a debt paid. And nothing changed the fact that someone had killed Dane's wife. And, Dane being who he was, was going after them, taking matters into his own hands—if all of this was as it appeared to be. And if roles were reversed, I couldn't guarantee I wouldn't do the same.

"Can you tell us anything? Did Dane give you any information? Did he say anything that could put us on, if not his track, then the killer's?"

"He was too smart for that." Shooter's hands balled into fists as his shoulders hunched up around his ears. He might have been good at controlling his frustration, but he sucked at hiding it. "He said he wouldn't pull me into it. Can you believe it? After all the shit we've been through?"

"I can believe it." The Lone Ranger, great. Dane would probably get himself killed, which I was feeling ambivalent about at this particular moment. "What can you tell us about his wife?"

Shooter pulled a stool from behind the counter and straddled it. "Sylvie," he said, his voice flat, resigned. He shook his head.

"The one and only, unless there were others?"

"No others." Shooter shook his head. "She was enough."

"You knew her?" Jeremy interjected.

Shooter shifted his attention and he visibly relaxed. Guys talking about women, locker-room talk. I got it. Relinquishing the lead to Jeremy, I stepped into the background.

"Sure. I never really got that relationship. I mean I did and I didn't, you know?" Shooter turned away from me, putting his back to me. "She was one exceptional piece of ass, you know?" He shifted on the stool. "Excuse me, ma'am," he threw over his shoulder as an afterthought.

Somehow that made me smile, just a little, and it broke the tension. Either we'd be in time to rescue Dane from his own stupidity, assuming that was even possible, or we wouldn't. He was a big boy. My job was to ensure no more dead bodies turned up at the Babylon. And that was proving to be more difficult than I had imagined.

Jeremy nodded at Shooter, encouraging him to continue.

"It started out great, all piss and vinegar and white-hot sex," Shooter said, his voice growing soft, drifting into the past.

I resisted pointing out that his definition of a great relationship and mine were a wee bit off. I didn't think it would be helpful.

"Then, I don't know, it sorta went screwy, you know?" He swiveled to look at me, catching me off guard. I nodded, but I hadn't a clue. "I don't know where it went off the tracks, but there was something . . ." Shooter trailed off as his look grew distant.

"Something?" I prompted, ignoring Jeremy's look. I knew "shut up" when I saw it.

"Yeah, even though she drove him nuts, he couldn't let her go. Know what I mean?"

"He couldn't let her go?" My heart sank. "What does that mean?"

"He kept telling her she needed to quit. To get out of the line of fire. To stop tilting at windmills, I believe was how he put it."

"Out of the line of fire?" I asked. "Wasn't she just a girl looking for a ride to the States?"

Shooter turned his full attention to me. "Ma'am, I don't know who told you that, but whoever it was, he was the biggest liar."

I resisted telling him that Dane had painted that picture of his wife. "If not that, then what was she doing in Afghanistan?"

"Working with the CIA."

Jeremy and I, neither one of us could speak for a moment as we stared at Shooter.

He didn't seem to be bothered by our looks of disbelief. "Dane wanted her to quit—a woman's place is in the home and that sort of thing. They used to have the most god-awful fights."

"I can imagine," I choked out between clenched teeth as my eyes threatened to go slitty again. A woman's place . . . I developed a grudging respect for Sylvie Dane's self-control—I would've been hard-pressed to resist pulling the trigger.

"When she left him, he was really pissed."

"Pissed enough to kill her?"

Shooter stopped and glared at me. "You oughta know the answer to that. You're friends of his, right? Friends. You understand?"

Yeah, light was dawning. Dane carried a torch and had a serious case of red-ass. Had he killed his wife? And had someone witnessed it? Is that what all this was about? Silencing a witness?

My heart raced and sweat beaded on my upper

lip as I thought through the possibilities. Someone gave Dane those scratches on his cheek and apparently, if the coroner was right and there was no trace under her nails, it wasn't Sylvie. Dane had time to clean the murder scene, but did he have enough time and skill to get rid of all the evidence? Who knew? And if he had killed his wife because of a personal dispute, what had happened to the Stoneman? And why? Who knew? I sure didn't. But one thing I was absolutely sure of, I'd better figure it out . . . and quick.

"So, where do we go from here?" Shooter asked.

I thought for a moment. "Well, we got three dead bodies, two murdered for sure, and the only real connection is poker. Why don't we start there?"

"Can you give us a direction?" Jeremy asked.

"Start turning over stones and see what crawls out." I chewed on my lip as I thought for a moment. "And for God's sake, find Dane before he digs himself in so deep it'll take a backhoe to get him out."

Thankfully, Jeremy knew me well enough not to require an explanation. He turned to Shooter. "You in, Moran?"

Shooter reached behind the counter and grabbed a handgun—it looked like an old Colt. He tucked it in his belt at the small of his back, then pulled his shirt-tail over it. "Count me in." Vengeance lit his eyes.

Great, now we had two crazies, locked and loaded and looking for justice.

. . .

TRAFFIC had thinned by the time Jeremy and I re-traced our steps back to Jamm's to retrieve his truck—there's something about a Hummer that cries out for a fifty-caliber gun mounted on the roof. Not a bad idea, all things considered, but I resisted sug-gesting it as I bid Jeremy farewell and headed to the office. Lost in thought, he didn't tell me where he was going and I didn't ask. With him, the less I knew, the better. He'd been known to cross a line or two in the name of justice—a fact I appreciated, but I didn't want the details. Becoming an accessory after the fact wouldn't enhance my résumé.

Miss P looked up when I staggered through the office door—the Jimmy Choos weren't exactly easy to walk in. For some reason, her presence bothered me. Since I'd used my couch as my bed last night, finding people in my office was like finding uninvited guests in my house—except she belonged there. Re-gardless, the whole thing got under my skin. Unrea-sonable, I know. Clearly I was swinging at the end of my rope. Nothing made sense.

"Teddie," she started.

I silenced her with a deadly look.

"Okay," she continued as she followed me through the construction zone into my little corner of the world. "Jean-Charles, is that better?" She lev-eled her gaze over the top of her cheaters at me.

"I'm not sure." I plopped down in my desk chair. "Why do I get the feeling that no matter what I say, it will be the wrong thing?"

"I have no idea." Miss P sat on the edge of the chair across from me. She perched like a bird, dainty and delicate, pecking away. "There were fourteen messages on the machine this morning from the person I am not supposed to mention, and one from a certain French chef wondering why you didn't sleep at home last night. He is looking for you and he is worried."

"Angry?"

"Not that I could tell. Just curious." Miss P glanced up, waiting, as if I should offer an explanation.

Part of me wanted him to be angry, the other part was afraid of the commitment that that indicated—conflicted to the end. At least I'm consistent. I struggled to keep a bland expression in light of her scowl and I refused to be goaded into providing her what she wanted. From now on, my life would be a closed book. Today was her day for disappointment; I refused to feel bad about it. In fact, I refused to feel anything. Avoidance, so helpful. "Is that all?"

"Of course not." She scowled as she read from the notepad she held in her lap. "Miss Becky-Sue stopped by. She said you told her to. Apparently Shady Slim is giving one last party—a Celebration of Life . . ." Miss P consulted her notepad, then looked up, amusement curling her lips into a bow. "Vegas themed. Miss Becky-Sue wants everything from the Mexican National Circus, which happens to be in town, to Mr. Magic himself, Marik Kovalenko, who is not."

"Do you want me to handle that?" I asked hopefully. "Something to do that doesn't involve dead bodies would be wonderful."

"I've got Brandy on it." She glanced up. "Don't worry, Cole is sleeping and Jeremy is posting some guy named Shooter to stand guard outside his door."

I nodded, mollified for the moment.

Miss P pushed her glasses up the bridge of her nose and continued reading from her notes. "For some reason, Brandy seems to be able to handle Miss Becky-Sue. I don't know what to make of it."

"It won't last." Experience had taught me that much. When I'd first met Miss Becky-Sue, I'd been young and impressionable, too. "Anything else?"

"Mr. Watalsky asked if you could meet him in the Poker Room any time after noon—apparently the cops thought he wouldn't go anywhere. I told him yes. Your mother called to remind you about her doctor's appointment tomorrow afternoon at four— she said she was giving you fair warning—she's counting on you."

Miss P must've seen my eyebrows snap down and my stellar mood heading further south as she started reading faster. "The media frenzy is starting as the poker folks arrive, but Brandy and I have it covered. The tournament starts tomorrow, you know. There'll be the warm-up game tonight. Let some of the names perform for the crowd before the stakes get high. We're taking care of that, too."

"Can't you be a bit less efficient?" I was a bit

player in a melodrama. Either I sat back and found amusement in my plight or I . . . what? I needed to get over myself. I opted to relax, take a deep breath, and try to smile at my fearless co-worker, who I'd best remember was very good at keeping my ass out of the fire, even though she liked to take a bite out of it from time to time.

"As titular head of this outfit, isn't it your job to delegate?" Miss P said, her manner a bit less wary. She knew my bark was 90 percent bullshit. "Besides, don't you have a hotel to build or something?"

"Ah yes, a mere trifle." I waved my hand expansively. "Demolition has started. The plans are in place and ready to go. Work has begun on Jean-Charles's kitchen, so he is somewhat mollified at the moment. Now, while all the balls are in the air, I'm thinking about relinquishing the crown and returning to serfdom—things were a lot more straightforward at the bottom of the food chain."

"We all would be wise to carefully consider what we ask for." She out-grinned my glare. "I'm sorry, I couldn't resist—it's so much fun to poke at you when you're all huffy." She rose to go, brushing down her skirt—why she decided to wear all white was beyond me. "Now, I know a chef in need of a hug and some reassurance—he's been very patient, if you ask me."

"I didn't."

"Yes, well, you know me. Offering unsolicited advice is my gift. Best of intentions, I assure you."

"I know. Thanks." I pushed myself back from the desk. "I assume you know where Jean-Charles is?"

"In the kitchen." We both said in unison.

When life got tough, Jean-Charles cooked.

Chapter

THIRTEEN

♡

"**A**re you hungry?" Jean-Charles had his back to me, yet he knew the minute I walked into the kitchen. As I leaned in to kiss him, he reached back, touching my cheek.

The jolt of his touch warmed me, chasing dread and death away. My heart softened just a little.

"Are you all right?" he asked. No recriminations lurked in the simple question. No games. I felt curiously untethered, yet at peace.

"Mmm." I lingered, enjoying the taste of him, the hint of exotic cologne underneath the eau de onion and hamburger. "That's debatable."

"I looked for you last night before I went home. It was late. You weren't at your apartment." He didn't even toss an accusatory glance my way. Instead he focused on the hamburgers sizzling over the coals, even though he could handle the few orders in front of him with his eyes shut.

"You would've found me if you'd checked my office."

"You were working?" He seemed shocked—guess he hadn't considered that angle, although it seemed pretty obvious to me.

"No, sleeping. I was working, then fell asleep on the couch—too tired to trudge upstairs, I guess." Needing the connection, I nuzzled his neck. "You didn't call?"

As I nibbled on his ear, I felt him shiver. "You will stop that." He had the charming habit of framing questions as if he were giving orders.

"I think not." I actually giggled when he laid the spatula down and turned to catch me in a hug. Me. Giggling! I'm not sure how I felt about that . . . I mean, besides somewhat giddy and marginally morti-fied.

"Then you will be prepared for the punishment," he whispered before his lips captured mine.

Bending my body, molding it to his, I lost myself in his kiss. Like a flame consuming oxygen, he left me breathless, my heart pounding, liquid fire racing through my veins. Wanting him, needing him, draw-ing life from him . . . giving it in return. No drama. No games. It couldn't last.

When I came up for air, Rinaldo shot me a wink as he stepped in to minister to the orders. I'd never fully appreciated his handiness before.

"Why didn't you call? I would've shared my couch."

Jean-Charles pulled back, clearly equally as

affected, which was a good thing . . . no, a great thing. He kept his arms around me. "I was thinking it was so late. Perhaps you were with another?"

"I'm not sure whether that is flattering or insulting." I worked my arms around his waist and held tight. "Really, another? Don't you know me well enough by now?"

"I did not wish to presume."

"Presuming is good, but getting it all out on the table is better."

My Frenchman looked confused as he tripped over another English idiom.

"What is it you want from me?" I asked, not really afraid of the answer. Time had come for me to seize life. Teddie had moved on, although now he was feeling remorse over hurting my feelings, and now he wanted back in. I'd let him off the hook . . . set him free. "Tell me."

"I want you," Jean-Charles said simply.

"I'm a one-guy gal, and I don't share."

"This is good. I am thinking you will be more than enough." He leaned in for another kiss, deeper this time—heat, expectation . . . and a promise.

As fate would have it, a stolen moment was all we had. The lunch crowd descended, demanding Jean-Charles's attention and somewhere in the mess of my life, I had a job to do.

River Watalsky had said he would be in the Poker Room any time after noon.

It was noon straight up.

Time to find out if Mr. Watalsky was a man of his word.

NOON was early for poker, a game of the dark, its battles best fought in the wee hours of a new day. I found River Watalsky holding court at a table in the back, surrounded by lesser luminaries and wannabes. He looked comfortable in the reflected glow of adoration. I guess Romeo hadn't been too hard on him. Of course, a seasoned veteran around the tables, River Watalsky would have little trouble playing the young detective.

Despite his small, angry eyes, River Watalsky had a kind face and a thousand-candlepower smile, which he focused on me as I walked up and pulled out a chair.

"Lucky!" He stood and took my chair, holding it for me as I sat, then helping me scootch it closer to the table. Southern manners from a Mississippi boy. "It's been a coon's age since I laid eyes on you. How the heck are you?" Although he was teasing, he seemed genuinely pleased to see me. Gunfire, the ultimate bonding experience? Who knew?

"Still kickin' and grinnin', which wasn't a sure thing last night." I motioned to the cocktail waitress hovering nearby. "Diet Coke, please."

"Folks," River addressed his former audience. "I'm gonna need some space here. Me and the lady need private time, if you know what I mean." He gave them an exaggerated wink, which got a laugh and willing cooperation. The table cleared and we were alone—or at least no one lingered within earshot.

"So, sweets, it looks like you're wranglin' a bushel of snakes." Mixing metaphors was part of his charm, so I didn't mention it. River took a sip of a beverage that looked like scotch, but I knew it was watered-down iced tea with the absolute maximum amount of sugar the liquid could hold. Gamblers and their games. Today he sported a Hawaiian shirt, khaki slacks, neatly creased, and sandals—the only things missing were a mai tai with a cute little umbrella and a tan. His hair stuck straight from his head as if he'd stuck his finger in an electrical socket, or Romeo had some newfangled interrogation equipment I needed to know about.

Despite our late night getting caught in the cross-fire and the relatively early hour, Watalsky's cheeks were clean shaven, his eyes clear. He didn't look the worse for wear, which was more than I could brag about.

"You want to fill me in on that poker game last night?" I asked.

"How's that guy you plugged? Slurry?" River's eyes latched on to me—small dark holes, like the barrels of six-shooters.

So much for my ability to steer the conversation. I gave him a less than appreciative smile as my stomach fell around my feet. "He came through surgery, but he's still critical." I always thought shooting the bad guy would be a rush. I was wrong. Shooting another human hit me on a visceral level—bypassing rational thought and justification—punching me in the gut.

Watalsky took a sip of iced tea as he glanced over my shoulder. "Too bad. He'd be pretty interesting to talk to."

"Assuming you could get the truth out of him, which is a darn sight more than I'm getting out of you." I squirmed in my chair. "You didn't really go to that game to ferret out the cheaters from the previous night, did you?"

"Hon, I went to that poker game because your buddy Cole told me Slurry would be there. I wanted to know what was between him and the dead girl."

"Did he tell you?"

"You shot him before I had a chance to ask." Watalsky gave me sort of a humorous glare, which I thought captured it all.

"Was Slurry the only reason you were there?"

"Hell, no. I was trying to keep the bad guys from perforating the deaf kid."

"So you weren't surprised to see Cole there?"

"No, Frank put me onto him. Said he was the key to finding the girl." A startled look crossed his face and he clammed up.

"The girl?" I leaned in. "You were looking for her? For Frank DeLuca?"

His eyes focused on mine—I'd hit a nerve. He weighed what he said next—I could see it on his face, hear it in his measured words when he finally spoke. "Yeah, Frank was all hot and bothered to find her."

I waited while the waitress delivered my Diet Coke and arranged it to her satisfaction in front of me and departed with a wan smile. "Why?"

"Hell, I don't know." River fished in his pocket and came out with a pair of nail clippers. He began to methodically clip each nail, a habit I found irritating. "After that gal was laid out on his Ferrari, Frank was real shook, you know?"

"Understandable." I watched one clipping as it arced away until I lost it in the patterned carpet.

"Yeah." His eyes glanced off mine. "He grabbed me, told me I needed to find some girl. He didn't know what she looked like. Didn't tell me what for. So he wasn't real helpful. I got the impression he was throwing knives in the dark hoping he hit something."

"Really?" I grabbed the clippers from River, then placed them on the table. When he reached for them, one glare from me had him pulling his hand back as if he'd touched a hot coal. "Did he say how he knew there was a girl?"

"Something about a pair of shoes."

"Shoes. We have several pairs. You wouldn't happen to know what they looked like?"

"Hell, shoes are shoes. It's the legs that differentiate, if you know what I mean."

"So helpful, thanks." I'd have to corner Frank myself, which, for some reason, didn't scare me . . . a fact that probably *should* have scared me, but I wasn't getting butterflies from that either. Only a fool is impervious to fear. Fool that I am, I settled back, watching Watalsky closely as I turned the glass in my hand. "What were you supposed to do with the girl when you found her? And, come to think of it, how'd you know you found the right one?"

"She started flashing that necklace of Sylvie's around—figured it had to be her. If not, she at least had some info."

"And?"

"I was just supposed to call Frank when I had her."

"Did you?"

"Didn't have the time. You people showed up and bullets started flying."

I sipped my Diet Coke as I eyed him. He still appeared unperturbed—one cool customer. But he'd made several fortunes keeping a poker face. "Can you offer any enlightenment on the last poker game Sylvie Dane played in?"

"Enlightenment is a rare thing."

Taking a sip of my Coke, I eyed River as he feigned disinterest in whatever was happening over my shoulder. I resisted the urge to turn around to see for myself. "Why don't you give me your take on the poker game night before last?"

I didn't have to spell it out—he knew what I wanted. "Yeah, okay. The broad was good, real good. She knew exactly what she was doing."

"Marking cards, I got that much." I took another sip of Coke, this time wishing I'd gotten the fully loaded kind, and relished River's admiring grin. "What I can't figure is, if she was cheating, why did all the money go to Slurry?"

"I found that right curious as well." River nervously fingered a strand of beads around his neck—puka shells, how'd I miss those? "By the end of the evening, the whole table was wise to their game."

I resisted asking for some Meyer's dark rum to add to my Diet Coke, just to prove I could. "How do you know?"

"Several of them tried to bring the matter to the room manager's attention, but he didn't do nothin'. A' course you know what my opinion is of him?"

"Universal contempt. The Stoneman might have been an ass, but you can't fault his consistency." His opinion was irrelevant to Marvin at his point, but apparently he hadn't gotten the memo that the rumors of Marvin's demise were true.

"We don't tolerate vermin like that where I come from." He gave me a knowing look. "And they used to take care of fellas like that around here as well. There's tons of 'em buried in the desert. You know they find bones out there all the time."

"And they still require dental records to be included in your employment file, just in case," I added in a feeble attempt to stay in the game.

"You're shittin' me." River looked surprised.

"You turn up stuffed into the trunk of a Cadillac, burned beyond recognition, they've got to identify your body somehow." Adopting a nonchalance I didn't feel, I shrugged, then leaned back and glanced around the room to see if anyone was taking an interest in our conversation. When I was sure no one was, I continued, but I kept my voice low. "When you think about it, it doesn't seem so over-the-top. And by the way, someone took a dim view of the Poker Room manger. They fed him a lethal dose of poison and left him to rot in the garage. For a non-contact sport, poker is proving to be rather harmful to your health, wouldn't you say?"

"The Stoneman? He's dead?" River paled, his expression dead serious.

"Stone-cold. The Poker Room manager everyone loved to hate. Curious, isn't it?" Only one of the many curiosities of late.

"And Shady Slim," River mused.

Lost in thought, I'd almost forgotten about him. Romeo seemed convinced there was no foul play, but nothing about any of this was what it seemed, so I wasn't ready to accept such an easy out. Now I *really* wished I had some rum for my Diet Coke.

"The lights dimmed in the poker world when his ticket got punched." Watalsky's eyes turned dark, his expression serious. "You think him kicking the bucket is related to the other two?"

"I don't know if any of this is related or if all of it is simply a harmonic convergence of bad card karma." I leaned forward, dropping my voice further. "But these dead bodies are raining on my Vegas magic parade. I'm starting to take it personal."

"This is sorta your backyard." River swallowed hard. "If it's enlightenment you want, mind you, I'm not for sure. But if I was you, I'd ask that deaf kid. Hell of a player, but lately he's been snooping around like goddamn James Bond or somethin'."

COLE Weston wasn't in his room—or at least he didn't respond when I pressed the button that would flash a light signaling someone was at the door.

And Shooter Moran wasn't watching Cole's door. My thoughts were tumbling like pebbles carried in a strong current, but I could have sworn someone told me he was standing guard. The flush of anger competed with a cold dread as I grabbed my phone and pushed to talk.

Miss P drew the short straw.

"Where's Cole Weston?" I took a breath and forged ahead before she could respond. "Didn't someone tell me that that blockhead Moran was standing guard outside his door while he slept?"

"That's right."

"I'm standing outside Cole's door, Room fifteen-four-thirty-two, right?"

"Just a sec." Voices were muffled as she put a hand over the mouthpiece, which ticked me off. She wasn't gone long. "That's right, fifteen-four-thirty-two. Brandy checked him in herself. Shooter was there when she left."

"Moran. The moron. Where?" Then it hit me. He wasn't the moron. I was. Little Miss Fell-off-a-Turnip-Truck-Yesterday. I'd taken Moran at his word; I'd just forgotten where his allegiance lay.

Dane.

The cold ball of dread exploded.

"Double fuck!" I shut my phone, ending the call. Pulling my set of master keys out of my pocket, I let myself into Cole's room.

His bed didn't appear to have been slept in. No trash in the trashcans. No orders from room service. No half-eaten pizza. His toiletries untouched. His vibrating alarm clock still sitting on his bed waiting to jostle him awake.

And no kid.

Hands on my hips, I tapped one toe in semiconscious effort to rid myself of the nervous energy that put rocks in my stomach, tensed the muscles of my neck, and soured my already abysmal mood. I stood in the middle of his empty room waiting, hoping for some stroke of divine luck, some insight that I was previously blind to. The clock ticked loudly then flipped to another number as a minute expired. Laughter echoed down the hallway. A door slammed shut. The elevator dinged, then doors closed on the laughter, leaving an eerie quiet. Noise normally filled my world. Quiet echoed—I didn't like it

And I'd been beaten silly with a stupid stick. No great thoughts, connections, insights. The world was dark. Oz had spoken and I was found wanting. Inspiration was shining a light on someone else's parade. Not that I was surprised or anything.

I sagged onto Cole's bed and lay back. Afraid to close my eyes, I stared at the ceiling. The light fixture was some Byzantine thing of filigreed gold—I didn't like it.

What would Dane want with Cole? Information, but he didn't have to take him for that. So where did they go? Who were they looking for? A number of possibilities sprung to mind. The girl? DeLuca? Slurry was in a coma at the hospital under the watchful eyes of Metro.

Despite really concentrating, I came up empty. I wasn't Dane. I didn't know what his plan was . . . other than to catch a killer . . . or kill a witness. Yes, somehow that girl in the shoes had put herself in the vortex of this maddening maelstrom. Everyone was after her, and I had no idea where to look. I had a feeling Cole might have had a clue, but as usual, Dane was ahead of me.

And I'd hit another dead end.

The innocent phrase hung over my head like a black cloud, ominous and foreboding. The sun was up and everyone knew poker players were nocturnal creatures. Cole should have been in his hole, resting up. Nothing good could explain his absence. Well, maybe there was a good reason, but I couldn't think of one.

I only hoped the kid was having a better run of luck than me.

My eyelids sagged as I surrendered. On the verge of giving up, I gave in. No longer able to stuff my random thoughts into their compartments, they hammered in my head, beating me into submission. Most days, being me was pretty decent, darn good on occasion, but some days it sucked. Today was one of those days. A card-carrying Pollyanna, today even I found it next to impossible to find a toehold of peace on earth and goodwill toward man.

Too many dead bodies. Too many questions. Where was the connection?

And why did Sylvie Dane get caught in the cross-fire?

A gentle vibration shook me. I shifted and ignored it. A few moments, the vibrations grew stronger, irritating. Opening my eyes, it took me several seconds to get my bearings. Pushing myself up, I paused on the edge of the bed and brushed my hair out of my eyes. Falling asleep on the job was becoming a habit. I reached over and slapped the alarm clock, turning the vibrating feature off. The thing read two o'clock. The alarm had been set. Cole had intended to come back to the room.

Why hadn't he?

Oh yeah, Dane.

As I was struggling with reality, a knock sounded at the door. Still a bit groggy, for a moment I couldn't figure out what to do. Explaining my presence might be a bit dicey. After all, hotel execs aren't supposed to go parading through a guest's room without an invitation, or at least, a good reason, but I had to know who else was looking for Cole. If I needed an explanation, I'd do what I always did—I'd lie.

Finding my balance on the staggeringly high heels—perhaps the Jimmy Choos had not been the best choice—I brushed down my satin pants and rearranged the sweater, exposing one shoulder with a hot pink bra strap. Attitude. If I didn't feel it, I could at least look it. And as Flash said, if you pretend long enough, it becomes true or something to that effect. That girl had a way with words.

I turned the knob and pulled open the door. "What the . . ." I caught a glimpse. Hand raised. Arm coming forward. Instinctively I ducked down into the crook of my arm. Closing my eyes, I recoiled. I felt it before my mind could register. Liquid. Rivulets ran down my face. Cold. Not blood. No, something sweet. Like Coke. "Hey!" With the back of my hand, I swiped the liquid out of my eyes.

A hooded figure, shadows obscuring a face, paused for a moment in front of me, hand raised, fist clenched. Then whoever it was turned and ran. I got a flash of jeans. A gray hoodie. Tennis shoes. In seconds, the assailant disappeared into the elevator that stood open at the end of the hall.

Instinct took over and I bolted after the figure. "Wait." Two steps and my ankle twisted. I crumpled to the floor. Walking in the stilettos was a skill only recently acquired—running in them was out of the question. "Fuck." I grabbed my phone and began barking instructions to the hapless security person who had the misfortune of answering. Hot to the touch, my ankle swelled before my eyes. Kneading it didn't seem to be helping. Ice was clearly in order, then a good shower. This day had me on the ropes already.

Arm in arm, a couple strode out of another elevator and turned in my direction. They parted to walk around me, one on either side, but said nothing. In Vegas, inanimate objects don't attract interest.

With Security alerted and on the lookout for my hooded Coke hurler, there was nothing more for me to do. I pocketed my phone and pushed myself unsteadily to my feet, then limped to Cole's room to attempt repairs—I could only imagine what I looked like. Scaring the guests was against hotel policy.

"WHAT the hell happened to you?" Miss P actually looked taken aback when I eased through the office door and she got a good look at me.

"Get Romeo on the phone. Dane's taken Cole." I raised my hand at her unspoken question. "No, I don't have any proof. Which seems to be par for the course." I reached over her desk and gave the top right-hand drawer a tug. When it opened, I grabbed the spare set of keys to my apartment. Straightening, I tossed them to her. "Then, will you be so kind as to get me another outfit to wear today? This one has seen better days." I glanced down at the brown stain covering my chest. My clothes were ruined, my hair matted. My skin itched under its sugary crust—too bad they couldn't have hit me with Diet Coke. So much for Flash's theory that the world would be mine. "And some ice and a fistful of Baggies, sandwich-size."

She picked up the phone. I stopped listening when I heard her say, "Room Service, please."

"Oh, and a gun," I added. At Miss P's startled

look I continued, "There's a hooded Coke-wielding madman loose in this hotel. I'd sure like to pepper his ass with some double-aught buckshot."

The door opened behind me. I didn't bother to turn—I didn't care who it was. If I had to smile and be nice to one more person today, well, it probably was a good thing I wasn't locked and loaded. Instead, with one hand on the wall for support, I limped toward my office.

"That wouldn't be Coke, would it?" Romeo's voice sounded grim.

"What's left of one."

With one hand holding my arm and the other planted firmly in my back, he propelled me toward my office. "Quick. You've got a shower back here, right?"

He caught me by surprise. Thrown off balance, I staggered. "Ow." Pain shot up my leg, weakening my knee as my twisted ankle caught my weight. "Easy. What's got you all lathered up?"

He thrust me into the small cubicle. "Get out of those clothes."

"Why, Romeo, I thought you'd never ask." I didn't grin—I wasn't amused.

Pressing his lips into a thin line, he reached around me and turned the taps on the shower. Quickly the room started to fill with steam. Grabbing me by the shoulders, he pushed me into the stream of water, clothes, shoes, and all.

"What the hell are you doing?" I spluttered as I came up for air.

"Saving your life." He started rubbing my hair under the water. "You do it. Get it all off. I mean it."

"What the hell do you mean saving my life?" The look on his face wiped the smirk off mine, and my pithy reply fled.

"Cyanide." He slapped a bar of soap in my hand, whirled on his heel, and left. "For once, do as you're told."

The three of them, Miss P, Brandy, and Romeo, were waiting for me when I emerged, a towel wrapped around my head and the rest of me wrapped in a Babylon bathrobe of thick Turkish terry cloth. Miss P, a scowl on her face, her eyes filled with concern, held up some clothes on hangers. "I didn't know what you wanted, so I picked what I thought would be appropriate." A peach sweater, white jeans, gold sandals with a flat heel.

I reached for them, but she pulled them out of my reach. "I'll hang them up. Brandy, make her sit and let's get some ice on that ankle."

Romeo perched on the arm of a plush chair that cocooned Brandy. His hand on her shoulder, he idly traced the line of her jaw with his thumb and glared at me, relief softening the bite.

"How the hell did you translate Coke into cyanide?"

"I was just coming to tell you that the coroner's report came back on Mr. Johnstone."

"The Poker Room manager," I added for Brandy's benefit. The rest of us had the displeasure of knowing him.

"Right." Romeo continued. "On a hunch we tested your Poker Room manger's clothes and personal items, looking for any trace of poisoning. We found it on the dirty shirt from his locker. Coke with enough cyanide residue to kill him . . . eventually."

"What do you mean, eventually?"

"The poison had to have been absorbed through his skin. It would take a while for that to happen, but he would've exhibited symptoms for some time before the poison built up to lethal levels."

"Symptoms? Like what?" I was starting to feel sick, nauseous.

"Vertigo, light-headedness, confusion, giddiness, difficulty breathing. You know, all the oxygen-deprivation kinds of things."

"Thinking back on it, when I fired him, he was acting sort of weird."

"How so?" Romeo reached for his notebook. "What time was this?"

"About four, I guess. It was after I left you and Dane in the showroom. Then I took a shower." I hooked my thumb at my office behind me. "Same place. It wasn't long after that that I hit the Poker Room and Marvin was abusing Cole."

Romeo made a few notes, then looked up. "You said he was acting weird. What do you mean?"

"He was sweating, flushed, pulling at his collar. To be honest, the thought that he might've been drinking crossed my mind—he did smell like amaretto or Frangelico, something like that. Something nutty. But now . . . I guess it could've been the poison."

"You're not feeling any of those symptoms, are you?"

At the thought, a squirt of adrenaline surged through me. But after taking stock of how I felt, I started to relax. I was tired and angry, hurt and homicidal, but not light-headed or confused—and certainly not giddy. In fact, the pain and anger cleared my head and focused my resolve like the red dot of a laser sight on a target pistol. "No. Thank you very much."

Romeo nodded and gave me a quick, knowing smile. "Where could the Stoneman have been doused with Coke?" Romeo asked.

The question sounded vaguely rhetorical, but I actually had something to add. "I can't tell you exactly where—I have Jerry checking some of the other feeds to see where he went, but I can tell you when." I filled him in on Rachael's story about Marvin leaving the Poker Room as the high-stakes game was getting under way.

"And you think she was telling the truth?"

"One of the stewards corroborated." I adjusted the ice bags on my ankle—the skin had gone numb. "They both said he wasn't gone long. He couldn't have gone far." A chill washed over me. "The Ferrari dealership?"

Romeo let out a breath. "So maybe he did notice Sylvie was cheating?"

"Or they were in it together?"

"But what were they up to?" Defeat tinged the detective's voice.

"Don't give up yet, grasshopper. We're getting more pieces to the puzzle, surely the picture will start to become clear." Okay, I wasn't sure I believed me either, but although I might have been a fool, I wasn't a quitter. Especially when folks were messing with my Vegas mojo. "What about Cole Weston?"

"I'm ahead of you there." Romeo looked pleased—and capable. As I suspected, he had grown into his badge. "I put an APB out on him—we're beating the bushes but he hasn't surfaced."

"That Coke wasn't meant for me," I stated, trotting out my flair for the obvious. But this time I wasn't looking for answers. . . . I was looking for reassurance. Nothing like being mistaken by a killer to suck the joy out of a dismal day. But being targeted by one would be worse.

"I'd say Mr. Weston is a marked man," Romeo agreed, giving me what I wanted. "We'd better find him first."

"I don't know what else to do." I carefully extricated my foot from its shell of ice—the whole thing was blue and numb. I wiggled it, testing the limits. Better, but well below my normal championship levels—I was going to need a pinch hitter, or at least a designated runner. "Ladies, let's get back to work." I levered myself to my feet.

Romeo rushed to my side. "Where do you want to land?"

"Desk chair, but I can make it on my own, thanks." I rotated my foot, making several circles. The range of motion seemed to be increasing—at least, that's what I told myself. With the current body count at three, I did not have the time to baby a recalcitrant body part. "If I don't tackle some of that paperwork, I won't be able to find my desk tomorrow." Stymied, thwarted at every turn, I was in desperate need of accomplishing something. Paperwork. I *must* have been desperate.

Miss P drifted out of my office.

When I was sure they were out of earshot, I turned to Romeo. "What's the word on Kevin Slurry?"

"No change. Still critical. Although he's stable, he's not out of the woods. The docs told me they were going to keep him under for a while—a medically induced coma they called it. It could be a couple of days before he's strong enough to talk. And then there's no guarantees what he'll remember."

That took a moment to process. The fact that I had actually shot someone still burned a hole through my brain. The visual hit me every time I closed my eyes. How would I get over that? Especially if he died? So he deserved it—small comfort. With nothing more to do at this point, I tried to shelve it. As I said, compartmentalizing is one of my best things.

Romeo settled himself in the couch, pulling a pillow across his stomach, then holding it tightly. "They told me you were snooping around Cole's room, but he's gone. If you've got any ideas as to how all these pieces fit, I'm all ears."

"Outta gas and outta ideas, I'm a permanent resident of clueless county."

Brandy jumped up and made a fuss out of settling

me in my chair, then getting another one to put my injured leg up. After packing Baggies of ice around my now pumpkin-sized ankle—okay, a small pumpkin—she lurked, nervously wringing her hands. Romeo motioned for Brandy to join him. The girl didn't seem to be the worse for wear after the excitement last night.

But, having a mile-wide mothering streak, I had to ask. "Brandy, are you okay?"

She shrugged, then brushed away my concern. "When you dance in the cages you get used to bad shit."

"Not a sugar-and-spice-and-everything-nice kind of gal, are you?"

"Just like you. That's why you hired me."

Man, the whole world was reading me far too easily. "Did Security get the hoodie guy?"

My young disciple shook her head. "He got out of the hotel and disappeared into the crowd on the Strip before Security could lock his position down. They're checking with Metro now to see if anything showed up on their cameras."

"I won't hold my breath." Cameras covered most of the Strip, but it would take time to work through the bureaucratic snafus and patience to check all the footage. And they wouldn't jump through hoops to catch an assailant tossing Coke—heck, it happens all the time on the Strip and most of the people so assaulted don't even notice.

"Romeo, stick a pillow in your ear and take a

couple of hours in the horizontal position on that couch. No one knows you're here."

"I couldn't." He eyed the length of the sofa wistfully.

"Lie down before you fall down." I gave a quick nod to Brandy, who apparently got the hint. After giving Romeo a quick kiss, she said, "Do what Lucky tells you. What good will you be with no sleep?"

He watched her as she sashayed out of the office, waving good-bye with a little waggle of her fingers.

I cleared my throat to get the besotted detective's attention. "You just did me a huge favor, let me do you a small one. Trust me, I'll cover for you—if the president calls, I'll put him through."

Romeo chewed on his lip for a moment, then eased farther into the plush cushions, kicked off his shoes, and laid back, pulling a pillow under his head. He was out cold in less than a minute. Breathing heavily, his mouth open, he didn't snore—another advantage of youth. And even in repose, he looked cute . . . so innocent and young. Why I felt like smoothing his hair out of his eyes, I didn't know. Besides, he'd probably shoot me or something. Not that I cared. Maybe I needed the comfort of human contact. Maybe I just needed reorientation, a confirmation of the good in the world. Whatever it was, for a moment, I gave in.

Risking bodily harm, not to mention embarrassment to us both, I rose and limped over to the couch, then bent and gently brushed down his cowlick. Soft

to the touch, yet resilient, the feel of his hair surprised me. And yet, it fit. Smiling, I remembered the
first time I'd met him. Another murder. Another lifetime.

He stirred and I froze, afraid to move, afraid to
breathe. He repositioned, tucking one hand under
his head and throwing the other arm over his eyes. A
few ticks of the clock, then he quieted, his breathing
once again settling into a slow rhythm.

I tiptoed—okay I limp-toed—around my desk
and slowly settled back into the chair. Wincing at its
squeak of complaint, I glanced at Romeo. He didn't
move.

I had work to do. Romeo needed his sleep.

Death could wait.

ROMEO still slept when I reached the last paper in the
pile. After signing my name with a flourish, I tossed
it in my out-box with the others. The outer office
was quiet. No one stirred, not even the friggin' bird.
I leaned back in my chair, put my head back, and
savored the moment of peace and quiet, the satisfaction of a job done. Even though it was as insig-
nificant as plowing through a pile of papers, it was
something.

My eyelids sagged like sails in the doldrums. My
muscles loosened. Completely played out, I was beyond tired. Perhaps just a few winks . . .

"Lucky?" My father's voice boomed, shattering
the peace and jump-starting my heart.

I bolted upright in the chair and my hand flew to my chest. "Christ!"

"Lucky? Are you in here?" He sounded angry. No, he sounded pissed. Terrific.

"If I said no, would you believe me and go away?"

At full throttle, he burst through the opening, raising a cloud of dust. "This is all your fault." He stopped in front of my desk, his face the color of marinara sauce, his chest heaving.

I leaned to the side to look around him at Romeo. Dead to the world, the kid hadn't moved. I motioned to a chair. "Why don't you take a load off? If you're going to unload on me, we both might as well be comfortable."

For a moment, my father stood glaring down at me, his mouth opening and closing like a fish gulping for air. Then he did as I suggested.

I waited. Then, when he opened his mouth to speak, I shushed him with a finger to my lips. A lifetime of dealing with my father had taught me that, once he was caught in the vortex of a good rage, he needed two things to calm down: time and alcohol. I bought one while going in search of the other. I was right: The ankle only hurt when I tried to walk normally. If I walked on the ball of my foot, it only twinged. When I returned with a tall glass filled to the brim with Wild Turkey 101—granted it was a Flintstone's jelly jar but it was the best I could find— his face was a lighter shade of pink. If he noticed the hitch in my get-along or my interesting office attire—it was a rare day that I showed up to work in a bathrobe—he didn't let on.

Silently he took the glass and drained half of it. "It's your mother," he started in a loud voice.

"Quiet. The kid's one of the walking dead." We both swiveled to look at Romeo, who slept on.

"I think most of the world will agree that I had nothing to do with Mona's current predicament," I whispered.

My father didn't smile—not a good sign. But he did modulate his voice. "You're deflecting."

"A survival skill." The smell of the whiskey in his glass exerted an inexorable pull. I leaned forward, but paragon of virtue that I am, that's as far as I let it go. "She hasn't shot anyone, has she? Put a double-barrel loaded with rock salt in her hands and she could do some damage. Just ask the sheriff back in Pahrump—she's peppered his hide a time or two."

"No." My father glared at me, momentarily side-tracked by my question. His glare softened. "I heard you saved your young assistant's ass last night."

I tried a half grin, but it ended up as a sigh. "I may have killed someone in the process." My voice cracked when I said it.

My father covered my hand with his. "Life can be tough, honey. You did what you had to do. And the right people woke up this morning. Remember that."

"Yeah, but . . ."

"No buts. Why do you think you run this place? You make the tough decisions, and yet you still lead with your heart. Would it offend you if I told you I was proud of you? It sounds sort of condescending. I hope you don't take it that way."

I wanted to crawl into his lap and hug his neck, but not only would that be physically impossible, but also the time for that had long since passed, which made me sad. Life, one giant timing issue—too bad I always seemed to zig when everyone else zagged.

"You're just trying to make me feel better." I pulled my hand out from under his, giving it a pat as I disengaged. "Now, why don't you tell me about Mother? We've established she didn't shoot anybody, so how bad could it be?"

"You have no idea." Pretending to be fascinated, he held his glass by the lip with three fingers, then rotated his wrist and watched the liquid swirl.

I gave him a moment. The problem was, I could imagine—horrible possibilities whirled through my head like a cloud of bats in a cave.

When he looked up at me, his face was serious but the hint of humor lit his eyes. "That woman has thrown her hat in the ring."

"The ring? Oh, please tell me she wants to run away with the circus." I couldn't take my eyes off his glass as he lifted it to his lips. "Life would be much simpler if you let her go."

"Cute." My father fought a grin and lost. "She's decided to campaign for an appointment to the Paradise Town Advisory Board." Most folks thought the Strip, the most important real estate in Las Vegas, was part of the city of Las Vegas. Not so. In fact, most of it was part of an unincorporated census data area known as Paradise . . . which was sorta perfect, if you ask me. The former mayor of Las Vegas, even though he had appeared everywhere with a showgirl on each arm and had announced more than once that he was King of the World, had no authority over the Strip. Instead it was managed by the Clark County Commission under advisement from the Paradise Town Advisory Board. Together they controlled the flow of a serious chunk of change—not to mention a huge portion of the income of the state of Nevada.

I motioned to my father's drink. "Give me some of that."

He pushed the glass across the desk, then watched me drain it dry. "I don't need to point out that you seem to be drinking a bit more than normal these days."

"Life has been a bit more than normal lately." I set down the glass carefully and resolved to slow down, although I wasn't making any guarantees. "Politics and Mona. It's so absurd it sorta makes sense."

My father nodded, his eyes holding a faraway look. "Like how everyone says one of those rat dogs is so ugly it's cute."

"If you value your hide, I wouldn't run that little analogy by Mother."

"God, no." My father's gaze returned to me as he pushed himself to his feet. "You keep the hootch back there?" He motioned to the kitchenette.

"Top shelf on the right in the back."

He disappeared into the gloom to get us both a glass of liquid courage, leaving me to contemplate Mona as a humble public servant. Just another Vegas entertainment extravaganza. Heck, if a former mob defender could be mayor and a former dancer the lieutenant governor, then a former hooker on a town council wasn't that far-fetched. But Mona?

"Christ." With shaking hand, I took the glass my father offered as he maneuvered around the desk and sat back in his chair, clutching tightly a glass of his own.

"I want front-row seats when she takes on the Clark County Commission." Pride tinged his voice.

"And a flak jacket." I took a sip of whiskey, a small sip. We both grinned.

"I know I really shouldn't ask." I put the glass on the table, then pushed it to arm's length, putting distance between us. "But how is this my fault?"

"I'm not a hundred percent sure—I couldn't really follow your mother's logic." My father leaned back, stretching, then settled in, his arms resting lightly on the arms of the chair. "That woman takes the scenic route."

"Circuitous on her best days."

"But she gets to her point . . . eventually." My father regrouped. "This time it has something to do with your friend Carl. I forget his last name. You know, the one who lives in the storm drains?"

"Carl Colson?" Most people referred to him as Crazy Carl Colson, but I just couldn't bring myself to call him that. Besides, he wasn't crazy *all* of the time.

"That's the one—the Air Force discharged him on psychological grounds, if I recall correctly." The Big Boss raised an eyebrow at me but didn't wait for a response. "Anyway, there was an article today in the *R-J*—did you know there is a whole city the homeless have set up underground in the storm drains?"

"I've been taking them blankets and coats for years. Food when I thought they needed it." My father's stunned look told me he needed some enlightenment. "Vegas isn't all bright lights and magic."

"I should've known you'd be hip-deep."

I thought I detected a hint of honest pride in his voice, not the make-me-feel-better kind. A hint was enough.

"Then I'm sure you remember when the city council made it a crime to give food to the homeless in the city parks?" he continued.

"A banner day for our fair city. But the council caved under a heaping pile of negative publicity, as I recall."

"Yes, but that and your friend Carl boosted Mona onto her soapbox."

"A hooker and a mind reader—now there's a platform," I groused. My overblown sense of righteous indignation reared its ugly head. A former Air Force pawn, Carl happened to have amazing psychic powers, but that was another story. I wondered if a psychic adviser would violate political ethics rules, to the extent any still existed. "Throw in the Amazing Kreskin, and Mona will have an act she can take on the road."

"Careful." My father's eyebrows snapped into a frown. "She's a *former* hooker, and I don't think she meant to use Carl literally, just figuratively." Even as he said it my father didn't look convinced. "She *does* mean well."

"You know what they say about good intentions." I picked up a pen and started doodling on the back of one of the random memos on my desk. A heart with a dagger through it. "I'll straighten it out," I assured him, as if it would be a mere trifle for someone with my superpowers. "I've got something else I need your help with."

"A sponsor in AA?"

"Cute." I pretended to be perturbed but even I knew my life was spinning out of control and I was self-medicating. "It is my understanding that our stalwart Paxton Dane is under investigation by the Gaming Control Board for monetary improprieties."

That wiped the smug look off my father's face. "What? What kind of improprieties?"

I recognized his battle as he struggled to wrap his mind around the possibility that Dane might not be one of the white hats. Been there, still working on it. "That's what I need you to find out. Details would be good. Can you do it?"

"Sure, sure. I got a few markers I can pull in." His

eyes took on a distant look as he pinched his lower lip. "You think he did it?" His voice had lost its warmth.

"Did what? Kill his wife? Play fast and loose with the house money? To be honest, I haven't a clue." A chill chased down my spine, competing with a flush of rising anger. "I don't want to believe it, but where there's smoke . . ."

The Big Boss shrugged in ambivalence. He didn't want to believe it either. "And Marvin?" Betrayal flashed across his face, pulling his mouth into a taut line. "After all I've done. If that slimy little bastard was pulling a fast one . . ." He let the threat hang. I didn't need to tell him Marvin had moved beyond its reach.

But Dane hadn't.

For some reason a picture of Teddie flashed across my synapses. My hands itched to circle a neck and squeeze. "Let me handle it," I said, my tone matching my father's. "Slimy little bastards are my specialty."

"Which slimy little bastards are we talking about?" Romeo asked, his voice fuzzy with sleep. I'd forgotten about him. "What time is it? And why the hell am I here?" He pushed himself to a sitting position, stockinged feet on the floor, head in his hands. When he looked up and his eyes focused, the light went on. "Oh, sorry, sir," he stammered when he caught my father's eye. Leaning around my father, he threw a silent plea in my direction.

"You've been here a few hours," I explained.

"Probably longer than you planned, but I didn't have the heart to awaken you."

Romeo rubbed his face as if trying to restore circulation to his brain. "The time?"

I pulled my phone from its perch on my hip. "Just finishing the cocktail hour."

"Looks like you started without me."

"A head start is the only way I can stay in front," I said, pretending it wasn't true.

"I'm not sure that's a race I'd want to win."

"Glibness. I like it."

Romeo gave me a knowing grin. "I've been sitting at the feet of a master."

"You are wise beyond your years, Grasshopper."

"Would you two stop?" My father pushed himself to his feet and stepped to the side so his back was no longer aimed at the young detective. "I'll tell you what," he said as he rubbed his hands together, hatching a plan. "I'm thinking we all could use a good meal. I'll go roust your mother. Surely she can take a break from plotting the overthrow of Clark County and the rise of the downtrodden." His gaze touched on me. For the first time this evening he seemed to take in my attire. "Did I barge in on something?" His face colored a bit. So did Romeo's.

"God, no." Romeo sounded offended, and slightly horrified. "Sir, I would never . . . She's old enough . . ." Glancing at me, he ground to a halt.

On any other day I probably would have been amused. "Thank you." My voice could've cut glass.

Turning to my father, I said, "I fought a losing battle with a can of Coke."

"Fine, you can tell me about it over dinner—that and why you are limping around like a retired tight end. Detective, you come, too. Say, twenty minutes at Tigris."

"I'd like a tight end, but I don't want to be one." I groused as my father disappeared out the door.

Romeo's eyes widened. "Tigris?" A grin lifted the corner of his mouth as he nodded at me. Tigris, our five-star eatery, was the toughest table in town.

My father poked his head back in through the door. "And Lucky, why don't you bring your chef? Your mother and I would love the chance to get to know him better."

My chef. *My* father. Still new concepts.

"You think you have enough stroke to get us a table?" I teased. My father had discovered Chef Omer, the executive chef at Tigris, slaving away in the bowels of some obscure Turkish eatery and made him the toast of Vegas.

A table wouldn't be too much to ask.

Chapter

FOURTEEN

♡

Opinions differed as to which location in a restaurant was the most coveted. Some thought that a table tucked away in the back room, far from prying eyes, shouted your importance to the world. Others considered being parked out front, sort of like the Ferrari by the door, meant you had climbed to the top rung of the social ladder. In this see-and-be-seen world, I ascribed to the latter theory. Apparently so did the Big Boss.

Romeo and I were the first to arrive. Somehow, I'd managed to squirm into the outfit Miss P had found for me—my ankle, still twice its normal size and hot to the touch, was practically immobile. No matter how I tried to walk, I still came out lumbering like Igor with his hump. Romeo was pressed-and-polished as well . . . sort of. I'd helped him with some quick freshening—somehow we'd managed to tame his cowlick with a serious application of hairspray. I'd even found a tie and a pressed sports coat that fit him, sort of. And it really didn't matter as long as he felt presentable. That was the key, wasn't it?

Accustomed to the slick elegance and pretention of most top-of-the-line troughs, Romeo was a bit taken aback when we stepped through the double bronze doors. "Wow," he managed to splutter.

I knew how he felt. Tigris was so unexpected, yet so perfect. Loops of brightly dyed silks hung from the ceiling. Flame under glass imbued the intimate space with warmth. Date palms grew from patches of soil. Tightly woven mats covered a mahogany floor burnished to a rich, dark sheen. The tabletops of intricate inlaid mosaics were cloth-free. The glassware was sturdy and blue—hand-blown and proud of its imperfections. Somewhere, hanging from one of the pillars, was a very early Greek reproduction of the Code of Hammurabi, but I didn't see it as I pointed Romeo in the right direction, then followed him. My father would have the best table—the one in the middle of the action—and the attention of the best of the stellar staff.

As I predicted, Roham, one of my very favorite people and the head of the waitstaff at Tigris, waited by a round table set for six in the center of the room, his hands crossed in front of him. Two bottles were already chilling in a silver stand at his elbow.

A shit-eating grin split his face when he saw me. "Lucky! Why are you walking like a lame camel?"

"To get attention."

"You are okay, then?" He held a chair for me, then helped push it in. I always found that whole thing a bit awkward, never knowing how to time my scootch with his push, but Roham handled it with a flourish.

"Okay about covers it."

Roham eyed Romeo, making him blush. "Every time a different man! This one, such a handsome *young* man." He emphasized the *young*. "I'm impressed. Where should the *young* mister sit?" Again a misplaced emphasis.

Romeo's eyes hardened.

I winked at the kid. "Don't mind him," I said to Romeo, not bothering to lower my voice. "He's just jealous." Then I turned my grin to the waiter. "Roham, let me introduce you to Detective Romeo with the Metropolitan Police Department. And he can sit here next to me."

Apparently that took enough wind out of the waiter's sails to satisfy Romeo as he grabbed the chair and sat.

Roham looked suitably impressed as he pulled the napkins from our wineglasses, shook them out with a flourish, then laid them across our laps. "I meant no offense, Detective. Lucky and I are good friends."

"None taken and I can see you two share some interesting traits."

"Perhaps a beverage while you wait?" Roham asked Romeo while he wrapped a white cloth around a bottle and he pulled it from the ice. He filled a crystal flute in front of me with champagne. Bubbles and alcohol, an imperfect Mona vaccine—it wouldn't keep her away, but it did make her easier to take. Roham got the medicine and the dosage just right, as usual.

"Ketel One martini, straight up with a twist," the detective announced after a moment of thought. I'm not sure I would have pegged Romeo as a martini drinker, but I couldn't argue with his taste.

Before he escaped, I stopped Roham with a hand on his arm. "Mother sits over there." I pointed to the opposite side of the table. "And remember . . ."

"No sharp knives," my friend finished with a grin.

"You know she can't be trusted."

"I was thinking no knives for *you*." He skittered away before I could react.

"I like him." Romeo worried with one of the knives as he watched Roham's retreat. "He's from someplace dark and swarthy, but where, exactly? I'm pretty sure he isn't from here."

"Please, nobody's *from* Vegas." I arranged my napkin in my lap. "This is a town of transients, which is part of the reason we have such trouble with our schools and all the other infrastructure. Nobody's invested in this city."

"Another one of your soapboxes, huh?" Romeo looked uncomfortable. "Sorry I asked," he groused. "And, for the record, *we* are from Vegas."

"Yeah, nobodies from Vegas." My champagne warmed as we waited, but I refused to drink alone—a girl had to have her standards. "Roham is Persian, from Iran, but his parents left the country when the shah fell. He was raised in Arizona, but don't tell anyone. Roham likes to keep his image as a true Persian alive and well. He says it works wonders with the women."

"Really? Maybe that's what I need—a story." Romeo relinquished the knife and fork and placed his hands in his lap as if he wasn't sure what to do with all the forks and knives in front of him.

"You're a detective, how much more cool factor do you need?" I made a show of smoothing my napkin in my lap, then picking an invisible piece of lint from it.

"Maybe." He didn't look convinced. "Why are there six places?"

"Even numbers are best, don't you think?"

"If you say so." He ran a finger between his collar and his neck as if loosening a noose. "I don't normally frequent these toffee-nose establishments."

"Not any different than eating at the Omelet House, just more expensive and attracts a higher class of riffraff."

"A few more forks and stuff, too." Tension pulled his voice tight, like the string on a bow, until it almost twanged.

"All show, meant to make those who care feel important. Just work from the outside in."

The young detective started to relax. "Emily Post CliffsNotes?"

"That's all I know. Remember, I learned my manners in a whorehouse." I squeezed his arm. "Enjoy yourself. Eat with your fingers if it suits you. No one will give a hoot."

Over his shoulder I caught sight of the Big Boss and Mona working their way toward us. "Showtime."

Mona had clearly recovered her mojo and was flexing her power-behind-the-throne position. Dressed in a flowing silk caftan and cocktail pants, both infused with threads of silver, flat silver sandals, and, curiously for her, an understated number of diamonds (although the carat weight was still sufficient to attract attention from the larcenous to the envious), she carried herself with regal bearing as she worked her way through the tables. If she noticed eyes shifting to her and the hushed whispers behind raised hands as she passed by, she didn't let on. Although fashionably disguised, her baby bump was clearly visible. I was no expert, but from the size of it, that kid was on serious grow-juice.

My father, one hand touching the small of his wife's back, followed closely behind. He'd changed uniforms since I last saw him. Now he was pressed and polished in a white collarless shirt open at the neck, a double-breasted blue blazer that accentuated his trim physique—Dunhill if I wagered a guess—and perfectly tailored steel-gray slacks. Broken-in loafers and no socks completed the ensemble. As a couple, my parents looked ready to attend a movie premiere at Cannes. Studied elegance—clearly a gene that had skipped the next generation—although I didn't feel too shabby in the new peach outfit Miss P had chosen.

After hurriedly setting down Romeo's drink, Roham rushed around the table to hold Mother's chair. "Mrs. Rothstein, you look radiant."

With my father holding one arm, Mother smiled as she lowered herself into the chair. Radiant, yes, but something else. Back straight, eyes alert, she reminded me of a mountain lion waiting to pounce on an unwary rodent. But then again, there had always been something feline about Mona.

Romeo and I had risen when my parents approached. I now retrieved my napkin from my chair, then let my father help me into it. He took the chair next to his wife, leaving an empty one between us.

"Mother, you know Detective Romeo."

Romeo nodded as he raised his filled-to-the-brim glass and took a tentative sip of his martini. Somehow he managed not to spill a drop, which was better than I could've done.

"Of course. So glad you could take a break from all your dead bodies." Mona tossed off the line as if she were trading small talk at a tea party, but I noticed she studiously avoided my glare as she arranged her napkin across her shrinking lap.

"No worries," Romeo adopted the same casual tone as Mona's, "they'll just cool it until I get back."

Leaning back, I grinned and raised my glass to Romeo.

Mona leaned forward, her eyes big. "I've never been to the morgue. Do they really just lay them out naked and all?"

"Mother!"

"What?" She feigned innocence as her eyes finally met mine. "I'm just making small talk."

"Cold, stiff, blue, with a toe tag and nothing else," Romeo said, adding fuel to the fire.

"Imagine." Mona leaned back, a faraway look in her eyes. "Stiff . . ."

She let the word dangle and frankly, I didn't

want to know what she was imagining. I gulped a bit of champagne and slammed my mind shut to the visuals . . . all of them.

Gives a whole new take on the term cold-cocked, doesn't it? The words rushed from my brain toward my mouth, threatening to bypass good taste altogether. I threw back another slug of champagne and choked, bringing tears to my eyes. One good thing—if I couldn't breathe, I couldn't talk.

My father narrowed his eyes at me. Yup, the whole world most definitely was reading me far too well.

"Well, if I'm ever in your refrigerated unit," Mona said, her eyes fixed on the young detective, "and you lay me out like that, I'll come back and haunt you."

My father sat back, out of the fray, with a semi-amused, semi-confused look on his face.

I knew the feeling. "Murder might well be in your future if you keep badgering the detective, Mother."

"I am not . . ." Mona stopped at the look on Romeo's face.

Staring over Mona's shoulder, Romeo caught sight of something that made him blanch and smile at the same time.

Mother swiveled around, then, once she caught sight of Brandy, she slowly turned back and graced me with a warm smile. Boy, first my father, now Mona, I was racking up serious daughter-of-the-year points. But with Mona it felt a bit like being seduced by the Dark Side.

Romeo jumped to his feet, his napkin falling to the floor. As I bent to retrieve it, I caught his questioning glance.

I handed him his napkin and I waggled my eyebrows. "Like I said, even numbers are the best for a nice dinner party, don't you agree?"

The look on his face was more reward than I deserved.

Brandy, stunning in one of those skintight things that only twenty-one–year-olds can get away with, and balancing on impossibly high heels, greeted everyone warmly, reserving a kiss for Romeo, which made him blush. She took the chair between her detective and Mother.

After making sure everyone knew each other, I leaned back and watched as my family and friends settled into comfortable conversation. Champagne bubbles tickled my nose as I took another sip, this time more carefully, suffused with the warmth of a full life. Thoughts of murderers and liars and slimy little bastards retreated until I found the old me again.

"I just love young love, don't you?" Mona asked, bringing me into the conversation as she watched Romeo and Brandy nuzzle.

The Big Boss reached around his wife, pulling her close. Whispering something in her ear, he made her blush. With pink cheeks, she looked almost demure, virginal, which was a *huge* stretch. *Huge*. The Game of Life had clearly gone on tilt.

One seat still sat empty. Odd numbers—I'd been

right about that much. As the fifth wheel, I was warming the bench. While the game of love was interesting as a spectator, it was far more fun to be a participant. At least that's what I'd been told, but recent history had left me bloodied and bruised, standing awkwardly on the sidelines.

Jean-Charles appeared in the doorway then paused, sweeping his gaze over the tables until his eyes met mine. A smile, warm and full of promise, split his face, summoning me into the game. Like the Grinch hearing the songs of Whoville, I smiled as my heart grew two sizes, at least.

Dodging tables, he worked his way closer. I could see his golden brown blazer, made of fine cashmere, had tiny pinstripes of blue—robin's-egg blue that matched his eyes. And those Italian slacks—formfitting, leaving just enough to the imagination. A silk scarf, also blue, knotted at his neck—a look that would appear calculated and insincere on anyone else—completed the perfection. Taking a deep breath, then letting it out slowly, I was very thankful I resisted drooling.

Instead of taking the open seat next to me, and before he greeted anyone else, Jean-Charles, his eyes never leaving mine, extended a hand. Taking mine, he urged me to stand in front of him. The table fell silent as he eased the crystal flute from my hand and set it down. Wrapping one arm around my waist, he pulled me to him. Merriment danced in his eyes, and something serious, too—I didn't know what.

"*Bonsoir,* my love," he whispered. His thumb

brushed lightly over my lips as he eased his hand behind my neck. Pulling me to him, his mouth captured mine. Slow and sensual, his lips assaulted mine, leaving me weak kneed and needing air. Where our skin touched, fire burned through me. A jolt. A sizzle. Heat. A long-burning blaze. Out of the frying pan into the fire. Resistance was futile.

Nobody died from a broken heart, right?

When he released me, I blinked a few times, trying to get my bearings. Way too difficult with him this close. My legs went all wobbly so I let him ease me back into my chair. Then he took the one to my left, between my father and me. He captured my hand in his, squeezing. When he turned to greet my parents, he didn't let go. Romeo, his face red, glanced away when my eyes caught his. Everyone else looked at me with bemused expressions.

My father raised his flute of champagne. "To love."

"And mind-blowing sex," Mona added as she raised her glass of soda water.

My father shook his head and chuckled, "That, too, my dear."

We all clinked glasses.

AS usual, my father let Omer and Roham make the selections for the evening, with one caveat—the salad must be my favorite. Who knew goat cheese, pine nuts, pears, and avocado, all nestled on a bed of baby spinach and drizzled with balsamic vinaigrette, could be so decadent?

Conversation flowed freely, almost as freely as the champagne and wine as the courses came and went. Even Jean-Charles seemed impressed as Roham and his staff removed the last of the plates. "Superb," he said to my father. "My compliments to the chef. And to you, sir."

"I have very little to do with what transpires here at the Babylon. Lucky's a big part of that, as are others. We have a good team," my father said as he reached for another bottle of wine. Leaning, he refilled Jean-Charles's glass. At my father's questioning look, I shook my head. Roham took the bottle from him and took care of the youngsters—Mona's delicate condition kept her on the wagon. I was impressed. "But," the Big Boss continued, "we are only as good as the members of our corporate family."

"Employees," I whispered in Jean-Charles's ear in translation.

He nodded and squeezed my knee. I don't think he'd stopped touching me since he arrived, not that I was complaining. "The longer a team is together, the more fluidly it works."

"Precisely." My father raised his glass in salute.

"This is why I bring my own staff for the restaurants here," Jean-Charles said.

"They are family," my father and Jean-Charles said in unison. Then both of them laughed.

"And I understand you are preparing for a competition soon?" Mona directed her question at Jean-Charles.

"Yes, there will be much publicity. I hope to represent the Babylon well."

"I'm sure our reputation is in good hands." Mona smoothed her napkin on the table, sounding for all the world like a co-owner of the hotel. "But where will you prepare your dishes? I'm sure the grill at the Burger Palais is insufficient, and your new kitchen is far from ready, or so Lucky tells me." She cast a quick glance my direction, burying the knife in my back with a sweet smile.

"Lucky, she is taking care of this problem." Jean-Charles squeezed my hand.

"Then you are in good hands," my father added, effectively shutting down that line of conversation.

"Sir, if I may?" Romeo stepped into the easy silence. "I'd like to offer my condolences. I understand Shady Slim was a good friend."

My father's face clouded but he didn't lose his smile. "We knew each other since Benny Binion invited six of his friends to a friendly game at the Horseshoe and started the whole thing rolling. Guess we both grew up with Vegas."

"Lotsa changes." Romeo nodded sagely.

I resisted scoffing. What could he know? He was so young he sparkled like a new penny.

"Slim lived pretty large, so I guess he had it coming." My father poured himself another glass of wine. "The timing was bad though, not that there's ever a good time to meet your Maker."

My father being so forthcoming raised every red

flag I had. If I didn't know better, I'd say he was reeling the kid in. But why? Looking for answers, I decided to play along. "Why was now any worse than any other?"

"The long hours of professional poker drove him out of the game—they practically play around the clock now—and it was get out or develop an amphetamine addiction. Without an outlet for those competitive juices, he'd been a bit lost." My father glanced around the table, his eyes coming to rest on me. "Recently, he'd found a way back in."

"What was that?" The rest of the table fell silent as I warmed to the role of straight man.

"The Internet. He was all gung ho about offshore poker sites. To hear him tell it, owning one was like printing money."

"He owned one?" Out of the corner of my eye, I saw Romeo ease his pad and pencil from his inside pocket. Flipping the pad open, he held the pencil poised.

"Part of one. A small consortium of his friends invited him in to buy a site from that amateur player Lucky perforated last night." My father chewed on his lip as he thought a moment. "What's his name?"

The words caught in my throat.

Romeo jumped to my rescue. "Kevin Slurry."

Brandy looked at me—her eyes had gone all slitty at the mention of his name. "I'm here tonight because of Lucky."

"Yes," my father said as he gave me a knowing look. "Slurry, he was a pretty good player. He won a WSOP bracelet a few years back. I think that's where he crossed paths with Slim. Anyway, the kid had been after Slim for a while. He said having a legend's name attached to the site would really grow the brand. I told Slim he should wait until we got some legislation passed that would bring Internet gaming back to this country. Of course, that would raise the price."

"He didn't listen."

"No, he wanted in while the price was low." My father's emotions filtered through as his voice caught. "They offered me a stake, but I didn't want it—at least not right now."

"How'd Slim take that?"

"No hard feelings. Besides, I left the door open."

"How?"

"We were working on a plan to bring it onshore, grow the site, offer in-room play to the guests. It's the wave of the future, why fight it?"

"But isn't that illegal?" Romeo always had a nose for nuance.

"Technically it's illegal for the banks and other monetary institutions to process payments from U.S. players to gambling sites. The actual site isn't illegal, but the result is the same." My father pushed his glass away and leaned back in his chair. Idly he stroked Mother's hand as it rested on his thigh. "It's just a matter of time before the legislation is over-turned. You'd think our lawmakers would under-stand it's more effective to tax vice than it is to try to eradicate it. But then again, those guys aren't known for playing with a full deck."

"Who got in with Slim?" Romeo asked, keeping his tone conversational.

I hid my grin—it would take far more than an easy manner—probably handcuffs and a stun gun—to lead that old dog down a path he didn't want to go. Romeo's naïveté was charming.

Unruffled, my father continued letting out the line, baiting the hook. "DeLuca and Watalsky. Those were the main two. There were others, but they didn't have much of a stake."

"Watalsky? River Watalsky?" Now it was my turn to be surprised. "Last I heard he didn't have two nickels to rub together."

"As you know, sweetheart," my father glanced at me, "all it takes is one hot streak and you're back in the game."

"An interesting group." I thought for a moment as the table fell silent. The good Mr. Watalsky had been a bit circumspect the last time we'd talked. Time to nail him down, literally, if that's what it took. Come to think of it, DeLuca had a lot of explaining to do as well, but that would be a bit touchier. "And Marvin Johnstone?"

"I haven't added that piece to the puzzle . . . yet." My father's eyes hardened. "All I know is there was a lot of smack involved. And where there's smack . . ."

"There's murder," I said, finishing his thought as if it were my own.

"Are you two suggesting someone killed Shady Slim?" Romeo couldn't hide his skepticism. If the Big

Boss wasn't here I'm sure the kid would be a little more sarcastic. I could hear him saying, "You can't be serious? You're pulling this out of thin air!" or something to that effect. Instead he calmly finished with "We have no reason to believe foul play was involved, sir."

The "sir" was a bit much, if you asked me, but my father took the bait. "Look more closely, Detective. Money brings out the worst in people."

An awkward silence descended over the group, each of us lost in our own thoughts.

"You don't have to tell me that!" Mona jumped into the fray. "The more money they flashed at the house, the more I worried about the girls." From gambling and murder to hookers. Apparently we were going to hit all the Vegas high points.

Brandy nodded at my mother and seized the opening. "I know what you mean. When the guys started stuffing Franklins through the bars of my cage, I knew it was going to get bad." Cage dancing had paid her tuition at UNLV.

"The men were not gentlemen?" Jean-Charles asked, sounding somewhat appalled. Poor man, he had a lot to learn about Vegas.

Brandy and Mother both looked at him for a moment as if trying to understand the concept of "gentlemen" in the world they both had worked in.

Finally Brandy shook her head. "No, the men were, well . . . men. Men are pretty simple, you know—you get what you expect, most of the time. But the other girls! Once they picked up the scent of easy money, they were like a pack of rabid coyotes eating their own."

HOLDING up a wall in the corner of the kitchen at Tigris, I worked my ankle, trying to increase the range of motion as I watched Jean-Charles and Omer, the urbane Frenchman and the rotund little Turk, their heads together as they traded culinary war stories. The rest of the dinner had passed in easy camaraderie, although I thought Mona and I might come to blows over the last of the vanilla crème brûlée.

After thanking the staff, we'd said our good-byes. Romeo and Brandy headed to Babel to dance for a bit. Mother wanted a warm bath and a foot rub. Father knew the bit part he would play and he'd looked thrilled at the prospect when he'd let his wife lead him toward home. Jean-Charles insisted he couldn't leave the restaurant without complimenting the chef. I agreed, so here we were.

Letting the chefs' conversation fade into the background, I marveled at how Brandy had gotten away with the "men are so simple" line at dinner. If I'd made that pronouncement, I would've been skewered and slow-roasted over an open pit.

Beauty and youth . . . an advantage and an excuse. If I knew where to shop, I'd buy me some of both.

"Hey, I'm glad I caught you." Romeo's voice jerked me back to the present.

At his hand on my arm, I turned to stare into the bright eyes of the young detective.

"I forgot what I had to tell you, what with dinner and . . . everything." He threw a furtive glance toward the front of the restaurant where, I assumed, Brandy waited for him. "I like your even numbers theory. Thank you, by the way."

"I'm a sucker for love."

His shy smile crept out of hiding. I bet he'd be shocked at the number of hearts he'd unwittingly broken with that grin. "Forgot to tell you. I ran the phone numbers from the plane's satellite phone."

"And?" My body had apparently gone into max-conserve mode. The flutter of hope in my chest didn't even come close to tripping a faster heartbeat.

"Somebody on that plane called Washington."

"Technically, you can't call Washington—it's a city, assuming we're talking D.C. Washington State presents a similar problem though." I wiped a hand across my face, then leaned my head back against the wall and closed my peepers. This was a dream, wasn't it? Sort of like that whole "Bobby Ewing died" thing. "Just for kicks, kid, when you call Washington, who answers the phone?"

"A wee bit pissy, are we?" Romeo said with a grin—I could hear it in his voice so I didn't waste the energy to look.

"One of my many charms."

"Shady Slim called two folks. One of them works for the DOJ. The other just got paroled out of Leavenworth."

"Why are there always two jokers in every deck?" I raised a hand. "Rhetorical. I already know the answer: The powers that be have serious issues with me. And I have a feeling you're just dangling the bait."

"The felon, he had a tie-in with Dane. Apparently our cowboy was the acting MP who busted the guy's ass on a charge of laundering money."

"Any specifics?"

"The guy gave me the runaround, so I requested the files from the army, but you know how that goes."

We'd get stonewalled, that's how every game was played inside the Beltway. "And the DOJ?"

"Not returning my calls."

"And we're all shocked, right? If the Beltway bozos can't share info in an effort to keep terrorists from our shores, why would they throw crumbs our way?" I blew at a strand of hair I felt tickling my eyelid. "Dane could clear all of this up, I have a feeling. Sure would be nice to find him and throw him on a rack or, even better, a Judas cradle." The thought of Dane being stretched or slowly impaled was somewhat appealing, which did sorta bother me . . . just a little.

"A Judas what?"

"Never mind. It's too late for torture. I'm thinking dismemberment."

"You scare me." The smile still warmed the kid's voice. He had way more confidence in me than I did.

"Heck, I scare myself. Any other glad tidings?"

"I wasn't going to tell you this, but . . ."

Opening one eye, I raised an eyebrow at him. "Withholding information? So unlike you."

"It's nothing like that. It's just . . ." He looked sort of stricken.

"Romeo, you're starting to scare me for real. Give it up."

"In running trace on the Coke spill in the doorway of Cole Weston's room, we found cyanide."

"That's not even a tiny surprise."

"And we found blood."

"Blood?" That got both my eyes open. "Whose?"

Romeo shrugged. "But if it's any consolation, we found it outside the room."

"None inside?"

"No."

Again, I blew at that annoying strand of hair. "Do you think we'll ever start coming up with answers instead of more questions?"

"Eventually." He sounded resolute. I took momentary comfort even though I didn't believe him for a nanosecond. I felt myself tumbling into the morass of cynicism—the first sign of the apocalypse.

Romeo pulled himself to his full height and worked the kinks out of his shoulders. "I'm hitting the dance floor. I do some of my best thinking there. Besides, I can't think of anything else to do."

As I watched him go, I didn't know whether he was pulling my leg or not. Not only had I apparently lost my ability to read people, I didn't have any answers or theories either. This whole thing was a mess—Dane on the lam, presumably with Cole

Weston in tow, although the blood confused things, Dane's wife dead, our Poker Room manager poisoned like a bit player in a Bogart black-and-white, Shady Slim taking a dump (no, I did not grin at that pun), Slurry fighting for his life, Watalsky and De-Luca lying by omission, a mysterious girl on the run, a killer on the loose . . . and poker the only connection.

Oh how I hated poker . . . and all the other games people played.

Chapter

FIFTEEN

" *I* am so sorry." The Frenchman's voice at my elbow startled me. I guess I had closed my eyes again. "You look like the standing dead. This is the right way to say this, no?"

"'Dead on my feet' is the idiom I believe you are reaching for."

"Yes, yes. This is it."

As I looked into his eyes, cloudy with concern, I had the same thought about something altogether different. This *is* it. He *is* it. But I'd been wrong before . . . so very, very wrong.

And he was right—I was in the middle of a whizzbang energy crisis and on the verge of emotional meltdown. It would probably take the Aztec calendar and an abacus to figure out when I'd last had any meaningful rest. A sadistic internal projectionist kept running the film of Kevin Slurry as he fell, leaving me little peace.

So this most definitely was not the time to make decisions about the rest of my life. To be honest, deciding *what* to wear to bed would be a sufficient challenge—deciding *whom* to take to bed was way outside my current capabilities. So I punted. "Walk me home?"

He extended an elbow. "With pleasure. But you must tell me what happened to your ankle."

"A brief but ugly battle with exceptionally high heels. I lost."

He looked at me for a moment as if weighing my words. "You must be more careful," he finally said. The look on his face left me with the distinct impression he saw way more than I told. Or maybe I was just being paranoid.

"Truer words were never spoken."

At this time of night, Vegas would be firing on all cylinders. We eased into the river of humanity in the Bazaar and let ourselves be carried along on the flow of enthusiasm toward the hotel lobby. Being surrounded by the chatter of excitement and captured in the crush of people intent on having a good time, did bolster my spirits—Vegas magic always had that effect. Too bad I couldn't tap into some of the everpresent energy.

"I know you are dead, and your ankle hurts, but perhaps we could rest in the Hanging Gardens for a bit?"

Even in my depleted state I wasn't so far gone that I'd turn down a romantic . . . rest . . . with a gorgeous Frenchman who suffered from the delusion that I was special. Clutching his arm with both of my hands, I squeezed and nodded. "The perfect antidote to a semi-dreadful day."

Leaning heavily on his arm, I hobbled next to him, sheltered in the bubble of our own little world. Jean-Charles bent and kissed my forehead, then murmured in my ear. "You did not tell me Chef Omer has allowed me to use his kitchen for the competition."

"His kitchen, he should be the one to tell you."

Jean-Charles was quiet for a moment as he digested that. "You can trust me, Lucky, just as I trust you. I will not hurt you. And someday you will tell me all these things you hold inside."

No one could make those kinds of promises about a fickle future, but I didn't want to spoil the mood so I didn't mention it. Instead, I rested my head on his shoulder.

One step at a time.

ONE of the Seven Wonders of the Ancient World, the original Hanging Gardens of Babylon had beckoned travelers from far and wide, requiring many days of travel by boat and beast. The thought alone made me hurt. Thankfully, the trip here in Vegas was much shorter and didn't involve camels. Even though I'd missed the original, I was pretty sure the Big Boss's rendition did the ancient version proud.

Night hung low and heavy under the canopy of trees high above as we pushed through the doors into the only tropical climate zone west of the Rockies. The dampness caressed my skin—skin that was used to being sucked dry in the Mojave furnace. I filled my lungs, savoring the high relative humidity. Water. As a species we hadn't traveled very far since the first of us abandoned fins and crawled out of the primordial stew. Some of us had moved further from our reptilian ancestry than others, but I didn't want to think about that now.

As I clutched my Frenchman's arm, his hand covering mine, I let him lead me down discreetly lit paths through lush vegetation. The scent of flowers mingled with the lingering aromas of suntan oil and fruity beverages—vestiges of a day long since put to bed. Water burbled in the darkness as our path followed the waterway that connected our three pools. The bars were closed, the pools abandoned, which suited me just fine. Silence was a welcomed contrast to the endless party called Vegas.

Even the birds were quiet, but snatches of music drifted past on a slightly cool breeze. Bats winged silently, feeding. I must've shivered as Jean-Charles paused and shrugged out of his jacket. Placing it over my shoulders, he wrapped an arm around me. Once again I settled my head on his shoulder, securing his nearness with an arm around his waist. The other hand, I placed on his stomach, comforted in his warmth, the regular rise and fall of each breath.

"Thank you," I whispered, afraid my voice would shatter the delicate peace.

He said nothing, but gave me a slight squeeze.

Time seemed to stand still—a perfect antidote to the mad rush of the day. I had no idea how long we wandered—for some reason my ankle didn't bother me that much. Jean-Charles pulled me toward a chaise, then extricated himself from my hold. After he grabbed a clean towel from the tall stack awaiting tomorrow's sun worshippers, he spread it on the chair and motioned for me to lie down. "We get such little time to enjoy each other's company."

Settling myself, I scootched over to allow room for Jean-Charles. Darkness shadowed his face as he eased in next to me. I couldn't see what lurked in his eyes, but his features looked relaxed with a pleasant emotion. "If I fall asleep, you won't be insulted."

"Having you fall asleep in my arms would be a dream," he whispered against my hair as he wrapped his arms around me, pulling me close.

Too tired to resist, I snuggled in, his body molding to mine. Why did he have to fit perfectly? Even the measure of my breath, the cadence of my heart, matched his.

"Christophe arrives tomorrow."

My stomach clenched—so much for relaxing. Jean-Charles's son. Although he looked like a charmer, if the kid didn't like me, he could be a deal breaker. While sucking up to adults was in my job description, navigating a five-year-old was way beyond my capabilities.

"So soon? I'd lost track of time."

"Yes, my niece, Chantal, she is bringing him. They arrive tomorrow night." A warm tenor infused his voice when he talked about his son.

Would there be room in their life and hearts for me? Another question with no easy answer. Why was I not surprised? "I don't need to ask if you are excited."

"To be a family again, it will be nice. Christophe, he will go to school. Life will find its song."

"Rhythm," I corrected reflexively. The warmth in his voice made me smile, and his love for his son filled my heart. Despite my fear, I wanted him to be happy. "And Chantal?"

"She is wearing my boots. She is only sixteen, but she will be a student at the Culinary Institute."

Overcome by surprise, this time I didn't bother correcting his idiomatic error. A five-year-old *and* a teenager. Just as my courage flagged, I heard Miss P's admonishing voice—"Remember, Lucky, the harder the struggle, the larger the prize"—and courage was restored. I could handle a five-year-old. Sure I could! Assuming I lived through the teenager. "I didn't know Chantal would be staying."

"My mother, she is not pleased. She says I am a Pied Piper stealing all the children."

And the hearts, I thought. The Game of Life. What I would give for an instruction manual. Or at least a list of rules. Or a crystal ball.

In the comfort of Jean-Charles's arms, I felt my eyelids grow heavy. My breathing slowed, and the wheels ground to a halt. The safe haven of sleep exerted its inexorable pull. Did I dare relinquish myself? He said it would be a dream.

I took him at his word.

A chill tickled the back of my neck, awakening me. For a moment, I lay still, remembering, enjoying. The night had darkened. The music had slipped from a pulsing rhythm to languid melodies. Hours had passed.

"You are awake, yes?" Somehow a male-timbered French accent made dreams unnecessary.

"And you have not slept."

"For a bit, perhaps. But sleep would rob me of these memories."

I pushed myself up to my elbow so I could look at him. A smile lifted the corner of his mouth. His eyes had turned all deep and delicious—an unfair advantage in my weakened state.

"You never say what I think you're going to say," I admitted as I traced the line of his jaw, then bent and brushed my lips over his.

Reaching a hand behind my head, he pulled me to him, deepening the kiss. Molten lava flowed through my veins, pooling in my core, where it exploded in a ball of desire. The guy was going to be the death of me. But I wasn't going down today . . . I cringed at the bad choice of words. Anyway, my demise would have to be rescheduled.

Both hands pressing against his chest broke his hold. "Walk me home?"

He grinned. "Is this not how we ended up here?"

"You expect me to remember?"

The crowd was much thinner now as we pushed through the doors back into the casino. We blinked against the assault of the light—casinos were the only places south of the Artic where daylight prevailed twenty-four hours a day. Smoke hung heavy in the air. Gamblers riding a hot streak or nursing hopes of a change in their luck clustered around a few tables. The remaining tables, like picnic tables after a party, sat forlorn, abandoned, surrounded by empty stools. Bees darting among blossoms, cocktail waitresses bounced between groups, keeping the participants well oiled. Casinos walked a fine line—allowing a severely intoxicated player to keep playing was a violation of gaming laws. But a slightly inebriated player would push his comfort zones, usually to the house's benefit.

In quiet corners, the cleaning crew labored surreptitiously with their spot cleaners. Cases of liquor and condiments were stacked next to the bars like sand bags bracing for an impending flood. A group of bored employees circled several slot machines as a rep from the Gaming Commission droned on about new ways cheaters rigged the machines and what to watch out for. Dane used to give that class—a lifetime ago.

Dane, the perfect strident note of reality to burst my joy balloon.

Poised to leap into the abyss of gloom, I concentrated on Jean-Charles's and my reflection in the double bronze doors as we waited for the elevator. My chef, quiet, handsome, sedately calm, holding himself in a relaxed, easy manner. Me, mussed, frazzled around the edges, held together with the epoxy of resolve. Proof that opposites attract.

My phone vibrated at my hip. Briefly I thought about ignoring it. But life had taught me that problems were like sparks in a dry forest—the sooner you threw water on them, the smaller the chance of an inferno. With a practiced motion, I pulled the phone from its holster and pushed to talk. "Yeah."

Jerry didn't waste time with pleasantries. "You wanted DeLuca. He's in Delilah's holding court."

"Got it. Thanks."

"You must leave?" Jean-Charles asked as I reholstered my phone.

"Duty calls. I'm sorry."

Jean-Charles took me in his arms. Reaching up, he brushed a strand of hair out of my face, then brushed his lips across mine, igniting the sting after a burn. A sensual tease leaving me wanting for more. "I am glad you got a bit of sleep. Your job, it is not healthy."

"Now there's an understatement." I gave a shaky laugh and waved away the look of worry that turned his eyes all dark and deep. "Gotta go."

With regret, and a bit more willpower than I thought it'd take, I pushed aside the lingering warmth left by the Frenchman and tried to concentrate. Frank had some questions to answer . . . if I could only remember what they were. I watched Jean-Charles as he disappeared through the doors to the garage, then I turned and headed into the casino.

Another call caught me halfway to Delilah's. "So, where is he now?"

"Who?" Romeo didn't sound confused, just tired, as if he couldn't understand the context or he didn't care.

"Sorry, I thought you were Jerry." Pressing my phone to one ear, I stopped next to an abandoned bank of slot machines and stuck a finger in the other ear. "Whatcha got?"

"A couple of your guests who got into a knock-down, drag-out with some folks as they were leaving Piero's. A cruiser picked them up and dropped them in my lap. I spend so much time here at the Detention Center, they're going to give me my own room."

"And you need me because . . . ?"

"Because"—Romeo chuckled—"you're going to love this. I need you because the male guest was arrested for soliciting." I started to say something, but Romeo said, "No, wait for it." He paused dramatically. "Your guest, he was arrested for soliciting his wife."

"Oh, you've met Toby and Myrna."

"How do you know everything?" The bravado had leaked out of Romeo's voice.

"It's my job." No way was I telling him how lucky I really was. "And what I don't know, I can figure out. Soliciting one's wife is not a crime, at least, not the last time I looked. So there must be something else."

"A piece . . . of jewelry. The other couple involved swears the necklace is theirs and that it was stolen out of their suite at the Babylon a few weeks ago."

"Really?"

"And what do Toby and Myrna say?"

"They won't say a word until you get here."

AS much as I wanted to, I didn't have the heart to leave guests cooling their heels in a cell while I went on a little fishing trip with Mr. Frank DeLuca. So I did an about-face and headed toward the lobby. Fresh out of vehicles, I grabbed a cab for the ten-minute ride to the Detention Center.

A young officer greeted me as I pushed through the doors and escorted me to the interrogation room. Somehow it seemed to be too sad a commentary on my life that I could find it by myself, so I didn't admit to it. Instead, I followed him dutifully, like a wide-eyed first-timer.

Probably too tired to stand, Romeo remained seated when I stepped inside the small room and shut the door behind me. Institutional gray coated every surface. Every time I stepped into the room I felt perpetually adrift in an ominous, storm-tossed sea. Whether that was by design or just my overactive imagination, the effect was unsettling. Of course, the blinking red eye of the video camera mounted in the corner didn't help.

Toby looked sheepish when his eyes caught mine. A red gash split his lower lip, which had swelled to twice its normal size. An ugly bruise colored his right cheek and a deepening circle of purple underscored his other eye. Myrna, on the other hand, looked angry, and relieved . . . and not the least bit embarrassed—even in her spandex tube top, which she nervously tugged. But the more she tugged at the top, the higher the bottom inched, threatening the lower threshold of decency.

Romeo kicked out the chair next to his. "Take a load off. Now that you're here, maybe the Jacobses will be so kind as to enlighten me as to how we came to be introduced this evening?" He looked expectantly at his charges as I sunk into the chair next to him.

"What is all of this about?" I asked the two of them in my best schoolteacher voice.

A glance passed between Toby and Myrna; then Toby gave a slight nod and Myrna started in. "Well," she said, her tone conspiratorial. "Everything was going to plan. I got all gussied up and went to the bar at Piero's as planned. They have the most wonderful bar. And the food! It's to die for. Anyway, I was sitting there and Toby—"

"I'm sure this is a good story, but could you fast-forward to the interesting part?"

She tugged at her skirt, another piece of spandex insufficient to cover the necessaries. "Well," she harrumphed. "It all started with the necklace Toby gave me."

I glanced at Romeo. He pulled the item in question out of his pocket and dribbled it on the table. "Is this the one?" he asked.

"Yes. It's so pretty, don't you think?"

Pretty if you like a huge diamond set in platinum, offset by an emerald of equal size, with the two stones then circled by smaller rubies. Distinctive. Pricey. Noticeable. The piece would be hard to miss, especially on Myrna's neck, uncluttered as it was with clothing.

"Can you tell me what happened?" Romeo pressed.

"We were standing out front of the restaurant, negotiating a price when this couple attacked us!" Myrna talked with her hands, making grand gestures as her voice escalated with indignation. "They accused us of stealing! Stealing! Us? Please, we're commodity traders from Chicago."

I almost asked what the going price for meat on the hoof was, but Romeo's daggered look shot me down. Instead I composed myself and asked, "If you didn't steal it, where did you get it?"

"I bought it at that high-end jewelry store at the Edelweiss." Toby sounded less than pleased, which was understandable, all things considered.

"A lot of people pay a lot more, get less, and end up in jail anyway," I offered. "You're not alone."

"You're not helping," Romeo hissed.

Toby gave me the grin I was hoping for. So I turned to Romeo to gloat. Leaning back, he shrugged and motioned for me to continue.

I leaned forward, my elbows on the table, arms crossed. "You bought it?"

"Of course. Those folks specialize in one-of-a-kind pieces, estate jewelry, pretty amazing stuff. I buy something there every year." He sure looked like he was telling the truth. Personally, I didn't know much about the jewelry store at the Edelweiss, but it was on my list of places to visit. As a boutique property catering to Eastern Europeans and Russians, the Edelweiss was a close competitor and it stood to reason they'd have something over-the-top.

I turned to Romeo. "I assume you questioned the couple who said the piece is theirs?"

"They even provided me with a video inventory they used for insurance purposes. The piece is there." He poked the necklace with his finger. "If this isn't the same one that was stolen outta your hotel, it's a damn fine forgery."

That stopped me. "Forgery? Hadn't thought of that. Did you check with Security to see if a report of the theft had been filed?"

"They said they'd fax it to me."

"Unique pieces stolen from the Babylon . . ." I turned to Romeo. "Are you thinking what I'm thinking?"

"Wouldn't hurt to check it out," he said with a noncommittal shrug, but I could see Myrna and Toby's story had piqued his interest.

"How're you going to handle that? The store is probably closed at this hour."

"True." He leaned forward, a glint in his eye. "I have a plan, but I need your help."

AS I staggered through the Babylon, Jerry confirmed my fear—Frank DeLuca was not on the property. I'd missed my chance.

Finally, I made it back to my temporary home—the top floor. The hall was empty, the atmosphere funereal. Much like my life, it was devoid of light, laughter, and fun—three of my staples that currently had gone wanting. The floor was private, with Mona, the Big Boss, and I its only residents, so I saw little need to throw the deadbolt. The knob turned easily in my hand and I stepped inside, closing the door behind me. Propping myself against the wall, I reached down and gingerly pulled the shoe from my foot with the huge ankle, then kicked off the other shoe. With my feet released from their prison, I sighed in relief. High heels were invented to make women more appreciative of simple pleasures. And although the theory worked, I'm not sure it had the far-reaching effects men hoped for.

The lights from the Strip painted the apartment in a multicolored glow sufficient for navigation so I left the interior lights off as I grabbed my shoes and made my way through the great room to my bedroom in the back.

And then I smelled it. Smoke. Cigarette smoke. What the hell?

"It's about time you showed up," a voice in the dark growled.

Dane! I whirled toward his voice as my heart leaped into my throat. The glow from the end of his cigarette brightened as he took another drag—I could hear the sizzle of the tobacco as the fire consumed it. An unreadable shadow backlit by the glow from the Strip, he eased forward from the deep embrace of a winged, high-back chair.

For a moment I froze. Should I be afraid? Defend myself? With what, my rapier wit? My gun? I had no idea where it was—stuffed in some box still waiting to be unpacked, I guessed, which didn't help. Should I fling my shoes at him and make a break for it? Unable to process, my brain ground to a halt. "How the hell did you get in here?"

"Your door was unlocked." He blew out the smoke in a perfect ring that glowed eerily in the half-light, which irritated me.

"And the elevator needed a special key." That comment was rhetorical. Dane had worked in Security—even I could connect those dots. I stood in the middle of the room unsure where to turn or what to do next. "Would you turn on a light or something? It's not like Metro is going to be looking in my windows." Come to think of it, they might, but I didn't say that part.

Dane flicked on a lamp.

I blinked against the light. Narrowing my eyes, I tried to measure his mood as he mashed the butt into a blown-glass bowl, a limited-edition Chihuly, on the table next to his chair. He looked tired, worried, angry, but not homicidal, as far as I could tell. I took that as a good thing. His shirt and jeans, now well into their second day of wear, appeared as if they'd been pulled from the bottom of the dirty laundry pile. A two-day stubble darkened his cheeks. His hair, on the other hand, had come through unscathed, beckoning for fingers to be run through it.

Either I was too tired to care, or just mad as hell, but the normal tickle of temptation was a no-show. "You've got one hell of a nerve coming here."

"I had nowhere else to go." His voice was flat, tired but with an edge. Absentmindedly he patted his pockets, then quit.

"I'm touched." Tossing my shoes under the side table, I staggered to the couch and curled myself into a corner, tucking my feet underneath me. Pulling the throw pillows around me, I created a pastel silk-and-foam fortification. Not much, but the illusion was all I needed. "You do know the police are beating every bush in this city looking for you?"

"They'd be incompetent if they weren't."

"Then I suggest you give them a shout. They get seriously irritated when you make them chase you." Dropping this whole mess in Romeo's lap would so simplify my life. But if Dane was concerned about anything, it sure wasn't my comfort level, so I didn't see any upside to pointing it out. "It'd be easier for you in the long run."

"It's the short run I'm worried about." Dane leaned forward. His elbows on his knees, he buried his face in his hands. "I've got to find Sylvie's killer." When he looked up, his face was pinched with anger, his eyes haunted by an emotion I couldn't read. Regret? Sadness? Perhaps he really had loved her.

What would I do if someone killed one of my loved ones? "Why are you here, Dane? I mean, besides trying to add harboring a fugitive to my résumé?"

"I need your help."

"You can't be serious!" Fury arced through me—white-hot, it sizzled and burned. I thought about jumping up and starting to pace, but I was too tired and my ankle had started to throb. "You're avoiding the police, stringing us all along, and you want my help." I stared at him for a moment—the guy was a head case. "Logic is clearly not one of your strong suits."

He leaned into the light. "You may be right, none of this makes sense."

At least he got that part right.

"But one thing I'm sure of . . ." He paused, milking the moment, making sure he had my attention. "I'm in way over my head."

"I fell for that game . . . once." I reached for my phone. "I'm calling Romeo."

"Wait." For a moment, Dane tensed, pulling into himself—a caged animal coiled to leap. But he didn't. He settled back, almost vibrating with the effort to still himself. "Hear me out, then call him if you want to."

The clock on the wall ticked the passing of the seconds, perhaps stretching to a minute, as I contemplated my predicament. There was not one good reason why I should listen to him . . . again. Not one. So, of course, bitten by the curiosity bug, I sorted through possible justifications. God, I must have had *stupid* written all over me. Perhaps I should consider changing my name to Patsy.

"Where's Cole Weston?" I tossed the question out there, chumming the waters.

The question clearly caught him off guard. "The deaf kid? With Shooter, last I knew."

"Yes, but where exactly?"

"His room on the fifteenth floor, west wing." Understanding reached Dane's eyes as they locked on mine. "They aren't there?"

"No. And the police found blood in the hallway."

He blinked a couple of times, absorbing the blow. "Fuck." That hint of homicidal I had been looking for now hit his eyes.

"Any ideas?" I asked, because sarcasm makes me feel good.

"The killer?"

"A shot in the dark, but that's one explanation." I pulled the pillows closer to me, finding comfort in the foam fortification. "How about this one? You and Shooter tried to take Cole with you. He resisted."

"Why would we take him?"

"You tell me."

"I really haven't a clue. What part does he play in this whole thing? Sylvie never mentioned him, not that she threw much my way." He clammed up, pressing his lips into a thin line as he looked over my shoulder.

"Who was Sylvie, really?" I had lots of ideas, and a few suppositions, but I wanted to hear Dane's story.

He leaned back, but kept his face in the light, where I could see it. His eyes flicked to mine. "My wife, but you know that." He paused.

I waited, absolutely certain he was weighing exactly how much to tell me. "Dane, now is not the time to hedge your bet. It's all in or I'm out."

"She worked for the government. Undercover. All that stuff I told you about her was really her cover story." He took a crumpled pack of cigarettes from the breast pocket on his shirt, shook one out, then rolled it between his fingers. A frown pulled his brows together and hardened his mouth. "She was in over her head. I was convinced the bad guys had made her, but she didn't believe me. She thought it was one more ploy to get her to quit. The more I pushed, the madder she got. One night she split."

"And she didn't leave a forwarding address?"

Dane glared at me. Confirmation enough.

"And that pissed you off?"

"It was her choice, not mine."

"Answer my question."

A tic worked in his cheek as his eyes narrowed. He stuck the cigarette between his lips. He thumbed the lighter, then held the flame to the tip, inhaling deeply. Tilting his head back, he blew the smoke out through the side of his mouth. "Yeah, it pissed me off. But I loved her, why would I bury a shoe in her neck?"

"Because she split. Men like you don't take no for an answer."

"Men like me?" Dane's voice held a knife-edge.

I was beyond caring. "Controlling. Arrogant. Chivalrous to cover a mile-wide chauvinistic streak." Why hadn't I seen what was so apparent now? I waited, watching his anger boil. "She didn't call you from the poker game, did she?"

"No. I called her."

"Why?"

"I wanted to get her out of there. Things were getting hot."

"You'd tried that before."

"Yeah, but this time she was scared, I could tell." He glared at me. "I knew her pretty well."

"From the video it looked like she was mad."

"Mad as a cornered coyote." Dane's voice had gone quiet. "She said I'd blow her cover."

"She got that part right."

He flinched, which should've made me feel better, but didn't.

"How'd you meet?" I modulated my voice, but I had to work to keep the mad out of it.

"Like I said, she worked for the government, more specifically the Department of Justice, chasing a money-laundering scheme involving American troops overseas. Our paths crossed."

"The DOJ? Money laundering?"

"Black-market profits pushed though an offshore

gaming site. The money went in as wagers, came out as winnings. Scrubbed clean. Untraceable."

"Gambling and money laundering, common bedfellows. Does this offshore gaming site have a name?"

"Yeah, it was that site run by Kevin Slurry—Aces Over Eights."

A dead man's hand. Sylvie's clue, Frank's code phrase. She had been telling us where to look. "How come the feds haven't shut it down as they have so many others?"

"If you want to catch a rat, it's better to bait a trap."

"A sting?" I couldn't keep the incredulity out of my voice. "In my limited experience dead bodies tend to make government types all twitchy. And as far as I know, Aces Over Eights is still up and running."

"With Sylvie . . ." He trailed off. After a moment, he found his voice. "I'm out of the loop, let's leave it at that."

"Okay, let's assume what you say is true, which, given your proclivities, is a huge leap. Let's say Kevin Slurry is guilty as sin. Who is he cleaning all this money for?"

"Don't know." Dane rubbed the stubble on his chin, making a sandpaper-on-wood sound. "Sylvie caught their scent in Iraq, but just when she thought she had them, they vanished. I can only assume that she caught the whiff of their scent and it led her here."

"And the guy you sent up? I understand Leavenworth isn't a garden spot. Bet he was pissed, but he didn't roll, did he?"

Dane's eyes widened. "You're good."

"I'd rather be lucky than good," I said, trotting out one of Miss P's platitudes—one I hated. Middle school kids could be vicious—apparently I still had the scars to prove it. "And, since I can't trust you, luck is something I'm gonna need in spades. That and a couple of Guardian Angels willing to work overtime." I squeezed the pillows close to me. Why did a friend's betrayal cut so deeply? "Your Leavenworth friend? Got any insight?"

"You're right; he didn't roll. We offered him the moon, but he wouldn't give his contact up. The guy was scared stupid."

"And the Gaming Commission, you didn't quit, did you?"

The change in topic caught him by surprise. "No, I was put on indefinite leave pending an investigation." He paused, taking a deep breath. When he started again, his voice was stronger, fueled with emotion. "There were some papers, some records. It looked like I was part of the scheme—the black market stuff and the laundering. Sylvie found them."

"You? One of the black hats? I'm shocked." Using sarcasm as a weapon was sort of like arguing the Constitution in court. If that was the best you had, you'd better run for cover. Curiously impervious to the warning, I tried not to think about it. "Now this is the part where you tell me it was all a setup, a misunderstanding."

"You wouldn't believe me." He shrugged as his

eyes flicked to mine, looking for confirmation, if I could hazard a guess.

"You have yourself to blame for that."

"I've made some mistakes."

"That's the first honest thing you said." I massaged my ankle as I watched the emotions parade across his face. What was I supposed to do? Oh, I knew what I was *supposed* to do, but really, I wanted answers almost as badly as he did. Would throwing him to the Metro wolves help? Doubtful. Yes, I'm the queen of justification. "What exactly was Sylvie doing here? Trying to pull your nuts out of the fire?"

"Hell, no. She was obsessed with bringing down the whole house of cards. Those guys were . . . well, money laundering was the least of their . . . businesses." He spat the word out like it was laced with poison. "She didn't give a rat's ass about me. I was collateral damage."

"I see," I said, although this whole thing was about as clear as the air downwind of a forest fire. "And the shoe, the mate to the one buried in your wife's neck, did the bad guys plant that in your truck, too?"

"No, Sylvie left it there. She only took the one. It was broken—something with the heel, I think she said. I don't know. She said the guy who shines shoes for the guests said he could fix it for her." Dane leaned on his elbows, his hands clasped in front. His knuckles were white.

So the killer had pawed through her purse and the shoe was handy? If so, what was he looking for? Or maybe Sylvie had pulled out the shoe, the only weapon she had? So many ways the whole thing could've gone down. "So you guys were still together?"

"She'd call when she needed something."

Sounded familiar. "And those scratches on your cheek? Did Sylvie give you those?"

Dane shot me a glance out of the corner of his eye. I tried to keep my face blank, my expression impassive. He started to nod, then he slowly shook his head. "No." He chewed on his lip for a moment. If he tried to hide his conflicting emotions, he wasn't very good at it. Finally he said, "There was this girl."

With Dane, there was always a girl. I so hoped it was our girl—the one with Sylvie's shoes. Then, at least we'd know who we were looking for, sort of. "Where?"

"Coming out of the showroom as I went in."

"A witness?" I asked, trying to keep my voice steady.

So he had seen the girl.

And she had seen him.

A fact that could cut either way.

"I don't know, but she fought like a hellcat." Absent-mindedly, he traced the marks on his cheek.

"What'd she look like?"

"You mean besides terrified?"

When my eyes went all slitty, Dane settled back to the truth, or at least his version of it. "Dark hair, Hispanic, medium build, big brown eyes, dressed as a cocktail waitress, but didn't smell like one."

Our girl. The girl in Sylvie's red shoes.

I rooted in my pocket until I found the picture Jerry gave me. I unfolded it, then thrust it at Dane. "Is this her?"

He half stood in order to reach across the gap between us, then settled back in the chair, the photo in his hand. I waited while he studied it.

"Yeah." Hope flashed in his eyes. "You have her?"

I shook my head. "She may have been dressed as an employee, but she doesn't work at the Babylon."

"Can you find her?" At my outstretched hand, Dane rose and returned the photo.

His reluctance to give it back was easy to see. I'm sure he wanted to flash it around, see if he could get a line on her. Maybe she was the killer. Maybe she could finger the killer. Maybe she could finger Dane. The thought made my blood run cold. Either way, I sure didn't want him taking off after the girl before I could find her—so I measured my response as I meticulously refolded the paper and put it back where I had found it. "No. But leave her to Romeo. That's his job."

"I can't believe I let her get away, but when I caught sight of Sylvie over the girl's shoulder, I froze."

"Understandable."

"Sylvie was already dead."

"And someone with some answers disappeared."

"So you really don't know where she is?" Dane asked.

"I told you before—I haven't a clue."

The light of hope in his eyes flashed out. He turned once again to stare at his hands, his head hanging in defeat.

Something was bothering me. Okay, a ton of somethings were bothering me, but this was something he had said. What was it? I mentally panned back over our conversation. Finally I had it. "She didn't smell like a cocktail waitress? What does that mean?"

"Most of the women who work here smell of cologne or flowers or something. But this girl, she smelled like smoke, charcoal, I'd say. We used to cook out a bunch in Texas when I was a kid. Just the smell makes my mouth water."

I waited while Dane finished his jaunt down memory lane.

"Charcoal smoke and something else," he said as he closed his eyes. When he opened them again they were empty dark holes. "A dank sort of smell."

"Dank?" In the middle of the Mojave that was a rarity.

"Yeah, like water. Sour, standing water. The odor of the mosquito pits after a summer storm."

Mosquito pits. Standing water. Sour. Dank. Charcoal smoke. "Oh, man!" I jumped to my feet, then crumpled a bit as my ankle screamed at me.

Startled, Dane jumped up a fraction of a second after I did. As I moved to go around him, this time more gingerly, he grabbed my arm, pulling me to a stop. "Wherever you're going, I'm going, too."

I pried his fingers from my arm. "You show your face, you'll get us both arrested. You're staying right here."

"I need to know what you're thinking, where you're going."

"Not a chance, cowboy. Stay here."

His face closed into a frown. "And do what?"

"I don't know. Sleep, get rid of the stink of fear and alleys that's clinging to you, whatever. I don't care. But I'll kill you myself if you dare even stick your nose out of the door while I'm gone. Got it?" I poked his chest with my forefinger for emphasis.

While he mulled that over, I charged toward my bedroom. First a shower and a new outfit.

The strappy gold flats would be out of place where I was going.

Chapter

SIXTEEN

♡

Dane had agreed to stay put a bit too easily.

I didn't trust him for a minute, which was a good thing. Maybe I was actually learning—doubtful, but possible. After a quick change of clothes, I laced on my Nikes, then headed out the door. As I passed the guest bedroom, I heard the shower running. Punching the lock, then securing the door behind me, I paused in the hallway, grabbed

my push-to-talk, and pressed the appropriate button. "Security? Who's running the show right now?"

"Who do you think?" came the pithy reply.

"Jerry." Relief flooded through me—handling Dane
would require the first-stringers. "I thought I sent
you home."

"Yeah, well, I take orders about as well as you do.
What's up?" I heard the click of his lighter then the
sizzle as he pulled the flame into the tobacco.

"Those things are going to kill you."

"If this job doesn't get me first. Between you and
me, it's a toss-up."

"Good point. Listen, I need you to post one of
your guys outside my apartment door. No one goes
in. No one comes out."

"Who you got in there?"

I lowered my voice—God knew who was listening. "Just a friend."

"You and me got differing opinions on friends."
Jerry's cigarette sizzled as he took another pull.
"You're diggin' a hole, girl."

"I'm a danger to myself and others—it's part of
my charm. Promise me you'll see to it I get the help
I need when this is over. But right now, just do as I
ask, okay? Just for a few hours?"

"If the cops come nosing around here . . ."

"Without a warrant, they can't get into my apartment."

"Technically . . ."

"I know, but they need good cause to go barging

in. And if you can keep my friend under wraps, they won't have any. Just a few hours, that's all I need." I started to ring off, then I stopped. "Jerry, my ass is on the line here."

"I got your ass, girl. You know that." I started to ring off again, then I heard his voice come back. "Lucky?"

"Yeah."

"One of my people found some footage of the Stoneman in the casino after he'd asked for personal time. It looked like he was tailing Sylvie Dane, but he was almost as good at dodging the cameras as Dane himself was."

"Did you see him by the dealership?"

"He was headed in that direction, but with the sign hanging in front of the cameras and all, I can't put him inside."

"Maybe not, but it's something. Thanks."

This time I did hang up—there was nothing else to say and banter wasn't the panacea it normally was.

When the security detail showed up, I made sure they had no problem with my shoot-first-ask-questions-later instructions, then I headed toward the elevator.

I needed sleep. I needed food. I needed a life. But most of all, right now I needed a plan.

Handling this by myself seemed the height of stupidity, so, of course, that's what I decided to do. Besides, I was fresh out of knights in shining armor.

The elevator deposited me in a curiously quiet lobby. All the smart people were tucked in bed.

Concentrating on repositioning my phone at my hip, I was startled by a body hurtling around the corner. Scowling, his stride purposeful, his jaw set, Jeremy stared straight ahead, unseeing. Distracted, he looked like a man on a mission.

Suffering from a lack of everything that does a body good, I was one step too slow. I braced for impact.

Nose to nose, we both skidded to a halt with inches to spare.

"What are you doing here?" Even at this godforsaken hour, Australian sounded good. And looked good.

"I work here." Boy, ask for a white knight and voilà! If I'd only known it was that easy. "How about you?"

"Trying to catch the scent of Shooter and the kid. Was on my way to go over video footage one more time." With one quick glance, he absorbed my jeans, sweatshirt, Nikes. "Is today casual day?"

I smiled, feeling the tension ease a smidge. "No, it's do-somebody-else's-dirty-work day."

Jeremy gripped my arm. Any tighter and I would've grimaced. "Dane's dirty work? Do you know where he is?"

I glanced around before answering. "Under wraps," I whispered as I eased my arm from his grasp. "Did Miss P tell you about Shooter and the kid?"

"Yeah, Lovey told me. I've been ringing them both, but no answer." Jeremy glanced around, probably a habit, then lowered his voice. "Does our boy have any news that might be helpful?"

"Sure," I scoffed. "Why he keeps acting like we are on opposite teams in this game, I'd like to know."

"Curious, I'll admit."

In my limited understanding, that statement was tantamount to treason in the Male Code of Ethics, which didn't give me a warm fuzzy. Friends were usually the last to bail.

I grabbed Jeremy's elbow. "I'm chasing a connection and I could use your help."

He matched my stride. "Where're we going?"

"Remember the storm drains?"

A maze of storm sewers crisscrossed under Las Vegas. Some said there were three hundred miles of the concrete pipes, most of them large enough to stand in. A rare storm in the summer could dump so much rain in the mountains to the west that flash flooding became a huge problem as the city grew. The storm drains were part of the elaborate system designed to keep the rampaging water off the streets and out of the casinos.

The other elements not wanted in the casinos—the homeless, the crazy, and the criminal—all took refuge in the drains when the water wasn't an issue. They built cities down there—hovels, kitchens, workspaces, all of it.

Absentmindedly, Jeremy rubbed the left side of

his torso. "The pipes. Man I hope I never go back there."

Couldn't say I blamed him—the last time I'd sent him down there, Crazy Carl had creased his side with a .30-30 bullet. Technically it wasn't my fault, but I blamed myself.

Jeremy gave me a sideways glance, narrowing his eyes. "Why?" He stretched the word out, giving me the impression he knew why, but didn't want to hear it.

"Hope you still have your gun and that Maglite."

He looked down at his nice slacks and leather loafers. "Bugger."

"This is really important, and time is not on our side." I fisted my hand in his shirt to get his attention. "Where's your truck?"

"Valet. It won't fit in the garage."

"Let's go." I turned on my heel and headed toward the lobby. "I'll explain on the way."

Shoulder to shoulder, Jeremy and I hurried, propelled by the sense that we were woefully behind.

LIGHTNING flashed in the western sky, jagged bright slashes ripping the dark fabric of the night. Great. Just what we needed. "I hope to hell it doesn't rain." Riding high, tucked comfortably into the passenger seat of Jeremy's Hummer, I felt invincible—a fleeting, foolish feeling, but I held on to it. To be honest, the storm drains scared the heck out of me. And rain made them death traps.

Jeremy shot me a glance, then refocused on the

road, both hands clutching the steering wheel, his shoulders hunched in concentration. "I've been here a couple of years and it hasn't rained at all. They say we're in a drought. How would you know—we live in a desert? Anyway, I wouldn't worry."

The first fat drop hit the windshield like a bullet. Other droplets followed, peppering the truck like shrapnel hurled from each violent explosion of thunder.

"Silly of me to worry." I had to raise my voice to be heard above the staccato beat of the rain, growing in intensity now until the windshield wipers could barely keep up. I had to squint to see. "Nice to see my luck is holding. You can see better than me, I hope."

Jeremy, his brow gathered in concentration, grunted. I didn't know whether that was a yes or a no, but decided I'd rather be left in the dark. We fell quiet, beaten into silence by the steady drumming. Puddles formed quickly, throwing sheets of spray as we splashed through. Rivulets of water raced down the sides of the streets, growing in speed and depth. Water in the desert—both life-giving and destructive. Too little or too much, both had devastating consequences.

"I hope we beat the police." I didn't realize I'd spoken out loud until Jeremy responded.

"The police? You called them?"

"No. On a night like tonight, raining as hard as it is, I'm sure a wash call went out."

"Wash call?"

"When the water runs like this, every unit is scrambled to try to get folks out of the storm drains. A couple inches of flowing water can take your feet right out from under you. People die in the drains every time it rains."

A streetlight illuminated Jeremy's wide-eyed glance as we passed underneath, then darkness engulfed his face once again as we drove on. "I'd prefer not to be one of them."

That made two of us.

He left the lights on as he pulled off Decatur and parked the car. Our breath fogged the windows as we took a moment to assess. It always amazed me how a good thunderstorm could drop the temperature thirty degrees. With the soft pad of my fist I cleared a spot on the glass in front of me and squinted into the darkness, timing the lightning strikes.

Water accumulated in the retention basin—it was filling fast. We didn't have much time before the torrent reached the storm drain at the far end. There, the relatively small opening of the pipes themselves would act as a Venturi. Forced through the pipes, the water would become a roiling, deadly surge that would scour the drainage system like a giant Roto-Rooter, spitting the limp, lifeless forms of previously living things out the other side.

Once trapped, you were as good as dead.

With a glance at Jeremy, I tugged on the door handle and eased the door open. "We'd better hurry."

"Wait." Before my feet hit the ground, his hand

fisted in my sweatshirt, pulling me back inside. "Who's that?"

I swiped at a trickle of rain and focused. A dark figure sprinted across the basin toward the drain. I knew that long thin, slice of a man—Dane. I grabbed my phone and punched a now-familiar button. "Jerry."

"I know. I know. Fuck." Homicide lurked in the depths of his tone. The guy would have to stand in line. "I just tried my team, but neither one answered. I'm heading to your place now, but I'd bet my left ball Dane is gone."

"Are your people okay?"

"If they aren't . . ." Jerry didn't finish the threat; he didn't have to.

I dropped my phone on the floorboard, leaped into the rain, and ran. My ankle be damned—fear and anger, the perfect antidotes to pain. Even with my loping stride, Jeremy was twenty feet ahead of me.

Shoulder to shoulder, we ducked through the drain opening. Being out of the rain was nice, but it did little to offset my fear at the ominous black hole leading away from us. Why hadn't I brought that gun? Because I'd left it somewhere in my apartment . . . with Dane. Fuck.

Jeremy clicked on the Maglite—the cone of light barely held back the Stygian darkness. Instead it pressed around us, lurking like a demon, just out of sight, waiting for a sign of weakness.

My hand lightly on his back, I followed him into the darkness. Water sloshed around our feet, seeping into my shoes. It was rising fast. "Carl's place." The water muffled the usual echo.

"Right." Jeremy's voice came back solid, strong.

While I was delighted to have him there, I was conflicted. He'd almost died once down here already. "Bugger." I hurled his word into the darkness because I couldn't think of anything else to say.

Half running, we sloshed on in silence. I thought I heard the sound of someone running in front of us, but I wasn't sure.

"Here's the turn." I pulled Jeremy up short. Apparently Carl didn't want company—he'd erected a wooden fence across the opening.

"No wonder I didn't see it." Jeremy attacked the makeshift barrier. Three kicks splintered it and we squeezed through.

A few feet farther then the pipes opened at a juncture point, creating a large open room—Carl's home. A weak glow from a dying fire glowed in the hibachi, which Carl had set on top of a crate to protect it from the rising water. "Carl?"

No answer.

Then I heard them: angry, animal sounds, unintelligible shouts. "Great, Carl's off his meds." I tossed the words over my shoulder as I moved toward the sounds. After briefly considering using Jeremy as a shield, I abandoned that idea as bad form. Instead, summoning a false courage, I strode into the center of the room.

"Carl?" I checked his bed. No one. Jeremy cast

the thin beam of light around, but it couldn't penetrate the corners. The noise seemed to be coming from the exit pipe on the far side of the room. I grabbed Carl's rifle lying across the foot of his bed and motioned to Jeremy. "Come on." I didn't bother to check to see if the old Browning .30-30 was loaded. Carl was a member of the what's-the-use-of-an-empty-gun school of thought—something I was grateful for at the moment.

Jeremy and I hadn't made it twenty feet into the pipe when a huge figure emerged from the darkness in front of us. "Carl?"

His matted dark hair was glued to his forehead. His beard, long and unkempt, hid the lower half of his face. Catching what little light there was, his eyes glowed like those of a wild animal stalking the periphery of sight. "Carl, it's Lucky."

"Lucky?" Confusion replaced the anger. "It's not safe down here. We need to go." He lumbered into the light.

Under one arm he held a squirming, fighting bunch of irate female. Her eyes wide with fear, her dark hair whipping like writhing snakes, she fought and pushed at the huge arm holding her. "Let me go." She kicked and hit, with no effect—she couldn't even get Carl's attention.

I moved closer. When she caught sight of me she stopped fighting. Her eyes widened in recognition.

"You," the girl and I said in unison. "From the casino."

I wanted to throw my arms around the big man. "Carl, you are my hero."

He beamed, even though he hadn't a clue. "This here *feline*"—he half lifted the girl still caught in the vise of his arm—"was stealing my hotdogs. She even took a gallon of milk out of the ice chest. Brand-new, too. Caught her red-handed."

Bending around Carl's elbow, the young woman stared at me. I saw fear—no, terror in her eyes. "My daughter," she whispered, her voice choked with the effort.

"Daughter? Where?" I put my hand on Carl's arm. "Let her go, Carl. Please."

He nodded, setting her down easy. Steadying herself on her feet, she pulled air deep into her lungs, then grabbed my arm, tugging me. "Please. Help me. She is so small."

I looked at the water swirling around my ankles. Gaining speed, it made walking a struggle.

"It's not far," the woman pleaded, her panic boiling to the surface. "I left her while I went to get us food. She was so hungry, but never complained."

Even Carl seemed to understand. "Show us."

The young woman disappeared into the pipe. I followed with Carl behind me and Jeremy bringing up the rear.

We hadn't gone far when an angry snarl sounded behind us.

I whirled, a split second behind Jeremy, who arced the flashlight toward the sound. Dane sprang into the light. His face twisted. His teeth bared. His eyes glued to the figure over my shoulder.

"You killed her!" Dane charged, a beast wild with bloodlust.

The girl screamed and shrank back.

Jeremy flicked the bright light, pointing it into Dane's eyes.

Momentarily blinded, he threw his arm up, shielding his eyes. Jeremy tensed, his muscles bunched. Then he unfurled them, like a home-run hitter swinging for the fence. The beam of light arced.

A meaty thunk. Then the world plunged into darkness.

"Not so fast, cowboy." Jeremy's voice. I didn't hear another.

"Jeremy?"

"I got the bugger. He's out cold, but he'll live. Unfortunately, I can't say as much for the light. Sorry."

The black void pulled at me, tugging me different directions, making my head spin. Without a purchase, a handhold, I felt my balance slipping. Panic clenched my stomach.

A huge hand closed around my arm, steadying me. "Lucky, I'm here. Don't worry." Carl's voice was calm, reassuring—an interesting turnabout if I'd had time to think about it.

"And the girl?"

"Gone, but I know where she goes. I can find her."

"I'm coming, too." Carl knew me well enough not to argue.

"Jeremy, can you get yourself and Dane out? He'll drown in here if we leave him." The prospect didn't sound all that unsavory, to be honest.

"No worries." I guess he knew me well enough not to argue either. I heard him grunt, then move away. And it was a good thing, too—another moment of reflection and I might have changed my mind and held Dane's face under the water myself.

DIZZY in the near-darkness, my eyes unable to find even a pinpoint of light as a balance point, I squeezed them shut and clung to Carl's shirt. One hand trailing along the wall, he moved quickly. I stumbled to keep up.

"Lucky, hurry." His breathing was labored. "Too much water."

Energy would have been wasted on a response, so I concentrated on matching my pace to his. The water was around our knees now, and starting to move more quickly. Even with Carl breaking the way, each step was a struggle. The air conspired with the water, and I struggled to pull oxygen into my lungs as I labored against the current.

"It's not far now." Carl's voice was a low, clear growl.

Focusing on the battle, my head bowed with the effort, I lost touch with anything around me. One foot. Shift my weight. Lean heavily on the front foot. Carefully lift the back foot. Fight the current. Lift my foot out of the water. Bring it forward. Step forcefully into the moving water. Then do the whole sequence again.

Without warning, Carl moved to the left. I lost my balance. The force of the water hit my leg. I fell. Instinctively, I shoved my hands out, bracing. Anchorless, I fought as the current pulled at me.

As my head went under, my hands scraped the floor—two feet, no more. But I was powerless—flotsam on a wild river. Shoving against the concrete, I got my head above the surface. Dragging air into my lungs, I fought panic.

As the water closed over my head, I felt a hand grab the back of my sweatshirt and pull. My foot found brief purchase and I pushed with all the energy I had left. Twisting as I surfaced, I grabbed Carl's arm.

"Pull, Lucky. Quickly. You can do this." Carl's voice. Calm. The illumination of hope. "I've got hold of a ladder. Can you find it?"

Like a demon dragging me to Hell, the current pulled at my legs. Hand over hand, I pulled my way up Carl's arm and across his chest. Finally my hand closed over metal. My teeth chattered—from fear or cold, or both—stealing my strength. I worked my other hand to the metal. Then a foot. Then the other. "I've got it."

"Stay here."

Two words, then he was gone.

THE water sucked and pulled, draining my strength. Clinging to the last vestiges of hope, I fought back. With my butt wedged between two rungs of the ladder, my hands fisted around one of the uprights, my toes curled around a lower rung, I held on. The water had risen—it was up over my feet now. Shrouded in darkness, I moved up one rung, repositioning myself. Numbness replaced the shivering. Calmness replaced fear.

Time passed. With no reference, I had no idea how many minutes filled what felt like an eternity. A dim glow above filtered into the gloom—pinpoints of light. The ladder led upward to a manhole. To safety.

But I wasn't leaving without Carl.

My head rested on my arms. My eyes shut. My breath came in shallow gasps. My strength trickled away, like sand in an hourglass, leaving me weak, my muscles slow to respond. The water swirled close to my knees now. Then I heard it—a faint noise altering the rush of the water.

Raising my head, I concentrated. There it was again.

"Carl?" I shouted.

Nothing. Was my mind playing tricks? I held my breath. The noise again. I was sure of it.

"Carl?" Extending one leg into the water, I shouted again. "Carl?" The water whipped my leg downstream, pulling me from my perch. I fought. Summoning strength I didn't know I had, I pulled myself back to safety.

"Lucky." Carl's voice. Weak. But close.

I strained into the darkness. I thought I saw a figure, but I wasn't sure. "Carl, I'm here."

The seconds ticked by, measured by the pounding of my heart.

Then I saw him. Keeping myself above the water, I extended my body. Reaching, my hand hit cloth, a body. Carl's hand found mine. I pulled. One step. Two. Closer. I could hear his ragged gasps.

Shifting his hand from mine to the ladder, he nudged me with something. "Here."

Taking the bundle in one arm, I moved up the ladder. One rung. Two. I felt the metal take Carl's weight.

The bundle shifted in my arm.

"Is the baby breathing?" Carl asked from below.

"Christ!" Without a hand to spare, I used my chin to work the blanket back. Cool skin under my lips. No movement. My heart stopped. Then a whimper. Energy flowed through me. "Barely. We need to hurry."

Hand up one rung, feet following, I worked my way up. The metal shook as Carl followed.

Pinpoints of light pulled me. Finally, my hand hit metal—the manhole cover. My arm already shook with the effort of climbing. Stepping up two rungs, I leaned my head to the side. Crouching, bundling the energy I had left into my legs, I pressed my shoulder to the metal. A deep breath. Hold it. Push.

The cover moved. Inches. Not enough.

Two deep breaths. Oh, the fresh air tasted good. Another push.

This time, I could squeeze through. With just

enough rational thought left, I stuck my head up to make sure I wasn't climbing into the middle of Las Vegas Boulevard or something—I had no desire to get all this way only to have my head taken off by a taxi.

Luck held. This manhole was in the sidewalk. I didn't recognize the neighborhood and I didn't care. Squirming as fast as I dared, I worked my body through and onto firm ground. Laying the baby in a safe place next to me, I pushed the manhole cover completely out of the way and reached in.

Carl lifted a body toward me. Dark hair. The girl. "Here, take her, she's gone, man."

"Shit."

Grabbing under her shoulders, I pulled her to safety and laid her out on the sidewalk. Smoothing her hair from her face, I put my cheek to her nose as I felt for a pulse in her neck. With neither breath nor pulse, her skin was clammy to the touch.

Carl pulled himself out of the hole and crouched next to me. "She's not movin'. I don't think she's breathin'. Dammit, have we lost her?"

Fingers laced, with one hand on top of the other, I pressed firmly into her sternum as I silently counted. "Come on."

Thirty seconds, then I shifted to her mouth. Opening it, I tilted her head back and pulled her jaw toward me, then felt to make sure her tongue wasn't blocking her airway. Pinching her nose, I covered her mouth with mine and blew while I watched her chest. Two breaths strong enough to make her chest rise, then back to the compressions. As I shifted, I glanced at Carl.

Eyes wide but calm, he picked up the baby and cradled it as he watched me. "I found her just going out, clinging to a piece of wood wedged in an opening. She had the baby above water even as she was going under."

Another thirty seconds of compressions. On autopilot now, I moved toward her head.

As I pinched her nose, I thought she moved. I slapped her face. "Come on. You can do it."

She coughed.

"Yes!" I rolled her onto her side and pounded her back.

She gagged. Water spewed out as she gagged again.

"That's right." Kneeling behind, with one hand on her shoulder, I held her.

Finally she took a deep, ragged lungful of air.

Shifting back, I sat. Pulling her into my lap, I held her tight as her breaths finally slowed.

Her body tensed. "My baby?"

"She's okay." I smoothed her hair. Looking up, my eyes found Carl's, tears welling.

He looked like a bedraggled lumberjack or something. What was that guy's name? Reruns on TV when I was kid. Grizzly Adams, that was it. I giggled as my body started to shake. Uncontrollable spasms. Shock.

My vision tunneled. I thought I felt a hand on my

shoulder. A voice in my ear said, "It's okay. We called nine-one-one. Help is on the way."

Sirens in the distance. I felt myself slipping. My world went dark.

Chapter

SEVENTEEN

♡

"**N**o!" A male voice. Angry. Shouting. Noise. "Sir, you are going to have to come with me." Something clattered. The smell. Oh God, the smell. Hospital.

My eyes fluttered open as my heart galloped. Bright lights. Squinting, I struggled to move, but a weight held me down. Panic. Why couldn't I move?

"Sir, you are not making this any easier."

My thoughts tumbled as memories flooded. The storm drains. Water. A baby. I focused on the source of the sound. I could just make out shadows and forms. Where was I?

"I. AM. NOT. LEAVING. LUCKY." Carl. He had been in the drains.

Blinking furiously, I felt like I was looking through a pair of binoculars as I thumbed the focus wheel. Hazy at first, my world slowly took shape. Bright lights. Too bright. And that smell, ammonia . . . and death. I squinted against the light. Two men dressed in purple scrubs held on to Carl. His shoulders bunched, his hands tight hammers of flesh, he shook the orderlies off as easily as a bear would a couple of dogs. They lunged for him again.

My mind formed the words, but I couldn't find the breath to give them sound. Sucking air into my lungs, I concentrated. "Carl." My voice came out all pinched and small.

The three men froze, their heads swiveling toward me.

Carl beamed. "Lucky!" He shrugged out of the orderlies' grasp and rushed to my side. Still wet and smelling of the storm drains, he leaned over me and grabbed my hand. "I thought we lost you."

"Forgot my Wheaties this morning," I whispered. Waves of cold rolled through me, chattering my teeth. Lying in bed, my cocoon of warm blankets helped, but it wasn't enough. Flashes of memory hit me—bits and pieces, jerky, like an old silent movie. "Jeremy?"

"Waterlogged but safe. The fool has a hero complex—something about coming back to save us. He damn near drowned. The cops fished him out." A huge tear trickled out of Carl's eye. "Lucky, don't go leaving me, okay?"

"How long have I been here?" Testing, I wiggled my feet. My ankle screamed, which I took as a good sign.

"You've been out a while." Carl touched me tentatively, like a child who wasn't sure he had permission.

"I wasn't worried. I knew you'd be okay. It wasn't your time."

I'd learn to trust Carl's odd assertions—this one I held on to like a drowning swimmer clung to a raft. "The girl and the baby?"

"They got the kid under some lamp thing, like they're trying to make her sprout. I'm sure her mama is close by. That detective friend of yours has gone to look for her. He made me promise not to leave you until he got back." Carl threw an angry look over his shoulders at the orderlies who shrank back, then turned tail and fled.

As if waiting for his cue, Romeo stepped through the doorway. He looked angry and relieved at the same time, which I sort of understood. I wasn't exactly happy with me either. "You and me have some talking to do," Romeo said, trying to keep the mad in his voice. He was marginally successful. "But we can cover that ground later." He pulled the girl from behind him. "This is Estella and I thought you might want to talk to her."

Without the heels, the uniform, and the makeup, Estella looked to be a fresh-faced nineteen, tops. With her hair dry, a bit of color back in her cheeks, and wearing a set of scrubs so large the sleeves and pant legs had to be rolled several times, the hardened girl I remembered had all but disappeared. Only the barest hint remained in the defiant tilt to her chin. "I did nothing wrong." And in the hard edge to her voice.

"Matter of opinion, I'm sure." Rolling, I pushed

myself up on an elbow. Struggling against the weight of the blankets took more strength than I thought possible—they felt as if they were made of lead. Romeo stuffed another pillow or two behind me and I leaned back. Half sitting, I looked at the girl with fresh eyes. Thin. Pale. Young. So very, very young. "The night before last, you were in the hotel, yes?"

She nodded, her arms folded across her chest. Like a cornered animal, she wanted to run. I could see it in the way she held her body, in the slightly wild look in her eyes.

"It wasn't the first time, was it?"

Shock flashed across her face, and fear. She shook her head.

"The uniforms, where did you get them?"

She swallowed hard, then glanced at Romeo.

"Tell her the truth, you owe her at least that much." He nodded in my direction. "Carl got you out of the sewers, but she breathed life back into you."

This time when the girl looked at me, the fight leaked out of her. "This ugly man, and not so nice."

"Describes Marvin Johnstone pretty well." I gave her his physical appearance and she nodded. ".Yes, that's him."

"So tell me how it went down."

"He'd give us the uniform, mostly they were from Housekeeping. We'd go from room to room looking for stuff."

"Stuff?"

"Jewelry, that's all he wanted."

"Then what?"

Estella pursed her lips and shrugged. "We'd give him what we found, he'd pay us."

"What'd he do with it?"

"I have no idea. Please believe me. I took the jewelry—he said insurance would pay for it. I didn't think it was so bad." She wrung her hands as the weight of her situation landed on her shoulders. "What's going to happen to my daughter? Who's going to take care of her if I'm in jail?"

I looked at Romeo and he shrugged. I was fresh out of answers myself. "God, what a mess." I sighed as I leaned back and closed my eyes. Kids falling through the cracks. Next time I saw my mother I'd give her a new spin on a political platform. "Estella, you know what you did was wrong, don't you?" Opening my eyes, I saw her nod. "I don't know what to do, but I'll try to think of something. And, Detective Romeo will help. Won't you?" I didn't need to look at him to see his wide-eyed look.

I ignored him. Turning instead back to the girl. "The cocktail waitress uniform was a departure. Did Mr. Johnstone say why? What were you supposed to do?"

"Watch."

"For what?"

"Not what, who." She dropped one hand, her fingers nervously tapping her thigh as she glanced around the cubicle.

"For whom, then?"

"A couple of the poker dudes. Watalsky, Slurry, DeLuca, Grady—if any of them wandered into view I was to give the heads-up."

"To Mr. Johnstone?"

"No, to Sylvie."

Romeo's head popped up. "Sylvie? But Mr. Johnstone gave you the uniform?"

"Yes."

"They were working together?" This time it was my turn to sound incredulous.

"Maybe that's not the right words." Estella paused, her brows crinkled in thought. "I don't know, but I felt Sylvie was forcing him to do something. I don't know what."

Well, that muddied the waters. I motioned to one of the two orderlies who had stuck their heads in the doorway. "A cup of hot tea? Would that be possible?"

Nodding, he looked thankful for a mission as he grabbed his compatriot, and both of them disappeared. Now I knew how many orderlies it took to make a cup of tea. There was a joke in there somewhere. Fighting with my wandering thoughts, I pulled them back.

"I'm not lying." Estella swiped at a tear, then threw her shoulders back as if a show of strength was needed to discount the sign of weakness. "Mrs. Dane, she was a nice lady."

"So, let me get this straight. Marvin wanted you to scout for Sylvie Dane?"

"*Sí.*" She shook her head. "Sorry, yes."

"And she wanted you to give her a warning if you saw any of those men?"

"Yes."

"Why?"

"She had something to do in the dealership and she didn't want them to see."

"Was she meeting someone?"

"Not that I could tell."

"You didn't see anyone go into the dealership?"

"No."

"What was she doing, then?" I couldn't get my mind around it—not enough sugar left in my system to fire my thinker.

Estella just shook her head. "She didn't tell me."

Romeo piped up. "She was looking for something? Or maybe hiding something?"

He looked at Estella, who shrugged. "Possibly."

"Or someone came in the back door?" I added. "But the tapes didn't show anyone," I continued, shooting that theory down. I turned my attention back to Estella. "Mrs. Dane was worried about all the men you named."

This time the girl paused before answering. "I don't think she knew who to be afraid of."

The orderly came back with the tea, which he put on a movable table that he rolled up to my bed. Pretending to be engrossed in adding fake sugar and a touch of milk, I took a few moments to process. I pushed myself up a bit more, then took a sip of tea. As the warmth washed through me, I succumbed to its restorative powers. Tea? Who knew? "And after she was dead you stole the necklace, ripping it from her neck."

"I stole it, yes. But not from her."

Romeo's head swiveled as he focused on the girl. "You didn't take it from Mrs. Dane?"

Estella toed the ground. "I took it from her, yes. But I had stolen it from one of the big rooms at the hotel a couple of weeks ago."

"Then how did Sylvie Dane get it?" I asked, beating Romeo to the punch.

Estella looked at the floor, grinding her toe into the linoleum. "She caught me," she whispered.

"Caught you? When? Doing what?" Losing interest in the tea, I set down the cup.

"That day. The day I stole the pretty watch. I tried one more room. I knew I shouldn't, I'd been there too long." She looked up at me—a furtive glance, her eyes deep and dark . . . intense. "Mrs. Dane got wise to me. She said she would go to the police if I didn't tell her the whole story."

"And did you?" Romeo asked.

"She had me cold. I gave her what she wanted."

"And then what?" I prompted.

The girl shrugged. "I gave her the watch—that's the only piece she wanted. And she let me go."

"That's it?" I asked, feeling there was a bit more to the story.

Estella let out her breath slowly. When she looked up, her eyes were clear, her gaze level. "Mrs. Dane wanted me to tell the ugly man what happened."

Romeo and I looked at each other—I could tell our minds were riding the same wavelength. "Do you think Sylvie was blackmailing Marvin into helping her?" I whispered to him.

He shrugged. "Could be. But help her with what?"

"Beats me," I added unnecessarily.

"I didn't kill her." Estella's voice, now brittle with fear, had lost its edge. "I just stole things."

The classic dodge—admit to a lesser crime.

"She was already dead when you took the necklace?" I confirmed.

"Yes, and the shoes. I took them, too." Estella's eyes were bright. "I needed the money. My baby was hungry and Mrs. Dane wasn't going to need those things anymore."

Harsh, her words underscored a toughness no teenager should have. The thought made me sad.

"Tell me why you ended up in the dealership and what you saw and did."

"I saw Slurry and Watalsky and tried to get Mrs. Dane on the phone."

"You called her?"

"Yes, on her cell."

"What did you use?"

She looked at me like I should have been in a remedial life class. "My cell, what else?" She punctuated my stupidity with one of those irritating teenage snorts that makes one almost understand why a parent could hit a child . . . almost.

"You don't have anywhere to live, but you have a cell."

"There's a charity or something that hands them out to all the homeless kids. We keep in touch to keep each other safe."

The phone number Sylvie called—things were starting to add up . . . a bit. There were still some pretty large holes in the puzzle.

"Mrs. Dane didn't answer and I got worried."

"And Slurry and Watalsky?"

"They argued for a bit, near Delilah's. I couldn't hear what they were talking about, but then they went back to the Poker Room."

"And the dealership?" Romeo prompted.

"Mrs. Dane was dead when I got there. All laid out on that car. Blood everywhere." Estella wiped her eyes with a trembling hand. "I freaked. I grabbed the necklace and stuck the shoes on my feet. Then I ran."

"And your shoes?"

"That man had given me a pair. They were too big. I tossed them in the red car, the one Mrs. Dane . . ." She shuddered. "I figured no one would look for them there. And if someone found them, they'd just think some guest had left them."

"And Mr. Dane? Was he there?"

Her eyebrows scrunched into a frown. "Mr. Dane? I don't know him."

"Tall, handsome, cowboy thing going on. The guy in the storm drains?"

Recognition bloomed across the girl's face. "*That* guy was her old man?"

"Did you see him in the dealership that night?" Romeo asked.

"He came through the door as I was leaving. He caught a glimpse of the body and went postal. I wasn't sticking around."

Romeo's eyes met mine and I could see we were riding the same wavelength. Dane might actually have been telling the truth about not killing his wife. So if he hadn't . . .

My head spun with all the facts and all the probabilities. Trying to make sense of the mess was like throwing darts at balloons. Of course, a brain needed sugar to function, and I couldn't remember my last meal. My muscles, drained by cold, exhausted through effort, and now deprived of their high-octane fuel, refused to budge no matter how hard my brain prodded. A hollow pit lurked at the bottom of my stomach. Like a rabid dog, sleep nipped at me, then sank in its teeth.

"You have no idea who Sylvie was meeting at the dealership?" That seemed to be the key, so I asked it again.

"No."

"Do you have any idea why she was meeting whoever she was meeting?"

"That's all I know." Keeping her eyes focused on her feet and hugging herself tightly, she turned inward. "Can I see my daughter now?" She asked in a small voice as she glanced at Romeo, directing her question to him.

The girl looked anxious, tired, hungry . . . and . . . I narrowed my eyes. Scared. Yes, she looked scared.

But scared of whom? Us? Somebody else? God knew, she had enough to be scared about. But me being me, I wanted the specifics.

"Okay," Romeo said. "But we'll have more questions later." He motioned to someone I couldn't see outside the door. A tall woman dressed in street-cop blues stepped into the room. "Officer Mendoza will show you the way. She's going to stay with you. Understand?"

"What are you going to do with me?" Estella's voice had lost its swagger.

Romeo glanced at me before answering. "I don't know yet. For now, keep you both safe and fed."

A weak smile lit the girl's eyes as she turned to the officer waiting patiently just inside the doorway.

When the two had gone, I leaned my head back. "Let me guess, we have no idea where Dane is."

Before Romeo could answer, Jeremy strode into the room brandishing his phone. "You may not, but I do."

ONLY tourists drove up or down the Strip, and maybe the occasional townie looking to waste time soaking up some atmosphere. In Jeremy's Hummer, we were neither, so we darted down the back streets, taking the local route.

I pulled at my sodden clothing, which I had allowed Romeo and Jeremy to help me squirm into, breaking the Code of Womanly Mystery all to Hell. Not only did I smell, but I itched as well. A serious dose of penicillin lurked in my future, as well as a probable arrest by the fashion police.

My body vibrated with the effort required to remain upright. While Jeremy drove and Romeo looked grim, I took the time to stoke the internal fires with a couple of muffins I had snagged from the patients' dinner trays stacked neatly on the cart next to the elevator. In survival-of-the-fittest mode, I didn't feel even a slight twinge of guilt as I stuffed first the cinnamon apple, followed quickly by the bran, into my mouth, chewed rapidly, swallowed, then chased it with apple juice—also purloined from the hospital.

"Where exactly did Shooter call you from?" I asked Jeremy, needing to get the story straight. My thoughts refused to unmuddle; I don't know why.

"The lobby of the Edelweiss. He'd trailed Cole to a jewelry store there."

"And Dane?"

"With Shooter. Both of them are waiting, as you requested before . . ."

"They do anything stupid, I know. But I'm not holding out much hope that they can resist." The apple juice drained dry, I peeled back the top on a similar little jug of OJ. Not a proud moment, but necessity trumped pride every time—at least, that's what I told myself. "Speaking of stupidities . . ." I trailed off as my thoughts derailed. "Is that even a word?" My eyes met Jeremy's in the rearview mirror. His thoughts were easy to read. "Sorry. So how'd they get there again?"

"Cole hit Shooter over the head, then ran," Jeremy said, his patience clearly wearing thin. "Shooter followed him. Dane called Shooter."

"And Dane? Didn't the police hold him?"

"When I went back to try to help you out of the tunnel, Dane came to and bolted. The police haven't caught up with him yet, but now I doubt they'll put too much effort into chasing him. He's the least of their worries."

"The Three Stooges." I scrambled for a handhold as we wheeled down an alley, then bumped over the curb. "I know I'm slow on the uptake, but if Cole hit Shooter over the head, then how did he follow him?"

"Please," Romeo snorted, then turned, gracing me with a condescending look, which, for the record, I didn't appreciate. "He's a marine."

"Well that explains everything."

"The blood in the hallway was his."

"Shooter's?" I asked, just to be ornery, then turned to Romeo. "I guess this isn't exactly how your plan to set up a sting at this jewelry store was to play out?"

The detective refused to look at me.

"How do you want to play it?" I asked.

He turned slowly, his eyes full of surprise. "You're going to let me play lead?"

"I figure you've earned it. But trust me, being the boss isn't all it's cracked up to be."

Jeremy jammed on the brakes. "Here we are."

A liveried bellman opened my door with a flourish. "Ma'am." He reached in to help me out. I took his hand and, to his credit, he didn't recoil. Not even when he got a good whiff of me.

The Edelweiss had a superlative staff.

We sashayed through the front entrance—no one gave us a passing look. The lobby was crowded, as usual. Jeremy took the lead. Romeo and I tried to match his pace as he darted and weaved through the throng in the Orangerie—the floral arrangers were just putting the finishing touches on the fall display, all reds and yellows, oranges and browns with a lovely water feature.

Past the ice cream store, he angled to the left. The jewelry store was two stores down.

Shooter, Dane, and Cole sat in wingback chairs on the opposite side of the hallway against the window. They were swallowed in the large chairs, and I would have missed them had they not called to us. I noticed Dane had changed clothes—a purple shirt to match the pretty vivid shiner around his left eye. He and Jeremy nodded to each other, most likely tabling their differences until later.

"So, what's the plan?" I asked, the last to arrive. Leaning over, my hands on my knees, I tried to catch my breath. Of course, it didn't help that my brain was spinning in my head like the tilt-a-whirl at Circus Circus.

"No plan," Shooter said. "But the kid here thinks somehow this store is tied in with the piece that gal lifted from the hotel."

Cole nodded in confirmation.

"Those dots I already connected. But how?" I asked him.

He shrugged.

Then it hit me. I whirled around and peered through the glass storefront. A tall woman with long blond hair and an artificially taut face, sporting those plumped lips that reminded me of the fat lip I gave Billy Wilson in the seventh grade, waited on a Chinese man obviously in the market for a watch sufficient to confer bragging rights back home. While the just-been-slapped-around lips changed the woman's appearance a bit, the look of insincere obsequiousness in her eyes left little doubt.

Carmen DeLuca—the fourth Mrs. Frank DeLuca.

"Let me handle this."

No one gave me any argument. Not even Romeo. Ignoring the stains, I brushed down my slacks and threw back my shoulders.

A discreet chime announced my presence as I pushed through the heavy glass door. Plush carpet, white and spotless, muffled my footfalls. A floral scent lingered in the air. Soft music provided suitable undertones. With the practiced eye of a high-end shopkeeper, Carmen took my measure with one glance, then discreetly waved away the waiter who stepped to greet me with a silver tray of champagne flutes appropriately filled. He stepped back into his corner, his eyes averted. Guess I didn't peg on her well-heeled meter. To his credit, a pink blush tinged his cheeks.

Not only did I not peg on Carmen's well-heeled meter, apparently I didn't spark any recognition either. "Hello, Carmen."

This time her glance lingered. Clearly taken by surprise, she adopted that feigned, overly friendly demeanor of a professional suck-up caught flat-footed. "I'm sorry." She extended her hand across the counter. "So good to see you." Her eyes flicked to my attire, but her expression remained bland.

When I took her hand, she didn't even cringe. Way better than I would've managed. "Lucky O'Toole. From the Babylon?"

"Oh," she sighed, deflating as the air of obsequiousness rushed from her. "Lucky, of course. How can I help you?"

"Have you seen Frank lately?"

"Frank?" A frown normally would've accompanied the tone in her voice, but her face had no movement. "He wouldn't dare show his face around here."

"Why not? I thought you were on good terms."

She motioned for another clerk to assist the Chinese gentleman, who was watching us with interest. Carmen stepped to the far end of the counter. I followed her.

Leaning across the jewelry case, she lowered her voice. "He's so far behind in alimony payments, I'd shoot him for the insurance, but now, not even that would cover what he owes me."

I adopted a conspiratorial, slightly aghast tone, the dialect of her tribe of money-grubbers. "Honey, I had no idea. I thought that man was made of money. What are you going to do?"

"Can you imagine? Leaving me high and dry?"

"So unappreciative."

She pulled at a lock of hair, then wrapped it around the forefinger of her right hand, worrying it so that more than a few golden strands floated to the counter. The harsh light highlighted the subtle lines around her eyes and mouth she worked so hard to camouflage. "At least the store is safe. Frank did get some investors to give me an infusion of cash. If he hadn't . . ." A little shiver shook her.

Romeo pressed his nose to the glass, catching my eye. I ignored him.

I glanced around the store, taking in the glistening sconces, the original art perfectly lit, the huge rocks under glass, the subtle aura of wealth beyond the dreams of avarice. "Nice place you have here. It sure would've been a shame to see it go."

"If we didn't have our own line of high-end costume jewelry, we'd've been shuttered long ago."

"Your own line?"

She nodded, her disinterest evident. "We copy exquisite pieces, one-of-a-kind things. Sometimes we do it for insurance purposes—the owners don't want to travel with the real piece—that sort of thing."

"And sometimes you copy the pieces to sell?"

Carmen's lids fluttered. "I didn't say that."

"Do you do repairs as well?"

Carmen shifted back into her High Priestess of

the Cult of Embarrassing Riches mode. "We have a certified gemologist, a designer and craftsman—he makes the most exquisite pieces."

"And replating? I have a guest at the hotel, which is really why I'm here. She has a watch . . ." I described Sylvie's watch in detail as I kept a close eye on Carmen's face. Not a flicker of recognition. Not even a furtive glance of guilt.

"The owner wishes the engraving to be removed, then the metal replated to hide the removal?" Carmen reiterated.

"Yes."

"Platinum, you say?"

"Yes."

"Not a problem." Finally, she stopped torturing that lock of hair. "If you get it to me by the end of business today, we could have it back to your guest perhaps by dinner tomorrow. If not, for sure the next day. We have all the materials on hand."

I thanked her, then took my leave. Fortunately Romeo had stopped the kid-in-a-toy-store routine.

The men circled around me. "So?" Dane asked.

I summarized the high points of my conversation.

"You think the cyanide could've come from here?" Romeo asked.

"I didn't mention cyanide specifically—it's about as hard to bring up in casual conversation as an STD. But she said she could do replating with a short turnaround—all the necessary materials are here."

"And Frank DeLuca?" Jeremy asked. "You don't think she'd give him any?"

"I got the impression she'd use it on him before she gave it to him, but who knows? The more we dig, the more Frank's name keeps popping up."

"Where do we go from here?" Dane asked the question, but the three of them looked at me as if I had a clue what I was doing. No way was I going to admit I was making it up as I went. We were close. I could feel it. And Frank was the key.

"Romeo, you go get all the pertinent warrants. Jeremy, take Cole back to the hotel. Get Jerry to put someone on him until we're sure he's out of danger." Jeremy disappeared down the hallway.

Romeo paused for a moment. "What about Frank DeLuca?"

"I'll find him and keep him busy until you show up with the paperwork."

That seemed to mollify him. He turned and followed Jeremy.

I turned my attention to Shooter and Dane. Bloodied and bruised, they looked a bit battle-weary. "Why don't you two go to the doc-in-a-box and see about those head wounds?"

After a moment's thought and without argument, they turned on their heels and sauntered toward the lobby. I wasn't convinced they'd do as I suggested—which didn't really bother me. If they both died of ptomaine it'd be too easy a death in my book.

I turned and ran the other way. The tram would be the quickest way back to the Babylon.

I was going to find Frank if it killed me.

Chapter

EIGHTEEN

♡

When I burst through the front doors of the Babylon loaded for bear, people filled every corner of the lobby, which caught me off guard. My internal clock had gone on the fritz—spending the better part of the day unconscious could do that. Although it felt much earlier, from the energy of the crowd I thought the cocktail hour might be upon us—or perhaps that was wishful thinking. A good jolt of joy-juice would have done wonders for my disposition, but I didn't have the time—although I certainly had the lack of conviction.

Amazingly enough, I had not only remembered I'd left my phone on the floorboard of Jeremy's Hummer, but I'd also managed to find it under the passenger seat hiding in a sack of half-eaten hamburgers from In-N-Out.

Jerry answered on the first ring. "Lucky, man! You good, girl?"

"Good as I'll ever be. How are your people? Did Dane hurt them?"

"Headaches and a good case of red-ass. They'll recover."

I guessed I could cross Dane off my hit list. "I really need Frank."

"Golden Fleece Room regaling the press."

"You're a good man, Jer. I don't care what they say."

That got a chuckle out of him. "Girl, whatever you do, don't go telling everybody."

"What, and ruin your reputation?" Eyeing the line in front of the elevators, I turned and headed for the escalators to the Mezzanine, nearly bowling over two little gray-haired ladies mesmerized by a sexy young man in very tight jeans. Come to think of it, his shirt didn't leave much to the imagination either. As I darted around the ladies, I tossed him a second look. I'd give him an eight on my eye-candy meter. "Jer, you know the truth is safe with me."

Before he could quibble, I terminated the call. Hitting the escalator, I took the steps two at a time.

The press rooms at major Vegas functions reminded me of the sea off the Great Barrier Reef after a heavy chumming. Like sharks in a bloodlust frenzy, media types circled, almost vibrating with energy threatening to explode. Then, when the unwary wandered near, they'd dash in for a bite, chew it, and hit the victim again.

The fact one of the unworthy, like me, might wander in, didn't matter—they'd feast on anything moving. Entering the fray, I was struck by the fact that this was one of the few times being big, tall, and angry were good things. Ignoring the mikes stuck in my face and the questions hurled my way, I charted a course for Frank, who had been swallowed by a school of hungry flesh-eaters on the far side of the room.

As I pushed through the feeding frenzy, I heard one of the reporters tossed aside and left in my wake, grouse, "Don't waste your time. You won't get any good sound bites outta her."

It was a proud moment.

Frank's eyes widened when he saw me. Giving my head a quick tilt to the side, I motioned for him to join me outside, in the hall. Beating him there, I tapped my toe impatiently, which made my sore ankle hurt. I didn't care.

Several media types followed Frank as he burst into the hallway. He started to say something, but I silenced him with a look. Grabbing his elbow, I pulled him into the service area at the end of the hall. After stuffing him into a linen closet, I followed and pulled the door closed behind us.

He whirled on me the minute the door shut—hard to do in the tight space. His head ended up under my chin. "Lucky. What the hell?"

With two hands to his chest, I pushed him back. "Shut up, Frank. It's my turn."

Surprise registered—just a flicker, but it was there, so I jumped on it. "Why did you kill her?"

He staggered back as if I'd hit him. "What?"

"Sylvie Dane." I closed the distance, looming over him. "Why'd you kill her?"

"I . . . I . . . I didn't." A hand clutched his chest. "Lucky, girl, it's Uncle Frank you're talking to. How could you think . . ."

"I'll tell you how." I started ticking off the evidence one finger at a time. "Your dealership. Your code word—interesting word by the way. The police have yet to make the connection between your code word and the name of Slurry's site. I'm still not sure what that means or why you'd be so stupid." I shook my head and got my thoughts back on track. "I'll figure it out. But you bought the shoes Sylvie was wearing—the ones that freaked you out when they weren't on her feet when you came back to the dealership. You knew there was a witness to it—the missing shoes plus the shoes in the car? Dead giveaways." I took a breath and steamed ahead. "And you put Watalsky on the witness's tail. Were you going to kill her, too?"

"Lucky, you got it all wrong." He rubbed the stubble on his chin nervously. "I didn't buy those shoes. Someone sent them to Sylvie saying they were from me. Apparently they were real hot items. She was real appreciative, so I didn't tell her they weren't from me. I didn't see the harm."

"One lie, then another, pretty soon you're buried in them," I growled. "And Slim! How could you?"

"Slim?" Frank's eyes went all slitty—I resembled the feeling. "Now you've gone too far—he was a friend."

"My point. You know how we handle that in this town."

"Slim was murdered?" His voice held the menacing hiss of a rattler.

"On a quick and dirty tox screen, the lab guys

found sildenafil citrate in his system. Lethal when mixed with the nitrates he popped like candy. You knew that, hell we all did. A clever way to drop someone's blood pressure and trigger a heart attack. Very clever actually. We all knew he was overdue, so when it happened, who would suspect anything other than natural causes?"

Frank let out his breath slowly. "Coulda been an accident. I'm bettin' guys take those meds together all the time. Nobody wants a pecker that won't rise to the occasion."

"I wouldn't know." I chewed on my lip as I watched him. "There's one other little complication."

"What's that?" Frank looked a little nervous—it didn't take a rocket scientist to see he was in deep shit.

"Slim had a penile implant. What would he need with Viagra?"

Frank fixed me with those slitty eyes—they looked feral and hungry. A chill chased up my spine. If he really was the killer . . . I didn't really quite believe it . . . or my Perry Mason act, for that matter. But if he really did do it, I'd just locked myself in a closet with the killer. Not bright. Consistent, though. What was that old Emerson quote? A foolish consistency is the hobgoblin of small minds? At the rate I was decompensating, my sudden foolish streak made sense.

"A penile implant? How in the world would you know that?"

"Miss Becky-Sue told me. . . ." My heart fell, daggered by a thought. I felt myself go a little woozy. Pressing a hand to my head, I braced myself against the wall with the other hand. I closed my eyes and marshaled my thoughts. There were a few missing pieces, key pieces.

Frank's face showed concern when I opened my eyes and looked at him, really looked at him. He looked angry.

"Slim didn't call you to meet him at the plane, did he?"

"No, it was Miss Becky-Sue." Frank rubbed the heavy five o'clock shadow he carefully groomed. "Come to think of it, Slim did seem sorta surprised to see me. Relieved. He didn't really want to go to the party. He said his heart had been acting up."

"Anything weird happen with your little pecker-power stash while you were there?"

Frank rolled his eyes. "Just like with you. I pulled out my phone, and the bag came with it. Becky-Sue grabbed it, was razzing me. When I grabbed it back, she didn't let go. The thing ripped and pills went flying. Embarrassing."

"And fatal." Miss Becky-Sue . . . Funny, could she actually be the viper I thought she was? "Tell me about the offshore poker site you guys are all into. Somehow it's the key. I know it."

"Yeah, it was going to be my ticket back to the big time. Get several ex-wives off my back. Carmen scares me." He stopped and shook his head. "Anyway, to answer your question. It was looking pretty good until Sylvie came to us."

"Kevin Slurry kept a back door in the algorithm."

If Frank was surprised, he didn't show it. "Yeah, said she had a source who was going to go public."

"The source goes public and overnight your investment would be worth zip-point-doodle." I gave an appreciative whistle. "Did you know who her source was?"

"None of us did, as far as I know."

"And Slim." I held up my hand, stopping him. "He wanted it public, didn't he?"

"Yeah, the sanctity of the game and all of that. Preserving not only the rep of the game but his own as well."

"So who stood to gain by silencing him?"

"All of us, I guess. If we kept him from spilling the beans, our investment value would hold up."

"If you also took out Sylvie Dane and her snitch." Hands on my hips, I glared at him. "Two down, one to go."

Frank looked at me. For the first time I saw just a wee bit of give-up. "I didn't kill him, Lucky. You know I couldn't. I didn't kill the girl either—that's not my style, you know that."

"In this town it'd be like signing your own death warrant." I chewed on my lip for a minute. "The thing I don't get is Marvin Johnstone. Did he have any connection to the Aces Over Eights Web site?"

"Not on a bet." Frank snorted. "Can't say I'm sad he's gone. How'd they do it?"

"Cyanide."

"You're shitting me." The look on my face strangled his laugh and his eyes went from slits to saucers. "Really?"

"Afraid so."

"Where the hell would you get your hands on something like that?"

I watched his face carefully. If he was lying, then I was in way over my head. I sidestepped his question with a noncommittal shrug. "Carmen said you got some investors for her store. You guys still close?"

"Hell, I'm way behind on her alimony. Had a bad run of luck lately." He smiled at the irony. "I asked some friends to stake her, keep the dagger out of my back while I wined and dined Lady Luck. Self-preservation. Last time I saw her was in court when we split the blanket. A few phone calls since then. A hate letter or two from her mongrel with a Bar card—that guy gives lawyers a bad name, if that's possible."

"Miss Becky-Sue's name wouldn't be on that list of investors, would it?" The look on his face told me all I needed to know. "And Carmen has cyanide on hand."

"She tell you that?" Frank looked like he's been sucker punched.

"Indirectly." I nodded at the disbelief I saw in his eyes. "Who stood to inherit Slim's stake with him out of the way?" I asked even though I was pretty sure I knew the answer. Turning the knob, I pulled open the door and ran. My ankle screamed but adrenaline dulled the pain. The rest, I ignored.

Frank followed me. "Why would Becky-Sue . . ." He forced the words through labored breathing as he struggled to keep up.

"He was a heart attack waiting to happen, everybody knew it. You guys sunk a pile into the poker site."

"Slim bought the biggest slice."

"I bet." I ignored a couple of reporters standing outside the Press Room who fell in behind us.

"And if he blew the whistle . . ." That was all Frank could manage as he wheezed after me.

People jammed the escalators, so I had to stop and take my turn. Lacking oxygen myself, I took advantage and filled my lungs. "What about Sylvie's source, Cole Weston?"

"The deaf kid?" Frank seemed surprised.

"You know him?"

"Yeah, sat at many a poker game with him. Hell of a player, but I had no idea he was involved in this. How does he factor in?"

"Right now he's a loose end. And if my hunch is right, Miss Becky-Sue went for him yesterday but got me instead."

Hitting the ground floor, I sidestepped the guests in front of me and took off.

Miss Becky-Sue was planning a going-away party in the Garden Arena.

I'd always wanted to rain on someone's parade.

· · ·

THE Garden Arena hosted rock concerts, title fights, Broadway shows, and now a Celebration of Life for poker's biggest star. The Babylon's largest venue, the arena had tiered seating for thirty thousand or more, depending on the configuration. The security guy standing guard at one set of main doors jumped to when I approached.

I slowed only slightly as I barked orders. "Stop the folks behind me. Call Metro, Detective Romeo. Get him down here, stat." Then I threw my weight against the doors and kept motoring, letting my momentum carry me down the stairs toward the arena floor.

The lights hanging from the catwalks high above trained their beams on the center of the arena where seats had been retracted to increase the floor size. Huge pieces of scenery dangled on wires at various heights above the floor, the winches above them whining in protest. A hand of playing cards caught my eye—aces and eights. Whether it was by design or someone's sick joke, I wasn't amused. A huge poker chip emblazoned with the Babylon's logo drifted slowly toward the ground, where workmen waited, their gloved hands outstretched, ready to maneuver the piece into place. A single beam illuminated a gleaming white baby grand on a raised platform to the left—presumably for the band. On hands and knees in the middle of the floor, several workers snapped sections of wooden flooring into place— perfect for dancing—which seemed out of place. In fact, it all seemed in bad taste for a funeral, but what did I know?

The crew had opened a huge trapdoor in the floor on the far side of the arena and installed a movable elevator to bring all the required party staples up from the underground storage areas. The set pieces that would fit, cases of liquor, mixers, and condiments, food from the banquet kitchens, linens from the laundry, tables from storage—all of it trundled up the elevator to be dispersed to the proper location.

I scanned the area for the floor manger in charge of directing traffic. I smiled when I caught sight of Moony Ridgeway, in her boots and overalls, barking orders. My smile fled and my eyes narrowed dangerously when I spied my target, Miss Becky-Sue, glued to Moony like a suckerfish on a shark. Both of them leaned over the railing around the elevator shaft, peering down through the hole in the floor. If they'd just keep that position for thirty seconds. Then I'd be within striking distance. If luck was with me . . .

"Hey!" Frank shouted from above me, his voice carrying across the vast expanse, cutting through the noise, turning heads. "Hey, Lucky! Wait."

Miss Becky-Sue stood and looked in my direction.

My foot hit the last step hard, almost buckling my ankle. I staggered, gasping in pain. When unsure, the guilty usually run. Miss Becky-Sue was no exception. With two hands on the top railing, she vaulted over. Pretty good for a bimbo in a long skirt and boots.

"Stop her," I shouted, but I was too late.

Miss Becky-Sue had vanished.

Thundering footsteps sounded behind me as I darted toward the opening. Pointing at Moony, who stepped out of my way, I said, "Tell Security to get busy securing all the exits from the basement floors. That's their first priority. If they have any manpower left over, they can help me—but not until we've sealed off all escapes. Got it?"

I caught her quick nod, then levered myself over the railing and fell.

Bending my knees, I braced for the fall. My feet hit solid wood, sending a jolt through me, jarring every bone I had. My ankle screamed. Tears leaked into my eyes as the breath left me in a whoosh. Jolts of adrenaline spiked through me. Pain . . . and anger . . . snapped across my synapses.

Miss Becky-Sue had a head start. Glancing around, my eyes locked on to those of a workman, opened in shocked surprise. At my questioning glance, he pointed around a corner. I sneaked through the lower railings. The workman offered me his gloved hand, which I gladly used to take the weight off my bum ankle. Only a moment, but it was enough.

Turning, I ran in the direction he had pointed.

Three underground floors formed a labyrinth beneath the Babylon. We'd landed on the first level, which left two below us. Miss Becky-Sue might make it to the next one down, but she'd be shot on sight on the third level down. That one was the money floor, which housed the counting room and various vaults. Heavily guarded, it was penetrable only by those with the highest clearance. To be honest, I wasn't even sure I had enough stroke to wander down there.

On the two accessible floors, I had the advantage. The place was a maze—endless wide hallways best traversed in golf carts. Of course, it was a bit like Oz with different colored center stripes painted on the floor and pointing the way to various corporate divisions. Human Resources, Payroll, Accounting, they were all stuck down here—beehives of activity caged by windowless walls. At this time of night, the corporate offices were down to a skeleton staff. In Vegas, the open sign remained lit 24/7.

While the corporate staff would be downsized, with the work slowing during the waning hours, the laundry, receiving dock, and freight storage, along with the employee grub hall, where employees could dine before their shifts started, would be working at full capacity.

Miss Becky-Sue would be like a fox in a rabbit warren. I knew my way. All I had to do was keep her running blind until I had her cornered. A daunting thought—nothing like being empty-handed when facing a cornered animal. Right now, I'd sell my mother for a stun gun—top dollar for Mona.

At the next intersecting hallway, a guy barreled into my periphery in a golf cart. Flashing my executive badge, I commandeered his ride and motored off. My ankle wouldn't take much more pounding.

Hopefully, Miss Becky-Sue was in as wretched a state as I was. Surely she'd have to be slowing down soon.

With the various department doors closed and locked, I followed the only path open to her. Silently I glided past the motor pool, where all the Babylon's vehicles were cleaned, serviced, spit, and polished. Being addicted to internal combustion, my heart soared at the sound of compressed-air impact wrenches. I wheeled in next to a mechanic busy removing lug nuts. "You see a woman running by here?"

"Cowboy-lookin' chick?" He had wavy black hair, blue eyes, and big muscles . . . and a way with cars.

I swallowed hard and nodded, not trusting myself to speak.

"She took a left at the next corner."

Pressing the accelerator, I glided away in hot pursuit. She'd turned left, toward the banquet kitchens, which provided food for everything from gala events to the staff mess hall. No golf carts allowed. I parked as close as I could and hoofed it through the double doors.

Sound and energy slammed me. From the quiet of the deserted hallways to the hustle and heat of commercial kitchens at full throttle, I paused to get my bearings. Preparing for a shift change, the chefs barked orders to their staffs. Sous chefs and other minions leaped to the task. Wonderful aromas hung in the air. Steam rose like cool-morning fog off a warm lake. At the far end, food was plated then passed through to the waitstaff on the other side. They then stacked covered plates on trays and disappeared through double doors into the mess hall.

I let my gaze sweep over the gleaming stainless counters, past the huge gas stoves, through the white-clad staff seemingly moving to a silent shared song in a perfectly choreographed dance. Where was the person out of step? I restarted my scan.

There! Just easing past the cold prep area. A flash of fringe, and she was gone.

"Someone stop her!" I shouted as I pointed, but not one head turned in my direction. Mine wasn't the voice their ears were listening for. Trying not to disrupt the flow too much, I pushed my way through. Hurrying, a sense of urgency prodding me like a pin left in my shirt, I made it to the far end without mishap. Bolting for the double doors, I met a waiter coming the other way.

As we collided, his tray went flying. Thankfully the dishes were empty—wasted food was almost as egregious a sin as wasted alcohol. "I'm so sorry." I didn't stop to help. I couldn't.

One quick scan and I spied Miss Becky-Sue. Afloat in the sea of uniformed staff, she stuck out like a clothed gawker in a nudist colony. Sauntering between rows of long tables where the staff ate communal-style, she was trying not to attract attention.

"Someone grab that friggin' woman!" I shouted as I pointed.

This time heads turned, cutlery hit plates with a tinny clang. For a moment, motion slowed as heads swiveled my direction, then followed my finger. Two big guys dressed in valet uniforms rose from their benches. Miss Becky-Sue hiked up her skirt, stepped on a bench, then up on one of the tables. Her skirt still in her hands, she turned and ran. Employees grabbed their plates and leaned back out of the way of flying glassware and serving pieces kicked by Becky-Sue as she ran past.

One look at the table, and I ruled out following her. With my bulk and bum ankle, it wouldn't be pretty. Instead, I stayed on the low road—I'd been traveling there a lot lately—and monitored her progress as a few more liveried bellmen joined the chase. So nice to have reinforcements.

A huge fish tank formed the center portion of the wall at the far end of the hall. Fish to be served at the high-end restaurants swam lazily, unaware of their impending fate. Lobsters crawled across the gravel bottom. I avoided meeting their eyes. Staring at my dinner face-to-face was a bit cold-blooded for my taste.

My pace slowed as Miss-Becky-Sue hit the end of the table at the fish tank. The men closed in on either side. Trapped with nowhere to go, she cast frantically around the room looking for an escape. Nothing.

One of the men reached for her. Tugging her skirt out of his reach, she turned and leaped. Grabbing the edge of the tank with both hands, she worked one foot up, then a leg, followed by the rest of her.

Her eyes caught mine as she disappeared.

I waited. It couldn't have been much more than a fraction of a second. Then I heard it. The splash as Miss Becky-Sue, in all her fringed leather finery, landed in the fish tank. If she could get to the other side, she might have a chance of continuing the race. But I wasn't too worried—Michael Phelps himself couldn't make it.

Not in leather. Not in boots.

She sank like a stone.

I took a deep breath as I pushed through the gathering crowd. Nose to nose with only the glass between us, Miss Becky-Sue and I stared at each other. Her anger apparent even as terror crept in around the edges, Miss Becky-Sue glared at me.

"If you wouldn't mind"—I motioned to two of the valets—"get her out of there before she kills the fish."

AFTER calling off Security and telling everyone the chase was over, the quarry caught, I settled in a chair at one of the banquet tables and perused the selections on the employee menu while I waited. I wasn't really hungry, but I had nothing better to do while the valets secured Miss Becky-Sue and brought her to me. Above the din of the dining room returning to normal, I heard occasional wails and shrieks, much like the sounds made by a cornered feline. Feigning disinterest, I smiled to myself. Better the men dealt with it than me.

Finally, the odd little trio presented itself in front

of me. The two hulking, water-drenched valets bracketed a tiny Miss Becky-Sue who, arms at her sides, was wrapped tightly in a tablecloth cinched with a rope. One of the valets sported fresh scratches on his cheek. The other had a red welt on his arm that looked suspiciously like a bite mark. Both wore angry expressions. Miss Becky-Sue looked ready to rip my throat out.

"You," she spat. Not particularly eloquent, but the message was clear.

I stood, slowly pushing myself to my full height. Stepping close, I looked down at her, checking surreptitiously that her arms were indeed tethered to her sides and the two men had her firmly pinned between them. Apparently Miss Becky-Sue was the exception to the old adage that one's bark is worse than their bite.

I reared back and slapped her across the face . . . hard, surprising us both. "That's for Slim."

She staggered back. The two men kept her from falling.

Pulling herself together, she looked at me with venomous eyes. "I didn't kill him."

The doors opened behind me and I glanced over my shoulder in time to see Frank huff into the room, red faced. He lumbered through the crowd, shouldering in next to me.

Miss Becky-Sue's face brightened. She nodded toward him. "He did it. Not me."

"You bitch," he roared.

A man standing near Frank grabbed him as he

coiled to launch himself at Miss Becky-Sue. "Hold on there," he growled. Amazingly, Frank did as he asked.

I turned back to Miss Becky-Sue. "Oh, you set him up pretty good. Except for one thing. Well, a couple of things, actually."

She tossed her head. Her eyes held a challenge. "What?"

"Sylvie Dane's source, for one"

"A kid," Becky-Sue scoffed.

"So you knew?"

"I saw them together."

"Know anything else about him?"

"No. Why should I? He didn't matter to me."

"Oh, but he did." I lowered my voice. "You do know there was a witness?"

A flicker of surprise crossed her face, but her smile stayed in place. "A witness?"

"Mmmm, to Sylvie's murder. I'll get to Slim in a minute." Time to see how my poker face would hold up. Lying isn't one of my best things. "A young woman. She saw everything."

That took a bit of the starch out of the bitch. I bit down on a gloat—that would ruin everything—as I dangled the bait. This was like trying to catch crabs—you put a chicken neck on the line, then lowered it into the water in front of them. They'd snatch it. Then you'd ever so slowly pull them up to within net reach. They were too focused on the prize to realize the danger. My fingers were crossed that Miss

Becky-Sue was a crab. My heart beat so fast I thought it'd leap out of my chest at any moment. Trying to maintain my composure gave me a new-found appreciation for Perry Mason.

"I don't believe you." She eyed me, assessing.

I shrugged. "I don't care," I lied. "But let me ask you about the shoes."

"Shoes?"

"The Loubous. The ones you bought." I glanced out of the corner of my eye at Frank. His eyes widened as I talked. "The ones Sylvie Dane was wearing when she died."

"I didn't buy those shoes. Red isn't my color."

"How'd you know they were red?" I asked, my voice going all quiet and deadly.

"Sylvie told me . . ." Miss Becky-Sue looked around, wild-eyed. "Before. She told me before."

"No, you'd just arrived in town." I stepped in closer. "And those shoes weren't at the scene, so you couldn't have learned about them from someone who was there. Nothing was mentioned in the paper. You had to have seen them on Sylvie, right before you killed her. They showed up on a young woman. She was there. She took them." I stared Miss Becky-Sue down. "You set Slim's death in motion, then left to deal with Sylvie. I think I know why. You wanted her proof of the back door in the algorithm." I paused. Slim. The coldhearted calculation, the planning, the conniving bitch. I wanted to circle her neck with my hands and squeeze the life out of her.

"Slim was a heart attack waiting to happen," Miss Becky-Sue countered. "You said so yourself more than once."

"Yes, but you accelerated the timetable. There was enough Viagra in his system to drop his blood pressure to the floor when he popped his usual nitro pill."

Miss Becky-Sue's eyes were still black holes in her pale face, ringed with mascara, but I could see just a hint of wild-eyed white.

"You got the pills from Frank when his packet of them spilled in the plane. You knew he'd have them, that's why you called him to come meet with Slim. The police found residue in Slim's beer bottle that he had been drinking from before he went to the can. Sort of an odd thing to find in a Lone Star longneck, don't ya think?"

"Why would I kill Slim?" She softened, blinking back invisible tears. "I loved him."

"Save it for the jury." I turned my back to her for a moment. My anger boiled to the surface. If I didn't get myself under control, the jury wouldn't have the opportunity to decide her fate. Turning back around to face her, I took a deep breath and unclenched my hands, letting them hang loosely at my sides. "You loved his money. Which he threw into Aces Over Eights."

That took a little bit of the starch out of her. "He was an old fool."

"An idealist, perhaps, but no fool. And when you got wind of the improprieties, the cheating going on, you took matters into your own hands." Reaching down, I plucked a knife off the table, but not before I saw Miss Becky-Sue flinch. "What I want to know is how did you find out that Kevin Slurry kept a back door?"

Her eyes darted around the room.

Casually, I turned the knife over in my hands, running a finger lightly down the blade. The thing couldn't cut butter, but Miss Becky-Sue didn't need to know that. "Here's what I think. Sylvie Dane got the better of you. She dangled the bait and, just as she knew you would, you swallowed it whole."

Becky-Sue glared at me.

"Hit a nerve, have I?" I stepped closer. She took a wide-eyed step backward. "You were played the fool."

"That bitch." Miss Becky-Sue unraveled before my eyes. Shaking with anger, seething and scared, she wanted to strike out. The only weapon she had was the truth. "She came sniffing around. Dropped that little stink bomb in our laps. Slim went all righteous on me."

"She wanted to see if anyone took her bait, I bet. He was going to tell."

"Sing like a canary. He said this was the sort of thing that gave poker a bad name."

I resisted the urge to point out he was right.

"We'd lose everything."

"So you started plugging the leaks. First Sylvie, or maybe first Marvin . . ."

"Who?"

"The bad comb-over." She'd killed him and she didn't even know who he was. "Wrong place, wrong time. He got the cyanide meant for Sylvie."

Miss Becky-Sue smiled—a benign smile, as if she were telling a cute little story at a garden party. "He was a dead man and he didn't even know it."

She scared the heck out of me. "So, with the cyanide gone, you had to use the shoe on her. Pretty clever, actually."

"She never saw it coming." Miss Becky-Sue gloated; then her eyes widened when she realized what she'd said.

"The cyanide you stole from Frank's wife's jewelry store—another part of the setup to try to hang this on Frank. Then, you tried to take out Sylvie's source, Cole Weston, today with it, but you got me instead."

"Shoulda used a stronger dose." She sounded like she would rip out my throat with one bite if she could.

THE Ferrari dealership. I had come full circle.

Thankfully it was only midnight and not 3 A.M. Jeremy, Cole, Brandy, Dane, Estella, and I were looking for the last piece to the puzzle. Romeo was running late—he had taken Miss Becky-Sue and Frank to the station. I felt that with a little digging, and another conversation with the clerk at the Christian Louboutin store, Romeo would cut Frank loose. As far as I knew, gross stupidity wasn't a punishable offense, although it probably should have been. The one major thing working in his favor was he knew Cole Weston was deaf. The person who tried to kill Cole but got me instead, hadn't known that. They had knocked on the door. Romeo would untangle it all. Hopefully, he could break away.

The door opened and Romeo strode through. Brandy stepped to greet him with a hug. The young detective looked happy, tired but happy, as he folded her into his arms and shot a frown over her shoulder at Cole, who smiled easily in return.

The frown disappeared from the detective's face as he stepped out of Brandy's embrace and took her hand in his. "You guys find anything yet?"

I swept my arm around the room, taking in the others. "We just got here. Glad you could make it." With Romeo's steadying presence, the place didn't creep me out quite as badly.

Someone had cleaned up the showroom. The same car still turned under the spot, minus the decoration. I wondered if the law required disclosure that blood had been spilled and a life lost on the hood? Show me the Carfax. How would one feng shui a car to get rid of the lingering angry spirits? Why did I care? So many questions, so few functioning brain cells.

Romeo clicked on the overhead lights which ruined the ambiance but settled my nerves. If something evil lurked in the corners, at least we'd see it coming.

The dealership empty, we drifted apart, separated by our memories, pulled by our fears. Jeremy drooled over the car. I couldn't look at it without seeing Sylvie Dane's lifeless body draped across it. Dane, his arms crossed tightly over his chest, his head wrapped in a glaring white bandage, his eyes half closed—probably due to a pounding headache—lurked in the doorway, like a vampire waiting to be invited in. Estella roamed the space like a mountain lion hunting dinner. Pulling Brandy with him, Romeo dogged her heels but gave her just enough leash to wander.

"I was sorta freakin' last time I was here," she murmured. Biting her lip, she wandered the showroom. "There are so many places to hide something. I wish Sylvie had told me where."

"Why did Sylvie want to meet you here?" I asked as I watched the scene unfolding in front of me. Although I was part of it, I felt disconnected.

"Privacy." Estella kept her eyes moving around the room. "Mrs. Dane said it was the only place in the hotel to meet where the cameras couldn't see."

"Did you hang the sign out front, then?"

The girl paused and glanced at me, guilt on her face, fear in her eyes.

"It's okay. I'd say that would be the least of your transgressions."

Estella tilted her head in a show of defiance. "It's not like your office is locked or anything. I slipped the form from the desk out front, then put it in the pile of papers you sign every day. You should be more careful about what you sign."

She had an aptitude for justification, I'd grant her that. And there weren't enough hours in the day to read all the shit I had to put my signature on—most of it was corporate CYA anyway. Guess I was pretty good at justification as well.

I parked my brain and waited. Thinking took way more effort than the results warranted. A shiver chased down my spine—I was cold. If the demand for high-end Italian iron dried up, Frank could always use this space as a meat locker. I let my brain continue to run free. Loose associations, often hidden, sometimes lit the way to enlightenment. Then it hit me—like a ball peen hammer between the eyes. "The car."

"What?" Multiple voices rose in unison as everyone in the room stopped where they stood and turned in my direction.

The more I thought about it, the more certain I became. I strode over to the car, then walked around it. "Let me play out a scenario. Let's assume Sylvie was cheating in the poker game to provide a laundered, seemingly innocent payoff to Slurry. But for what?"

No one said anything, choosing instead to let me circle that car another time as my thoughts raced. "He had to have some information she wanted. Maybe something he got using his back door into the poker site algorithm."

"But why the car?" Romeo asked.

"Frank told me he thought he had the car sold to Slurry, who had test-driven it earlier on the day Sylvie died."

"And then Sylvie ditches me to sneak into the dealership," Dane added, his voice tightened to an angry pitch.

"Why here?" Romeo asked as everyone gathered around the car.

"As Estella pointed out, privacy. No cameras. Who would see?" I guessed. A reasonable explanation, assuming I was right about the other.

Opening the driver's door, I eased into the seat. Both hands on the wheel, fingering the paddle shifters because I couldn't resist, I tried to imagine Slurry on a test-drive. "If I wanted to hide something where someone else, who knew where to look for it, could find it easily, where would that be?" I imagined the nooks and crannies of the car, a car I knew well. It was a tightly engineered racing machine, and there weren't many.

Pulling the hood latch, I then levered myself out of the car and walked around to the front. "Let's see what it has under the hood."

"Not much," Romeo scoffed. "The engine's in the back in Ferraris."

I smiled as I slid my fingers into the gap between the hood and the body, shifted the secondary latch to the side, then raised the hood. "Not this one. This is the first model with a midfront V-eight."

And there it was, the top of a metal cylinder, stuffed down the side. To the untrained eye, it would look like an oil spigot or something. Romeo handed me a handkerchief. Reaching in with two fingers, I worked the metal until it came free.

Without a word I handed it to Romeo. Using the cloth to protect prints and keep his off it, he unscrewed the top and shook out a sheaf of papers tightly bound with a string. He quickly scanned the pages. When he looked up his face held an emotion I couldn't read. Whatever it was, it was not good. "They're for you," he said as he handed the documents to Dane.

Dane seemed to pale, if that was possible. He looked like death as it was. When he reached for the papers, his hand shook. Nobody moved. Nobody seemed to breathe as we watched him read, turn a page, read, until he had finished. Without a word, he handed the sheaf to Jeremy and wandered over to the car, where he stood and stared.

Jeremy glanced through the pages. When he looked up, his eyes were glistening, his mouth set in a thin, hard line.

My patience long since exhausted, I could wait no more. "What?"

"Bugger."

"That's it? That's the only thing you can say?" He handed me the pages. After a quick scan, I dropped my hand and raised my eyes to Jeremy's. "Bugger." I wandered over to Dane.

When I snaked an arm around his waist, he didn't look up. Instead, he stared at the spot where his wife had died. "She died trying to prove my innocence."

"She did it, too."

"She squeezed Slurry to use his back door not to get the bad guys, but to prove I was still one of the good guys." He rubbed a hand roughly across his eyes. I could feel his body shudder. "Fuck."

"Her choices, cowboy."

He tilted his head back for a moment, fighting for control. Then he stepped away and turned on me, his voice raised. "You don't know shit."

"That's probably the first absolutely honest thing you've said to me since this whole thing started."

Chapter

NINETEEN

♡

"So, you think Marvin was killed because he was working with Sylvie?" Dane asked. The others had left, and Dane and I again had boosted our heinies up onto the parts counter. Once again we sat, hands under our thighs, our feet swinging. A different day, a different hour, different costumes, and thankfully no dead body on the car. The world had shifted slightly in the last forty-eight hours. And I'm sure something had shifted inside of Dane as well. A woman he had both loved and wrongfully vilified had lost her life while giving him back his.

"Either that or he followed Sylvie and spooked Miss Becky-Sue. She couldn't leave someone who might know something," I speculated. "We know he followed you two, heading this way. Wrong place, wrong time, he was expendable. And he got the cyanide meant for Sylvie."

"That would explain the shoe." Dane's voice was hollow, dead.

"Weapon of opportunity," I added unnecessarily.

He didn't say anything. What was there to say? Explanations at this point didn't really matter. Instead we both watched the car turn on its dais.

Finally Dane broke the silence. "How do I . . . ?" His voice cracked.

Out of the corner of my eye, I saw him swipe at a tear. This time, I was the one speechless. What could I say? What would help? I had no idea how a man would recover from the knowledge that his wife had died for him . . . and he had so misjudged her. And he could never make it right—not in this lifetime anyway.

Instead, I covered his hand with mine and gave it a squeeze.

DESPITE the late hour, energy and enthusiasm still burbled from the crowd, filling every corner of the casino. After all the turmoil, sleep wouldn't pay me a visit any time soon. So I wandered, seeking peace and perspective and hoping a bit of the joy refilled my empty stores. My eyes drifted over the crowd. A typical crowd for this time of night—a mix of the well-heeled and the jeans-clad onlookers ringed the tables. Drinks in hand, pressing buttons with the other, a cigarette dangling from their lips, slot players focused intently on the spinning cylinders in front of them. A couple of high-end girls sat at the bar, eyeing the crowd for their next mark. Too tired to run them off, I wandered on. Closing in on the far side of the casino, movement caught my eye.

A man. Rushing away from me. He darted through the crowd, frantic, as if looking for something.

Maneuvering for a better look, my heart soared and sank at the same time—Jean-Charles! What was he doing here? Something was wrong.

I chased after him. Dodging patrons as I ran through the crowd, I almost bowled over a woman waiting at one of the blackjack tables. "Sorry," I said as I righted her. Then I continued on, trying to keep Jean-Charles in sight.

Finally I was close enough to call to him and be heard over the crowd and the music. "Jean-Charles!"

Stopping at my shout, he turned, scanning the crowd.

I didn't like the look on his face.

Finally he saw me and worked his way in my direction. He reached out.

I took his hands—they were as cold as ice. "What's wrong?"

"It's Christophe. He's disappeared. I picked them up from the airport. We were home, just getting the children settled, when someone called me about a lady swimming in my fish tank?" He shot me a quizzical look.

I shrugged as if I had no idea.

"My son, he was right here one second, the next, poof, he was gone."

My heart skipped a beat. I'd never seen such anguish on anyone's face. Pulling him off to the side, out of the crush of people, I said, "Calm down. We'll find him. Tell me what happened."

"He had slept on the plane. Too excited to calm down, he wanted to see the hotel and the restaurant. We left Chantal at home—she was worn out." Jean-Charles ran a hand through his hair as his eyes scanned the crowd over my shoulder. "He loved the lobby, the river, the ski mountain. Just for a moment, I left him sipping a milkshake in a booth near the kitchen in the restaurant while I tried to deal with the fish tank problem. I told him not to move. When I returned, not five minutes later, he was gone. It's so unlike him."

I grabbed my phone. "What is he wearing?"

"Blue jeans. Tennis shoes. A green shirt—the one with the little alligator on it."

I keyed Security. "We have a missing person. Male. Five years old. Sandy brown hair. Blue eyes. Jeans, green Izod shirt, tennis shoes. Three and a half feet tall and forty-five pounds, give or take." I raised my eyebrows at Jean-Charles. He nodded. "His name is Christophe."

Jerry's voice came back. "Roger."

"Get your people on the exits first."

"Wilco."

I repocketed my phone, but kept one ear listening to the chatter as Jerry rallied the troops. "Go back to the restaurant," I said to Jean-Charles. "He'll probably find his way back there. As you head in that direction, take a peek at the toy store and the gelato stand and any other kid-friendly places you see."

Jean-Charles, his face white, his eyes haunted, nodded.

I squeezed his hand. "Try not to worry. We'll find him. I haven't lost a child yet."

Watching him go, I willed my mind to think like a five-year-old. A five-year-old who had never seen anything like the Babylon. I thought back over the details Jean-Charles had told me about his son.

Where would I go if I were Christophe?

A few moments of thought, then it hit me—I knew exactly where he had gone.

THANKFULLY, the lobby wasn't quite as crazy as the casino. Starting at one end of the Euphrates, I followed the winding stream as it meandered under bridges, around corners, through the vast expanse of the lobby. I was beginning to doubt my assumptions about my young Frenchman when I spied a flash of green and blue among the reeds on the opposite shore. Bolting to the nearest bridge, I crossed and raced back. Parting the reeds, I stuck my head through and found myself gazing at an almost hidden glen.

Christophe Bouclet sat cross-legged in the middle, his eyes as big as saucers as he watched a mother duck and her brood of babies. As immobile as a statue, only the boy's eyes moved as the ducks came closer and closer, unaware of the tiny human lurking there.

Keeping my eye on the boy, I backed away so as not to scare the ducks, and keyed my phone. "Jerry," I whispered. "I've got our missing boy."

"That was fast."

"I know it won't come as a surprise, but I have no trouble thinking like a five-year-old."

He rewarded me with a laugh.

"Please tell Chef Bouclet immediately that I have his son and will return him in a few. I'd like some time with the boy. Jean-Charles will understand."

"You got it."

"Take care of it personally, will you? Last I saw him, he was headed toward his restaurant. It's important and I want to be sure he gets notified quickly—he's frantic."

"Will do."

Turning down the volume, I repocketed the phone and took a deep breath.

Tiptoeing, and careful to move slowly, I stepped into the glade. Lifting the lid on a canister hidden among the bushes, I took a fist of duck food, then sat down, Indian-style, next to the boy.

He put a finger to his lips as he looked at me with his father's eyes, and crawled right into my heart. "Shhh," he said. "Don't scare the mama." His English was as good as mine, but with a much more attractive accent.

"Here." I opened his small fist and poured in a bit of food. "Toss it out there. Don't feed them from your hand—the big ducks will bite the poo out of you. Watch." I sprinkled a little food just beyond his feet, luring the ducks closer.

Christophe giggled as the ducklings swarmed around him—the mama duck quacking orders, which her babies seemed to be ignoring. Used to humans, the mother duck didn't seem too worried by our presence. When Christophe's hand was empty, he stuck it out for a refill without taking his eyes off the birds. My handful was about five of his. I kept dribbling food into his hand until, finally, we had exhausted the supply.

"Can we get more?" Christophe asked, giving me his full attention for the first time.

"We don't want to give them so much they pop."

The boy smiled. "Okay. But can we come back again?"

"Any time you want." We watched as the mother duck herded her brood through the reeds into the water. "Christophe, perhaps we should go find your father. He is very worried."

The boy turned to me, his face turning serious. "Worried?"

"You didn't tell him where you were going. He couldn't find you."

Tears welled in the boy's eyes. "I didn't mean to make him afraid. Do you think he will be mad?"

"Not too." I stood and held out my hand. Christophe tucked his in mine, and hit my heart—a child's hand strums a primal chord. "We'll find a way to make him laugh."

"What is your name?" Christophe asked as we stepped through the reeds and out of our own little world.

"Lucky."

A smile tickled his lips, chasing the worry from his eyes. "That's a funny name."

That's me, good for a laugh. "Yes, but it's the only one I've got."

"I like funny names. My friends think my name is funny."

"I think it's very unique and grown-up."

Pride puffed the boy's chest. "I like you."

"I like you too."

People filled the lobby, bumping into us and almost tripping over the small boy as we worked our way toward the entrance to the Bazaar. Pulling Christophe to a stop, I knelt down so we were eye to eye. "Would you mind if I carried you? I think it would be better that way."

He extended his arms to me.

Propping him on a hip, I held his body to mine. "Better?"

His hands gripped my sweater—one in the front, one in the back. "You are almost as tall as my father. Do you think I will be this tall when I grow up? I like it."

"Whatever you will be, it will be special."

We paused at the glass in front of the ski hill and watched the skiers. Christophe delighted in one man who skied effortlessly down the hill, graceful, as if the skis were extensions of his legs. "My father told me, when I get bigger, he will take me to ski in the big mountains near my grandparents' house."

"You can learn to ski here, then you can practice on a mountain north of here, Mount Charleston."

"Really?"

"The skiing is not like the Alps, but it's a good place to practice."

"Will you come?"

"Sure. That's where I learned to ski when I was your age."

He looked at me as if he couldn't imagine me being a five-year-old, but he took me at my word.

JEAN-CHARLES paced in front of the restaurant, working the crowd, his eyes scanning. Chatting with customers in line, greeting each of them with a handshake, or pausing for a picture, he looked relaxed, casual, but his posture belied his tension. When he caught sight of us, he visibly relaxed, his shoulders losing their hunched look, his face settling into a gentle smile, his eyes holding love—a little of which I hoped might be for me.

"Papa! I have made a friend!" Christophe shouted when we got close, turning heads.

"I see." Jean-Charles's eyes held mine as he ruffled his son's hair and gave him a kiss on his cheek. "But you and I must have a talk about disappearing like that. You know better."

"Yes, Papa." The boy's face fell.

"But not now. Rinaldo is making you a fresh milk-shake."

Christophe's smile returned. "Papa, this is Lucky. She showed me how to feed the baby ducks! They came right up to me. I wanted to touch them, but she said no, they bite. We are going to feed them again and then ski on the mountain!"

Christophe wiggled in my arms like a puppy, his excitement bubbling over . . . contagious.

"Really?" Jean-Charles smiled at his son, then gave me a wink. "You two are going to be busy."

"I found him down by the water in a clump of reeds—he'd been following the mother duck."

Jean-Charles stroked my cheek, the look in his eye a mixture of emotions I couldn't read. "Thank you for my son," he said, then, ignoring Christophe's shocked look, he leaned in for a very satisfying kiss.

If he kept doing that in public places, eventually I was going to embarrass myself.

"Papa!"

"Lucky is my friend, also."

"Really?" The boy cast a delighted look between us. "Then can we invite her over to play?"

"May we?" Jean-Charles corrected. "You're not tired?" he asked his son, who clung resolutely to me.

"No! Pleeeease?" Christophe drew out the word, pleading as five-year-olds do.

Jean-Charles, a smile lighting his face, and something altogether different lighting his eyes, turned to me. "Would you like to come home . . . to play?"

"I thought you'd never ask."

Chapter

TWENTY

♡

*C*hristophe proved to be a delightful host, squiring me around his house, showing me all the good places to hide. We looked at his toys—he was seriously into heavy equipment. We played several tennis matches on his Wii before the boy's energy began to flag. Seizing the moment, Jean-Charles bustled his son off to a bath—I got in on the sudsing—then we both put him to bed. Before I left his room, Christophe rewarded me with a kiss—one on each cheek. The kid was going to be a heartbreaker.

Waiting in the family room, I chose a modest Bordeaux from Jean-Charles's impressive collection, decanted it to breathe, and set two bowl-shaped wineglasses on the bar.

I was really getting in deep. Things were happening so fast. I felt adrift, yet strangely anchored. My mind shouted for me to run; my heart willed me to stay.

So I did what every self-respecting woman of a certain age would do in this situation—I poured myself a drink. A glass of wine, to be more precise—Jean-Charles would just have to catch up.

Sipping my wine, trying to make it last, I stared through the French doors to the patio and pool—

lights casting shadows that moved with the invisible wind—like ghosts . . . or angels, waiting, watching.

Jean-Charles snuck up behind me, wrapping his arms around my waist, putting his chin on my shoulder. Our reflection in the glass made me smile.

"You were a huge hit with my child, as I knew you would be." He took my wineglass and set it on the bar next to him.

"He is his father's son, delightful in every way." I leaned back, pressing against him, my head lying back on his shoulder, my cheek against his. "Would you like some wine?" I asked.

"Mmmm, that means I would have to move." He nuzzled my neck, sending delicious jolts to my core.

"Jean-Charles, right now all of this seems so fantastic, so perfect. But what if we don't work? We're adults and can deal with the fallout, but what about Christophe? Aren't we setting him up for a fall?"

"Is that what you believe the future holds for us?"

"If I did, I wouldn't be here. But I'm smart enough to know there are no sure things."

Jean-Charles turned me to face him, holding my body pressed to his. Gently, he brushed my cheek with the backs of his fingers. "None of us gets through life without a little heartbreak. I want to teach my son to seize life, squeeze the joy out of every day. Life is wasted if you let worry and fear make your choices for you. We are resilient—so is Christophe. Trust life, Lucky. Trust me."

His kiss was tender, with a hint of things to come. My body molded to his, my arms around his neck, my hands in his hair. He deepened the kiss and I lost myself.

Pulling back, his breath coming hard, he said, "The time must be right for you. You do not have to stay."

"No. I don't." I tried to calm the beat of my heart, but it wasn't happening. "Do you want me to stay?"

"More than anything." Jean-Charles met my gaze, his eyes dark and serious.

"Then ask me." I no longer cared whether this whole thing was too fast, or not fair to Christophe, or the wrong thing right now, or whether I was on the rebound, or would get my heart broken. I simply had to be here—I had to stay, to feel his arms around me, his flesh on mine.

"I know this seems so fast, too fast to be real," he said. "But when I look at you, when I hold you, I know in my heart this is right, this is good—it *is* real. Please stay with me. Let me show you how I've come to feel about you."

"Only if you let me do the same."

THE shades in his bedroom were closed, the lights dimmed, a few candles flickering softly. I gave him a grin as he led me inside then secured the double doors behind us.

"I had hopes," he said with a shy, half-embarrassed smile that warmed my heart. Opening the doors on the fireplace, he lit the logs, then extinguished the lights, leaving us bathed only in the glow from the flickering flames.

My hands moved to the buttons on my sweater.

Jean-Charles shook his head. "Let me." His head bowed, he concentrated on undoing each of the tiny buttons. His hands shook a little—I liked that.

Where his fingers brushed my skin, warmth radiated. If he didn't hurry, I wasn't going to have a functional sweater to wear home.

When he had my sweater undone, with both hands he pushed the delicate fabric back, over my shoulders, letting it drop to the floor. He swallowed hard when he looked at me.

From the look on his face I guessed the black lace had been a good choice.

"You are beautiful," he whispered as he hooked one finger under a strap. "Did you wear this for me today?" he asked as he slid both straps over my shoulders. His breath caught as the delicate fabric gapped away from my skin.

"I wear this every day—for me."

"You are more French than you think." His hands slipped around behind me and undid the catch, letting the lace fall away. His hands found my flesh—his thumb brushing an already taut nipple, taking my breath. "Every day, when I catch sight of you at work, this is what I will see." His hands drifted to the waistband of my slacks.

I stilled them. "Not yet. Now it's my turn."

He waited while I unbuttoned his shirt. His eyes never left mine as my hands roamed over his chest before pushing his shirt away. Warmth radiated from his skin, taut muscles rippled under my touch, his desire barely contained.

"You know what they say about not trusting a trim chef?" I teased as I delighted in him.

"In Europe, we know how to appreciate the finer things in life," he whispered as his eyes wandered the length of me, then recaptured mine. His hands filled with my flesh. "Quality over quantity."

"Show me."

His mouth captured mine, demanding, plundering, taking my breath and firing a need, a desire, like none before.

Finally, flesh on flesh, we fell on the bed, a tangle of limbs . . . feasting. His mouth, his hands, tasting, touching, for the first time . . . arousing, making me his own.

WRAPPED in Jean-Charles's arms, thoroughly sated, yet somehow knowing a lifetime of having him would never be enough, I felt my emotions tumbling through me. So fast, yet so perfect. Terrifying, yet comforting. A complete surrender.

A cool breeze wafted through the open doors—I vaguely remembered him opening them. Actually, what I remembered was a brief moment when his skin was not on mine, his hands were not teasing, arousing . . . pleasuring. I sighed and pulled him tighter to me, burrowing into him. My Frenchman and his emphasis on quality had been mind-blowing—but the quantity was pretty darn impressive as well.

As I nuzzled his neck, I felt him stir. "Are you asleep?"

"Drifting," he whispered as he nibbled my ear.

"From the first day I met you, this is what I have been dreaming about."

"As I recall, our first meeting was a shouting match."

He chuckled. "Yes, there was fire even then. And we will argue more—it is inevitable."

"Lovers and business partners," I mused. Life with the volatile Frenchman wouldn't be dull, if we lived through it. "I've heard make-up sex can be amazing."

"What is this? Make-up sex? I do not think imaginary sex would be so much fun."

"That would be *made*-up sex. I'm talking about where a couple fights, then reconciles—in colonial English that is called 'making up.'"

"Ah. Sex is about passion. Anger is passion. So, one could make the other better, *non*?"

"Between you and me," I whispered as I pulled his lips to mine. "I don't know how it could be any better."

A scratching noise jolted me awake. Disoriented, it took me a moment to remember where I was. Then the memories flooded back, warming me to my toes. Spooned around me, Jean-Charles breathed softly in my ear, the measured cadence of sleep.

The noise sounded again. Someone was at the door.

"Papa?" Christophe whispered as he worked the door handle.

Jean-Charles didn't stir. Clearly he was exhausted. For some reason, I didn't feel badly about that at all.

Easing myself from his arms, I rooted in his closet for a pair of sweatpants and a shirt. Clothed, I unlocked the door and greeted a very surprised little boy.

"Shhh. Your father is asleep." I took his hand. "Let's go to the kitchen. I'm starving."

Christophe allowed me to lead him across the great room. At the foot of the stairs curving upward to the second floor, he paused. "We have so many rooms. Why did you sleep in my father's bed?"

Formulating an answer, I stared into his wide, innocent eyes.

"You slept with Uncle Jean?" came a lilting female voice from the landing above. A trim young woman, with a tangle of brown curls, wide, knowing eyes, and a lush mouth, which was now curved into a huge grin, bounded down the stairs.

The two youngsters stared at me.

"You must be Chantal," I said to the beautiful girl standing in front of me. "My name is Lucky, and to answer your question . . . yes." I never had learned the subtle art of beating around the bush. "Would you happen to be hungry? I know it's only six A.M. here, but it must be dinnertime in France."

"Can you cook?" The girl eyed me warily.

"What I do in the kitchen would probably be a punishable offense in your family, but I can make pancakes. You two up for that?"

CHANTAL took my list of ingredients. Searching the cabinets, she found all the essentials—only a chef would have made sure his kitchen was fully stocked when he moved in—a chef and a father. I melted butter while the girl sifted all the dry ingredients together in a large bowl.

"I want to help," Christophe said from his perch on the edge of the counter. "Pancakes are my favorite."

"Your turn is coming up. You have the most important part." I caught Chantal looking at me and I gave her a wink. She rewarded me with a grin.

I turned on the griddle and plopped a wad of butter on it.

Handing me the bowl, Chantal asked, "So how was it? Uncle Jean is pretty good, *non*?"

Caught by surprise, I juggled the bowl, catching it in the nick of time. I gave her a wide-eyed look.

"I thought so," she announced, as if she knew what she was talking about. She couldn't be any more than fifteen. She gave me one of those shrugs. "He is French," she said, as if that explained everything—which perhaps it did.

"You, behave," I said to her with a grin. "And you," I said to Christophe. "Now it's your turn."

He moved to his knees on the counter, peering into the depth of the bowl. "What is my father good at?"

"Everything. Ignore your cousin; she is being precocious."

I corralled him with my body so he couldn't fall. "Take this"—I handed him a long-handled wooden spoon—"and mush down the middle so we have a little hole."

His face a mask of concentration, he did as I asked.

"Now pour in the milk." I handed him the measuring cup.

He spilled a little bit, and looked at me with worried eyes.

"If you don't make a mess, the pancakes won't turn out right. Now the butter."

He did as I instructed.

"Do you know how to crack an egg?" I asked.

He shook his head.

The egg was almost too large for his hand. Covering his with mine, I showed him how to rap the shell lightly on the edge of the bowl until it cracked. Then I pressed his thumbs inside the crack and he opened the shell over the bowl. "Perfect! The first time I did that, the egg squirted all over me."

Christophe beamed as I took the bowl and began mixing. Chantal moved the butter around the griddle, coating it as it heated.

"I like helping," Christophe announced. "My father doesn't let me help."

"When he sees what a wonderful job you did this morning, I'm sure he will change his mind." Pausing in my beating, I ruffled his hair.

Jean-Charles's voice sounded from the doorway. "You can be assured of that," he said, a grin lighting his eyes and splitting his face as he lounged in the doorway, arms folded over his chest. Dressed only in a pair of gym shorts, with his hair disheveled, a day's worth of stubble, his lips a little swollen, Jean-Charles looked good enough to eat . . . again.

"Papa!" Christophe shouted. Jumping to his feet, he bounded across the counter and launched himself into his father's arms.

My heart caught in my throat, but Jean-Charles snagged his son in midair with a practiced swoop. He gave him a squeeze, then a good tickle as he held him tight.

Yeah, another course of the incredibly delectable Frenchman would be perfect for my breakfast.

When his eyes caught mine, I could tell we were thinking along similar lines.

But we had entertaining to do, and hungry bellies to fill.

"How long have you been standing there?" I asked.

"A little while."

Chantal ambled over to him. Bussing him on both cheeks, she said, "Uncle," her tone amusingly accusatory.

Jean-Charles set Christophe down, then much to the delight of all present, he took the bowl from me, set it on the counter, then wrapped me in his arms and gave me the best wake-up kiss ever. "Good morning," he said when he had released my lips.

"Fabulous morning, actually," I said. The look in his eyes told me he agreed.

The butter started to sizzle, so I grabbed Christophe, deposited him on the counter once again, handed him a spatula, and said, "Be careful, it's hot. But I am going to teach you to toss pancakes."

Taking a stool across from us, his chin in his hand, his elbow on the counter, Jean-Charles watched, a smile tickling his lips. Christophe's first two attempts didn't turn out so well—one pancake landed on a burner, oozing into the pan below, the other landed half on, half off the griddle.

I glanced at Jean-Charles, but he didn't seem at all upset at the mess.

By the third, the boy had it figured out—gently moving the spatula under the cake, then flicking his wrist so it formed an arc, turning over before it again landed on the griddle. Kids ... so precocious these days.

"You're a natural," I said, giving him free rein with the batter but staying close to make sure he didn't get too near the hot surfaces.

On the next batch, we added chocolate morsels in the shape of a smiley face. Jean-Charles grimaced.

"Mr. Fancy-Pants Chef, I'll have you know, pancakes without chocolate are a crime against nature—like crepes without Nutella," I lectured as I raised my spatula to him.

"I'm willing to accept that Americans have less-cultured palates."

Chantal's voice cut right through our witty little banter like a razor blade through flesh.

"Hello? Grandmama? Uncle has a girlfriend. She's making us breakfast."

Jean-Charles bolted off the stool, but he was a few steps too slow. Cell phone pressed to her face, the young girl danced around the kitchen, keeping the center island between her uncle and herself as she rattled on to her grandmother in French.

I tried to corral her, but with a hot griddle and a little boy who squirmed in delight, I had my hands full. Although not fluent in the language, I knew enough to get the drift. Something about me sleeping over. I was tall and pretty . . . nice even. And her uncle had a smile on his face she had never seen.

Conceding defeat, Jean-Charles retreated to his stool, and shot me a grin and a shrug. He didn't seem upset, merely amused. "My love life is a family concern," he said. "Don't worry, they will adore you and, in time, you will get used to the meddling—my family has elevated it to an art form."

Chantal said her good-byes, then extended the phone to her uncle. "She wants to talk to you."

His smile negated the dirty look he shot his niece as he took the phone. "*Oui?*" he said, pretending to be annoyed. Then, unable to continue the charade and with warmth in his voice, he regaled his mother with his version of the events.

I especially liked the part about me being special and him being happy.

BREAKFAST was a big hit. The kids launched off to play video games, leaving Jean-Charles and me with KP duty—I washed, he dried and put away.

"Your pancakes were actually very good—light, sweet, with a hint of butter." He did a pretty good job at hiding his surprise.

"I keep my culinary aptitude a closely guarded secret."

After stowing the last of the pans, he circled my

waist as I rinsed my hands. "Any other hidden talents I should know about?"

"Well." I turned in his arms. "I'm pretty good in the shower."

A grin lifted the corner of his mouth.

I couldn't resist nibbling on his lower lip. "Mmmm, light, sweet, with just a hint of . . . chocolate."

He reached down and scooped me into his arms.

My arms around his neck, I let him carry me toward the bedroom. "What exactly are the rules concerning sex when young people are on the prowl?" I whispered.

"I'm making this up as I go." He laughed. "But I think several locked doors would be wise."

I had been exaggerating a bit about the shower part, but I needn't have worried—my Frenchman was very inventive. Bedroom doors secured. Bathroom door bolted. Water running. Music playing. Passions flaring. Clothes pooled at our feet, we fell on each other, hungry, driven. Boosting me to sit on the counter, Jean-Charles feasted at will on my exposed flesh. Leaning back, I offered myself to him. His fingers, his tongue driving me to the edge of sanity. He lowered me onto him, filling me fully. My legs around his waist, my back against the wall, our eyes locked, he drove into me.

God, animal sex in the bathroom—I could so get used to this.

Then my body shattered.

. . .

STILL on the floor of the bathroom where we had collapsed, Jean-Charles lay across my legs. With strength I didn't know I possessed, I pushed myself to a seated position.

"I don't think I can stand," he said. Rolling over, he cast an eye at me, then threw his arms across his face. "Sweet Jesus, that was . . . unbelievable."

"Life-altering," I said, testing my legs. Shaky, but they held. "Heck of a way to burn off a high-carb breakfast." Turning the tap on the shower, I tested the water until I found a suitable temperature. Then I closed the tap to the tub. I flipped off the CD player. "I can honestly say that was the first time I've made love to the theme from *Thomas the Tank Engine*."

"That was all I had."

"Well, I have no doubt my future Thomas the Tank viewing pleasure has been permanently altered."

Joining me in an upright position, he pulled me to him, giving me a tender kiss where he had nipped my lip and drawn blood. "I'm sorry."

"You don't look sorry. In fact I'd say you look pretty satisfied."

"That, too." His head on my shoulder, he held me tight for a moment. "Lucky, be mine."

"I don't know how I could be any more yours."

"Live here with us. When you are here, whether in my bed or my kitchen, magic happens."

"You know, if I didn't have the context for that remark, I might accuse you of being chauvinistic."

His eyes probed mine. "You joke. Is this what you meant by a defense mechanism?"

"Prime example." Needing time to think, I kissed him. Stupid idea. Being naked, in his arms . . . rational thought wasn't even close to a possibility. I stepped away. "Jean-Charles, let's not screw this up. One step at a time, okay?" Of course we'd just taken about ten giant steps, but I chose to overlook that part. I needed some semblance of control—even if I had to pull it out of thin air.

He nodded, but I didn't see agreement in his eyes.

"DO you have a busy day?" Jean-Charles asked as he drove me to work. Christophe, belted in a child safety seat in the back, was mesmerized by a DVD.

My body still humming with sexual pleasure, I tried to focus. "One of the worst of the year." I glanced at my phone: no messages . . . nine fifteen. "In my line of work, who knows? Every day is a whole new set of problems." I secretly prayed that today would not serve up another dead girl on a Ferrari.

Holding my hand, he maneuvered through traffic . . . like an unseasoned rookie. I wasn't too sure about only one hand on the wheel, but I decided to live dangerously—the reward of his hand holding mine was worth total terror. As it turned out, my worry was misplaced: He scared me only once.

After kissing him good-bye for longer than was wise, I climbed out of the car. "Will I see you later?" I asked, leaning back in for one more kiss, earning a honk from the valet waiting to park the car behind us.

"I am running the kitchen tonight. I'll be in by three." He glanced back at Christophe, who still was transfixed. "I've got a few things to do at the restaurant right now, but they won't take me long."

As I closed the door, I glanced at my watch. Only a little more than five hours until I could kiss him again.

Chapter

TWENTY-ONE

♡

*L*ife had returned to normal.

Well, let me rephrase. Still basking in a warm French glow, I was once again ensconced behind my desk, signing my way through a stack of papers—this time a bit more mindful of exactly what I was signing.

Christophe perched happily on one of my knees as he drew a picture for his father. Apparently, the boy refused to stay in the restaurant, instead wanting to share my space. To be honest, I'd never considered myself a kid magnet before, so I was enjoying the ride while it lasted. And there was something so visceral about holding a child. Something so soothing about the softness of his skin, the smell of his hair. Something that greased the rusty cogs of my biological clock. I felt a subtle stirring, which surprised the heck out of me. Me? A mother? Heck, I wasn't finished being a child yet. Besides, Mona was in the baby business, not this gal, thank you very much. That reminded me—Mona's doctor's appointment—I'd promised to go with her, but I just couldn't remember when it was scheduled. A small snag in the fabric of a perfect day, but I could deal with it. She'd been awfully coy about the purpose of the visit, a fact that worried me just a bit.

"Miss P, you out there?" I called through the open doorway.

I heard the squeak of her chair, then her head appeared in the doorway, followed by her body. She smiled at Christophe, then gave me an amused look.

"Mona's appointment?"

"Today at four."

"The poker tournament?"

"Under control. Moving at its normal glacial pace." She shifted and leaned against the doorjamb. "Have you seen your mother today?"

My blood pooled in my feet, leaving me momentarily light-headed. The Mona effect, I called it. "No. Why?"

"She hasn't told you about her plans to let the girls from the whorehouse in Pahrump hold a bake sale to raise funding for her fledgling run at the Advisory Board appointment?" Miss P kept her expression bland, but I could see the laughter in her eyes.

"Where does she want to hold this . . . affair?"

"In the parking lot at Smokin' Joe's XXX Video Emporium."

"My father will blow a gasket." I shook my head and sighed. "Oh well, his problem." At Miss P's surprised look I added, "Delegation, I'm getting the hang of it."

She nodded and turned to go, but stopped when I said, "Today is Sunday, right?"

"All day."

"Do you have a copy of the *R-J*?"

"Sure." She disappeared then returned, handing me the paper.

"Thanks. Now go on home."

She smiled, her cheeks coloring. "Jeremy's waiting in Delilah's."

"Then get a move on." I grinned as she disappeared.

I took another whiff of Christophe, then kissed him lightly on the head. He reached up and patted my cheek with his tiny hand. My heart flipped.

I was a goner.

With just one free hand, it took me longer than it should have to find the legal announcements in the paper. I scanned them . . . twice.

Not one mention of Dane's divorce proceedings.

I guess he'd loved her after all. The thought made me sad. He'd gotten so mad at her when she wouldn't do as he asked, when she wouldn't take herself out of harm's way. He'd had no way of knowing she was doing it for him. If he had, maybe none of this would've happened. Maybe it still would've turned out the way it did. Sylvie Dane had a mind of her own—a tough thing for a control freak like Dane.

But he'd have to find his own peace.

Life had sure taken an interesting turn. Thinking of my Frenchman—both of my Frenchmen—I smiled. My heart filled. Life was just about perfect

My phone sang out at my hip. It had a bad habit of doing that just when my happiness quotient was peaking. To make matters worse, it played a snippet of the song Teddie had written for me, "Lucky for Me." I was certain I had changed that ringtone, but I guessed not. The song broke my heart a little each time I heard it.

Before I could answer the call, a voice from the doorway stopped my heart.

"They're playing our song."

Teddie.

ABOUT THE AUTHOR

DEBORAH COONTS's mother tells her she was born in Texas a very long time ago, though she's not totally sure—her mother can't be trusted. But she was definitely raised in Texas on barbecue, Mexican food, and beer. She currently resides in Las Vegas, where family and friends tell her she can't get into too much trouble. Silly people. Coonts has built her own business, practiced law, flown airplanes, written a humor column for a national magazine, and survived a teenager.

Visit her online at www.deborahcoonts.com.

NEED A LITTLE MORE LUCK IN YOUR LIFE?
DON'T MISS ANY OF LUCKY O'TOOLE'S
VEGAS ADVENTURES.

. . . .

Wanna Get Lucky?

Lucky Stiff

So Damn Lucky

Lucky Bastard

♡

NOVELLAS

Lucky in Love

Lucky Bang

A FORGE BOOK

Tom Doherty Associates

Forge

Award-winning authors
Compelling stories

· ·

Please join us at the website
below for more information
about this author and other great
Forge selections, and to sign up for
our monthly newsletter!

· · · · www.tor-forge.com · · · ·

creating MOTION GRAPHICS with after effects

3rd Edition

Volume 2: Advanced Techniques

Trish & Chris Meyer

CMP Books

San Francisco, CA

DEDICATED

*to the memory of **Vera McGrath**,*
who always said I could do anything I put my mind to – Trish

*and to the memory of **Leroy Meyer**,*
who taught me to be curious about how all things worked – Chris

Published by CMP Books
An imprint of CMP Media LLC
CMP Books, 600 Harrison St., San Francisco, California 94107 USA
Tel: 415-947-6615; Fax: 415-947-6015
www.cmpbooks.com
Email: books@cmp.com

Copyright © 2000, 2003, 2005 by Trish and Chris Meyer. All rights reserved. No part of this publication may be reproduced or distributed in any form or by any means, or stored in a database or retrieval system, without the prior written permission of the publisher.

Designations used by companies to distinguish their products are often claimed as trademarks. In all instances where CMP is aware of a trademark claim, the product name appears in initial capital letters, in all capital letters, or in accordance with the vendor's capitalization preference. Readers should contact the appropriate companies for more complete information on trademarks and trademark registrations. All trademarks and registered trademarks in this book are the property of their respective holders.

The programs in this book are presented for instructional value. The programs have been carefully tested, but are not guaranteed for any particular purpose. The publisher does not offer any warranties and does not guarantee the accuracy, adequacy, or completeness of any information herein and is not responsible for any errors or omissions. The publisher assumes no liability for damages resulting from the use of the information in this book or for any infringement of the intellectual property rights of third parties that would result from the use of this information.

For individual orders, and for information on special discounts for quantity orders, please contact:
   CMP Books Distribution Center, 6600 Silacci Way, Gilroy, CA 95020
   Tel: 1-800-500-6875 or 408-848-3854; Fax: 408-848-5784
   Email: cmp@rushorder.com; Web: www.cmpbooks.com

Distributed to the book trade in the U.S. by: Publishers Group West, 1700 Fourth Street, Berkeley, California 94710

Distributed in Canada by: Jaguar Book Group, 100 Armstrong Avenue, Georgetown, Ontario M6K 3E7 Canada

Library of Congress Cataloging-in-Publication Data
Meyer, Trish
     Creating motion graphics with after effects / Trish & Chris Meyer.
   – 3rd ed.
          p. cm.
     Includes index.
     ISBN 1-57820-249-3 (softcover with dvd : alk. paper)
1. Cinematography–Special effects–Data processing. 2. Computer animation. 3. Computer graphics. 4. Adobe After Effects.
I. Meyer, Chris II. Title.
   TR858.M49 2004
   778.5'2345'028553–dc22   2004017343

ISBN: 1-57820-269-8 (volume 2)

Printed in the United States of America

05 06 07 08 09   5 4 3 2 1